Praise for the Jason Bourne series

'A first-rate thriller with grit and intrigue to spare' *Variety*

'A rollicking blockbuster ride' *Empire*

'Ludlum has never come up with a more head-spinning, spine-jolting, intricately mystifying, Armageddonish, in short Ludlumesque, thriller than this . . . Every chapter ends with a cliff-hanger; the story brims with assassination, torture, hand-to-hand combat, sudden surprise and intrigue within intrigue' *Publishers Weekly*

'The story unfolds at a whirring pace' *New York Times*

'Move over 007, Bourne is back' *Daily Mirror*

'This is the most satisfying thriller of the year'
Chicago Tribune

Praise for Robert Ludlum

'Robert Ludlum is an ingenious storyteller with a wonderful and convincing imagination. His place as a bestselling novelist is assured' Mario Puzo, author of *The Godfather*

'Robert Ludlum has the storytelling gift' *TLS*

'Don't ever begin a Ludlum novel if you have to go to work the next day' *Chicago Sun-Times*

'Ludlum stuffs more surprises into his novels than any other six-pack of thriller writers combined' *New York Times*

'Ludlum is light years beyond his literary competition in piling plot twist upon plot twist, until the mesmerized reader is held captive' *Chicago Tribune*

'Robert Ludlum is an acknowledged superstar of the political thriller' Amazon.co.uk

Robert Ludlum is one of the world's bestselling authors and there are more than 300 million copies of his books in print. He is published in 32 languages and 50 countries. He is best known for the Jason Bourne series: *The Bourne Identity*, *The Bourne Supremacy*, *The Bourne Ultimatum*, *The Bourne Legacy*, *The Bourne Betrayal* and *The Bourne Sanction*. The first three titles have been made into critically acclaimed movies, with *The Bourne Ultimatum* winning three Academy Awards. Visit Robert Ludlum's website at www.orionbooks.co.uk/Ludlum.

Eric Van Lustbader was born in Greenwich Village. He is the author of more than twenty bestselling novels, and his work has been translated into more than twenty languages.

Also Available

The Bourne Series
The Bourne Identity
The Bourne Supremacy
The Bourne Ultimatum
The Bourne Legacy
The Bourne Betrayal
The Bourne Sanction
The Bourne Deception
The Bourne Objective

The Covert-One Series
The Hades Factor
The Cassandra Compact
The Paris Option
The Altman Code
The Lazarus Vendetta
The Moscow Vector
The Arctic Event

Road to . . . Series
The Road to Gandolfo
The Road to Omaha

The Matarese Series
The Matarese Circle
The Matarese Countdown

Standalone Novels
The Scarlatti Inheritance
The Osterman Weekend
The Matlock Paper
Trevayne
The Rhinemann Exchange
The Cry of the Halidon
The Gemini Contenders
The Chancellor Manuscript
The Holcroft Covenant
The Parsifal Mosaic
The Aquitaine Progression
The Icarus Agenda
The Scorpio Illusion
The Apocalypse Watch
The Prometheus Deception
The Sigma Protocol
The Janson Directive
The Tristan Betrayal
The Ambler Warning
The Bancroft Strategy

Robert Ludlum's™

THE
BOURNE
BETRAYAL

A New **Jason Bourne** Novel by
Eric Van Lustbader

An Orion paperback

First published in Great Britain in 2007
by Orion
This paperback edition published in 2008
by Orion Books Ltd,
Orion House, 5 Upper St Martin's Lane,
London WC2H 9EA

An Hachette UK company

13 15 17 19 20 18 16 14

Reissued 2010

A CIP catalogue record for this book
is available from the British Library.

ISBN 978-1-4091-1763-6

Printed and bound in the UK by
CPI Mackays, Chatham ME5 8TD

The Orion Publishing Group's policy is to use papers
that are natural, renewable and recyclable products and
made from wood grown in sustainable forests. The logging
and manufacturing processes are expected to conform to
the environmental regulations of the country of origin.

www.orionbooks.co.uk

In memory of Adam Hall (Elleston Trevor),
a literary mentor:

The roses are for you, too

Thanks to

Ken Dorph, my Arabist
Jeff Arbital

And a special thank-you to Victoria,
for the title

PROLOGUE

The Chinook came beating up into a blood-red sky. It shuddered in the perilous crosscurrents, banking through the thin air. A web of clouds, backlit by the failing sun, streamed by like smoke from a flaming aircraft.

Martin Lindros stared intently out of the military copter carrying him upward into the highest elevations of the Semien mountain range. While it was true that he hadn't been in the field since the Old Man had appointed him to the position of deputy director of Central Intelligence four years ago, he'd made sure that he'd never lost his animal edge. He trained three mornings a week at the CI field agent obstacle course outside Quantico, and every Thursday night at ten he washed away the tedium of vetting electronic intel reports and signing action orders by spending ninety minutes at the firing range, reacquainting himself with every manner of firearm, old, current, and new. Manufacturing action of his own served to assuage his frustration at not being more relevant. All that changed, however, when the Old Man approved his operations proposal for Typhon.

A thin keening knifed through the interior of the CI-modified Chinook. Anders, the commander of Skorpion One, the five-man squad of crack field operatives, nudged him, and he turned. Peering out the window at the shredding clouds, he saw the wind-ravaged north slope of Ras Dejen. There was something distinctly ominous about the forty-five-hundred-meter mountain, tallest in the Simien range.

Perhaps that was because Lindros remembered the local lore: legends of spirits, ancient and evil, who supposedly dwelled on its upper reaches.

The sound of the wind rose to a scream, as if the mountain were trying to tear itself from its roots.

It was time.

Lindros nodded and moved forward to where the pilot sat strapped securely into his seat. The deputy director was in his late thirties, a tall, sandy-haired graduate of Brown who had been recruited into CI during his doctorate in foreign studies at Georgetown. He was whip-smart and as dedicated a general as the DCI could ask for. Bending low so he could be heard over the noise, Lindros gave the pilot the final coordinates, which security dictated he keep to himself until the last possible moment.

He had been in the field just over three weeks. In that time, he'd lost two men. A terrible price to pay. Acceptable losses, the Old Man would say, and he had to retrain himself to think that way if he was to have success in the field. But what price do you put on human life? This was a question that he and Jason Bourne had often debated, without an acceptable answer being reached. Privately, Lindros believed there were some questions to which there was no acceptable answer.

Still, when agents were in the field, that was another matter altogether. 'Acceptable losses' had to be accepted. There was no other way. So, yes, the deaths of those two men were acceptable, because in the course of his mission he had ascertained the veracity of the report that a terrorist organization had gotten its hands on a case of triggered spark gaps somewhere in the Horn of Africa. TSGs were small, ultra-high-energy switches, used to turn on and off enormous levels of voltage: high-tech escape valves to protect electronic components such as microwave tubes and medical testing devices. They were also used to trigger nuclear bombs.

Starting in Cape Town, Lindros had followed a twisting trail that led from Botswana, to Zambia, through Uganda, to Ambikwa, a tiny agricultural village – no more than a fistful of buildings, a church and a bar among them – amid alpine pastureland on the slope of Ras Dejen. There he had obtained one of the TSGs, which he had immediately sent back to the Old Man via secure courier.

But then something happened, something extraordinary, something horrifying. In the beaten-down bar with a floor of dung and dried blood, he had heard a rumor that the terrorist organization was transshipping more than TSGs out of Ethiopia. If the rumor was true, it had terrifying implications not only for America, but for the entire world, because it meant the terrorists had in their possession the instrument to plunge the globe into nightmare.

Seven minutes later, the Chinook settled into the eye of a dust storm. The small plateau was entirely deserted. Just ahead was an ancient stone wall – a gateway, so the local legends went, to the fearsome home of the demons that dwelled here. Through a gap in the crumbling wall, Lindros knew, lay the almost vertical path to the giant rock buttresses that guarded the summit of Ras Dejen.

Lindros and the men of Skorpion One hit the ground in a crouch. The pilot remained in his chair, keeping the engine revved, the rotors turning. The men wore goggles to protect them from the swirling dust and hail of small pebbles churned up by their transportation, and tiny wireless mikes and earpieces that curled into their ears, facilitating communication over the roar of the rotors. Each was armed with an XM8 Lightweight Assault Rifle capable of firing a blistering 750 rounds per minute.

Lindros led the way across the rough-hewn plateau. Opposite the stone wall was a forbidding cliff face in which there appeared the black, yawning mouth of a cave. All else was dun-colored, ocher, dull red, the blasted landscape of another planet, the road to hell.

Anders deployed his men in standard fashion, sending them first to check obvious hiding places, then to form a secure perimeter. Two of them went to the stone wall to check out its far side. The other two were assigned to the cave, one to stand at the mouth, the other to make certain the interior was clear.

The wind, rising over the high butte that towered over them, whipped across the bare ground, penetrating their uniforms. Where the rock face didn't drop off precipitously, it towered over them, ominous, muscular, its bare skull magnified in the thin air. Lindros paused at the remnants of a campfire, his attention shifting.

At his side, Anders, like any good commander, was taking readings of the area perimeter from his men. No one lurked behind the stone wall. He listened intently to his second team.

'There's a body in the cave,' the commander reported. 'Took a bullet to the brain. Stone-dead. Otherwise the site's clean.'

Lindros heard Anders's voice in his ear. 'This is where we start,' he said, pointing. 'The only sign of life in this godforsaken place.'

They squatted down. Anders stirred the charcoal with gloved fingers.

'There's a shallow pit here.' The commander scooped out the cindered debris. 'See? The bottom is fire-hardened. Means someone's lit not just one fire but many over the last months, maybe as long as a year.'

Lindros nodded, gave the thumbs-up sign. 'Looks like we might be in the right place.' Anxiety lanced through him. It appeared more and more likely that the rumor he'd heard was true. He'd been hoping against hope that it was just that, a rumor; that he'd get up here and find nothing. Because any other outcome was unthinkable.

Unhooking two devices from his webbed belt, he turned them on, played them over the fire pit. One was an alpha radiation detector, the other a Geiger counter. What he was looking for, what he was hoping not to find, was a combination of alpha and gamma radiation.

There was no reading from either device at the fire site.

He kept going. Using the fire pit as a central point, he moved in concentric circles, his eyes glued to the meters. He was on his third pass, perhaps a hundred meters from the fire pit, when the alpha detector activated.

'Shit,' he said under his breath.

'Find something?' Anders asked.

Lindros moved off axis and the alpha detector fell silent. Nothing on the Geiger. Well, that was something. An alpha reading, at this level, could come from anything, even, possibly, the mountain itself.

He returned to where the detector had picked up the alpha radiation. Looking up, he saw that he was directly in line with the cave. Slowly, he began walking toward it. The reading on the radiation detector remained constant. Then, perhaps twenty meters from the cave mouth, it ramped up. Lindros paused for a moment to wipe beads of sweat off his upper lip. Christ, he was being forced to acknowledge another nail in the world's coffin. Still – *No gamma yet*, he told himself. That was something. He held on to that hope for twelve more meters. Then the Geiger counter started up.

Oh, God, gamma radiation in conjunction with alpha. Precisely the signature he was hoping not to find. He felt a line of perspiration trickle down his spine. Cold sweat. He hadn't experienced anything like that since he'd had to make his first kill in the field. Hand-to-hand, desperation and determination on his face and on that of the man trying his best to kill him. Self-preservation.

'Lights.' Lindros had to force out the word through a mouth full of mortal terror. 'I need to see that corpse.'

Anders nodded and gave orders to Brick, the man who had made the first foray into the cave. Brick switched on a xenon torch. The three men entered the gloom.

There were no dead leaves or other organic materials to leaven the sharp mineral reek. They could feel the dead-weight of the rock massif above them. Lindros was reminded of the feeling of near suffocation he had experienced when he'd first entered the tombs of the pharaohs down in the depths of Cairo's pyramids.

The bright xenon beam played over the rock walls. In this bleak setting, the male corpse did not look altogether out of place. Shadows fled across it as Brick moved the light. The xenon beam drained it of any color it might have had, making it seem less than human – a zombie out of a horror film. Its position was one of repose, of utter peace, belied by the neat bullet hole in the center of its forehead. The face was turned away, as if it wished to remain in darkness.

'Wasn't a suicide, that's for sure,' Anders said, which had been the starting point of Lindros's own train of thought. 'Suicides go for something easy – the mouth is a prime example. This man was murdered by a professional.'

'But why?' Lindros's voice was distracted.

The commander shrugged. 'With these people it could be any of a thousand—'

'Get the hell back!'

Lindros shouted so hard into his mike that Brick, who had been circling toward the corpse, leapt back.

'Sorry, sir,' Brick said. 'I just wanted to show you something odd.'

'Use the light,' Lindros instructed him. But he already knew what was coming. The moment they had stepped inside the cave both the rad detector and the Geiger counter had beat a terrifying rat-tat-tat against his eyes.

8

Christ, he thought. *Oh, Christ.*

The corpse was exceedingly thin, and shockingly young, not out of its teens, surely. Did he have the Semitic features of an Arab? He thought not, but it was nearly impossible to tell because—

'Holy Mother of God!'

Anders saw it then. The corpse had no nose. The center of his face had been eaten away. The ugly pit was black with curdled blood that foamed slowly out as if the body were still alive. As if something were feasting on it from the inside out.

Which, Lindros thought with a wave of nausea, *is precisely what is happening.*

'What the hell could do that?' Anders said thickly. 'Tissue toxin? Virus?'

Lindros turned to Brick. 'Did you touch it? Tell me, did you touch the corpse?'

'No, I—' Brick was taken aback. 'Am I contaminated?'

'Deputy Director, begging your pardon, sir, what the hell have you gotten us into. I'm used to being in the dark on black-ops missions, but this has crossed another boundary altogether.'

Lindros, on one knee, uncapped a small metal canister and used his gloved finger to gather some of the dirt near the body. Sealing the container tightly, he rose.

'We need to get out of here.' He stared directly into Anders's face.

'Deputy Director—'

'Don't worry, Brick. You'll be all right,' he said with the voice of authority. 'No more talk. Let's go.'

When they reached the cave mouth and the glare of the blasted, blood-red landscape, Lindros said into his mike, 'Anders, as of now that cave is off limits to you and your men. Not even to take a leak. Got it?'

The commander hesitated an instant, his anger, his

concern for his men evident on his face. Then it seemed he shrugged mentally. 'Yessir.'

Lindros spent the next ten minutes scouring the plateau with his rad detector and Geiger counter. He very much wanted to know how the contamination had gotten up here – which route had the men carrying it taken? There was no point in looking for the way they had gone. The fact that the man without a nose had been shot to death told him that the group members had discovered in the most horrifying way that they had a radiation leak. They would surely have sealed it before venturing on. But he had no luck now. Away from the cave, both the alpha and gamma radiation vanished completely. Not a hint of a trace remained for him to determine its path.

Finally, he turned back from the perimeter.

'Evacuate the site, Commander.'

'You heard the man,' Anders shouted as he trotted toward the waiting copter. 'Let's saddle up, boys!'

'*Wa'i*,' Fadi said. He knows.

'Surely not.' Abbud ibn Aziz stirred his position beside Fadi. Crouched behind the high butte three hundred meters above the plateau, they served as advance guard for a cadre of perhaps twenty armed men lying low against the rocky ground behind them.

'With these I can see everything. There was a leak.'

'Why weren't we informed?'

There was no reply. None was needed. They had not been informed because of naked fear. Fadi, had he known, would have killed them all – every last one of the Ethiopian transporters. Such were the wages of absolute intimidation.

Fadi, peering through powerful 12x50 Russian military binoculars, scanned to his right to keep Martin Lindros in his sights. The 12x50s provided a dizzyingly small field of view but more than made up for it in their detail. He had seen that the leader of the group – the deputy director of CI – was using both a rad detector and a Geiger counter. This American knew what he was about.

Fadi, a tall, broad-shouldered man, possessed a decidedly charismatic demeanor. When he spoke, everyone in his presence fell silent. He had a handsome, powerful face, the color of his skin deepened further by desert sun and mountain wind. His beard and hair were long and curling, the inky color of a starless midnight. His lips were full and wide. When he smiled the sun seemed to have come down from its place in the heavens to shine directly on his disciples. For Fadi's avowed mission was messianic in nature: to bring hope where there was no hope, to slaughter the thousands that made up the Saudi royal family, to wipe their abomination off the face of the earth, to free his people, to distribute the obscene wealth of the despots, to restore the rightful order to his beloved Arabia. To begin, he knew, he must delink the symbiotic relationship between the Saudi royal family and the government of the United States of America. And to do that he must strike at America, to make a clear statement that was as lasting as it was indelible.

What he must not do was underestimate the capacity of Americans to endure pain. This was a common mistake among his extremist comrades, this is what got them into trouble with their own people, this more than anything else was the source of a life lived without hope.

Fadi was no fool. He had studied the history of the world. Better, he had learned from it. When Nikita Khrushchev had said to America, 'We will bury you!' he had meant it in his heart as well as in his soul. But who was it that had been buried? The USSR.

When his extremist comrades said, 'We have many lifetimes to bury America,' they were referring to the endless supply of young men who gained their majority each year, from whom they could choose the martyrs to die in battle. But they gave no thought whatsoever to the deaths of these young men. Why should they? Paradise lay waiting with open arms for the martyrs. Yet what, really, had been gained? Was America living without hope? No. Did these acts push America toward a life without hope? Again, no. So what was the answer?

Fadi believed with all his heart and his soul – and most especially with his formidable intellect – that he had found it.

Keeping track of the deputy director through his 12x50s, he saw that the man seemed reluctant to leave. He felt like a bird of prey as he gazed down on the target site. The arrogant American soldiers had climbed into the helicopter, but their commander – Fadi's intel did not extend to his name – would not allow his leader to remain on the plateau unguarded. He was a canny man. Perhaps his nose smelled something his eyes could not see; perhaps he was only adhering to well-taught discipline. In any case, as the two men stood side by side talking, Fadi knew he would not get a better chance.

'Begin,' he said softly to Abbud ibn Aziz without taking his eyes from the lenses.

Beside him, Abbud ibn Aziz took up the Soviet-made RPG-7 shoulder launcher. He was a stocky man, moon-faced with a cast in his left eye, there since birth. Swiftly and surely, he inserted the tapered, finned warhead into the rocket propulsion tube. The fins on the rotating grenade provided stability, assurance that it would hit its target with a high degree of accuracy. When he depressed the trigger, the primary system would launch the grenade at 117 meters per second. That ferocious burst of energy would, in turn, ignite the rocket propulsion system within the trailing tube, boosting the warhead speed to 294 meters per second.

Abbud ibn Aziz put his right eye against the optical sight, mounted just behind the trigger. He found the Chinook, thought fleetingly that it was a pity to lose this magnificent war machine. But such an object of desire was not for him. In any event, everything had been meticulously planned by Fadi's brother, down to the trail of clues that had compelled the deputy director of CI out of his office and into the field, that led him a tortuous route to northwestern Ethiopia, thence here to the upper reaches of Ras Dejen.

Abbud ibn Aziz positioned the RPG-7 so that it was aimed at the helicopter's front rotor assembly. He was now one with the weapon, one with the goal of his cadre. He could feel the absolute resolve of his comrades flowing through him like a tide, a wave about to crash onto the enemy shore.

'Remember,' Fadi said.

But Abbud ibn Aziz, a highly skilled armorist, trained by Fadi's brilliant brother in modern war machinery, needed no reminder. The one drawback of the RPG was that upon firing, it emitted a telltale trail of smoke. They would immediately become visible to the enemy. This, too, had been accounted for.

He felt the tap of Fadi's forefinger on his shoulder, which meant their target was in position. His finger curled around the trigger. He took a deep breath, slowly exhaled.

There came the recoil, a hurricane of superheated air. Then the flash-and-boom of the explosion itself, the plume of smoke, the twisted rotor blades rising together from the opposite camps. Thunderous echoes, like the dull ache in Abbud ibn Aziz's shoulder, were still resounding when Fadi's men rose as one and rushed to the butte, a hundred meters east of where he and Abbud ibn Aziz had been perched and were now scrambling away, where the telltale smoke plume rose. As the cadre had been taught, it fired a massed fusillade of shots, the expressed rage of the faithful.

Al-Hamdu lil-Allah! Allah be praised! The attack had begun.

*

One moment Lindros had been telling Anders why he wanted two more minutes on site, the next he felt as if his skull had been crushed by a pile driver. It took him some moments to realize that he was flat on the ground, his mouth filled with dirt. He lifted his head. Burning debris swung crazily through the smoky air, but there was no sound, nothing at all but a peculiar pressure on his eardrums, an inner whooshing, as if a lazy wind had started up inside his head. Blood ran down his cheeks, hot as tears. The sharp, choking odor of burned rubber and plastics filled his nostrils, but there was something else as well: the heavy underscent of roasting meat.

It was when he tried to roll over that he discovered Anders half lying atop him. The commander had taken the brunt of the blast in an effort to protect him. His face and bared shoulder, where his uniform was burned away, were crisped and smoking. All the hair on his head had been burned off, leaving little more than a skull. Lindros gagged, with a convulsive shudder pushed the corpse off him. He gagged again as he rose to his knees.

A kind of whirring came to him then, strangely muted, as if heard from a great distance. Turning, he saw the members of Skorpion One piling out of the wreckage of the Chinook, firing their semiautomatics as they came.

One of them went down under the withering hail of machine-gun fire. Lindros's next move was instinctual. On his belly, he crawled to the dead man, snatched up his XM8, and began firing.

The battle-hardened men of Skorpion One were both courageous and well trained. They knew when to take their shots and when to take refuge. Nevertheless, as the crossfire started up they were totally unprepared, so concentrated were they on the enemy in front of them. One by one they were shot, most multiple times.

Lindros soldiered on, even after he was the last man standing. Curiously, no one shot at him; not one bullet even came close. He had just begun to wonder about this when his XM8 ran out of ammo. He stood with the smoking assault rifle in his hand, watching the enemy coming down from the butte above him.

They were silent, thin as the ravaged man inside the cave, with the hollow eyes of men who had seen too much blood spilled. Two broke off from the pack and slipped into the smoldering carcass of the Chinook.

Lindros jerked as he heard shots being fired. One of the cadre spun through the open door of the blackened Chinook, but a moment later the other man dragged the bloody pilot out by his collar.

Was he dead or merely unconscious? Lindros longed to know, but the others had enclosed him in a circle. He saw in their faces the peculiar light of the fanatic, a sickly yellow, a flame that could be extinguished only by their own death.

He dropped his useless weapon and they took him, pulling his hands hard behind his back. Men took up the bodies on the ground and dumped them into the Chinook. In their wake, two others advanced with flamethrowers. With unnerving precision, they proceeded to incinerate the helicopter and the dead and wounded men inside it.

Lindros, groggy and bleeding from a number of superficial cuts, watched the supremely coordinated maneuvers. He was surprised and impressed. He was also frightened. Whoever had planned this clever ambush, whoever had trained this cadre was no ordinary terrorist. Out of sight of his captors, he worked the ring he wore off his finger and dropped it into the rocky scree, taking a step to cover it with his shoe. Whoever came after him needed to know that he'd been here, that he hadn't been killed with the rest.

At that moment, the knot of men around him parted and he saw striding toward him a tall, powerful-looking Arab with a bold, desert-chiseled face and large, piercing eyes. Unlike the other terrorists Lindros had interrogated, this one had the mark of civilization on him. The First World had touched him; he had drunk from its technological cup.

Lindros stared into the Arab's dark eyes as they stood, confronting each other.

'Good afternoon, Mr. Lindros,' the terrorist leader said in Arabic.

Lindros continued to stare at him, unblinking.

'Silent American, where is your bluster now?' Smiling, he added: 'It's no use pretending. I know you speak Arabic.' He relieved Lindros of both radiation detector and Geiger counter. 'I must assume you found what you were looking for.' Feeling through Lindros's pockets, he produced the metal canister. 'Ah, yes.' He opened it and poured out the contents between Lindros's boots. 'Pity for you the real evidence is long gone. Wouldn't you like to know its destination.' This last was said as a mocking statement, not as a question.

'Your intel is first-rate,' Lindros said in impeccable Arabic, causing a considerable stir among everyone in the cadre, save two men: the leader himself and a stocky man whom Lindros took to be the second in command.

There came the leader's smile again. 'I return the compliment.'

Silence.

Without warning, the leader hit Lindros so hard across the face his teeth snapped together. 'My name is Fadi, the redeemer, Martin. You don't mind if I call you Martin? Just as well, as we're going to become intimates over the next several weeks.'

'I don't intend to tell you anything,' Lindros said, abruptly switching to English.

'What you intend and what you *will* do are two separate things,' Fadi said in equally precise English. He inclined his head. Lindros winced as he felt the wrench on his arms, so savage it threatened to dislocate his shoulders.

'You have chosen to pass on this round.' Fadi's

disappointment appeared genuine. 'How arrogant of you, how truly unwise. But then, after all, you are American. Americans are nothing if they are not arrogant, eh, Martin. And, truly, unwise.'

Again the thought arose that this was no ordinary terrorist: Fadi knew his name. Through the mounting pain shooting up his arms, Lindros fought to keep his face impassive. Why wasn't he equipped with a cyanide capsule in his mouth disguised as a tooth, like agents in spy novels? Sooner or later, he suspected, he'd wish he had one. Still, he'd keep up this front for as long as he was able.

'Yes, hide behind your stereotypes,' he said. 'You accuse us of not understanding you, but you understand us even less. You don't know me at all.'

'Ah, in this, as in most things, you're wrong, Martin. In point of fact I know you quite well. For some time I have – how do American students put it? – ah, yes, I have made you my major. Anthropological studies or realpolitik?' He shrugged as if they were two colleagues drinking together. 'A matter of semantics.'

His smile broadened as he kissed Lindros on each cheek. 'So now we move on to round two.' When he pulled away, there was blood on his lips.

'For three weeks, you have been looking for me; instead, I have found you.'

He did not wipe away Lindros's blood. Instead, he licked it off.

BOOK ONE

ONE

'When did this particular flashback begin, Mr. Bourne?' Dr. Sunderland asked.

Jason Bourne, unable to sit still, walked about the comfortable, homey space that seemed more like a study in a private home than a doctor's office. Cream walls, mahogany wainscoting, a vintage dark-wood desk with claw feet, two chairs, and a small sofa. The wall behind Dr. Sunderland's desk was covered with his many diplomas and an impressive series of international awards for breakthrough therapy protocols in both psychology and psychopharmacology related to his specialty: memory. Bourne studied them closely, then saw the photo in a silver frame on the doctor's desk.

'What's her name?' Bourne said. 'Your wife.'

'Katya,' Dr. Sunderland said after a slight hesitation.

Psychiatrists always resisted giving out any personal information about themselves and their family. *But in this case*, Bourne thought . . .

Katya was in a ski suit. A striped knit cap was on her head, a pom-pom at its top. She was blond and very beautiful. Something about her suggested that she was comfortable in front of the camera. She was smiling into the camera, the sun in her eyes. The crinkles at their outside corners made her seem peculiarly vulnerable.

Bourne felt tears coming. Once he would have said that they were David Webb's tears. But the two warring personalities – David Webb and Jason Bourne, the day and night of his soul – had finally fused. While it was true that David Webb, sometime professor of linguistics at Georgetown University, was sinking deeper into shadow, it was just as true that Webb had softened Bourne's most paranoid and antisocial edges. Bourne couldn't live in Webb's world of normalcy, just as Webb couldn't survive in Bourne's vicious shadow world.

Dr. Sunderland's voice intruded on his thoughts. 'Please sit down, Mr. Bourne.'

Bourne did so. There was a kind of relief in letting go of the photo.

Dr. Sunderland's face settled into an expression of heartfelt sympathy. 'The flashbacks, Mr. Bourne, they began following your wife's death, I imagine. Such a shock would—'

'Not then, no,' Jason Bourne said quickly. But that was a lie. The memory shards had resurfaced the night he had seen Marie. They had woken him out of sleep – nightmares made manifest, even in the brilliance of the lights he had turned on.

Blood. Blood on his hands, blood covering his chest. Blood on the face of the woman he is carrying. Marie! No, not Marie! Someone else, the tender planes of her neck pale through the streams of blood. Her life leaking all over him, dripping onto the cobbled street as he runs. Panting through the chill night. Where is he? Why is he running? Dear God, who is she?

He had bolted up, and though it was the dead of the night he'd dressed and slipped out, running full-out through the Canadian countryside until his sides ached. The bone-white moonlight had followed him like the bloody shards of memory. He'd been unable to outrun either.

Now he was lying to this doctor. Well, why not? He didn't trust him, even though Martin Lindros – the DDCI and Bourne's friend – had recommended him, showed Bourne his impressive credentials. Lindros had gotten Sunderland's name from a list provided by the DCI's office. He didn't have to ask his friend about that: Anne Held's name on the bottom of each page of the document verified his hypothesis. Anne Held was the DCI's assistant, stern right hand.

'Mr. Bourne?' Dr. Sunderland prompted him.

Not that it mattered. He saw Marie's face, pale and lifeless, felt Lindros's presence beside him as he took in the coroner's French-Canadian-accented English: *'The viral pneumonia had spread too far, we couldn't save her. You can take comfort in the fact that she didn't suffer. She went to sleep and never woke up.'* The coroner had looked from the dead woman to her grief-stricken husband and his friend. *'If only she'd come back from the skiing trip sooner.'*

Bourne had bitten his lip. *'She was taking care of our children. Jamie had turned an ankle on his last run. Alison was terribly frightened.'*

'She didn't seek a doctor? Suppose the ankle was sprained – or broken.'

'You don't understand. My wife – her entire family are outdoors people, ranchers, hardy stock. Marie was trained from an early age to take care of herself in the wilderness. She had no fear of it whatsoever.'

'Sometimes,' the coroner had said, *'a little fear is a good thing.'*

'You have no right to judge her!' Bourne had cried out in anger and grief.

'You've spent too much time with the dead,' Lindros had berated the coroner. *'You need to work on your people skills.'*

'My apologies.'

Bourne had caught his breath and, turning to Lindros, said, *'She phoned me, she thought it was just a cold.'*

'A natural enough conclusion,' his friend had said. *'In any event, her mind was clearly on her son and daughter.'*

'So, Mr. Bourne, when did the memory flashes begin?' There was the distinct tinge of a Romanian accent to Dr. Sunderland's English. Here was a man, with his high, wide forehead, strong-lined jaw, and prominent nose, that one could easily have confidence in, confide in. He wore steel-rimmed glasses and his hair was slicked back in a curious, old-fashioned style. No PDA for him, no text-messaging on the run. Above all, no multitasking. He wore a three-piece suit of heavy Harris tweed, a red-and-white polka-dot bow tie.

'Come, come.' Dr. Sunderland cocked his large head, which made him look like an owl. 'You'll forgive me, but I feel quite sure you're – how shall I put it – hiding the truth.'

At once, Bourne was on the alert. 'Hiding . . . ?'

Dr. Sunderland produced a beautiful crocodile-skin wallet, from which he slipped a hundred-dollar bill. Holding it up, he said, 'I'll wager that the memory flashes began just after you laid your wife to rest. However, this wager will be invalid if you elect not to tell the truth.'

'What are you, a human lie detector?'

Dr. Sunderland wisely kept his own counsel.

'Put your money away,' Bourne said at length. He sighed. 'You're right, of course. The memory flashes began the day I saw Marie for the last time.'

'What form did they take?'

Bourne hesitated. 'I was looking down at her – in the funeral home. Her sister and father had already identified her and had her transferred from the coroner's. I looked down at her and – I didn't see her at all . . .'

'What did you see, Mr. Bourne?' Dr. Sunderland's voice was soft, detached.

'Blood. I saw blood.'

'And?'

'Well, there was no blood. Not really. It was the memory surfacing – without warning – without . . .'

'That's the way it always happens, isn't it?'

Bourne nodded. 'The blood . . . it was fresh, glistening, made bluish by street lamps. The blood covered this face . . .'

'Whose face?'

'I don't know . . . a woman . . . but it wasn't Marie. It was . . . someone else.'

'Can you describe this woman?' Dr. Sunderland asked.

'That's the thing. I can't. I don't know . . . And yet, I know her. I know I do.'

There was a small silence, into which Dr. Sunderland interjected another seemingly unrelated question. 'Tell me, Mr. Bourne, what is today's date?'

'That's not the kind of memory problem I have.'

Dr. Sunderland ducked his head. 'Indulge me, please.'

'Tuesday, February third.'

'Four months since the funeral, since your memory problem began. Why did you wait so long to seek help?'

For a time, there was another silence. 'Something happened last week,' Bourne said at length. 'I saw – I saw an old friend of mine.' Alex Conklin, walking down the street in Alexandria's Old Town where he'd taken Jamie and Alison for the last outing he'd have with them for a long time. They had just come out of a Baskin-Robbins, the two of them loaded with ice-cream cones, and there was Conklin big as life. Alex Conklin: his mentor, the mastermind behind the Jason Bourne identity. Without Conklin, it was impossible to imagine where he'd be today.

Dr. Sunderland cocked his head. 'I don't understand.'

'This friend died three years ago.'

'Yet you saw him.'

Bourne nodded. 'I called his name, and when he turned around he was holding something in his arms – someone, actually. A woman. A bloody woman.'

'*Your* bloody woman.'

'Yes. At that moment I thought I was losing my mind.'

That was when he'd decided to ship the kids off. Alison and Jamie were with Marie's sister and father in Canada, where the family maintained their enormous ranch. It was better for them, though Bourne missed them terribly. It would not be good for them to see him now.

Since then, how many times had he dreamed of the moments he dreaded most: seeing Marie's pale face; picking up her effects at the hospital; standing in the darkened room of the funeral home with the director beside him, staring down at Marie's body, her face still, waxen, made up in a way Marie never would have done herself. He had leaned over, his hand reaching out, and the director had offered a handkerchief, which Bourne had used to wipe the lipstick and rouge off her face. He had kissed her then, the coldness of her lips running right through him like an electric shock: *She's dead, she's dead. That's it, my life with her is over.* With a small sound, he'd lowered the casket lid. Turning to the funeral director, he'd said, *'I've changed my mind. No open casket. I don't want anyone to see her like this, especially the children.'*

'Nevertheless you went after him,' Dr. Sunderland persisted. 'Most fascinating. Given your history, your amnesia, the trauma of your wife's untimely death set off a particular memory flashback. Can you think in what way your deceased friend is connected with the bloody woman?'

'No.' But of course that was a lie. He suspected that he was reliving an old mission – one that Alex Conklin had sent him on years ago.

Dr. Sunderland steepled his fingers together. 'Your memory flashes can be triggered by anything providing it's vivid enough: something you saw, smelled, touched, like a dream resurfacing. Except for you these "dreams" are real. They're your memories; they actually happened.' He took up a gold fountain pen. 'There's no doubt that a trauma such as you've suffered would be at the top of that list. And then to believe you've seen someone you know to be dead – it's hardly surprising the flashbacks have become more numerous.'

True enough, but the escalation of the flashbacks made his

mental state that much more unbearable. On that afternoon in Georgetown, he'd left his children. It was only for a moment, but . . . He'd been horrified; he still was.

Marie was gone, in a terrible, senseless moment. And now it wasn't only the memory of Marie that haunted him, but those ancient silent streets, leering at him, streets that possessed knowledge he didn't, that knew something about him, something he couldn't even guess at. His nightmare went like this: The memory flashes would come and he'd be bathed in cold sweat. He'd lie in the darkness, absolutely certain he'd never fall asleep. Inevitably he did – a heavy, almost drugged sleep. And when he rose from that abyss, he'd turn, still in the grip of slumber, searching as he always did for Marie's warm, delicious body. Then it would hit him all over again, a freight train slamming him full in the chest.

Marie is dead. Dead and gone forever . . .

The dry, rhythmic sound of Dr. Sunderland writing in his notebook brought Bourne back from his black oblivion.

'These memory flashes are literally driving me crazy.'

'Hardly surprising. Your desire to uncover your past is all-consuming. Some might even term it obsessive – I certainly would. An obsession often deprives those suffering with it of the ability to live what might be termed a normal life – though I detest that term and use it infrequently. In any event, I think I can help.'

Dr. Sunderland spread his hands, which were large and callused. 'Let me begin by explaining to you the nature of your disability. Memories are made when electrical impulses cause synapses in the brain to release neurotransmitters so that the synapses fire, as we say. This creates a temporary memory. To make this permanent a process called consolidation needs to occur. I won't bore you by detailing it. Suffice it to say that consolidation requires the synthesis of new proteins, hence it takes many hours. Along the way the process can be blocked or altered by any number of things – severe trauma, for instance, or unconsciousness. This is what happened to you. While you were unconscious, your abnormal brain activity turned your permanent memories into temporary ones. The proteins that create temporary memories degrade very quickly. Within hours, or even minutes, those temporary memories disappear.'

'But my memories occasionally do surface.'

'That's because trauma – physical, emotional, or a combination of the two – can very quickly flood certain synapses with neurotransmitters, thus resurrecting, shall we say, memories previously lost.'

Dr. Sunderland smiled. 'All this is to prepare you. The idea of full memory erasure, though closer than ever before, is still the stuff of science fiction. However, the very latest procedures are at my disposal, and I can confidently say that I can get your memory to surface completely. But you must give me two weeks.'

'I'm giving you today, Doctor.'

'I highly recommend—'

'Today,' Bourne said more firmly.

Dr. Sunderland studied him for some time, tapping his gold pen contemplatively against his lower lip. 'Under those circumstances . . . I believe I can *suppress* the memory. That's not the same as erasing it.'

'I understand.'

'All right.' Dr. Sunderland slapped his thighs. 'Come into the examination room and I'll do my best to help you.' He lifted a long, cautionary forefinger. 'I suppose I needn't remind you that memory is a terribly slippery creature.'

'No need at all,' Bourne said as another glimmer of foreboding eeled its way through him.

'So you understand there are no guarantees. The chances are excellent that my procedure will work, but for how long . . .' He shrugged.

Bourne nodded as he rose and followed Dr. Sunderland

into the next room. This was somewhat larger than the consultation room. The floor was doctor's standard-issue speckled linoleum, the walls lined with stainless-steel equipment, counter, and cabinets. A small sink took up one corner, below which was a red plastic receptacle with a BIOHAZARD label prominently affixed to it. The center of the room was taken up by what looked like a particularly plush and futuristic dentist chair. Several articulated arms depended from the ceiling in a tight circle around it. There were two medical devices of unknown origin set on carts with rubber wheels. All in all, the room had the efficient, sterile look of an operating theater.

Bourne sat on the chair and waited while Dr. Sunderland adjusted its height and inclination to his satisfaction. From one of the rolling carts, the doctor then affixed eight electronic leads to different areas of Bourne's head.

'I'm going to perform two series of tests of your brain waves, one when you're conscious, one when you're unconscious. It's crucial that I be able to evaluate both states of your brain activity.'

'And then what?'

'It depends on what I find,' Dr. Sunderland said. 'But the treatment will involve stimulating certain synapses in the brain with specific complex proteins.' He peered down at Bourne. 'Miniaturization is the key, you see. That's one of my specialties. You cannot work with proteins, on that minuscule level, without being an expert in miniaturization. You've heard of nanotechnology?'

Bourne nodded. 'Manufactured electronic bits of microscopic size. In effect, tiny computers.'

'Precisely.' Dr. Sunderland's eyes gleamed. He appeared very pleased by the scope of his patient's knowledge. 'These complex proteins – these neurotransmitters – act just like nanosites, binding and strengthening synapses in areas of your brain to which I will direct them, to block or make memories.'

All at once Bourne ripped off the electronic leads, rose, and, without a word, bolted out of the office. He half ran down the marble-clad hall, his shoes making small clicking sounds as if a many-legged animal were pursuing him. What was he doing, allowing someone to tinker with his brain?

The two bathroom doors stood side by side. Hauling open the door that said MEN, he rushed inside, stood with his arms rigid on either side of the white porcelain sink. There was his face, pallid, ghostly in the mirror. He saw reflected the tiles behind him, so like those in the funeral home. He saw Marie – lying still, hands crossed on her flat, athlete's belly. She floated as if on a barge, as if on a swift river, taking her away from him.

He pressed his forehead against the mirror. The flood-gates opened, tears welled up in his eyes, rolled freely down his cheeks. He remembered Marie as she had been, her hair floating in the wind, the skin at the nape of her neck like satin; when they'd whitewater-rafted down the Snake River, her strong, sun-browned arms digging the paddle into the churning water, the big Western sky reflected in her eyes; when he'd asked her to marry him, on the stolid granite grounds of Georgetown University, she in a black spaghetti-strap dress beneath a Canadian shearling coat, holding hands, laughing on the way to a faculty Christmas party; when they'd said their vows, the sun sliding behind the jagged snowcapped peaks of the Canadian Rockies, their newly ringed hands linked, their lips pressed together, their hearts beating as one. He remembered when she'd given birth to Alison. Two days before Halloween, she was sitting at the sewing machine, making a ghost pirate costume for Jamie, when her water broke. Alison's birth was hard and long. At the end, Marie had begun to bleed. He'd almost lost her then, holding on tight, willing her not to leave him. Now he had lost her forever . . .

He found himself sobbing, unable to stop.

And then, like a ghoul haunting him, the unknown woman's bloody face once again rose from the depths of his memory to blot out his beloved Marie. Blood dripped. Her eyes stared sightlessly up at him. What did she want? Why was she haunting him? He gripped his temples in despair and moaned. He desperately wanted to leave this floor, this building, but he knew he couldn't. Not like this, not being assaulted by his own brain.

Dr. Sunderland was waiting with pursed lips, patient as stone, in his office. 'Shall I?'

Bourne, the bloody face still clogging his senses, took a breath and nodded. 'Go ahead.'

He sat in the chair, and Dr. Sunderland reattached the leads. He flipped a switch on the movable cart and began to ramp up dials, some quickly, others slowly, almost gingerly.

'Don't be apprehensive,' Dr. Sunderland said gently. 'You will feel nothing at all.'

Bourne didn't.

When Dr. Sunderland was satisfied, he threw another switch and a long sheet of paper much like the one used in a EEG machine came rolling out of a slot. The doctor peered at the printout of Bourne's waking brain waves.

He made no notations on the printout but nodded to himself, his brow roiled like an oncoming thunderhead. Bourne could not tell whether any of this was a good sign or a bad one.

'All right then,' Dr. Sunderland said at length. He switched off the machine, rolled the cart away, and replaced it with the second one.

From a tray on its gleaming metal top he picked up a syringe. Bourne could see that it was already loaded with a clear liquid.

Dr. Sunderland turned to Bourne. 'The shot won't put

you all the way out, just into a deep sleep – delta waves, the slowest brain waves.' In response to the practiced movement of the doctor's thumb, a bit of the liquid squirted out the end of the needle. 'I need to see if there are any unusual breaks in your delta wave patterns.'

Bourne nodded, and awoke as if no time had passed.

'How do you feel?' Dr. Sunderland asked.

'Better, I think,' Bourne said.

'Good.' Dr. Sunderland showed him a printout. 'As I suspected, there was an anomaly in your delta wave pattern.' He pointed. 'Here, you see? And again here.' He handed Bourne a second printout. 'Now here is your delta wave pattern after the treatment. The anomaly is vastly diminished. Judging by the evidence, it is reasonable to assume that your flashbacks will disappear altogether over the course of the next ten or so days. Though I have to warn you there's a good chance they might get worse over the next forty-eight hours, the time it takes for your synapses to adjust to the treatment.'

The short winter twilight was skidding toward night when Bourne exited the doctor's building, a large Greek Revival limestone structure on K Street. An icy wind off the Potomac, smelling of phosphorus and rot, whipped the flaps of his overcoat around his shins.

Turning away from a bitter swirl of dust and grit, he saw his reflection in a flower shop window, a bright spray of flowers displayed behind the glass, so like the flowers at Marie's funeral.

Then, just to his right, the brass-clad door to the shop opened and someone exited, a gaily wrapped bouquet in her arms. He smelled . . . what was it, wafting out from the bouquet? Gardenias, yes. That was a spray of gardenias carefully wrapped against winter's chill.

Now, in his mind's eye, he carried the woman from his unknown past in his arms, felt her blood warm and pulsing on his forearms. She was younger than he had assumed, in her early twenties, no more. Her lips moved, sending a shiver down his spine. She was still alive! Her eyes sought his. Blood leaked out of her half-open mouth. And words, clotted, distorted. He strained to hear her. What was she saying? Was she trying to tell him something? Who *was* she?

With another gust of gritty wind, he returned to the chill Washington twilight. The horrific image had vanished. Had the scent of the gardenias summoned her from inside him? Was there a connection?

He turned around, about to go back to Dr. Sunderland, even though he had been warned that in the short run he might still be tormented. His cell phone buzzed. For a moment, he considered ignoring it. Then he flipped open the phone, put it to his ear.

He was surprised to discover that it was Anne Held, the DCI's assistant. He formed a mental picture of a tall, slim brunette in her middle twenties, with classic features, rosebud lips, and icy gray eyes.

'Hello, Mr. Bourne. The DCI wishes to see you.' Her accent was Middle Atlantic, meaning that it lay somewhere between her British birthplace and her adopted American home.

'I have no wish to see him,' Bourne responded coldly.

Anne Held sighed, clearly steeling herself. 'Mr. Bourne, next to Martin Lindros himself nobody knows your antagonistic relationship with the Old Man – with CI in general – better than I do. God knows you have ample cause: They've used you countless times as a stalking horse, and then they were sure you'd turned rogue on them. But you really must come in now.'

'Eloquently said. But all the eloquence in the world won't sway me. If the DCI has something to say to me, he can do it through Martin.'

'It's Martin Lindros the Old Man needs to talk to you about.'

Bourne realized he was holding the phone with a death grip. His voice was ice cold when he said: 'What about Martin?'

'That's just it. I don't know. No one knows but the Old Man. He's been closeted in Signals since before lunchtime. Even I haven't seen him. Three minutes ago, he called me and ordered me to have you brought in.'

'That's how he put it?'

'His precise words were, "I know how close Bourne and Lindros are. That's why I need him." Mr. Bourne, I implore you, come in. It's Code Mesa here.'

Code Mesa was CI-speak for a Level One emergency.

While Bourne waited for the taxi he'd called, he had time to think about Martin Lindros.

How many times in the past three years had he spoken of the intimate, often painful subject of his memory loss with Martin. Lindros, the deputy director of CI – the least likely confidant. Who would have expected him to become Jason Bourne's friend? Not Bourne himself, who had found his suspicion and paranoia coming to the fore when Lindros had shown up at Webb's campus office nearly three years ago. Surely, Bourne had figured, he was there to once more try to recruit Bourne into CI. It wasn't such an odd notion. After all, Lindros was using his newfound power to reshape CI into a leaner, cleaner organization with the expertise to take on the worldwide threats that radical, fundamentalist Islam presented.

Such a change would have been all but unthinkable five years ago, when the Old Man ruled CI with an iron hand. But now the DCI truly was an old man – in reality as well as in name. Rumors swirled that he was losing his grip; that it was time for him to retire honorably before he was fired. Bourne would wish this were so, but chances were that these particular rumors had been started by the Old Man himself to flush out the enemies he knew were hiding in the Beltway brush. He was a wily old bastard, better connected to the old-boy network that was the bedrock of Washington than anyone else Bourne had ever come across.

The red-and-white taxi pulled to a halt at the curb; Bourne got in and gave an address to the driver. Settling himself into the backseat, his thoughts returned inward.

To his complete surprise, the subject of recruitment had never come up in the conversation. Over dinner, Bourne began to get to know Lindros in an entirely different way from their time in the field together. The very fact of his changing CI from the inside had turned him into a loner within his own organization. He had the absolute, unshakable trust of the Old Man, who saw in Lindros something of his own younger self, but the head of the seven directorates feared him because he held their futures in the palm of his hand.

Lindros had a girlfriend named Moira, but otherwise had no one close to him. And he had a particular empathy for Bourne's situation. *'You can't remember your life,'* he had said over that first of many dinners. *'I have no life to remember . . .'*

Perhaps what drew them unconsciously was the deep, abiding damage each of them had suffered. From their mutual incompleteness came friendship and trust.

Finally, a week ago, he'd taken a medical leave from Georgetown. He'd called Lindros, but his friend was unavailable. No one would tell him where Lindros was. Bourne missed his friend's careful, rational analysis of Bourne's increasingly irrational state of mind. And now his friend was at the center of a mystery that had caused CI to go into emergency lockdown mode.

*

The moment Costin Veintrop – the man who called himself Dr. Sunderland – received confirmation that Jason Bourne had, indeed, left the building, he neatly and rapidly packed his equipment into the gusseted outside compartment of a black leather briefcase. From one of the two main sections he produced a laptop computer, which he fired up. This was no ordinary laptop; Veintrop, a specialist in miniaturization, an adjunct to his study of human memory, had customized it himself. Plugging a high-definition digital camera into the Firewire port, he brought up four photo enlargements of the laboratory room taken from different angles. Comparing them with the scene in front of him, he went about ensuring that every item was as he had found it when he'd entered the office fifteen minutes before Bourne had arrived. When he was through, he turned off the lights and went into the consult room.

Veintrop took down the photos he'd put up, giving a lingering look at the woman he'd identified as his wife. She was indeed Katya, his Baltic Katya, his wife. His ingenuous sincerity had helped him sell himself to Bourne. Veintrop was a man who believed in verisimilitude. This was why he'd used a photo of his wife and not a woman unknown to him. When taking on a legend – a new identity – he felt it crucial to mix in bits of things he himself believed. Especially with a man of Jason Bourne's expertise. In any event, Katya's photo had had the desired effect on Bourne. Unfortunately, it had also served to remind Veintrop of where she was and why he could not see her. Briefly, his fingers curled, making fists so tight his knuckles went pale.

Abruptly he shook himself. Enough of this morbid self-pity; he had work to do. Placing the laptop on the corner of the real Dr. Sunderland's desk, he brought up enlargements of the digital photos he'd made of this room. As before, he was meticulous in his scrutiny, assuring himself that every single detail of the consult room was as he had found it. It was essential that no trace of his presence remain after he'd left.

His quad-band GSM cell phone buzzed, and he put it to his ear.

'It's done,' Veintrop said in Romanian. He could have used Arabic, his employer's native language, but it had been mutually decided that Romanian would be less obtrusive.

'To your satisfaction?' It was a different voice, somewhat deeper and coarser than the compelling voice of the man who'd hired him, belonging to someone who was used to exhorting rabid followers.

'Most certainly. I have honed and perfected the procedure on the test subjects you provided for me. Everything contracted for is in place.'

'The proof of it will occur shortly.' The dominant note of impatience was soured by a faint undertone of anxiety.

'Have faith, my friend,' Veintrop said, and broke the connection.

Returning to his work, he packed away his laptop, digital camera, and Firewire connector, then slipped on his tweed overcoat and felt fedora. Grasping his briefcase in one hand, he took one final look around with exacting finality. There was no place for error in the highly specialized work he did.

Satisfied, he flipped the light switch and, in utter darkness, slipped out of the office. In the hallway he glanced at his watch: 4:46 PM. Three minutes over, still well within the time-frame tolerance allotted to him by his employer. It was Tuesday, February 3, as Bourne had said. On Tuesday, Dr. Sunderland had no office hours.

TWO

CI headquarters, located on 23rd Street NW, was identified on maps of the city as belonging to the Department of Agriculture. To reinforce the illusion, it was surrounded by perfectly manicured lawns, dotted here and there with ornamental shade trees, divided by snaking gravel paths. The building itself was as nondescript as was possible in a city devoted to the grandeur of monumental Federal architecture. It was bounded to the north by huge structures that housed the State Department and the Navy Bureau of Medicine and Surgery, and on the east by the National Academy of Sciences. The DCI's office had a sobering view of the Vietnam Veterans Memorial, as well as a slice of the shining, white Lincoln Memorial.

Anne Held hadn't been exaggerating. Bourne had to go through no less than three separate security checkpoints before he gained admittance to the inner lobby. They took place in the bomb- and fireproof public lobby, which was, in effect, a bunker. Hidden behind decorative marble slabs and columns were half-meter-thick meta-concrete blast walls, reinforced with a mesh of steel rods and Kevlar webbing. There was no glass to shatter, and the lighting and electrical circuits were heavily shielded. The first checkpoint required him to repeat a code phrase that changed three times a day; at the second he had to submit to a fingerprint scanner. At the third, he put his right eye to the lens of a sinister-looking matte-black machine, which took a photo of his retina and digitally compared it with the photo already on file. This added layer of high-tech security was crucial since it was now possible to fake fingerprints with silicone patches affixed to the pads of the fingers. Bourne ought to know: He'd done it several times.

There was another security check just before the elevator bank, and still another – a jury-rigged affair as per Code Mesa regs – just outside the DCI's suite of offices on the fifth floor.

Once through the thick, steel-plated, rosewood-clad door he saw Anne Held. Uncharacteristically, she was accompanied by a whey-faced man with muscles rippling beneath his suit jacket.

She gave him a small, tight smile. 'I saw the DCI a few moments ago. He looks like he's aged ten years.'

'I'm not here for him,' Bourne said. 'Martin Lindros is the only man in CI I care about and trust. Where is he?'

'He's been in the field for the last three weeks, doing God alone knows what.' Anne was dressed in her usual impeccable fashion in a charcoal-gray Armani suit, a fire-red silk blouse, and Manolo Blahniks with three-inch heels. 'But I'll wager high money that whatever signals the DCI has received today are what's caused the extraordinary flap around here.'

The whey-faced man escorted them wordlessly down one corridor after another – a deliberately bewildering labyrinth through which visitors were led via a different route every time – until they arrived at the door to the DCI's sanctum sanctorum. There his escort stood aside, but did not leave. Another marker of Code Mesa, Bourne thought as he smiled thinly up at the tiny eye of the security camera.

A moment later, he heard the electronic lock clicking open remotely.

The DCI stood at the far end of an office as large as a football field. He held a file in one hand, a lit cigarette in the other, defying the building's federally mandated ban. *When did he start smoking again?* Bourne wondered. Standing beside him was another man – tall, beefy, with a long scowling face, light brush-cut hair, and a dangerous stillness about him.

'Ah, you've come at last.' The Old Man strode toward Bourne, the heels of his handmade shoes clicking across the polished wood floor. His shoulders were up around his ears, hunched as if against heavy weather. As he approached, the floodlights from outside illuminated him, the moving images of his past exploits written like soft white explosions across his face.

He looked old and tired, his cheeks fissured like a mountainside, his eyes sunken into their sockets, the flesh beneath them puddled and yellow, a candle burned too low. He jammed the cigarette between his liver-colored lips, underscoring the fact that he would not offer to shake hands.

The other man followed, clearly and deliberately at his own pace.

'Bourne, this is Matthew Lerner, my new deputy director. Lerner, Bourne.'

The two men shook hands briefly.

'I thought Martin was DDCI,' Bourne said to Lerner, puzzled.

'It's complicated. We—'

'Lerner will brief you following this interview,' the Old Man interrupted.

'If there is to be a briefing after this.' Bourne frowned, abruptly uneasy. 'What about Martin?'

DCI hesitated. The old antipathy was still there – it would never disappear. Bourne knew that and accepted it as gospel. Clearly the current situation was dire enough for the Old Man to do something he'd sworn never to do: ask for Jason Bourne's help. On the other hand, the DCI was the ultimate pragmatist. He'd have to be to keep the director's job for so long. He had become immune to the slings and arrows of difficult and, often, morally ambiguous compromise. This was, simply, the world in which he existed. He needed Bourne now, and he was furious about it.

'Martin Lindros has been missing for almost seven days.' All at once the DCI seemed smaller, as if his suit were about to fall off him.

Bourne stood stock-still. No wonder he hadn't heard from Martin. 'What the hell happened?'

The Old Man lit another cigarette from the glowing end of the first, grinding out the butt in a cut-crystal ashtray. His hand shook slightly. 'Martin was on a mission to Ethiopia.'

'What was he doing in the field?' Bourne asked.

'I asked the same question,' Lerner said. 'But this was his baby.'

'Martin's people have gotten a sudden increase in chatter on particular terrorist frequencies.' The DCI pulled smoke deep into his lungs, let it out in a soft hiss. 'His analysts are expert at differentiating the real stuff from the disinformation that has counterterrorist divisions at other agencies chasing their tails and crying wolf.'

His eyes locked with Bourne's. 'He's provided us with credible evidence that the chatter is real, that an attack against one of three major cities in the United States – D.C., New York, L.A. – is imminent. Worse still, this attack involves a nuclear bomb.'

The DCI took a package off a nearby sideboard and handed it to Bourne.

Bourne opened it. Inside was a small, oblong metallic object.

'Know what that is?' Lerner spoke as if issuing a challenge.

'It's a triggered spark gap. It's used in industry to switch on tremendously powerful engines.' Bourne looked up. 'It's also used to trigger nuclear weapons.'

'That's right. Especially this one.' The DCI's face was

grim as he handed Bourne a file marked DEO – Director's Eyes Only. It contained a highly detailed spec sheet on this particular device. 'Usually triggered spark gaps use gases – air, argon, oxygen, SF_6, or a combination of these – to carry the current. This one uses a solid material.'

'It's designed to be used once and once only.'

'Correct. That rules out an industrial application.'

Bourne rolled the TSG between his fingers. 'The only possible use, then, would be in a nuclear device.'

'A nuclear device in the hands of terrorists,' Lerner said with a dark look.

The DCI took the TSG from Bourne, tapped it with a gnarled forefinger. 'Martin was following the trail of an illicit shipment of these TSGs, which led to the mountains of northwestern Ethiopia where he believed they were being transshipped by a terrorist cadre.'

'Destination?'

'Unknown,' the DCI said.

Bourne was deeply disturbed, but he chose to keep the feeling to himself. 'All right. Let's hear the details.'

'At 17:32 local time, six days ago, Martin and the five-man team of Skorpion One choppered onto the upper reaches of the northern slope of Ras Dejen.' Lerner passed over a sheet of onionskin. 'Here are the exact coordinates.'

The DCI said, 'Ras Dejen is the highest peak in the Semien Range. You've been there. Better yet, you speak the language of the local tribespeople.'

Lerner continued. 'At 18:04 local time, we lost radio contact with Skorpion One. At 10:06 AM Eastern Standard Time, I ordered Skorpion Two to those coordinates.' He took the sheet of onionskin back from Bourne. 'At 10:46 EST today, we got a signal from Ken Jeffries, the commander of Skorpion Two. The unit found the burned-out wreckage of the Chinook on a small plateau at the correct coordinates.'

'That was the last communication we had from Skorpion

Two,' the DCI said. 'Since then, nothing from Lindros or anyone else in the party.'

'Skorpion Three is stationed in Djibouti and ready to go,' Lerner said, neatly sidestepping the Old Man's look of disgust.

But Bourne, ignoring Lerner, was turning over possibilities in his mind, which helped him put aside his anxiety regarding his friend's fate. 'One of two things has happened,' he said firmly. 'Either Martin is dead or he's been captured and is undergoing articulated interrogation. Clearly, a team is not the way.'

'The Skorpion units are made up of some of our best and brightest field agents – battle-hardened in Somalia, Afghanistan, and Iraq,' Lerner pointed out. 'You'll need their firepower, believe me.'

'The firepower of two Skorpion units couldn't handle the situation on Ras Dejen. I go in alone, or not at all.'

His point was clear, but the new DDCI wasn't buying it. 'Where you see "flexibility," Bourne, the organization sees irresponsibility, unacceptable danger to those around you.'

'Listen, you called me in here. You're asking a favor of me.'

'Fine, forget Skorpion Three,' the Old Man said. 'I know you work alone.'

Lerner closed the file. 'In return, you'll get all the intel, all the transportation and support you need.'

The DCI took a step toward Bourne. 'I know you won't pass up the chance to go after your friend.'

'In that you're right.' Bourne walked calmly to the door. 'Do whatever the hell you want with the people you command. For myself, I'm going after Martin without your help.'

'Wait.' The Old Man's voice rang out in the huge office. There was a note to it like a whistle on a train passing through a dark and deserted landscape. Sadness and cynicism venomously mixed. 'Wait, you bastard.'

Bourne took his time turning around.

The DCI glared at him with a bitter enmity. 'How Martin gets along with you is a goddamn mystery.' Hands clenched behind his back, he strode in full military fashion to the window, stood staring out at the immaculate lawn and, beyond, the Vietnam Veterans Memorial. He turned back and fixed Bourne in his implacable gaze. 'Your arrogance disgusts me.'

Bourne met his gaze mutely.

'All right, no leash,' the DCI snapped. He was shaking with barely suppressed rage. 'Lerner will see that you have everything you need. But I'm telling you, you'd damn well better bring Martin Lindros home.'

THREE

Lerner led Bourne out of the DCI's suite, down the hall, into his own office. Lerner sat down behind his desk. When he realized that Bourne had chosen to stand, he leaned back.

'What I'm about to tell you cannot under any circumstances leave this room. The Old Man has named Martin director of a black-ops agency code-named Typhon, dealing exclusively with countering Muslim extremist terrorist groups.'

Bourne recalled that *Typhon* was a name out of Greek mythology: the fearsome hundred-headed father of the deadly Hydra. 'We already have a Counterterrorist Center.'

'CTC knows nothing about Typhon,' Lerner said. 'In fact, even inside CI, knowledge of it is on a strict need-to-know basis.'

'So Typhon is a *double-blind* black op.'

Lerner nodded. 'I know what you're thinking: that we haven't had anything like this since Treadstone. But there are compelling reasons. Aspects of Typhon are – shall we say – extremely controversial, so far as powerful reactionary elements within the administration and Congress are concerned.'

He pursed his lips. 'I'll cut to the chase. Lindros has constructed Typhon from the ground up. It's not a division, it's an agency unto itself. Lindros insisted that he be free of administrative red tape. Also, it's by necessity worldwide – he's already staffed up in London, Paris, Istanbul, Dubai,

Saudi Arabia, and three locations in the Horn of Africa. And it's Martin's intention to infiltrate terrorist cells in order to destroy the networks from the inside out.'

'Infiltration,' Bourne said. So that's what Martin had meant when he'd told Bourne that save for the director, he was completely alone inside CI. 'That's the holy grail of counterterrorism, but so far no one's been able to even come close.'

'Because they have few Muslims and even fewer Arabists working for them. In all of the FBI, only thirty-three out of twelve thousand have even a limited proficiency in Arabic, and none of those works in the sections of the bureau that investigate terrorism within our borders. With good reason. Leading members of the administration are still reluctant to use Muslims and Western Arabists – they're simply not trusted.'

'Stupid and shortsighted,' Bourne said.

'But these people exist, and Lindros has been quietly recruiting them.' Lerner stood up. 'So much for orientation. Your next stop, I believe, will be Typhon ops itself.'

Because it was a *double-blind* counterterrorist agency, Typhon was down in the depths. The CI building sub-basement had been recast and remodeled by a construction firm whose every worker had been extensively vetted even before they had been made to sign a confidentiality agreement that would assure them a twenty-year term in a federal maximum-security facility if they were foolish or greedy enough to break their silence. The supplies that had been filling up the sub-basement had been exiled to an annex.

On his way out of the DCI's office, Bourne briefly stopped by Anne Held's domain. Armed with the names of the two case officers who had eavesdropped on the conversation that had sent Martin Lindros halfway around the world on the trail of transshipped TSGs, he took the private elevator that shuttled between the DCI's floor and the sub-basement.

As the elevator sighed to a stop, an LCD panel on the left-hand door activated, an electronic eye scanning the shiny black octagon Anne had affixed to the lapel of his jacket. It was encoded with a number invisible save to the scanner. Only then did the steel doors slide open.

Martin Lindros had reimagined the sub-basement as, basically, one gigantic space filled with mobile workstations, each with a braid of electronic leads spiraling up to the ceiling. The braids were on tracks so they could move with the workstations and the personnel as they relocated from assignment to assignment. At the far end, Bourne saw, was a series of conference rooms, separated from the main space by alternating frosted-glass and steel panels.

As befitted an agency named after a monster with two hundred eyes, the Typhon office was filled with monitors. In fact, the walls were a mosaic of flat-panel plasma screens on which a dizzying array of digital images were displayed: satellite chartings, closed-circuit television pictures of public spaces, transportation hubs such as airports, bus depots, train stations, street corners, cross sections of snaking highways and suburban rail lines, metropolitan underground platforms worldwide – Bourne recognized metros in New York, London, Paris, Moscow. People of all shapes, sizes, religions, ethnicities walking, milling mindlessly, standing undecided, lounging, smoking, getting on and off conveyances, talking to one another, ignoring one another, plugged into iPods, shopping, eating on the run, kissing, cuddling, exchanging bitter words, oblivious, cell phones slapped to their ears, accessing e-mail or porno, slouched, hunched, drunk, stoned, fights breaking out, first-date embarrassments, skulking, mumbling to themselves. A chaos of unedited video from which the analysts were required to find specific patterns, digital omens, electronic warning signs.

Lerner must have alerted the case officers to his arrival, because he saw a striking young woman whom he judged to be in her midthirties detach herself from a view screen and come toward him. He at once knew that she was or had been, at any rate, a field agent. Her stride was not too long, not too short, not too fast, not too slow. It was, to sum it up in one word, anonymous. Because an individual's stride was as distinctive as his fingerprints, it was one of the best ways to cull an adversary out of a swarming pack of pedestrians, even one whose disguise was otherwise first-rate.

She had a face that was both strong and proud, the chiseled prow of a sleek ship knifing through seas that would capsize inferior vessels. The large, deep blue eyes were set like jewels in the cinnamon dusk of her Arabian face.

'You must be Soraya Moore,' he said, 'the senior case officer.'

Her smile showed for a moment, then was quickly hidden behind a cloud of confusion and abrupt coolness. 'That's right, Mr. Bourne. This way.'

She led him down the length of the vast, teeming space to the second conference room from the left. Opening the frosted-glass door, she watched him pass with that same odd curiosity. But then considering his often adversarial relationship with CI, perhaps it wasn't odd after all.

There was a man inside, younger than Soraya by at least several years. He was of middling height, athletic, with sandy hair and a fair complexion. He was sitting at an oval glass conference table working on a laptop. The screen was filled with what looked to be an exceptionally difficult crossword puzzle.

He glanced up only when Soraya cleared her throat.

'Tim Hytner,' he said without rising,

When Bourne took a seat between the two case officers, he discovered that the crossword Hytner was trying to solve was, in fact, a cipher – and quite a sophisticated one at that.

'I have just over five hours until my flight to London departs,' Bourne said. 'Triggered spark gaps – tell me what I need to know.'

'Along with fissionable material, TSGs are among the most highly restricted items in the world,' Hytner began. 'To be precise, they're number two thousand six hundred forty-one on the government's controlled list.'

'So the tip that got Lindros so excited he couldn't help going into the field himself concerned a transshipment of TSGs.'

Hytner was back to trying to crack the cipher, so Soraya took over. 'The whole thing began in South Africa. Cape Town, to be exact.'

'Why Cape Town?' Bourne asked.

'During the apartheid era, the country became a haven for smugglers, mostly by necessity.' Soraya spoke quickly, efficiently, but with an unmistakable detachment. 'Now that South Africa is on our "white list," it's okay for American manufacturers to export TSGs there.'

'Then they get "lost,"' Hytner chimed in without lifting his head from the letters on the screen.

'Lost is right.' Soraya nodded. 'Smugglers are more difficult to eradicate than roaches. As you can imagine, there's still a network of them operating out of Cape Town, and these days they're highly sophisticated.'

'And the tip came from where?' Bourne said.

Without looking at him, Soraya passed over sheets of computer printouts. 'The smugglers communicate by cell phone. They use "burners," cheap phones available in any convenience store on pay-as-you-go plans. They use them for anywhere from a day to, maybe, a week, if they can get their hands on another SIM card. Then they throw them away and use another.'

'Virtually impossible to trace, you wouldn't believe.' Hytner's body was tense. He was putting all he had into breaking the cipher. 'But there is a way.'

'There's always a way,' Bourne said.

'Especially if your uncle works in the phone company.' Hytner shot a quick grin at Soraya.

She maintained her icy demeanor. 'Uncle Kingsley emigrated to Cape Town thirty years ago. London was too grim for him, he said. He needed a place that was still full of promise.' She shrugged. 'Anyway, we got lucky. We caught a conversation regarding this particular shipment – the transcript is on the second sheet. He's telling one of his people the cargo can't go through the usual channels.'

Bourne noticed Hytner looking at him curiously. 'And what was special about this "lost" shipment,' Bourne said, 'was that it coincided with the specific threat to the U.S.'

'That and the fact that we have the smuggler in custody,' Hytner said.

Bourne ran his finger down the second page of the transcript. 'Was it wise to bring him in? Chances are you'll alert his customer.'

Soraya shook her head. 'Not likely. These people use a source once, then they move on.'

'So you know who bought the TSGs.'

'Let's say we have a strong suspicion. That's why Lindros went into the field himself.'

'Have you heard of Dujja?' Hytner said.

Bourne accessed the memory. 'Dujja has been credited with at least a dozen attacks in Jordan and Saudi Arabia, the most recent being last month's bombing that killed ninety-five people at the Grand Mosque in Khanaqin, 144 kilometers northeast of Baghdad. If I remember right, it was also allegedly responsible for the assassinations of two members of the Saudi royal family, the Jordanian foreign minister, and the Iraqi chief of internal security.'

Soraya took back the transcript. 'It sounds implausible, doesn't it, that one cadre could be responsible for so many attacks? But it's true. One thing links them all: the Saudis. There was a secret business meeting going on in the mosque that included high-level Saudi emissaries. The Jordanian foreign minister was a personal friend of the royal family; the Iraqi security chief was a vocal supporter of the United States.'

'I'm familiar with the classified debrief material,' Bourne said. 'Those were all sophisticated, highly engineered attacks. Most of them didn't include suicide bombers, and none of the perpetrators has been caught. Who's the leader of Dujja?'

Soraya put the transcript back in its folder. 'His name is Fadi.'

'Fadi. The redeemer, in Arabic,' Bourne said. 'A name he must have taken.'

'The truth is we don't know anything else about him, not even his real name,' Hytner said sourly.

'But we do know some things,' Bourne said. 'For one, Dujja's attacks are so well coordinated and sophisticated, it's safe to assume that Fadi either has been educated in the West or has had considerable contact with it. For another, the cadre is unusually well armed with modern-day weaponry not normally associated with Arab or Muslim fundamentalist terror groups.'

Soraya nodded. 'We're all over that angle. Dujja is one of the new generation of cadres that has joined forces with organized crime, drug traffickers out of South Asia and Latin America.'

'If you ask me,' Hytner chipped in, 'the reason Deputy Director Lindros got the Old Man to approve Typhon so quickly was that he told him our first directive is to find out who Fadi is, flush him out, and terminate him.' He glanced up. 'Each year, Dujja's become stronger and more influential among Muslim extremists. Our intel indicates that they're flocking to Fadi in unprecedented numbers.'

'Still, as of today no agency has been able to get to first base, not even us,' Soraya said.

'But then, we've only recently been organized,' Hytner added.

'Have you contacted the Saudi secret service?' Bourne asked.

Soraya gave him a bitter laugh. 'One of our informants swears the Saudi secret service is pursuing a lead on Dujja. The Saudis deny it.'

Hytner looked up. 'They also deny their oil reserves are drying up.'

Soraya closed her files, stacked them neatly. 'I know there are people in the field who call you the Chameleon because of your legendary skill at disguising yourself. But Fadi – whoever he is – is a true chameleon. Though we have corroborating intel that he not only plans the attacks but is also actively involved in many of them, we have no photo of him.'

'Not even an Identi-Kit drawing,' Hytner said with evident disgust.

Bourne frowned. 'What makes you think Dujja bought the TSGs from the supplier?'

'We know he's holding back vital information.' Hytner pointed to the screen of his laptop. 'We found this cipher on one of the buttons of his shirt. Dujja is the only terrorist cadre we know of that uses ciphers of this level of sophistication.'

'I want to interrogate him.'

'Soraya's the AIC – the agent in charge,' Hytner said. 'You'll have to ask her.'

Bourne turned to her.

Soraya hesitated only a moment. Then she stood and gestured toward the door. 'Shall we?'

Bourne rose. 'Tim, make a hard copy of the cipher, give us fifteen, then come find us.'

Hytner glanced up, squinting as if Bourne were in a glare.

'I won't be near finished in fifteen minutes.'

'Yes, you will.' Bourne opened the door. 'At least, you'll sell it that way.'

The holding cells were accessed via a short, steep flight of perforated steel stairs. In stark contrast with Typhon's light-drenched ops room, the space here was small, dark, cramped, as if the bedrock of Washington itself were reluctant to give up any more of its domain.

Bourne stopped her at the bottom of the stairs. 'Have I done something to offend you?'

Soraya stared at him for a moment as if she couldn't believe what she was seeing. 'His name is Hiram Cevik,' she said, pointedly ignoring Bourne's question. 'Fifty-one, married, three children. He's of Turkish descent, moved to Ukraine when he was eighteen. He's been in Cape Town for the last twenty-three years. Owns an import-export firm. For the most part, the business is legit, but every once in a while, it seems, Mr. Cevik gets a whole other thing going.' She shrugged. 'Maybe his mistress has a taste for diamonds, maybe it's his Internet gambling.'

'It's so hard to make ends meet these days,' Bourne said.

Soraya looked like she wanted to laugh, but didn't.

'I rarely do things by the book,' he said. 'But whatever I do, whatever I say, goes. Is that clear?'

For a moment she stared deep into his eyes. What was she looking for? he wondered. What was the matter with her?

'I'm familiar with your methods,' she said in an icy tone.

Cevik was leaning against one wall of his cage, smoking a cigarette. When he saw Bourne approaching with Soraya, he blew out a cloud of smoke and said, 'You the cavalry or the inquisitor?'

Bourne watched him as Soraya unlocked the cage door.

'Inquisitor, then.' Cevik dropped the cigarette butt and ground it beneath his heel. 'I should tell you that my wife knows all about my gambling – and about my mistress.'

'I'm not here to blackmail you.' Bourne stepped into the cage. He could feel Soraya behind him as if she were a part of him. His scalp began to tingle. She had a weapon and was prepared to use it on the prisoner before the situation got out of hand. She was a perfectionist, Bourne sensed that about her.

Cevik came off the wall and stood with his hands at his side, fingers slightly curled. He was tall, with the wide shoulders of a former rugby player and gold cat's eyes. 'Judging by your extreme fitness, it's to be physical coercion, then.'

Bourne looked around the cage, getting a feel for what it was like to be pent up in it. A flare of something half remembered, a feeling of sickness in the pit of his stomach. 'That would get me nowhere.' He used the words to bring himself out of it.

'Too true.'

It wasn't a boast. The simple statement of fact told him more about Cevik than an hour of vigorous interrogation. Bourne's gaze resettled on the South African.

'How to resolve this dilemma?' Bourne spread his hands. 'You need to get out of here. I need information. It's as simple as that.'

Cevik let a thin laugh escape his lips. 'If it were that simple, my friend, I'd be long gone.'

'My name is Jason Bourne. You're talking to me now. I'm neither your jailor nor your adversary.' Bourne paused. 'Unless you wish it.'

'I doubt I'd care for that,' Cevik said. 'I've heard of you.'

Bourne gestured with his head. 'Walk with me.'

'That's not a good idea.' Soraya planted herself between them and the outside world.

Bourne gave her a curt hand signal.

She pointedly ignored him. 'This is a gross breach of security.'

'I went out of my way to warn you,' he said. 'Step aside.'

She had her cell phone to her ear as he and Cevik went past. But it was Tim Hytner she was calling, not the Old Man.

Though it was night, the floodlights turned the lawn and its paths into silver oases amid the many-armed shadows of the leafless trees. Bourne walked beside Cevik. Soraya Moore followed five paces behind them, like a dutiful duenna, a look of disapproval on her face, a hand on her holstered gun.

Down in the depths, Bourne had been gripped by a sudden compulsion, fired by the lick of a memory – an interrogation technique used on subjects who were particularly resistant to the standard techniques of torture and sensory deprivation. Bourne was suddenly quite certain that if Cevik tasted the open air, experienced the space after being holed up in the cage for days, it would bring home to him all he had to gain from answering Bourne's questions truthfully. And all he had to lose.

'Who did you sell the TSGs to?' Bourne asked.

'I've already told this one behind us. I don't know. It was just a voice on the telephone.'

Bourne was skeptical. 'Do you normally sell TSGs over the phone?'

'For five mil, I do.'

Believable, but was it the truth?

'Man or woman?' Bourne said.

'Man.'

'Accent?'

'British, like I told them.'

55

'Do better.'

'What, you don't believe me?'

'I'm asking you to think again, I'm asking you to think harder. Take a moment, then tell me what you remember.'

'Nothing, I . . .' Cevik paused in the crisscross shadows of an Adams flowering crab apple. 'Hang on. Maybe, just maybe, there was a hint of something else, something more exotic, maybe Eastern European.'

'You lived for a number of years in Ukraine, didn't you?'

'You have me.' Cevik screwed up his face. 'I want to say possibly he was Slavic. There was a touch . . . maybe southern Ukraine. In Odessa, on the northern Black Sea coast, where I've spent time, the dialect is somewhat different, you know.'

Bourne, of course, did know, but he said nothing. In his mind, he was on a countdown to the moment when Tim Hytner would arrive with the 'decoded' cipher.

'You're still lying to me,' Bourne said. 'You must've seen your buyer when he picked up the TSGs.'

'And yet I didn't. The deal was done through a dead drop.'

'From a voice on the phone? Come on, Cevik.'

'It's the truth. He gave me a specific time and a specific place. I left half the shipment and I returned an hour later for half the five mil. The next day, we completed the deal. I saw no one, and believe me when I tell you I didn't want to.'

Again, plausible – and a clever arrangement, Bourne thought. If it was true.

'Human beings are born curious.'

'That may be so,' Cevik said with a nod. 'But I have no desire to die. This man . . . his people were watching the dead drop. They would have shot me on sight. You know that, Bourne. This situation is familiar to you.'

Cevik shook out a cigarette, offered Bourne one, then took one himself. He lit it with a book of matches that was almost empty. Seeing the direction of Bourne's gaze, he said, 'Nothing to burn in the hole so they let me keep it.'

Bourne heard an echo in his mind, as if a voice were speaking to him from a great distance. 'That was then, this is now,' he said, taking the matchbook from Cevik.

Cevik, having made no move to resist, pulled the smoke into his lungs, let it out with a soft hiss, the sound of the cars rolling by beyond the moat of grass.

Nothing to burn in the hole. The words bounced around in Bourne's head as if his brain were a pinball machine.

'Tell me, Mr. Bourne, have you ever been incarcerated?'

Nothing to burn in the hole. The sentence, once evoked, kept repeating, blocking out thought and reason.

With a grunt almost of pain, Bourne pushed Cevik on and they resumed walking; Bourne wanted him in the light. Out of the corner of his eye, he saw Tim Hytner hurrying their way.

'Do you know what it means to have your freedom taken from you?' Cevik flicked a bit of tobacco off his under-lip. 'All your life to live in poverty. Being poor is like watching pornography: Once you start, there's no way out. It's addictive, d'you see, this life without hope. Don't you agree?'

Bourne's head was hurting now, each repetition of each word falling like a hammer blow on the inside of his skull. It was with extreme difficulty that he realized Cevik was merely trying to regain a measure of control. It was a basic rule of the interrogator never to answer a question. Once he did, he lost his absolute power.

Bourne frowned. He wanted to say something; what was it? 'Make no mistake. We have you where we want you.'

'I?' Cevik's eyebrows lifted. 'I'm nothing, a conduit, that's all. It's my buyer you need to find. What do you want with me?'

'We know you can lead us to the buyer.'

'No I can't. I already told you—'

Hytner was approaching through inky shadow and glazed light. Why was Hytner here? Through the pounding in his head, Bourne could scarcely remember. He had it; it slipped away like a fish, then reappeared. 'The cipher, Cevik. We've broken it.'

Right on cue, Hytner came up and handed the paper to Bourne, who almost dropped it, such was his preoccupation with the ringing in his brain.

'It was a bitch all right,' Hytner said a bit breathlessly. 'But I finally got it licked. The fifteenth algorithm I used proved to be—'

The last part of what he was going to say turned into a ragged shout of shock and pain as Cevik jammed the glowing end of his cigarette into Hytner's left eye. At the same time he spun the agent around in front of him, locking his left forearm across his throat.

'Take one step toward me,' he said low in his throat, 'and I'll break his neck.'

'We'll take you down, right enough.' Soraya, with a quick glance at Bourne, was advancing, her gun arm straight out, her other hand cupped beneath the gun butt, its barrel aimed, questing. Waiting for an opening. 'You don't want to die, Cevik. Think of your wife and three children.'

Bourne stood as if poleaxed. Cevik, seeing this, showed his teeth.

'Think of the five mil.'

His golden eyes flicked toward her for an instant. But he was already backing away from her and from Bourne, his bleeding human shield held tight to his chest.

'There's nowhere to go,' Soraya said in a most reasonable tone. 'Not with all the agents we have around. Not with him slowing you down.'

'I'm thinking of the five mil.' He kept edging away from them, away from the glare of the sodium lights. He was heading toward 23rd Street, beyond which rose the National Academy of Sciences.

More people there – tourists especially – to hamper the agents' pursuit.

'No more prisons for me. Not one more day.'

Nothing to burn in the hole. Bourne wanted to scream. And then a sudden explosion of memory obliterated even those words: He was running across ancient cobblestones, a sharp mineral wind in his nostrils. The weight in his arms seemed suddenly too heavy to bear. He looked down to see Marie – no, it was the unknown woman's bloody face! Blood everywhere, streaming from her though he frantically tried to stanch the flow . . .

'Don't be an idiot,' Soraya was saying to Cevik. 'Cape Town? You'll never be able to hide from us. There or anywhere else.'

Cevik cocked his head. 'But look what I've done to him.'

'He's maimed, not dead,' she said through gritted teeth. 'Let him go.'

'When you hand me your gun.' Cevik's smile was ironic. 'No? See? I'm already a dead man in your eyes, isn't that true, Bourne?'

Bourne seemed to be coming very slowly out of his nightmare. He saw Cevik step into 23rd Street now with Hytner skidding off the curb like a recalcitrant child.

Just as Bourne lunged at him, Cevik pitched Hytner at them.

Then everything happened at once. Hytner staggered pitifully. Brakes screeched from a black Hummer close by. Just behind it a trailer-truck filled with new Harley-Davidson motorcycles swerved to avoid a collision. Air horns blaring, it almost struck a red Lexus, whose driver spun in terror into two other cars. In the first fraction of a second it appeared as if Hytner had stumbled over the curb, but then a plume of blood spat out of his chest and he twisted with the impact of the bullet.

'Oh, God!' Soraya moaned.

The black Hummer, rocking on its shocks, had pulled up. Its front window was partly open, the ugly gleam of a silencer briefly glimpsed. Soraya squeezed off two shots before answering fire sent her and Bourne diving for cover. The Hummer's rear door flew open and Cevik ducked inside. It sped off even before he'd pulled the door closed behind him.

Putting up her gun, Soraya ran to her partner, cradling his head in her lap.

Bourne, hearing the echo of the gunshot in his memory, felt himself released from a velvet prison where everything around him was muffled, dim. He leapt past Soraya and the crumpled form of Hytner, ran out onto 23rd Street, one eye on the Hummer, the other on the trailer-truck. The truck's driver had recovered and sent his gears clashing as he resumed speed. Bourne sprinted toward the back of the trailer, grabbed the chain across the lifted ramp, and hauled himself aboard.

His mind was racing as he clambered up onto the platform on which the motorcycles were chained in neat, soldierly rows. The guttering flame in the darkness, the flare of the match: Cevik lighting his cigarette had two purposes. The first, of course, was to provide him with a weapon. The second was as a signal. The black Hummer had been waiting, prepared. Cevik's escape had been meticulously planned.

By whom? And how could they have known where he'd be, and when?

No time for answers now. Bourne saw the Hummer just ahead. It was neither speeding nor weaving in and out of the traffic; its driver secure in the assumption that he and his passengers had made a clean escape.

Bourne unchained the motorcycle closest to the rear of the trailer and swung into the saddle. Where were the keys?

Bending over and shielding it from the wind, he lit a match from the matchbook Cevik had tossed to him. Even so, the flame lasted only a moment, but in that time it revealed the keys taped to the underside of the gleaming black tank console.

Jamming the key into the ignition, Bourne fired up the Twin Cam 88B engine. He gunned the engine, shifted his weight to the rear. The front end of the motorcycle rose up as it shot forward off the rear edge of the trailer.

While he was still in free fall the cars behind the trailer jammed on their brakes, their front ends slewing dangerously. Bourne hit the pavement, leaned forward as the Harley bounced once, gaining traction as both wheels bit into the road. In a welter of squealing tires and stripped rubber, he made an acute U-turn and sped off after the black Hummer.

After a long, anxiety-filled moment, he spotted it going through the traffic-clogged square where 23rd Street intersected with Constitution Avenue, heading south toward the Lincoln Memorial. The Hummer's profile was unmistakable. Bourne kicked the motorcycle into high gear, blasting into the intersection on the amber, zigzagging through it to more squeals and angry horn blasts.

He shadowed the Hummer as it followed the road to the right, describing a quarter of a circle around the arc-lit memorial slowly enough that he made up most of the distance between them. As the Hummer continued on around toward the on-ramp to the Arlington Memorial Bridge, he gunned up, nudged its passenger-side rear bumper. The vehicle shrugged off the motorcycle's maneuver like an elephant swatting a fly. Before Bourne could drop back, the driver stamped on his brakes. The Hummer's massive rear end collided with the motorcycle, sending Bourne toward the guardrail and the black Potomac below. A VW came up on him, horn blaring, and almost finished the job the Hummer had started – but at the last instant Bourne was able to regain control. He swerved away from the VW, snaking back through traffic after the accelerating Hummer.

Above his head he heard the telltale *thwup-thwup-thwup* and, glancing up, saw a dark insect with bright eyes: a CI helicopter. Soraya had been busy on her cell phone again.

As if she were in his mind, his cell phone rang. Answering it, he heard her deep-toned voice in his ear.

'I'm right above you. There's a rotary on the center of Columbia Island just ahead. You'd better make sure the Hummer gets there.'

He swerved around a minivan. 'Did Hytner make it?'

'Tim's dead because of you, you sonovabitch.'

The chopper landed on the island rotary, and the infernal noise level dropped abruptly as the pilot cut the motor. The black Hummer kept on going as if nothing were amiss. Bourne, threading his way through the last of the traffic between him and his quarry, once again drew close to the vehicle.

He saw Soraya and two other CI agents emerge from the body of the helicopter with police riot helmets on their heads and shotguns in their hands. Swerving abruptly, he drew alongside the Hummer. With his cocked elbow, he smashed the driver's-side window.

'Pull over!' he shouted. 'Pull over onto the rotary or you'll be shot dead!'

A second helicopter appeared over the Potomac, angling in very fast toward their position. CI backup.

The Hummer gave no indication of slowing. Without taking his eyes off the road, Bourne reached behind him and opened the custom saddlebag. His scrabbling fingers found a wrench. He'd have one chance, he knew. Calculating vectors and speed, he threw the wrench. It slammed into the front of the driver's-side rear-wheel well. The wheel, revolving at speed, went over the wrench, launched it up with sickening power into the rear-wheel assembly.

At once the Hummer began to wobble, which only jammed the wrench deeper into the assembly. Then something cracked, an axle possibly, and the Hummer decelerated in a barely controlled spin. Mostly on its own momentum, it ran up over the curb onto the rotary and came to a stop, its engine ticking like a clock.

Soraya and the other agents spread out, moving toward the Hummer with drawn guns aimed at the passenger cabin. When she was close enough, Soraya shot the two front tires flat. One of the other agents did the same with the rear tires. The Hummer wasn't going anywhere until a CI tow truck hauled it back to HQ for forensics.

'All right!' Soraya shouted. 'Out of the vehicle, all of you! Out of the vehicle now!'

As the agents closed the circle around the Hummer, Bourne could see that they were wearing body armor. After Hytner's death, Soraya wasn't taking any chances.

They were within ten meters of the Hummer when Bourne felt his scalp begin to tingle. Something was wrong with the scene, but he couldn't quite put his mental finger on it. He looked again: Everything seemed right – the target surrounded, the approaching agents, the second helicopter hovering above, the noise level rising exponentially . . .

Then he had it.

Oh, my God, he thought, and viciously twisted the handlebar accelerator. He yelled at the agents, but over the noise of the two copters and his own motorcycle there was no chance they could hear him. Soraya was in the lead, closing in on the driver's door as the others, spread apart, hung back, providing her with a crossfire of cover should she need it.

The setup looked fine, perfect, in fact, but it wasn't.

Bourne leaned forward as the motorcycle sped across the rotary. He had a hundred meters to cover, a route that would take him just left of the Hummer's gleaming flank. He took his right hand off the handlebar grip, gesturing frantically at the agents, but they were properly concentrated on their target.

He gunned the engine, its deep, guttural roar at last cutting through the heavy vibrational *thwup-thwup-thwup* of the hovering copter. One of the agents saw him coming, watched him gesturing. He called to the other agent, who glanced at Bourne as he roared past the Hummer.

The setup looked right out of the CI playbook, but it wasn't, because the Hummer's engine was ticking over – cooling – *while it was still running*. Impossible.

Soraya was less than five meters from the target, her body tense, in a semi-crouch. Her eyes opened wide as she became aware of him. Then he was upon her.

He swept her up in his extended right arm, swung her back behind him as he raced off. One of the other agents, now flat on the ground, had alerted the second chopper, because it abruptly rose into the spangled night, swinging away.

The ticking Bourne had heard hadn't come from the engine at all. It was from a triggering device.

The explosion took the Hummer apart, turned its components into smoking shrapnel, shrieked behind them. Bourne, with the motorcycle at full speed, felt Soraya's arms wrap around his ribs. He bent low over the handlebars, feeling her breasts pressing softly against his back as she molded herself to him. The howling air was blast-furnace hot; the sky, bright orange, then clogged with oily black smoke. A hail of ruptured metal whirred and whizzed all around them, plowed into the ground, struck the roadway, fizzed into the river, shriveling.

Jason Bourne, with Soraya Moore clinging tightly to him, accelerated into the light-glare of monument-laden D.C.

FOUR

Jakob Silver and his brother appeared from out of the dinner-time night, when even cities such as Washington appear deserted or, at least, lonely, a certain indigo melancholy robbing the streets of life. When the two men entered the hushed luxury of the Hotel Constitution on the northeast corner of 20th and F Streets, Thomas, the desk clerk on duty, hurried past the fluted marble columns and across the expanse of luxurious carpeting to meet them.

He had good reason to scurry. He, as well as the other desk clerks, had been given a crisp new hundred-dollar bill by Lev Silver, Jakob Silver's brother, when he had checked in. These Jewish diamond merchants from Amsterdam were wealthy men, this much the desk clerk had surmised. The Silvers were to be treated with the utmost respect and care, befitting their exalted status.

Thomas, a small, mousy, damp-handed man, could see that Jakob Silver's face was flushed as if in victory. It was Thomas's job to anticipate his VIP clients' needs.

'Mr. Silver, my name is Thomas. It's a pleasure to meet you, sir,' he said. 'Is there anything I might get for you?'

'That you may, Thomas,' Jakob Silver replied. 'A bottle of your best champagne.'

'And have the Pakistani,' Lev Silver added, 'what's his name—?'

'Omar, Mr. Silver.'

'Ah, yes, Omar. I like him. Have him bring up the champagne.'

'Very good.' Thomas all but bowed from the waist. 'Right away, Mr. Silver.'

He hurried away as the Silver brothers entered the elevator, a plush cubicle that silently whisked them up to the executive-level fifth floor.

'How did it go?' Lev Silver said.

And Jakob Silver answered, 'It worked to perfection.'

Inside their suite, he shrugged off his coat and jacket, went directly into the bathroom, and turned on all the lights. Behind him, in the sitting room, he heard the TV start up. He stripped off his sweat-stained shirt.

In the pink-marble bathroom, everything was prepared.

Jakob Silver, naked to the waist, bent over the marble sink and took out his gold eyes. Tall, with the build of a former rugby player, he was as fit as an Olympian: washboard abdomen, muscular shoulders, powerful limbs. Snapping closed the plastic case in which he had carefully placed the gold contact lenses, he looked into the bathroom mirror. Beyond his reflection, he could see a good chunk of the cream-and-silver suite. He heard the low drone of CNN. Then the channel was switched to Fox News, then MSNBC.

'Nothing.' Muta ibn Aziz's vibrant tenor voice emerged from the other room. Muta ibn Aziz had picked his cover name – Lev – himself. 'On any of the all-news stations.'

'And there won't be,' Jakob Silver said. 'CI is extremely efficient in manipulating the media.'

Now Muta ibn Aziz appeared in the mirror, one hand gripping the door frame to the bathroom, the other out of sight behind him. Dark hair and eyes, a classic Semitic face, a zealous and inextinguishable resolve, he was Abbud ibn Aziz's younger brother.

Muta dragged a chair behind him, which he set down opposite the toilet. After glancing at himself in the mirror, he said: 'We look naked without our beards.'

'This is America.' He gestured curtly with his head. 'Go back inside.'

Alone again, Jakob Silver allowed himself to think like Fadi. He had jettisoned the identity of Hiram Cevik the moment he and Muta had exited the black Hummer. Muta, as previously instructed, had left the Beretta semiautomatic pistol with its ugly M9SD Suppressor on the front seat as they had tumbled onto the sidewalk. His aim had been true, but then he'd never had a doubt about Muta ibn Aziz's marksmanship.

They had run out of sight as the Hummer sped up again, slipped around a corner, and walked quickly up 20th Street to F Street, vanishing like wraiths inside the warmly glowing facade of the hotel.

Meanwhile, not a mile away, Ahmad, with his load of C-4 explosives that had filled up the front foot well of the Hummer's cabin, was already martyred, already in Paradise. A hero to his family, his people.

'Your objective is to take out as many of them as you can,' Fadi had told him when Ahmad had volunteered to martyr himself. In truth, there had been many volunteers, with very little difference among them. All were absolutely reliable. Fadi had chosen Ahmad because he was a cousin. One of a great many, admittedly, but Fadi had owed his uncle a small favor, which this decision repaid.

Fadi dug into his mouth and removed the porcelain tooth sheaths he'd used to widen Hiram Cevik's jaw. Washing them with soap and water, he returned them to the hard-sided case that merchants used to transport gems and jewelry. Muta had thoughtfully placed it on the generous rim of the bathtub so that everything in it would be within easy reach: a warren of small trays and custom compartments filled with every manner of theatrical makeup, removers, spirit gums, wigs, colored contact lenses, and various prosthetics for noses, jaws, teeth, and ears.

Squeezing a solvent onto a broad cotton pad, he methodically wiped the makeup off his face, neck, and hands. His natural, sun-darkened skin reappeared in streaks, a good decade peeled away, until the Fadi he recognized was whole again. A short time as himself, precious as a jewel, in the center of the enemy camp. Then he and Muta ibn Aziz would be gone, lifting through the clouds to their next destination.

He dried his face and hands on a towel and went back into the sitting room of the suite where Muta stood, watching *The Sopranos* on HBO.

'I find myself repelled by this creature Carmela, the leader's wife,' he said.

'As well you should. Look at her bare arms!'

Carmela was standing at the open door to her obscenely huge house, watching her obscenely huge husband get into his obscenely huge Cadillac Escalade.

'And their daughter has sex before her marriage. Why doesn't Tony kill her, as the law dictates. An honor killing, so that he and his family's honor won't be dragged through the mud.' In a fit of disgust, Muta ibn Aziz went over to the TV, switched it off.

'We strive to inculcate in our women the wisdom of Muhammad, the Quran, the true faith as their guides,' Fadi said. 'This American woman is an infidel. She has nothing, she is nothing.'

There came then a discreet knock on the door.

'Omar,' Muta said. 'Let me.'

Fadi gave his silent assent before he slipped back into the bathroom.

Muta crossed the plush carpet and drew open the door for Omar to enter. He was a tall, broad-shouldered man of no more than forty, with a shaven head, a quick smile, and a penchant for telling incomprehensible jokes. On his shoulder was a silver tray laden with a bottle in an enormous ice bucket, two flutes, and a plate of freshly sliced fruit. Omar filled the doorway, Muta thought, much as Fadi would, for the two men were of the same approximate height and weight.

'Your champagne,' Omar said superfluously. Crossing the room, he set his burden down on the glass top of the cocktail table. The ice made a shivery sound as he pulled the bottle free.

'I'll open it,' Muta said, grasping the heavy champagne bottle from the waiter.

When Omar proffered the leather-bound folder with the chit to sign, Muta called, 'Jakob, the champagne's here. You must sign.'

'Tell Omar to come into the bathroom.'

Even so, Omar looked at the other questioningly.

'Go on.' Muta ibn Aziz smiled winningly. 'I assure you, he won't bite.'

With the small leather folder held before him like an offering, Omar plodded toward the sound of Fadi's voice.

Muta dropped the bottle back into its bed of shaved ice. He had no idea what champagne tasted like and wasn't in the least interested. When he heard the sudden loud noise from the bathroom, he used the remote to turn the TV back on, cranking up the volume. Switching channels because *The Sopranos* was over, he stopped when he recognized the face of Jack Nicholson. The actor's voice filled the room.

'Here's Johnny!' Nicholson crowed through the rent in the bathroom door he'd made with an ax.

Omar, his hands tied behind his back, was bound to the chair in the bathtub. His large brown liquid eyes were staring up at Fadi. There was an ugly bruise on his jaw just beginning to inflate.

'You're not Jewish,' Omar said in Urdu. 'You're Muslim.'

Fadi ignored him and went about his business, which, at the moment, was death.

'You're Muslim, just like me,' Omar repeated. To his utter surprise, he wasn't frightened. He seemed to be in something of a dream state, as if from the moment he was born he was fated for this encounter. 'How can you do this?'

'In a moment, you will be martyred to the cause,' Fadi said in Urdu, which his father had made certain he learned as a child. 'What is your complaint?'

'The cause,' Omar said calmly, 'is your cause. It isn't mine. Islam is a religion of peace, and yet here you are waging a terrible, bloody war that devastates families, whole generations.'

'We are given no choice by the American terrorists. They suck at our oil tit, but that isn't enough for them. They want to *own* the oil tit. So they make up lies and use them to invade our land. The American president claims, of course falsely, that his god has spoken to him. The Americans have revived the era of the Crusades. They are the world's chief infidels – where they lead Europe follows, either willingly or grudgingly. America is like a colossal engine rolling across the world, its citizens grinding whatever they find into shit that all looks the same. If we don't stop them, they will be the end of us. They want nothing less. Our backs are against the wall. We have been driven into this war of survival, unwilling. They have systematically stripped us of power, of dignity. Now they want to occupy all of the Middle East.'

'You speak with a terrible hatred.'

'A gift of the Americans. Cleanse yourself of all Western corruption.'

'And I say that as long as your focus is hatred, you're doomed. Your hatred has blinded you to any possibility but the one you have created.'

A tremor of barely suppressed rage rippled through Fadi. 'I have created nothing! I am defending what *must* be defended.

70

Why can you not see that our very way of life hangs in the balance.'

'It is you who cannot see. There is another way.'

Fadi threw his head back, his voice corrosive. 'Ah, yes, now you have opened my eyes, Omar. I shall renounce my people, my heritage. I will become like you, a servant waiting on the decadent whims of pampered Americans, dependent on the crumbs left on their table.'

'You see only what you want to see.' Omar's expression was sad. 'You've only to look at the Israeli model to know what can be done with hard work and—'

'The Israelis have the money and the military might of America behind them,' Fadi hissed into Omar's face. 'They also have the atomic bomb.'

'Of course, that is what you see. But Israelis themselves are Nobel laureates in physics, economics, chemistry, literature; prizewinners in quantum computing, black-hole thermo-dynamics, string theory. Israelis were founders of Packard Bell, Oracle, SanDisk, Akamai, Mercury Interactive, Check Point, Amdocs, ICQ.'

'You're talking gibberish,' Fadi said, dismissively.

'To you, yes. Because all you know how to do is destroy. These people created a life for themselves, for their children, for their children's children. This is the model you need to follow. Turn inward, help your people, educate them, allow them to make something of themselves.'

'You're insane,' Fadi said in fury. 'Never. Finished. The end.' The flat of his hand cut through the air. It held a shining blade that slit Omar's throat from side to side.

With a last look at Nicholson's manically grinning face, Muta ibn Aziz followed Omar into the grotesque pink-marble bathroom, which looked to him like flesh after the skin had been stripped off. There was Omar, sitting on the chair he had placed in the bathtub. There was Fadi bent over, studying Omar's face as if to memorize it. Fadi's makeup case had been overturned when Omar had kicked it during his death throes. Small jars, broken bottles, prosthetics were all over the place. Not that it mattered.

'He looks so sad, slumped there on the chair,' Muta said.

'He's beyond sadness,' Fadi said. 'He's beyond all pain and pleasure.'

Muta stared into Omar's glassy eyes, the pupils fixed and dilated in death. 'You broke his neck. So neat, so precise.'

Fadi sat down on the lip of the tub. After a moment's hesitation, Muta retrieved an electric hair shearer from the tile floor. Fadi had affixed a mirror to the wall at the back of the tub by means of suction cups. He stared into this, scrutinizing every motion, as Muta began to take off his hair.

When the task was done, Fadi rose. He stared at himself in the mirror over the sink, then back at Omar. He turned to one side, and Muta moved Omar's head so the same side was visible. Then the other side.

'A little more here—' Fadi pointed at a spot on the top of his own scalp. '—where Omar is already bald.'

When he was satisfied, he began to give himself Omar's nose, Omar's slight overbite, Omar's elongated earlobes.

Together they stripped Omar of his uniform, socks, and shoes. Fadi did not forget the man's underwear, putting those on first. The idea was to be absolutely authentic.

'*La ilaha ill allah.*' Muta grinned. 'You look every inch the Pakistani servant.'

Fadi nodded. 'Then it's time.'

As he went through the suite, he picked up the tray Omar had brought. Out in the corridor, he took the service elevator to the basement. He drew out a handheld video device, brought up the schematics for the hotel. Locating the room housing the electronic panels for the HVAC, electrical power, and sprinkler systems took less than three minutes. Inside, he removed the cover to the sprinkler panel and replaced the wires for the fifth floor. The color coding would look correct to anyone who checked, but the wires were now shorted out, rendering the fifth-floor sprinklers inoperable.

He returned to the fifth floor the way he had come. Encountering a maid who entered the service lift on the second floor, he tried out his imitation of Omar's voice. She got out on the fourth floor without suspecting a thing.

Returning to the Silvers' suite, he went into the bathroom. From the bottom drawer of his case, he pulled out a small spray can and two metal containers of carbon disulfide. He emptied one container into Omar's accommodating lap, the odor of rotten eggs pervading the air. Back in the living room, he poured out the second just below the window, where the hem of the thick curtains fell. Then he sprayed the curtains with a substance that would turn the fabric from fire-retardant to flammable.

In the sitting room, he said, 'Do you have everything you need?'

'I have forgotten nothing, Fadi.'

Fadi ducked back into the bathroom and lit the accelerant in Omar's lap. Virtually no trace of him, not a recognizable bone nor a bit of flesh, would survive the intense heat of the inferno the accelerants would generate. With Muta watching, Fadi lit the bottom of the curtains in the living room, and they left the suite together. They parted almost immediately, Muta ibn Aziz to the stairwell, Fadi once again to the service elevator. Two minutes later, he exited the side entrance: Omar on a cigarette break. Forty-three seconds later, Muta joined him.

They had just turned off 20th Street onto H Street, protected by the bulk of one of the buildings at George Washington University, when, with a thunderous roar, the fire blew out the fifth-floor window, on its way to completely incinerating all three rooms of the Silvers' suite.

They strolled down the street to the sounds of shouts, cries, the mounting wail of sirens. A flickering red heat rose into the night, the heartbreaking light of disaster and death.

Both Fadi and Muta ibn Aziz knew it well.

A world away from both luxury and international terrorism, Northeast quadrant was rife with its own homegrown disasters arising from poverty, inner-city rage, and disenfranchisement – toxic ingredients of existence so familiar to Fadi and Muta ibn Aziz.

Gangs owned much of the territory; drug- and numbers-running were the commerce that fed the strong, the amoral. Vicious turf wars, drive-by shootings, raging fires were nightly occurrences. There wasn't a foot patrolman on the Metro D.C. Police who would venture onto the streets without armed backup. This held true for the squad cars as well, which were without exception manned by two cops; sometimes, on particularly bloody-minded nights or when the moon was full, by three or four.

Bourne and Soraya were racing through the night along these mean streets when he noted for the second time a black Camaro behind them.

'We picked up a tail,' he said over his shoulder.

Soraya didn't bother looking back. 'It's Typhon.'

'How d'you know?'

Over the sighing wind he heard the distinct metallic *snik!* of a switchblade. Then the edge of the blade was at his throat.

'Pull over,' she said in his ear.

'You're crazy. Put the knife away.'

She pressed the blade into his skin. 'Do as I tell you.'

'Don't do this, Soraya.'

'You're the one who needs to think about what he's done.'

'I don't know what you—'

She gave him a shove in the back with the heel of her hand. 'Dammit! Pull over now!'

Obediently, he slowed down. The black Camaro came roaring up on his left to trap him between it and the curb. Soraya noted this with satisfaction and, as she did so, Bourne jammed his thumb into the nerve on the inside of her wrist. Her hand opened involuntarily and he caught the falling switchblade by the handle, closed it, and stuck it into his jacket.

The Camaro, following procedure to the letter, had now angled in to the curb just in front of him. The passenger door swung open even as it rocked on its shocks, and an armed agent leapt out. Bourne twisted the handlebars and the motorcycle's engine screamed as he turned to his right, cutting across a burned-out lawn, slipping into a narrow alley between two houses.

He could hear shouts behind him, the slamming of a door, the angry roar of the Camaro, but it was no use. The alley was too narrow for the car to be able to follow the motorcycle. It might try to find him on the other side, but Bourne had an answer for that as well. He was intimate with this part of Washington, and he was willing to bet everything that they weren't.

On the other hand, he had Soraya to contend with. He might have stripped her of her knife, but she could still use every part of her body as a weapon. This she did with an economy of movement and an efficiency of application. She dug knuckles into his kidneys, repeatedly slammed her elbow into his ribs, even tried to gouge out an eye with her thumb, in obvious retaliation for what had happened to poor Tim Hytner.

All these assaults Bourne suffered with a grim stoicism, fending her off as best he could while the motorcycle rocketed through the narrow lane between the stained building walls on either side. Garbage cans and passed-out drunks were only the most frequent obstacles he had to negotiate at speed.

Then three teens appeared at the end of the alley. Two had baseball bats, which they brandished with chop-licking menace. The third, just behind the others, leveled a Saturday-night special at him as the motorcycle neared.

'Hang on!' he shouted at Soraya. Feeling her arms wrapped tightly around his waist, he leaned back, shifting their center of gravity sharply, at the same time gunning the engine. The front end of the motorcycle lifted off the ground. They rushed at the thugs reared up like a lion on the attack. He heard a shot fired, but the underside of the motorcycle protected them. Then they were in the midst of it. He snatched a bat from the grip of the thug on the left, slammed it down onto the wrist of the third teen, and the gun went flying.

They burst out of the end of the alley. Bourne leaned forward, guiding the motorcycle back onto two wheels just in time for the sharp turn to the right, down a street seething with garbage and stray dogs, yelping at the Harley's thunderous passage.

Bourne said, 'Now we can straighten—'

He never finished. Soraya had locked the crook of her arm across his windpipe and was bringing to bear a lethal pressure.

FIVE

'Damn you, damn you, damn you!' Soraya chanted like an exorcist.

Bourne scarcely heard her. He was far too busy trying to stay alive. The motorcycle was hurtling at a hundred kilometers an hour down the street, the wrong way, as it happened. He managed to swerve out of the way of an old Ford, horn blaring, a deep voice shouting obscenities. But in the process he sideswiped a Lincoln idling at the opposite curb. The motorcycle hit, bouncing off the long dented slash in the Continental's front fender. Bourne's windpipe, almost entirely blocked by the choke hold Soraya had on him, was allowing next to no air into his lungs. Stars twinkled at the periphery of his vision, and he was blacking out for microseconds at a time.

Even so, he was aware that the Lincoln had awakened and, making a sharp U-turn, was now in fast pursuit of the motorcycle that had done it damage. Up ahead, a truck lumbered toward him, taking up most of the street.

Putting on a shocking burst of speed, the Continental came abreast of him, its blackened window rolled down and a moon-faced black man scowling and howling a string of curses. Then the voracious snout of a sawed-off shotgun showed itself.

'This'll teach yo, muthafucka!'

Before Moon-face had a chance to pull the trigger, Soraya kicked upward with her left leg. The edge of her boot struck the shotgun barrel; it swung wildly upward, the blast exploding into the treetops lining the street. Taking advantage, Bourne twisted the handlebars to full speed and took off down the street directly toward the huge truck. The driver saw their suicide maneuver and panicked, turning the wheel hard over as he simultaneously downshifted and stood on the air brakes. The truck, howling in protest, slewed broadside across the road.

Soraya, seeing death approaching with appalling speed, cried out in Arabic. She relinquished her choke hold to once again swing her arms tight around Bourne's waist.

Bourne coughed, sucked sweet air into his burning lungs, leaned all the way over to his right, cut the engine an instant before they were sure to slam into the truck.

Soraya's scream was cut short. The motorcycle went down on its side in a welter of sparks and blood from skin flayed off Bourne's right leg as they slid between the truck's madly spinning axles.

On the other side Bourne brought the engine to life, using the momentum and the weight of their combined bodies to return the motorcycle to its normal upright position.

Soraya, too dazed to immediately resume her attack, said, 'Stop, please stop now.'

Bourne ignored her. He knew where he was going.

The DCI was in conference with Matthew Lerner, being debriefed on the particulars of Hiram Cevik's escape and its fiery aftermath.

'Hytner aside,' Lerner said, 'the damage was light. Two agents with cuts and abrasions – one of those also with a concussion from the blast. A third agent missing. Minor damage to the bird on the ground' – he meant the helicopter—'none to the one that had been hovering.'

'That was a public arena,' the Old Man said. 'It was fucking amateur hour out there.'

'What the hell was Bourne thinking, bringing Cevik out into the open?'

The director's gaze rose to the portrait of the president that hung on one wall of the conference room. On the other wall was a portrait of his predecessor. *You only get your portrait painted after they've hung you out to dry,* he thought sourly. The years had piled up on him, and some days – like today – he could feel every grain of sand in the hourglass burying him slowly, surely. Atlas with bowed shoulders.

The DCI shuffled through some papers, held one to the light. 'The chief of D.C. Metro's called, ditto the FB fucking I.' His eyes bored into Lerner's. 'You know what they wanted, Matthew? They wanted to know if they could help. Can you beat that? Well, I can.

'The president phoned to ask what the hell was going on, if we were under attack by terrorists, if he should head for Oz.' Another name for the Hidden Seat of Power, the secret place from which the president and his staff could run the country during a full-fledged emergency. 'I told him everything was under control. Now I'm asking you the same question, and by God I'd better get the answer I want.'

'In the end, we return to Bourne,' Lerner said, reading from the hastily prepared research notes his chief of staff had thrust into his fist just moments before the meeting convened. 'But then the recent history of CI is riddled with snafus and disasters that somehow always have their origin with Jason Bourne.

'It pains me to say I told you so, but this whole mess could've been avoided had you kept Lindros here at HQ. I know he was once a field operative, but that was some time ago. The animal edge is quickly dulled by administrative concerns. He's got his own shop to run. Who's going to run it if he's dead? The Cevik debacle was the direct result of

Typhon being without a head.'

'Everything you say is true, dammit. I never should've allowed Martin to talk me into this. Then disaster upon disaster at Ras Dejen. Well, at least this time Bourne won't disappear off the grid.'

Lerner shook his head. 'But I have to wonder whether that's enough.'

'What d'you mean?'

'There's more than a fair chance that Bourne had a hand in Cevik's escape.'

The Old Man's eyebrows knit together. 'You have proof of this?'

'I'm working on it,' Lerner said. 'But it stands to reason. The escape was planned in advance. What Cevik's people needed to do was to get him out of the cage, and Bourne accomplished that quite efficiently. He's nothing if not efficient, this we already knew.'

The Old Man slammed his hand on the table. 'If he's behind Cevik's escape, I swear I'll skin him alive.'

'I'll take care of Bourne.'

'Patience, Matthew. For the moment we need him. We must get Martin Lindros back, and Bourne is now our only hope. After due consideration, the Operations Directorate sent the Skorpion Two team in after Skorpion One, and we lost them both.'

'With my contacts, I told you I could gather a small unit—'

'Of freelancers, former NSA operatives now in the private sector.' The DCI shook his head. 'That idea was DOA. I could never sanction a bunch of mercenaries, men I don't know, men not under my command, for such a sensitive mission.'

'But Bourne – dammit, you know his history, and now history is repeating itself. He does whatever the hell he wants whenever it suits him and fuck anyone else.'

'Everything you say is true. Personally, I despise the man.

He represents everything that I've been taught is a menace to an organization like CI. But one thing I know about him is that he's loyal to the men he bonds with. Martin is one of those. If anyone can find him and extract him, it's Bourne.'

At that moment, the door swung open and Anne Held poked her head in.

'Sir, we have an internal problem. My clearance has been busted. I called Electronic Security and they said it wasn't a mistake.'

'That's right, Anne. It's part of Matthew's reorganization plan. He felt you didn't need top clearance to do the work I give you.'

'But, sir—'

'Clerical staff has one set of clearance priorities,' Lerner said. 'Operational staff another. Neat and clean, no ambiguities.' He looked at her. 'Still a problem, Ms. Held?'

Anne was furious. She looked to the Old Man, but realized at once that she'd get no help from that quarter. She saw his silence, his complicity, as a betrayal of the relationship she'd worked so long and hard to forge with him. She felt compelled to defend herself, but knew this was the wrong time and place to do it.

She was about to close the door when a messenger from Ops Directorate came up behind her. She turned, took a sheet of paper from him, turned back.

'We just got a read on the missing agent,' she said.

The DCI's mood had darkened considerably in the last few minutes. 'Who is it?' he snapped.

'Soraya Moore,' Anne told him.

'You see,' Lerner said sternly, 'another one of our people transferred out of my jurisdiction. How am I expected to do my job when people I have no control over slide off the grid? This is directly attributable to Lindros, sir. If you would give me control of Typhon at least until he's either found or confirmed dead—'

'Soraya's with Bourne,' Anne Held said to her boss before Lerner could say another word.

'Goddamm it!' the DCI exploded. 'How the hell did that happen?'

'No one seems to know,' Anne said.

The DCI was standing, his face empurpled with rage. 'Matthew, I do believe Typhon needs an acting director. As of now, you're it. Go forth and get the fucking job done ASAP.'

'Stop the motorcycle,' Soraya said in his ear.

Bourne shook his head. 'We're still too close to the—'

'Now.' She put the blade of a knife against his throat. 'I mean it.'

Bourne turned down a side street, pulled the cycle over to the curb, engaged the kickstand. As they both got off, he turned to her. 'Now what the hell is this all about?'

Her eyes blazed with an ill-contained fury. 'You killed Tim, you sonovabitch.'

'What? How could you even think—?'

'You told Cevik's people where he'd be.'

'You're insane.'

'Am I? It was your idea to take him out of the cell block. I tried to stop you, but—'

'I didn't have Hytner killed.'

'Then why did you just stand there while he was shot?'

Bourne didn't give her an answer because he had none to give. He recalled that at the time he'd been assaulted by sound, and – he rubbed his forehead – a debilitating head-ache. Soraya was right. Cevik's escape, Hytner's death. How had he allowed it all to happen?

'Cevik's escape was meticulously planned and timed. But how?' Soraya was saying. 'How could Cevik's people know where he was? How *could* they know, unless you told them?'

She shook her head. 'I should've listened more closely to the stories about you going rogue. There were only two men in all of CI you were able to buffalo: One's dead and the other's missing. Clearly you can't be trusted.'

With an effort, Bourne willed his head to clear. 'There's another possibility.'

'This should be good.'

'I didn't call anyone while we were down in the cells or outside—'

'You could've used hand signs, anything.'

'You're right about the method, wrong about the messenger. Remember when Cevik struck the match?'

'How could I forget?' she said bitterly.

'That was the final signal for the waiting Hummer.'

'That's just the *point*, the Hummer was *already* waiting. You *knew* because it was your setup.'

'If it was my setup, would I be telling you about it? Think, Soraya! You called Hytner to tell him we were going outside. It was *Hytner* who called Cevik's people.'

Her laugh was harsh and derisive. 'What, so then one of Cevik's people shot Tim to death? Why on earth would they do that?'

'To cover their tracks absolutely. With Hytner dead, there was no chance of him being caught and giving them up.'

She shook her head stubbornly. 'I knew Tim a long time; he was no traitor.'

'Those are usually the guilty ones, Soraya.'

'Shut up!'

'Maybe he wasn't a willing traitor. Maybe they got to him in some way.'

'Don't say one more thing against Tim.' She brandished the knife. 'You're just trying to save your own skin.'

'Look, you're absolutely right that Cevik's escape was planned in advance. But I didn't know where Cevik was being held – I didn't even know you were holding *anyone* until you told me not ten minutes before you took me to see Cevik.'

This stopped her in her tracks. She looked at him oddly. It was the same look she'd given him when he'd first seen her down in the Typhon ops center.

'If I was your enemy, why would I save you from the explosion?'

A little shiver went through her. 'I don't pretend to have all the answers—'

Bourne shrugged. 'If your mind's made up, maybe I shouldn't confuse you with the truth.'

She took a breath, her nostrils flared. 'I don't know what to believe. Ever since you came down to Typhon—'

In a flash he reached out, disarmed her. She stared at him wide-eyed as he reversed the knife, handing it back to her butt-first.

'If I was your enemy . . .'

She looked at it a long time, then up at him as she took it, slid it back into its neoprene sheath at the small of her back.

'Okay, so you're not the enemy. But neither was Tim. There's *got* to be another explanation.'

'Then we'll find it together,' he said. 'I have my name to clear, you have Hytner's.'

'Give me your right hand,' she said to Bourne.

Gripping Bourne's wrist, she turned the hand over so that the palm was faceup. With her other hand, she laid the flat of the blade on the tip of Bourne's forefinger.

'Don't move.'

With one deft motion she flicked the blade forward, along his skin. Instead of drawing blood, she lifted off a minute oval of translucent material so thin Bourne had not felt or noticed it.

'Here we go.' She held it up in the fitful glow of the streetlight for Bourne to see. 'It's known as a NET. A nano-electronic tag, according to the tech boys from DARPA.' She meant the Defense Advanced Research Projects Agency, an arm of the Department of Defense. 'It uses nanotechnology – microscopic servers. This is how I tracked you with the copter so quickly.'

Bourne had fleetingly wondered how the CI copter had picked him up so quickly, but he'd assumed it was the Hummer's distinctive profile they'd spotted. He considered for a moment. Now he recalled with vivid clarity the curious look Tim Hytner had given him when he had handled the transcript of Cevik's phone conversation: That was how they'd planted the NET on him.

'Sonovabitch!' He eyed Soraya as she slid the NET into a small oval plastic case and screwed down the lid. 'They were going to monitor me all the way to Ras Dejen, weren't they?'

She nodded. 'DCI's orders.'

'So much for the promise to keep me off the leash,' Bourne said bitterly.

'You're off now.'

He nodded. 'Thanks.'

'How about returning the favor?'

'Which would be . . . ?'

'Let me help you.'

He shook his head. 'If you knew me better, you'd know I work alone.'

Soraya looked as if she was about to say something, then changed her mind. 'Look, as you said yourself, you're already in hot water with the Old Man. You're going to need someone on the inside. Someone you can trust absolutely.' She took a step back toward the motorcycle. 'Because you know as sure as we're both standing here that the Old Man's going to find ways to fuck you every which way from Sunday.'

SIX

Kim Lovett was tired. She wanted to go home to her husband of six months. He was too new to the district and they were too new to each other for him to have yet succumbed to the crushing separation dictated by his wife's job.

Kim was always tired. The D.C. Fire Investigation Unit knew no typical hours or workdays. As a consequence, agents like Kim, who were clever, experienced, and knew what they were doing, were called on to labor hours akin to those of an ER surgeon in a war zone.

Kim had caught the call from DCFD during a brief lull in the mind-numbing drudgery of filling out paperwork on a phalanx of arson investigations, one of the few moments during the past weeks when she'd allowed herself to think about her husband – his wide shoulders, his strong arms, the scent of his naked body. The reverie didn't last long. She had picked up her kit and was on her way to the Hotel Constitution.

She engaged the siren as she headed out. From Vermont Avenue and 11th Street to the northeast corner of 20th and F took no more than seven minutes. The hotel was surrounded by police cars and fire engines, but by now the fire had been contained. Water streamed down the facade from the open wound at the end of the fifth floor. The EMT vehicles had come and gone, and there was about the scene the brittle, jittery aftermath of cinders and draining adrenaline Kim's father had described to her so well.

Chief O'Grady was waiting for her. She got out of the car and, displaying her ID, was admitted past the police barricades.

'Lovett,' O'Grady grunted. He was a big, beefy man with short but unruly white hair and ears the size and shape of a thick slice of pork tenderloin. His sad, watery eyes watched her guardedly. He was one of the majority who felt that women had no place in the DCFD.

'What've we got?'

'Explosion and fire.' O'Grady lifted his chin in the direction of the gaping wound.

'Any of our men killed or injured?'

'No, but thanks for asking.' O'Grady wiped his forehead with a dirty paper towel. 'There was a death, however – probably the occupant of the suite, though with the tiny fragments I've found I can tell you it will be impossible to make an ID. Also, the cops say one employee is missing. Damn lucky for a fireworks display like this one.'

'You said *probably* the guest.'

'That's right. The fire was unnaturally hot, and it was one bitch to put out. That's why FIU was called in.'

'Any idea what caused the explosion?' she asked.

'Well, it wasn't the fucking boiler,' the chief said shortly. He stepped closer to her, the burned rubber-and-cinder smell coming off him in waves. When he spoke again, his voice was low, urgent. 'You've got about an hour up there before Metro Police hand everything over to Homeland Security. And you know what's gonna happen when those boyos start tramping through our crime scene.'

'Gotcha.' Kim nodded.

'Okay. Go on up. A Detective Overton is waiting.'

He strode off in his rolling, slightly bandy-legged gait.

The lobby was filled with cops and firemen milling around. The cops were taking the temperature of the staff and guests, huddled in separate corners like plotting factions. The firefighters were busy dragging equipment across the blackened runner and marble floor. The place smelled of anxiety and frustration, like a stalled subway car at rush hour.

Kim rode the elevator up, stepping out into a charred and ruined fifth-floor corridor that, except for her, was utterly deserted. Just inside the suite, she found Overton, a stoop-shouldered detective with a long, mournful face, squinting at his notes.

'What the hell happened?' she said after introducing herself. 'Any ideas?'

'Possibly.' Detective Overton flipped open a notebook. 'The occupants of this corner suite were Jakob and Lev Silver. Brothers. Diamond merchants from Amsterdam. They came in at seven forty-five or thereabouts. We know that because they had a brief conversation with a concierge—' He flipped a page. '—named Thomas. One of them ordered a bottle of champagne, some kind of celebration. After that, Thomas didn't see them. He swears they didn't leave the hotel.'

They went into the suite proper.

'Can you give me the lowdown on what caused the explosion?'

'That's what I'm here for.' She snapped on latex gloves, went to work. Twenty minutes went by as she hunted down the epicenter of the blast and worked her way outward from there. Normally she'd take carpet samples – if an accelerant had been used, it was most likely to be a highly inflammable hydrocarbon-based liquid, such as turpentine, acetone, naphtha, or the like. Two telltale signs: The liquid would have seeped into the carpet, even into the underlayer. Also, there would be what was commonly called headspace – short for headspace gas chromatography – which would pick up the traces of the gases released when the accelerants ignited. Since each compound released a unique fingerprint, the headspace could determine not only if an accelerant had been used but also which one.

Here, however, the fire was of such intensity that it had eaten through the carpet and the underlayer. No wonder O'Grady and his men had had difficulty putting it out.

She examined every scrap of metal, splinter of wood, fiber of cloth, and pile of ash. Opening her kit, she exposed parts of this detritus to myriad tests. The rest she carefully put into glass containers, sealed them with airtight lids, and placed each container in its foam padding in her kit.

'I can tell you now that an accelerant was definitely used,' she said as she continued to stow evidence. 'I won't know what it was precisely until I get back to the lab, but I'll say this much: It wasn't your garden-variety accelerant. This heat, this level of destruction—'

Detective Overton interrupted her. 'But the explosion—'

'There's no trace of explosive residue,' she said. 'Accelerants have flashpoints that often cause explosions in and of themselves. But again, I won't be sure until I can conduct tests back at the lab.'

By this time, she had moved on in an ever-widening circle surrounding the point of explosion.

All at once, she sat back on her haunches and said, 'Have you found out why the sprinklers didn't come on?'

Overton flipped through his notes. 'As it happens, the sprinklers engaged on every floor of the hotel but this one. When we went down to the basement, we discovered that the system had been tampered with. I had to call in an electrician to find out, but the bottom line is that the sprinklers on this floor were disabled.'

'So the entire episode was deliberate.'

'Jakob and Lev Silver were Jews. The waiter who brought him the bottle of champagne – the one employee who's missing – is Pakistani. Hence my duty to turn this sucker over to Homeland Security.'

She looked up from her work. 'You think this waiter is a terrorist?'

Overton shrugged. 'My bet's on a business vendetta against the Silvers, but I sure as hell want to know before Homeland Security does.'

She shook her head. 'This setup is too sophisticated by half for a terrorist attack.'

'Diamonds are forever.'

She rose. 'Let's see the body.'

'*Body* would be the wrong word for what we got left.'

He took Kim into the bathroom, and together they stared down at the bits of charred bone scattered about the porcelain tub.

'Not even a skeleton.' Lovett nodded to herself. She did a complete 360. 'Here lies either Jakob or Lev Silver, fair enough. But where's the other brother?'

'Could be cindered. No?'

'In this heat, a definite possibility,' Kim said. 'It'll take me days, if not weeks to sift through the debris for any human ash. But then again I might not find anything at all.'

She knew he'd combed the entire suite, but she went through every nook and cranny herself.

He glanced nervously at his watch as they returned to the bathroom. 'This gonna take much longer? Time's running out on me.'

Kim climbed into the bathtub with the bits and pieces of charred bone. 'What's with you and Homeland Security?'

'Nothing, I just . . .' He shrugged. 'I've tried five times to make it as an HS agent. Five times they turned me down. That's my stake in this case. If I show them what I can do, they'll have to take me when I reapply.'

She crawled around with her equipment. 'There was accelerant here,' she said, 'as well as in the other room. You see, porcelain, which is created in fierce heat, tolerates it better than anything else, even some metals.' She moved down.

'Accelerants are heavy, so they tend to seep. That's why we look for them in the underlayer of a carpet or between the cracks of a wood floor. Here an accelerant would seek the lowest point in the tub. It would seep down into the drain.'

She swabbed out the drain, moving deeper with each separate swab she produced from her kit. All at once she stopped. She withdrew the swab, bagged it, put it away. Then she shone the xenon beam of a pencil flash into the hole.

'Ah, what have we here?'

She lowered a pair of needle-nose pliers into the drain. A moment later, she withdrew it. Clamped between its steel tips was something that looked quite familiar to both of them.

Detective Overton leaned forward until his head and torso were over the bathtub. 'A pair of one of the Silver brothers' teeth.'

Kim was scrutinizing them as she turned them in the cool, penetrating light of her pencil flash. 'Maybe.' She was frowning. *Then again maybe not*, she thought.

The olive-colored house just off 7th Street NE, looked much like its neighbors – dingy, time-worn, in desperate need of a new front porch. The skeleton of the house to its right was still standing, more or less, but the rest of it had been gutted by arson long ago. The worn stoop to its right was inhabited by a clutch of teens, jangly with hard-core hip-hop roaring from a battered ghetto blaster. They were illuminated by a buzzing streetlight in desperate need of refitting.

As one, the teens came off the stoop as the motorcycle drew up to the curb in front of the olive-colored house, but Bourne waved them off as he and Soraya climbed slowly off.

Bourne, ignoring the ripped right leg of his trousers and the blood seeping through it, touched knuckled fist with the tallest of the teens. 'How's it going, Tyrone.'

'It goin',' Tyrone said. 'Yo know.'

'This is Soraya Moore.'

Tyrone gave Soraya the once-over with his large black eyes. 'Deron, he gonna be pissed. Ain't no one should be here 'cept yo.'

'It's on me,' Bourne said. 'I'll make it right with Deron.'

At that moment, the front door of the olive-colored house opened. A tall, slim, handsome man with skin the color of light cocoa stepped out onto the front porch.

'Jason, what the hell?' Deron frowned deeply as he came down off the porch toward them. He was dressed in jeans and a chambray work shirt with the sleeves rolled up to expose his forearms. He seemed impervious to the cold. 'You know the rules. You made them yourself with my father. No one but yourself comes here.'

Bourne stepped between Deron and Soraya. 'I've got just over two hours to make my flight to London,' he said in a low tone. 'I'm in a pile of it. I need her help as much as I do yours.'

Deron came on in his long, languid strides. He was close enough now for Soraya to see that he had a gun in his hand. And not just any gun: a .357 Magnum.

As she began to take an involuntary step backward, Deron said, *'Ah, who is nigh? come to me, friend or foe, And tell me who is victor, York or Warwick?'* in a very fine British accent. *'Why ask I that? my mangled body shows, My blood, my want of strength, my sick heart shows. That I must yield my body to the earth And, by my fall, the conquest to my foe.'*

Soraya replied, *'See who it is: and, now the battle's ended, If friend or foe, let him be gently used.'*

'I see you know your Shakespeare,' Deron said.

'*Henry the Sixth, Part Three*, one of my favorites at school.'

'But is the battle truly ended?'

'Show him the NET,' Bourne said.

She handed over the small oval case.

Stashing the Magnum in the waistband of his jeans, Deron extended the delicate long-fingered hand of a surgeon, or a pickpocket, to open the case.

'Ah.' His eyes lit up as he plucked out the beacon to study.

'The newest CI leash,' Bourne said. 'She dug that little devil off me.'

'DARPA-engineered,' Deron said. You could almost see him smack his lips in delight. There was nothing he liked better than new technology.

Deron was neither a surgeon nor a pickpocket, Bourne informed Soraya as they followed him into the olive-colored house. He was one of the world's foremost forgers. Vermeers were a specialty – Deron had a knack with light – but in truth he could reproduce virtually anything, and often did, for an astronomically high price. Every one of his clients said his work was worth the money. He prided himself on satisfied customers.

Deron led them into the entryway, shut the front door behind them. The unexpected heavy clangor startled Soraya. This was no ordinary door, though that was how it appeared from the outside. From this side, the metal sheathing reflected the warm lamplight.

She looked around, astonished. Directly ahead was a curving tiger-oak staircase; to the left, a corridor. To her right was a large living room. The polished wood floors were covered in costly Persian carpets, the walls hung with masterpieces out of the storied history of fine art: Rembrandt, Vermeer, van Gogh, Monet, Degas, many others. Of course, they were all forgeries, weren't they? She peered at them closely, and while she was no expert she thought them all brilliant. She was certain that if she had viewed them at a museum or auction she would have had no doubt as to their authenticity. She squinted harder. Unless some of them *were* the originals.

Turning back, she saw that Deron had clasped Bourne in a warm embrace.

'I never had a chance to thank you for coming to the funeral,' Bourne said. 'That meant a lot to me. I know how busy you are.'

'My dear friend, there are things in life that outweigh commerce,' Deron said with a sad smile, 'no matter how pressing or lucrative.' Then he pushed Bourne away. 'First thing, we take care of the leg. Upstairs, first door on the right. You know the drill. Get cleaned up. New duds for you up there as well.' He grinned. 'Always the finest selection at Deron's.'

Soraya followed Deron down a yellow enameled hallway, through a large kitchen, into what must once have been the house's washroom and pantry. Here were waist-high cabinets topped by zinc-wrapped counters, banks of computers, and stacks of incomprehensible electronic instruments.

'I know what he's looking for,' Deron said as if Soraya had ceased to exist. Methodically he began to open cabinet doors and drawers, taking out an item here, a handful there.

Soraya, looking over his shoulder, was startled to see noses, ears, and teeth. Reaching out, she picked up a nose, turning it over in her hand.

'Don't worry,' Deron said. 'They're made of latex and porcelain.' He picked up what looked like a piece of dental bridgework. 'Lifelike, though, don't you think?' He showed her one edge. 'Reason being, there's little difference between this prosthetic and the real thing, except here on the inside. The real thing would have a small recess in order to fit over the ground-down tooth. This, as you can see, is just a porcelain shell, meant to fit over normal teeth.'

Soraya couldn't help herself – she put on the latex nose,

making Deron laugh. He rummaged around another drawer, handing her a much smaller model. This did feel better. Just for demonstration, he used some theatrical gum to mold it on.

'Of course, in real life you'd use another kind of glue, and makeup, to hide the edges of the prosthetic.'

'Isn't that a problem when you sweat or – I don't know, swim, maybe?'

'This isn't makeup from Chanel,' Deron said with a laugh. 'Once you apply it, you need a special solvent to get it off.'

Bourne returned just as Soraya was peeling off the fake nose. His leg wound was cleaned and bandaged, and he was dressed in new trousers and shirt.

Bourne said, 'Soraya, you and I need to talk.'

She followed him into the kitchen, where they stood by a huge stainless-steel refrigerator against the wall farthest from Deron's lab.

Bourne turned to her. 'You and Deron have a pleasant visit while I was gone?'

'You mean did he try to pump me for information?'

'You mean did I ask him to pump you.'

'Right.'

'As a matter of fact, I didn't.'

She nodded. 'He didn't.' Then she waited.

'There's no good way to get into this.' Bourne searched her face. 'Were you and Tim close?'

She turned her head away for a moment, bit her lip. 'What d'you care? To you he's a traitor.'

'Soraya, listen to me, it's either Tim Hytner or me. I know it's not me.'

Her expression was deliberately confrontational. 'Then tell me why you took Cevik outside?'

'I wanted him to get a taste of the freedom he no longer had.'

'That's it? I don't believe you.'

Bourne frowned. It wouldn't be the first time since Marie's death that he'd wondered if his latest trauma had somehow impaired his judgment. 'I'm afraid it's true.'

'Forget about my believing you,' she snapped. 'How d'you think that's going to play with the Old Man?'

'What does it matter? The Old Man hates loose cannons.'

She looked at her boots, shook her head. She took a breath, let it all out. 'I nominated Tim for Typhon, now he's dead.'

Bourne was silent. He was a warrior, what did she expect? Tears and regret? No, but would showing a smidgen of emotion kill him? Then she remembered his wife's recent death, and she felt immediately ashamed.

She cleared her throat, but not her emotions. 'We were in school together. He was one of those boys girls made fun of.'

'Why not you?'

'I wasn't like the other girls. I could see he was sweet and vulnerable. I sensed something.' She shrugged. 'He liked to talk about his younger childhood; he was born in rural Nebraska. To me, it was like hearing about another country.'

'He was wrong for Typhon,' Bourne said bluntly.

'He was wrong for the field, that's no lie,' she said just as bluntly.

Bourne put his hands in his pockets. 'So where does all this leave us?'

She started as if he'd pricked her with the business end of her switchblade. 'All what?'

'We've saved each other's lives, you've tried to kill me twice. Bottom line: We don't trust each other.'

Her eyes, large and liquid with incipient tears, bored into his. 'I gave up the NET; you brought me here to Deron's.

What's *your* definition of trust?'

Bourne said, 'You took photos of Cevik when he was detained.'

She nodded, waiting for the ax to fall. What would he require of her now? What, exactly, did she require of him? She knew, of course, but it was too painful to admit to herself, let alone tell him.

'Okay, call Typhon. Get them to upload the photos to your phone.' He began to walk down the corridor, and she paced him step for step. 'Then have them upload the cipher Hytner took off Cevik.'

'You forget that all of CI is still locked down. That includes data transfers.'

'You can get me what I want, Soraya. I have faith in you.'

The curious look came back into her eyes for a moment, then vanished as if it had never existed. She was on the phone to Typhon by the time they entered Deron's workroom, an L-shaped space carved out of the old kitchen and pantry. His artist's studio was upstairs, in the room that gathered the most daylight. As for Deron himself, he was bent over a worktable, poring over the NET.

No one in Typhon save its director had the clearance to upload sensitive data during lockdown. She knew she'd have to search elsewhere to get what Bourne needed.

She heard Anne Held's voice and identified herself.

'Listen, Anne, I need your help.'

'Really? You won't even tell me where you are.'

'It's not important. I'm not in any danger.'

'Well, that's a relief. Why did the beacon stop transmitting?'

'I don't know.' Soraya was careful to keep her voice level. 'Maybe it's defective.'

'Since you're still with Bourne, it shouldn't be too difficult to find out.'

'Are you crazy? I can't get that close to him.'

'And yet you need a favor. Tell me.'

Soraya did.

Silence. 'Why is it you never ask for anything easy.'

'I can ask other people for those things.'

'Too true.' Then, 'If I get caught . . .'

'Anne, I think we have a lead to Cevik, but we need the intel.'

'Okay,' Anne said. 'But in return you've got to find out what happened to that beacon. I've got to tell the Old Man something that'll satisfy him. He's out for blood and I want to make certain it's not mine.'

Soraya thought for a moment, but couldn't come up with another alternative. She'd just have to come back to Anne with something more detailed, something plausible. 'All right. I think I can work something out.'

'Good. By the way, Soraya, when it comes to the new DDCI, I'd watch my back if I were you. He's no friend of Lindros, or of Typhon.'

'Thanks, Anne. Thanks very much.'

'It's done,' Soraya said. 'The data's been uploaded successfully.'

Bourne took her cell and handed it to Deron, who dragged himself away from his new toy to plug the phone into his computer network and download the files.

Cevik's face popped up on one of the many monitors.

'Knock yourself out.' Deron went back to studying the NET.

Bourne sat down in a task chair and studied the photos for a long time. He could feel Soraya leaning over his right shoulder. He felt – what? – the ghost of a memory. He rubbed his temples, willing himself to remember, but the sliver of light eeled away into darkness. With some disquiet, he returned to his scrutiny of Cevik's face.

There was something about it – not any single feature, but an overall impression – that swam in his memory like the shadow of a fish out of sight beneath the surface of a lake. He zoomed in on one area of Cevik's face after another – mouth, nose, brow, temple, ears. But this only served to push the impressionistic memory farther into the unknown recesses of his mind. Then he came to the eyes – the golden eyes. There was something about the left one. Zooming in closer, he saw a minute crescent of light at the outer edge of the iris. He zoomed in again, but here the resolution failed him and the image began to blur. He zoomed out until the crescent of light sharpened. It was tiny. It could be nothing – a reflection of the illumination in the cell. But why was it at the edge of the iris? If it was a reflection off the iris, the light would be a mote nearer the center, where the eyeball was most prominent, and therefore most likely to pick up the light. This was at the edge where . . .

Bourne laughed silently.

At that moment Soraya's cell phone buzzed. He heard her on it briefly. Then she said: 'The prelim from forensics indicates that the Hummer was packed with a shitload of C-Four.'

He turned to her. 'Which is why they wouldn't respond.'

'Cevik and his crew were suicide bombers.'

'Maybe not.' Bourne turned back to the photo, pointing at the tiny crescent of light. 'See that? It's a reflection off the edge of a contact lens, because it's slightly raised above the surface of the iris and has caught the light. Now look here. Notice this tiny fleck of the gold intruding on the curving left edge of the pupil? The only way that's possible is if Cevik was wearing colored contacts.'

He peered up into her face. 'Why would Cevik disguise himself unless he wasn't Cevik at all.' He waited for her response. 'Soraya?'

'I'm thinking.'

'The disguise, the meticulous planning, the deliberate bomb attack.'

'In the jungle,' she said, 'only a chameleon can spot another chameleon.'

'Yes,' Bourne said, staring at the photo. 'I think we had Fadi under our thumb.'

Another pause, this one shorter. Her brain was working so fiercely he could hear it.

'Chances are, then, Cevik didn't die in the blast,' she said at length.

'That would be a good bet.' Bourne thought a moment. 'He wouldn't have had much time to get out of the Hummer. The only time I didn't have it in sight was when I was starting up the motorcycle. That means before the Twenty-third and Constitution intersection.'

'He might have had another car waiting.'

'Check it out, but, frankly, I doubt it,' Bourne said. Now he understood why Fadi had used the high-profile Hummer. He *wanted* it followed and, finally, surrounded by CI personnel. He wanted to inflict maximum damage. 'There was no way for him to predict where he needed to bail.'

Soraya nodded. 'I'll grid it out from the point the Hummer picked Fadi up.' She was already dialing Typhon. 'I'll start a couple of teams canvassing right away.' She gave her instructions, listened gravely for a moment, then disconnected. 'Jason, I have to tell you there's a growing internal rift. The DCI's gone ballistic over the Cevik fiasco. He's blaming you.'

'Naturally.' Bourne shook his head. 'If it wasn't for Martin, I'd have nothing more to do with CI or Typhon. But he's my friend – he believed in me, fought for me when the agency was out for my blood. I won't turn my back on him. Still. I swear this is my last mission for CI.'

*

For Martin Lindros, the shadows resolved themselves into the undersides of clouds, reflected in the still waters of the lake. There was a vague sensation of pain – what you might feel if a dentist drilled into a partially Novocained tooth. The pain, far off on the horizon, failed to disturb him. He was far too concentrated on the trout at the business end of his fishing line. He reeled in, lifted the rod high so that it bent like a bow, then reeled in more line. Just as his father had taught him. This was the way to tire out a fish, even the most vigorous fighter. With discipline and patience, any hooked fish could be landed.

The shadows seemed to cluster right above him, blotting out the sun. The growing chill caused him to concentrate on this fish even harder.

Lindros's father had taught him many other things besides how to fish. A man of singular talents, Oscar Lindros had founded Vaultline, turning it into the world's foremost private security firm. Vaultline's clients were the super-conglomerates whose businesses often took their personnel into dangerous parts of the world. Oscar Lindros or one of his personally trained operatives was there to protect them.

Lindros, bending over the side of the boat, could see the flashing rainbow-and-silver of the trout. It was a big one, all right. Bigger than any he'd caught to date. Despite the fish's thrashing, Lindros could see the triangular head, the bony mouth opening and closing. He hauled up on the rod and the trout came halfway out of the water, spraying him with droplets.

Early on, Martin Lindros had developed an interest in being a spy. It went without saying that this desire had thrilled his father. And so Oscar Lindros had set about teaching his son everything he knew about the business of clandestine work. Chief among this knowledge was how to survive any form of capture or torture. It was all in the mind, Oscar Lindros told his son. You had to train your mind to withdraw from the outside world. Then you had to train it to withdraw from those sections of the brain that transmitted pain. To do this, you needed to conjure up a time and a place, you needed to make this place real – as real as anything you could experience with your five senses. You had to go there and you had to stay there for the duration. Otherwise, either your will would eventually be broken or you would go mad.

This was where Martin Lindros was, where he had been ever since he had been taken by Dujja, brought to this place where his body now lay twitching and bleeding.

Out on the lake, Lindros finally landed the trout. It flopped and gasped in the bottom of the boat, its eye fixed on him even as it grayed over. Bending down, he removed the barbed hook from the hard cartilage around the trout's mouth. How many fish had he landed since he'd been out on the lake? It was impossible to know since they'd never stayed around long afterward; they were of no use to him once they were off the hook.

He baited the hook, cast out the line. He had to keep going, he had to keep fishing. Otherwise the pain, a dim cloudbank on the horizon, would rush at him with the fury of a hurricane.

Sitting in the business-class section of the overnight flight to London, Bourne put up the DO NOT DISTURB sign and took out the Sony PS3 Deron had given him, modified with expanded memory and ultra-high-resolution screen. The hard drive was preloaded with a bunch of new goodies Deron had concocted. Art forgeries might pay the rent, but his real love was dreaming up new miniaturized gadgets – hence his interest in the NET, which Bourne now had safely tucked away in its case.

Deron had provided Bourne with three separate passports beyond his diplomatic-CI passport. In each of the photos

Deron had on file, Bourne looked completely different. He had with him makeup, colored contact lenses, and the like, along with one of Deron's new-generation guns made of rubber-wrapped plastic. According to Deron, the Kevlar-coated rubber bullets could bring down a charging elephant if put in the right spot.

Bourne brought up the photo of Hiram Cevik. Fadi. How many other identities had this mastermind assumed over the years? It seemed probable that surveillance cameras, closed-circuit TV cameras, in public places, had recorded his image, but he'd doubtless looked different every time. Bourne had advised Soraya to go over all the tapes or still photos available of the areas just before and after the Dujja attacks, comparing the faces etched there with this photo of Cevik, although he had little hope she'd find anything. He himself had had his photo taken by surveillance cameras and CCTV over the years. He had no worries because the Chameleon had looked different in every one. No one could spot any similarities; he'd made damn sure of that. So Fadi, the chameleon.

He stared at the face for a long time. Though he fought it, exhaustion overtook him, and he slept . . .

. . . *Marie comes to him, in a place of mature acacia trees and cobbled streets. There is a sharp mineral tang in the air, as of a restless sea. A humid breeze lifts her hair off her ears, and it streams behind her like a banner.*

He speaks to her. 'You can get me what I want. I have faith in you.'

There is fear in her eyes, but also courage and determination. She will do what he asks of her, no matter the danger, he knows it. He nods in farewell, and she vanishes . . .

He finds himself on the same street of looming acacias that he's summoned up before. The black water is in front of him. And then he's descending, floating through air as if from a parachute. He's sprinting across a beach at night. On his left is a dark line of kiosks. He's carrying . . . there is something in his arms. No, not some-

thing. *Someone. Blood all over, a pounding in his veins. A pale face, eyes closed, one cheek on his left biceps. He sprints along the beach, feeling terribly exposed. He's violated his covenant with himself and because of that they'll all die: him, the figure in his arms . . . the young woman covered in blood. She's saying something to him, but he can't hear what. Running footsteps behind him, and the thought, clear as the moon riding low in the sky:* We've been betrayed . . .

When Matthew Lerner walked into the outer office of the DCI's suite, Anne Held took a moment before she looked up. She had been working on nothing special. Nothing, in fact, that required her attention, yet it was important that Lerner think so. Privately, Anne likened the Old Man's outer office to a moat around a castle keep; she, the large-toothed carnivore that swam in it.

When she deemed that Lerner had waited long enough, she looked up, smiled coolly.

'You said the DCI wants to see me.'

'In point of fact, *I* want to see you.' Anne stood up, running her hands down her thighs to flatten any wrinkles that might have developed while she had been sitting. Pearly light spun off her perfectly manicured nails. 'D'you fancy a cup of coffee?' she added as she crossed the room.

Lerner arched his eyebrows. 'I thought it was tea you Brits liked.'

She held the door open for him to pass through. 'Just one of the many misconceptions you have about me.'

In the metal-clad elevator going down to the CI commissary, silence reigned. Anne looked straight ahead while Lerner, no doubt, tried to figure out what this was all about.

The commissary was unlike that of any other governmental agency. Its atmosphere was hushed, the floors carpeted with deep pile in presidential blue. The walls were white, the banquettes and chairs red leather. The ceiling was constructed of a series of acoustic baffles that dampened all sound, especially voices. Waistcoated waiters glided expertly and soundlessly up and down the generous aisles between tables. In short, the CI dining room was more like a gentlemen's club than a commissary.

The captain, recognizing Anne instantly, showed the pair to the DCI's round corner table, almost entirely surrounded by one of the high-backed banquettes. She and Lerner slid in, coffee was served, then they were discreetly left alone.

Lerner stirred sugar into his cup for a moment. 'So what's this all about?'

She took a sip of the black coffee, rolled the liquid around in her mouth as if it were a fine wine, then, satisfied, swallowed and put down her cup.

'Drink up, Matthew. It's single-estate Ethiopian. Strong and rich.'

'Another new protocol I've instituted, Ms. Held. We do not address each other by our Christian names.'

'The problem with some strong coffee,' she said, ignoring him, 'is that it can be quite acidic. Too much acid will turn the strength against itself, upset the entire digestive system. Even burn a hole in the stomach. When that happens, the coffee must be thrown out.'

Lerner sat back. 'Meaning?' He knew she wasn't talking about coffee.

She allowed her eyes to rest on his face for a moment. 'You were named DDCI, what, six months ago? Change is difficult for everyone. But there are certain protocols that cannot be—'

'Get to the point.'

She took another sip of coffee. 'It's not a good idea, Matthew, to be bad-mouthing Martin Lindros.'

'Yeah? What makes him so special?'

'If you'd been at this level longer, you wouldn't need to ask.'

'Why are we talking about Lindros? Chances are he's dead.'

'We don't know that,' Anne said shortly.

'Anyway, we're not really talking about Lindros's territory, are we, Ms. Held?'

She flushed then, despite herself. 'You had no good cause to lower my clearance level.'

'Whatever you might think your title entitles you to, it doesn't. You're still support personnel.'

'I'm the DCI's right hand. If he needs intel, I fetch it for him.'

'I'm transferring in Reilly from Ops Directorate. He'll be handling all the Old Man's research from now on.' Lerner sighed. 'I see the look on your face. Don't take these changes personally. It's standard operational procedure. Besides, if you get special treatment, the other support personnel start to resent it. Resentment breeds distrust, and that we cannot tolerate.'

He pushed his coffee cup away. 'Whether you choose to believe it or not, Ms. Held, CI is moribund. It has been for years. What it needs most is a high colonic. I'm it.'

'Martin Lindros has been put in charge of revamping CI,' she said icily.

'Lindros is the Old Man's weakness. His way isn't the right way. Mine is.' He smiled as he rose. 'Oh, and one other thing. Don't ever mislead me again. Support staff have no business wasting the deputy director's time with coffee and opinions.'

Kim Lovett, in her lab at FIU headquarters on Vermont Avenue, was at the most crucial stage of her tests. She had to transfer the solid material she'd collected on the fifth-floor suite of the Constitution Hotel from its airtight vials for the headspace gas chromatography. The theory was this: Since all known fire accelerants were highly volatile liquid hydrocarbons, the gases that the compounds gave off often remained at the scene for hours afterward. The idea was to capture the gases in the headspace above the solid material that had been impregnated with the accelerants: bits of charred wood, carpet fibers, lines of grout she'd dug out with a dentist's tool. She would then take a chromatogram of each of the gases based on its individual boiling point. In this way, a fingerprint of the accelerant emerged to be identified.

Kim stuck a long needle into the lid of each container, drew out the gas that had formed above the solid material, and injected it into the cylinder of the gas chromatograph without exposing it to the air. She ensured that the settings were correct, then slipped the switch that would begin the process of separation and analysis.

She was making notes as to the date, time, and sample number when she heard the lab door whoosh open and, turning, saw Detective Overton enter. He wore a fog-gray overcoat and carried two paper coffee cups in his hands. He set one down in front of her. She thanked him.

He seemed more morose than before. 'What news?'

Kim savored the hot, sweet burn of the coffee in her mouth and her throat. 'We'll know in a minute what accelerant was used.'

'How's that going to help me?'

'I thought you were handing the case over to Homeland Security?'

'Magnificent bastards. Two agents were in my captain's office this morning, demanding my notes,' Overton said. 'Not that I wasn't expecting it. So I made two sets, because I mean to break this case and shove it in their faces.'

A beep sounded.

'Here we go.' Kim swiveled around. 'The results are

ready.' She peered at the chromatograph's readout. 'Carbon disulfide.' She nodded. 'This is interesting. Typically, we don't see this particular accelerant in arson cases.'

'Then why choose this one?'

'Good question. My guess is because it burns hotter and has an explosive limit of fifty percent – way higher than other accelerants.' She swiveled around again. 'You remember I found accelerants in two places – in the bathroom and under the windows. This interested me, and now I know why. The chromagraph gave me two separate readouts. In the bathroom, all that was used was the carbon disulfide. But at the other spot, the one in the living room near the windows, I found another compound, a rather complex and odd one.'

'Like what?'

'Not an explosive. Something more unusual. I had to do some checking, but I discovered that it's a hydrocarbon compound that counteracts fire retardants. This explains how the curtains caught fire, this explains why the explosion blew out the windows. Between the oxygen feeding the flames and the sprinklers being disabled, the maximum amount of damage in the minimum amount of time was virtually ensured.'

'Which is why we were left with nothing, not even an intact skeleton or a set of teeth from which to make a definite ID of the body.' He rubbed the blue stubble on his chin. 'The perps thought of everything, didn't they?'

'Maybe not everything.' Kim held up the two porcelain teeth she'd extracted from the bathtub drain. She had cleaned them of the coating of ash, so that they gleamed an ivory color.

'Right,' said Overton. 'We're trying to find out through channels in Amsterdam whether Jakob or Lev Silver wore a dental bridge. At least then we could make a positive ID.'

'Well, the thing of it is,' Kim said, 'I'm not at all sure this is a dental bridge.'

Overton plucked it out of her hand, studied it under a

high-intensity lamp. So far as he could see, there wasn't anything out of the ordinary. 'What else could it be?'

'I've got a call in to a friend of mine. Maybe she can tell us.'

'Oh, yeah? What's she do?'

Kim looked at him. 'She's a spook.'

Bourne traveled from London to Addis Ababa; Addis Ababa to Djibouti. He rested very little, slept even less. He was too busy poring over the intel of Lindros's known movements that Soraya had provided him. Unfortunately, much of it was lacking details. Not altogether surprising. Lindros had been tracking the world's most deadly terrorist cadre. Communications of any kind would have been exceedingly difficult and would have compromised security.

When he wasn't memorizing the data, Bourne was reviewing the video intel Anne Held had uploaded to Soraya's cell, which now resided in the PS3, most especially Tim Hytner's attempt to break the cipher Typhon had found on Cevik's person. But now Bourne had to wonder about that cipher itself: Was it an authentic Dujja communication or was it a fake, planted, for some reason, for Typhon to find and decode? A bewildering labyrinth of duplicity had opened in front of him. From now on, each step he took was fraught with peril. A single false assumption could drag him under like quicksand.

It was at this moment that Bourne realized that he was up against a foe of extraordinary intelligence and will, a master-mind to rival his old nemesis Carlos.

He closed his eyes for a moment and immediately Marie's image came to him. It was she who had been his rock, who had helped him get through the tortures of the past. But Marie was gone. Every day that passed, he felt her fading. He tried to hold on, but the Bourne identity was relentless; it would not allow him to dwell on sentimentality, on sorrow and despair. All these emotions dwelled in him, but they were shadows, held at bay by Bourne's exceptional concentration and relentless need to solve deadly puzzles no one else could tackle. Of course, he understood the wellspring of his singular ability; he'd known it even before Dr. Sunderland had so succinctly summed it up: He was driven by his burning need to unravel the enigma of who he was.

In Djibouti a CI copter, fueled and ready, was waiting for him. He ran across the wet tarmac beneath an angry sky filled with bruised clouds and a humid, swirling wind, and climbed in. It was the morning of the third day since he'd set out from D.C. His limbs felt cramped, muscles bunched tight. He longed for action and was not looking forward to the hour-long flight to Ras Dejen.

Breakfast was served on a metal tray, and he dug in as the copter took off. But he tasted nothing and saw nothing, for he was totally inside his mind. He was, for the thousandth time, running Fadi's cipher, looking at it as a whole, because he'd gotten nowhere following the algorithm route that Tim Hytner had chosen. If Fadi had, indeed, turned Hytner – and Bourne could not come up with another reasonable conclusion – Hytner would have no incentive to actually break the cipher. This was why Bourne had wanted the cipher and Hytner's work. If he saw that Hytner's work was bogus, he'd have his proof of the man's culpability. But of course, that wouldn't answer the question of whether the cipher contained real intel or disinformation meant to confuse and misdirect Typhon.

Unfortunately, he was no closer to solving the cipher's algorithm or even knowing whether Hytner had been on the right track. He had, however, spent two restless nights filled not with dreams, but memory shards. He was disappointed that Dr. Sunderland's treatment had had such a short-term effect, but he couldn't say he hadn't been warned. Worse, by far, was the sense of impending calamity. All the shards revolved around the tall trees, the mineral scent of the water, the desperate flight across sand. Desperate not only for him, but for someone else as well. He'd violated one of his own cardinal rules, and now he was going to pay for it. Something had set off this series of memory fragments, and he had a strong suspicion that this origin was the key to understanding what had happened to him before. It was maddening to have no – or at best limited – access to his past. His life was a blank slate, each day like the day he'd been born. Knowledge denied – essential knowledge. How could he begin to know himself when his past had been taken away from him?

The copter, soaring below the thick cloud layer, swung northwest, heading toward the Simien mountain range. When Bourne finished his breakfast, he climbed into an extreme-weather jumpsuit and specially made snow boots with extra-thick soles studded with metal blades meant to give him support on icy and rocky terrain.

As he stared out the curved window, his thoughts turned inward again, this time toward his friend Martin Lindros. He'd met Lindros after his old mentor, Alex Conklin, was found murdered. It was Lindros who'd stood behind Bourne, believed in him when the Old Man had put out a worldwide sanction against him. Ever since, Lindros had been his faithful backup at CI. Bourne steeled himself. Whatever had happened to Lindros – whether he was alive or dead – Bourne was determined to bring him home.

Just over an hour later, he arrived on the north slope of Ras Dejen. Brilliant sunlight made shadows sharp as razor blades on the mountainside, which seemed to exist in a curling sea of cloud through which, now and again, vultures could be seen, soaring on the thermals.

Bourne was just behind Davis's right shoulder when the young pilot pointed down. There was the wreckage of both Chinooks, pillowed in fresh snow, streaked with black, metal stripped back, twisted off as if with a mammoth can opener wielded by a maniacal demon.

'Damage is consistent with ground-to-air missiles,' Davis said.

So Soraya had been right. This kind of war matériel was expensive, a high cost only an alliance with organized crime could pay for. Bourne peered more closely as they neared the site. 'But there's a difference. The one on the left—'

'From what's left of the markings, the chopper carrying Skorpion One.'

'Look at the rotors. That one was shot as it was about to take off. The second chopper hit the ground with a great deal of force. It must've been hit as it was coming in for a landing.'

Davis nodded. 'Roger that. The opposition's well armed, all right. Odd for this neck of the woods.'

Bourne couldn't have agreed more.

Taking up a pair of field glasses, he directed Davis to circle the site. The moment the terrain came into focus, he was gripped with an intense feeling of déjà vu. He'd been to this part of Ras Dejen before, he was certain of it. But when? And why? He knew, for instance, where to look for hiding enemies. Directing the pilot, he searched every nook and crevice, every shadowed place around the periphery of the landing site.

He knew also that Ras Dejen, the highest peak in the Simien mountain chain, was within Amhara, one of the nine ethnic divisions within Ethiopia. The Amhara people made up 30 percent of the country's population. Amharic was Ethiopia's official language. In fact, after Arabic, it was the world's second most spoken Semitic language.

He was familiar with the Amhara mountain tribes. None of them had the means – either financially or technically – to inflict such sophisticated damage. 'Whoever it was isn't here now. Take her down.'

Davis brought the copter to rest just north of the wreckage. It slipped sideways a bit on the ice beneath the layer of fresh powder; then he had it under control. The moment they were on solid ground, he handed Bourne a Thuraya satellite phone. Just slightly larger than a normal cell phone, it was the only kind that would work in this mountainous terrain, where normal GSM signals were unavailable.

'Stay here,' Bourne said as the pilot began to unstrap himself. 'No matter what, wait for me. I'll check in every two hours. Six hours go by without hearing from me, you take off.'

'Can't do that, sir. I've never left a man behind.'

'This time is different.' Bourne gripped his shoulder. 'Under no circumstances are you to go after me, got it?'

Davis looked unhappy. 'Yessir.' He took up an assault rifle, opened the chopper door. Bitter-cold air shouldered its way in.

'You want something to do? Cover that cave mouth. Anything unknown to you moves or comes out, shoot first. We'll ask questions later.'

Bourne leapt out. It was frigid. The high terrain of Ras Dejen was no place to be in winter. The snow was thick enough, but so dry that the constant wind had pushed it about, causing high dunes of Saharan proportions. In other areas, the plateau had been swept clean, revealing patches of burned-out grass and rocks irregularly spaced like the rotting teeth of an old man.

Even though he'd done a 360 visual from the air, Bourne moved cautiously toward the wreckage of the two Chinooks. He was most concerned about the cave. It could hold good news – wounded survivors of either of the crashes – or bad news, namely members of the cadre that had taken out the two Skorpion units.

As he came abreast of the Chinooks, he saw bodies inside – nothing more than charcoaled skeletons, bits of singed hair. He resisted the urge to look inside the hulks for any sign of Lindros. Securing the site came first.

He reached the cave without incident. The wind, slithering through knuckles of rock, sent up an eerie, keening cry that sounded like someone being tortured. The cave mouth leered at him, daring him to enter. He stood against the bone-chilling rock face for a moment, taking deep, controlled breaths. Then he leapt, rolling into darkness.

Switching on a powerful flashlight, he sent the beam into niches and corners where those lying in wait were sure to secrete themselves. No one. Rising to his feet, he took a step, then, nostrils flared, came to an abrupt halt.

Once, in Egypt, he'd been led through an underground maze by a local conduit. There had come to him an odd scent – at once sweet and spicy – something utterly beyond his previous experience. When he'd voiced his question, the conduit had switched on a battery-powered flashlight for perhaps ten seconds, and Bourne saw the bodies, dark skin stretched like leather, drying, awaiting burial.

'*What you smell,*' his conduit had said as he switched off the flashlight, '*is human flesh after all the fluids are gone.*'

This was what Bourne smelled now in the cave punched into the north slope of Ras Dejen. Desiccated human flesh, and something else: the nauseating stench of decomposition trapped in the rear of the cave like swamp gas.

Fanning the high-intensity beam out in front of him, he moved forward. There came from underfoot a sharp, crunching sound. Redirecting the beam, he discovered that the floor was covered in bones – animal, bird, human alike. He continued, until he saw something stuck up from the rock bed. A body sat with its back against the rear wall.

Hunkering down on his haunches brought him to eye level with the head. Or what was left of it. A pit had begun in the center of the face, fountaining its poison outward like a volcano spewing lava, obliterating first the nose, then the eyes and cheeks, peeling away the skin, eating the flesh beneath. Now even parts of the skull – the bone itself – was pitted and scarred by the same force that had feasted on the softer human materials.

Bourne, his heart thudding hard against his rib cage, realized that he was holding his breath. He'd seen this particular kind of necrosis before. Only one thing could cause it: radiation.

This answered many questions: what had so suddenly, compellingly brought Martin Lindros into the field; why this area was so important, it had been defended by ground-to-air missiles and God only knew what other ordnance. His heart sank. Everyone from Skorpion One and Two – including Martin – would have to have been killed to protect the mind-numbing secret. Someone was transshipping more than triggered spark gaps via this route; someone had in their possession uranium ore. That was what this person had died of: radiation poisoning from a leak in the uranium container he was transporting. By itself, yellowcake uranium ore meant nothing: It was cheap, fairly easy to obtain, and impossible to refine into HEU unless you had a facility more than a kilometer square and four floors high, not to mention almost unlimited funds.

Also, yellowcake would not have left this radiation signature. No, without doubt, what Dujja had somehow gotten its hands on was uranium dioxide powder, only one easy step away from weapons-grade HEU. The question he was asking himself now was the same one that must have launched Lindros so precipitously into harm's way: What would a terrorist cadre be doing with uranium dioxide and triggered spark gaps *unless it had a facility somewhere with the personnel and the capability of manufacturing atomic bombs?*

Which could mean only one thing: Dujja was more extraordinary than anyone at Typhon realized. It was at the heart of a covert international nuclear network. Just such a network had been shut down in 2004, when Pakistani scientist Abdul Qadeer Khan admitted selling atomic technology to Iran, North Korea, and Libya. Now the terrifying specter had been resurrected.

Dizzied by this revelation, Bourne rose and backed out of the cave. He turned, took several deep breaths, even though the wind knifed into his lungs, and shivered. Giving the all-clear sign to Davis, he made his way back to the crash site. He could not stop his mind from buzzing. The threat to America that Typhon had intercepted was not only real, it was of a scope and consequence that was absolutely devastating.

He recalled the single-use triggered spark gap – the smoking gun of Martin's recent investigation. Unless he could stop Fadi, a nuclear attack would be carried out on a major American city.

SEVEN

Anne Held corralled Soraya the moment she appeared back at CI headquarters.

'Ladies,' she said under her breath. 'Now.'

Once inside the ladies' room in the lobby, Anne went through the cubicles one by one, making sure they were alone.

'My part of the bargain,' Soraya began. 'The NET came in contact with fire, which destroyed half of the circuits.'

'Well, that's something I can give the Old Man,' Anne said. 'He's out for Bourne's blood – and so is Lerner.'

'Because of what happened with Cevik.' Soraya frowned. 'But what's Lerner's involvement?'

'That's why I called you in here,' Anne said sharply. 'While you were with Bourne, Lerner staged a coup.'

'He did what?'

'He convinced the Old Man to name him acting director of Typhon.'

'Oh, Jesus,' Soraya said. 'As if things aren't screwed up enough as it is.'

'I have a feeling you haven't seen anything yet. He's hell-bent on reorganizing everything in CI, and now that he's got his claws into Typhon he's going to shake that up as well.'

Someone tried to come in, but Anne discouraged the intrusion. 'There's a flood in here,' she said with authority. 'Try upstairs.'

When they were alone again, she continued: 'Lerner's

going to come after everyone he doesn't trust. And because of your association with Bourne, I'd bet the house you're at the top of his list.' She went to the door. 'Heads up, poppet.'

Bourne sat, head in hands, trying to think his way out of this growing nightmare. The trouble was, he didn't have enough information. There was nothing he could do other than keep going, trying to find Lindros or, failing that – if his friend was already dead – continue his mission to find and stop Fadi and Dujja before they made good on their threat.

At length, he rose. After inspecting the outside of the Chinooks, he bypassed the one closest to the cave and clambered into the copter that had brought Lindros.

The interior looked surreal, like a painting by Dalí: plastic melted into puddles, metal fused to metal. Seared beyond anything he could have imagined. This interested him. At this high elevation, there wasn't enough oxygen to support a fire of such intensity for long, certainly not long enough to do this kind of damage. The fire must have come from another source – a flamethrower.

Bourne saw Hiram Cevik's face in his mind's eye. Fadi was behind the ambush. The advanced weaponry, the precise coordination of the attacks, the high level of tactics that had caused two of CI's crack field teams to be killed: All evidence pointed to it.

But another question gnawed at him. Why had Fadi allowed himself to be captured by CI? Several answers presented themselves. The most likely one was that he was sending CI a message: *You think you have me in your sights, but you don't know who you're dealing with.* To some extent, Bourne knew that Fadi was correct: They knew next to nothing about him. But it was exactly this act of bravado that might provide Bourne with the opening he needed. Bourne's success had come from being able to get inside his adversaries' heads. Experience had taught him that it was impossible to do this with someone who remained in the shadows. Now, however, Fadi had emerged into the light of Bourne's vision. He'd shown his face. For the first time, Bourne had a template – rough and imprecise as it might be – from which to begin his pursuit.

Bourne returned his full attention to the interior of the Chinook. He counted four skeletons. This was nothing short of a revelation. Two people were missing from the dead. Could they be alive? Was Martin one of them?

The CI's Skorpion units were run military-style. All the men wore dog tags that identified them as being attached to an Army Ranger unit that didn't exist. As quickly as he could, he collected the four dog tags. He rubbed off the snow, ash, and soot to read their names, which he'd memorized from the packet of intel he'd gotten from Typhon. Martin wasn't here! The pilot – Jaime Cowell – was also unaccounted for.

Moving to the final resting place of Skorpion Two, he discovered the five skeletons of the Skorpion complement. Judging by the number of limb bones strewn about, it was safe to say none of them was in operational condition when the Chinook crashed. They'd been sitting ducks. Bourne hunted around, gathering up their dog tags.

All at once there came the hint of movement in the shadows of the interior, then the brief glitter of eyes before a head turned away. Bourne reached into the recessed space beneath the instrument panel. He felt a sharp pain in his hand, then a blur rushed him, knocking him backward.

Regaining his feet, he followed the figure out of the shell of the Chinook and took off after it, all the while waving at Davis to hold his fire. He glimpsed the bloody semicircle of tooth marks on the back of his hand just as the figure slipped over the low stone wall on the northeast side of site.

Bourne flung himself into the air, came down feet-first on

the top of the wall, and, orienting himself, leapt off it onto the back of the figure.

They both went down, rolling, but Bourne kept a firm grip on the hair, yanking it back to see the face. He was confronted with a boy of no more than eleven.

'Who are you?' Bourne said in the local Amharic dialect. 'What are you doing here?'

The boy spat into his face, clawed him, trying to get away. Holding his crossed wrists behind his back, Bourne sat him down in the lee of the wall, out of the howling wind. The boy was thin as a spike, the bones prominent in his cheeks, shoulders, and hips.

'When was the last time you ate?'

No response. At least the boy didn't spit at him again, but possibly that was because he was as dry inside as the snow crunching beneath their feet. With his free hand, Bourne unhooked a canteen, opened it with his teeth.

'I want to let you go. I've no wish to hurt you. Would you like some water?' The boy opened his mouth wide like a chick in the nest.

'Then you must promise to answer my questions. Is that fair?'

The boy looked at him for a moment with his black eyes, then nodded. Bourne let go of his wrists, and he reached out for the canteen, tipped it, drank the water in great, convulsive gulps.

While he drank, Bourne built up snow walls on either side of them, to reflect back their own heat. He took back the canteen.

'First question: Do you know what happened up here?'

The boy shook his head.

'You must've seen the flash of weapons, the balls of smoke rising up over the mountain.'

A small hesitation. 'I saw them, yes.' He had the high voice of a girl.

'And naturally enough, you were curious. You climbed up here, didn't you?'

The boy looked away, bit his lip.

This wasn't working. Bourne knew he had to find another way to get the boy to open up.

'My name is Jason,' he said. 'What's yours?'

Again that hesitation. 'Alem.'

'Alem, did you ever lose anyone? Someone you cared about a great deal?'

'Why?' Alem asked suspiciously.

'Because I've lost someone. My best friend. That's why I'm here. He was in one of the burned-out birds. I need to know if you saw him or know what happened to him.'

Alem was already shaking his head.

'His name is Martin Lindros. Have you heard it spoken by anyone?'

Alem bit his lip again, which had begun to tremble slightly, but not, Bourne thought, from the chill. He shook his head.

Bourne reached down, scooped snow onto the back of his hand where Alem had bitten it. He saw Alem's eyes following his every movement.

'My older brother died six months ago,' Alem said after a time.

Bourne went on with packing the snow. *Best to act casual*, he reasoned. 'What happened to him?'

Alem drew his knees up to his chest, crossed his arms over them. 'He was buried in a rockslide that crippled my father.'

'I'm sorry,' Bourne said, meaning it. 'Listen, about my friend. What if he's alive? Would you want him to die?'

Alem was trailing his fingers in the icy rubble at the base of the wall. 'You'll beat me,' he muttered.

'Why would I do that?'

'I scavenged something.' He jerked his head in the

121

direction of the crash site. 'From there.'

'Alem, I promise you. All I care about is finding my friend.'

Without another glance at Bourne, Alem produced a ring. Bourne took it, held it in the sunlight. He recognized the shield with an open book in each quadrant: the coat of arms of Brown University.

'This is my friend's ring.' Carefully, he gave it back to Alem. 'Will you show me where you found it?'

Alem took him over the wall, then tromped through the snow to a spot several hundred meters away from the crash site. He knelt down, Bourne with him.

'Here?'

Alem nodded. 'It was under the snow, half buried.'

'As if it had been ground into the dirt,' Bourne finished for him. 'Yet you found it.'

'I was up here with my father.' Alem's wrists rested on his bony knees. 'We were scavenging.'

'What did your father find?'

Alem shrugged.

'Will you take me to him?'

Alem stared down at the ring in his grimy palm. He curled his fingers over it, put it back in his pocket. Then he looked up at Bourne.

'I won't tell him,' Bourne said quietly. 'I promise.'

Alem nodded, and they rose together. From Davis, Bourne got antiseptic and a bandage for his hand. Then the boy led him down from the small, bleak alpine meadow via a heart-stoppingly steep path that twisted along the iced rock face of Ras Dejen.

Anne wasn't kidding about Lerner being out for blood. There were two glowering agents waiting for Soraya at Typhon level as she stepped out of the elevator. Even to be here, she knew, they had to have Typhon-issued ID. Bad news, getting worse every second.

'Acting Director Lerner wants a word,' the one on the left said.

'He asks that you come with us,' the one on the right said.

She used her lightest, flirtatious voice. 'D'you think I could freshen up first, boys?'

The one on the left, the taller one, said: '"ASAP." That was the acting director's order.'

Stoics, eunuchs, or both. Soraya shrugged and went with them. In truth, there wasn't much else she could do. As she marched down the corridors between the two animated pillars, she tried not to worry. The best thing she could do now was to keep her head while those around her were losing theirs. Lerner would no doubt needle her, do his best to drive her to the wall. She'd heard stories about him, and he had been at CI, what, all of six months? He'd know she resented him, and he'd work on that like a sadistic dentist clamped onto her molar.

At the end of the corridor, she confronted the corner office. The taller agent beat a brief military tattoo on the door with his callused knuckles. Then he opened the door and stood aside for her to enter. But he and his doppelgänger didn't leave. They stepped into the office behind her, closed the door, and took a step back, as if holding the wall up with their brawny shoulders.

Soraya's heart sank. In the blink of an eye, Lerner had taken over Lindros's office, swept all of Lindros's personal mementos into God only knew where. The photos were down, their faces turned to the wall, as if already in exile.

The acting director was sitting behind Lindros's desk, his beefy ass in Lindros's chair, leafing through a pale green folder, a CAD – a current action dossier – while he fielded Lindros's calls as if they were his own. They *were* his own,

Soraya reminded herself, and was instantly depressed. She longed for Lindros to return, prayed for Bourne to find him and bring him back alive. What other outcome should she hope for?

'Ah, Ms. Moore.' Lerner hung up the phone. 'Good of you to join us.' He smiled but did not offer her a seat. Clearly he wanted her to stand, like a pupil brought before the vice principal for disciplinary action.

'Just where have you been?'

She knew he knew because she'd checked in via her cell. Apparently, it was a personal confession he wanted. He was a man, she saw, for whom the world existed as a series of boxes, all the same size, into which he could fit everything and everyone, each to its own neat cubbyhole. In that way he fooled himself into believing that he could control the chaos of reality.

'I've been consoling Tim Hytner's mother and sisters in Maryland.'

'There are certain procedures,' Lerner said stiffly. 'They're there for a reason. Or didn't that occur to you?'

'Tim was my friend.'

'You were presumptuous to assume CI incapable of caring for its own.'

'I know his family. It was better the news came from me. I made it easier for them.'

'By lying, by telling them Hytner was a hero, instead of an inept bungler who allowed himself to be used by the enemy?'

Soraya was desperately trying to keep herself on an even keel. She hated herself for feeling intimidated by this man.

'Tim wasn't a field op.' At once, she knew she'd made a tactical error.

Lerner picked up the CAD. 'And yet your own written report states that Hytner was drawn into the field directly by Jason Bourne.'

'Tim was working to decode the cipher we found on Cevik

124

– the man we now know was Fadi. Bourne wanted to use that fact to make him talk.'

Lerner's face grew hard and tight as a drumhead. His eyes seemed to her like bullet holes – black, deadly, ready to erupt. Other than that he seemed to her quite ordinary. He could have been a shoe salesman, a middle-aged office drone of any flavor. Which, she supposed, was just the point. A good field agent needed to be forgotten almost as soon as he was seen.

'Let me get this straight, Ms. Moore. You're defending Jason Bourne?'

'It was Bourne who identified Fadi. He's given us a starting point to—'

'Curious that he made this so-called ID *after* Hytner was killed, *after* he allowed Cevik to escape.'

Soraya was incredulous. 'Are you saying you don't think Cevik was Fadi?'

'I'm saying all you have is the say-so of a rogue agent, whose word is as far from gospel as it's possible to get. It's damn dangerous to allow your personal feelings to get in the way of your professional judgment.'

'I'm sure that's not the—'

'You cleared this little excursion to Hytner's family with whom?'

Soraya tried to keep her equilibrium through his abrupt shifts of topics. 'There was no one to clear it with.'

'There is now.' With a flourish, he closed the CAD. 'Here's a bit of advice, Ms. Moore: Don't wander off the reservation again. Are we clear on that point?'

'Quite clear,' she said shortly.

'I wonder. You see, you haven't been here the last several days, so you missed an important staff meeting. Would you care to hear the gist of it?'

'Very much,' she said through gritted teeth.

'Here it is in a nutshell,' Lerner said amiably. 'I'm changing Typhon's mission.'

'You're doing *what*?'

'You see, Ms. Moore, what this agency needs is less navel-gazing and more action. It doesn't matter in the least what the Islamic extremists think or feel. They want us dead. Therefore, we're going to go out and kick their butts into the Red Sea. It's as simple as that.'

'Sir, if I may say, there's nothing simple about this war. It's not like other—'

'Now you've been brought up to speed, Ms. Moore,' Lerner said sharply.

An acid churning had begun in Soraya's guts. This couldn't be happening. All of Lindros's planning, all of their hard work, was going down the drain. Where was Lindros when they all needed him? Was he even alive? She had to believe that he was. But for the moment, at least, it was this monster from the field who was calling the shots. At least this interrogation was over.

Elbows on the desk, Lerner steepled his fingers. 'I wonder,' he said, once again turning on a dime, 'if you could clear up a matter for me.' He wagged the CAD up and down as if it was an admonishing finger. 'How on earth did you fuck things up so royally?'

She stood stock-still, despite the rage running through her. He'd led her to believe the interview was over. In fact, it was just starting. She knew that he was just getting around to the real reason he'd called her in.

'You allowed Bourne to take Hiram Cevik out of the cage. You were on site when Cevik made his escape. You ordered the choppers into action.' He dropped the dossier onto the desktop. 'What have I gotten wrong so far?'

Soraya briefly thought about remaining mute, but she didn't want to give him that measure of satisfaction. 'Nothing,' she said dully.

'You were the agent in charge for Cevik. You were responsible.'

Nothing for it now. She squared her shoulders. 'Yes, I was.'

'Grounds for firing, Ms. Moore, isn't it?'

'I wouldn't know.'

'That's just the trouble. You *should* know. Just as you should've known better than to let Cevik out of his cage.'

No matter what she said, he found a way to turn it against her. 'Begging your pardon, but I had orders from the DCI's office to accommodate Bourne in every way.'

Lerner stared at her for a long moment. Then he gestured in an almost avuncular fashion. 'Why the hell are you standing?' he said.

Soraya settled into a chair facing him.

'On the subject of Bourne.' His eyes locked on hers. 'You would seem to be something of an expert.'

'I wouldn't say that.'

'Your file says that you worked with him in Odessa.'

'I suppose you could say I know Jason Bourne better than most agents.'

Lerner sat back. 'Surely, Ms. Moore, you don't think you've learned all there is to know about your craft.'

'I don't. No.'

'Then I have full confidence that we'll get along, that eventually you'll be as loyal to me as you were to Martin Lindros.'

'Why are you talking as if Lindros is dead?'

Lerner ignored her. 'For the moment, I have to respond to the unfolding situation. As AIC, the fiasco with Cevik was your responsibility. Therefore, I have no recourse but to ask for your resignation.'

Soraya's heart leapt up into her throat. 'Resignation?' she barely got out.

Lerner, gimlet-eyed, said, 'A resignation will look better on your records. Even you should be able to understand that.'

Soraya jumped up. He'd played her cruelly and beauti-fully, which infuriated her all the more. She hated this man and she wanted him to know it. Otherwise nothing would be left of her self-esteem. 'Who the hell are you to come in here and throw your weight around?'

'That's it, we're done here, Ms. Moore. Clear out your things. You're fired.'

EIGHT

The narrow path, treacherous with ice, down which Alem led him went on so long that Bourne felt it would never end. All at once, however, it did, winding inward from the dizzying face of the mountain to emerge into an alpine meadow many times the size of the one onto which the two Chinooks had been brought down. Much of this one was clear of snow.

The village was little more than a grouping of ramshackle structures, none of them very large. A gridwork of streets appeared to be made of tramped-down manure. A flock of brown goats lifted their triangular heads as the two approached but, apparently recognizing Alem, shortly returned to munching clumps of brittle brown grasses. Farther away, horses whinnied, shaking their heads as the men's scents reached them.

'Your father is where?' Bourne said.

'In the bar, as usual.' Alem looked up at him. 'But I won't take you to him. You must go alone. You can't let him know that I said anything to you about his scavenging.'

Bourne nodded. 'I promised you, Alem.'

'Or even that you met me.'

'How will I recognize him?'

'By his leg – his left leg is thin, and you can see it's shorter than his right. His name is Zaim.'

Bourne was about to turn away when Alem pressed Lindros's ring into his hand.

'You found this, Alem—'

'It belongs to your friend,' the boy said. 'If I return it to you maybe he won't be dead.'

It was time to eat. Again. No matter how else you resisted, Oscar Lindros had told his son, you could not refuse to eat. You needed to keep up your strength. Your captors could starve you, of course, but only if they wanted to kill you, which quite clearly Dujja didn't. They could drug your food, of course, and after the torture proved fruitless Martin Lindros's captors had done just that. To no avail. Ditto for sensory deprivation. His mind was vaulted up; his father had seen to that. Sodium Pentothal, for instance, had made him babble like a baby, but about nothing useful. Everything they wanted to know was inside the vault, unavailable to them.

They were on a timetable, so now they more or less left him alone. They did feed him regularly, though sometimes his jailers spat in his food. One of them would not clean him up when he soiled himself. When the stink became unbearable, they pulled out a hose. The resulting blast of ice-cold water lifted him off his feet, slammed him against the rock wall. There he would lie for hours, blood and water mingling in pink rivulets, while he reeled trout out of the peaceful lake, one by one.

But that was weeks ago – at least he thought so. He was better now. They'd even had a doctor look at him, stitch up the worst of the cuts, bandage him, feed him antibiotics for the fever that had raged through him.

Now he could let go of the lake for longer and longer periods of time. He could take in his surroundings, understand that he was in a cave. Judging by the chill, the howling of the wind that swirled in the cave mouth, he was high up, presumably still somewhere on Ras Dejen. He did not see Fadi, but from time to time he saw Fadi's chief lieutenant, the man called Abbud ibn Aziz. This man had been his chief interrogator after Fadi had failed to break him in the first few days of his incarceration.

For Lindros, Abbud ibn Aziz was a familiar type. He was essentially feral – that is to say, he was a stranger to civilization. He always would be. His comfort came from the trackless desert, where he had been born and raised. This much Lindros surmised from the form of Arabic he spoke – Abbud ibn Aziz was a Bedouin. His understanding of right and wrong was perfectly black-and-white, carved in stone. In this sense, he was exactly like Oscar Lindros.

Abbud ibn Aziz seemed to enjoy talking with Lindros. Perhaps he relished the prisoner's helplessness. Perhaps he felt that if they talked long enough Lindros would come to see him as a friend – that the Stockholm syndrome would set in, making Lindros identify with his captor. Perhaps he was simply being the Good Cop, because it was he who always toweled Lindros off after the hose attacks, it was he who changed Lindros's clothes when Lindros was too weak or out of it to do it himself.

Lindros was not a person to be affected by the temptation to reach out from his isolation, to become friends. Lindros had never made friends easily; he found that it was far easier to be a loner. In fact, his father had encouraged it. Being a loner was an asset if you aspired to be a spy, Oscar had said. This tendency had also been noted in Lindros's personnel file when he'd gone through the grueling monthlong vetting process thought up by the sadistic CI psych wonks just before his acceptance into the agency.

By now he knew very well what Abbud ibn Aziz wanted from him. It had come as something of a mystery to him that the terrorist sought information on a mission CI had mounted years ago against Hamid ibn Ashef. What did Hamid ibn Ashef have to do with Abbud ibn Aziz?

They had wanted more from him, of course. Much more. And despite Abbud ibn Aziz's apparent single-mindedness,

Lindros had noted with interest that the interrogation about the CI mission against Hamid ibn Ashef occurred only when Abbud was alone with him.

From this, he had deduced that this particular line of questioning was a private agenda that had nothing at all to do with Dujja's reason for kidnapping him.

'How are you feeling today?'

Abbud ibn Aziz stood in front of him. He had brought two identical plates of food. He put one in Lindros's hands. When it came to food, Lindros knew his way around the Quran. All food fell into one of two categories: *haram* or *halal*, forbidden or allowed. All the food here was, of course, strictly *halal*.

'No coffee today, I'm afraid,' Abbud said. 'But the dates and buttermilk curds are fine.'

The dates were a bit on the dry side, and the curds had a strange taste. These things were small but, in Lindros's world, significant. The dates were drying up, the curds turning, and the coffee was gone. No more supplies were being delivered. Why?

They both ate with their right hands, their teeth bared as they bit into the dark flesh of the dates. Lindros's mind was racing.

'How is the weather?' he asked at length.

'Cold, and the constant wind makes it colder still.' Abbud shivered. 'Another front is coming in.'

Lindros knew that he was used to hundred-plus-degree temperatures, sand in his food, the molten-white glare of the sun, the blessed cool relief of a star-strewn night. This endless deep freeze was intolerable, to say nothing of the altitude. His bones and his lungs must be protesting like old men on a forced march. Lindros watched as he switched his Ruger semiautomatic in the crook of his left arm.

'Being here must be painful for you.' Lindros's question was not mere banter.

Abbud's shrug ended as another shiver.

'It's more than the desert you miss.' Lindros put his plate aside. Taking an almost constant beating day after day did terrible things to the appetite. 'It's the world of your fathers that you miss, isn't it?'

'Western civilization is an abomination,' Abbud said. 'Its influence on our society is like an infectious disease that needs to be wiped out.'

'You're afraid of Western civilization, because you don't understand it.'

Abbud spat out a date pit, white as a baby's bottom. 'I would say the same of you Americans.'

Lindros nodded. 'You wouldn't be wrong. But where does that leave us?'

'At each other's throats.'

Bourne surveyed the interior of the bar. It was much like the outside: the walls bare stone and wood, mortared together by wattle. The floor was hard-pressed dung. It smelled of fermentation, of both the alcoholic and human variety. A dung fire roared in the stone hearth, adding heat and a particular odor. There were a handful of Amhara inside, all in varying degrees of drunkenness. Otherwise Bourne's appearance in the doorway would have kicked up more of a stir. As it was, it caused barely a ripple.

He tromped up to the bar, trailing snow. He ordered a beer, which, promisingly, came in a bottle. While he drank the thin, oddly brackish brew, he took the measure of the place. In truth, there wasn't much to see: just a rectangular room with a scattering of rude tables and backless chairs more like stools. Nevertheless, he marked them all in his memory, making of the area a sort of map in his head, should danger raise its head or he need a quick escape. Not long after that, he spied the man with the maimed leg. Zaim was sitting by himself in a corner, a bottle of rotgut in one hand and a

133

filthy glass in the other. He was beetle-browed, with the burned, crusty skin of the mountain native. He looked at Bourne vaguely as the other approached his table.

Bourne hooked a boot around one of the stool legs, pulled it out, sat down across from Alem's father.

'Get away from me, you fucking tourist,' Zaim muttered.

'I'm no tourist,' Bourne responded in the same dialect.

Alem's father opened his eyes wide, turned his head, spat on the floor. 'Still, you must want something. No one dares summit Ras Dejen in winter.'

Bourne took a long swig of his beer. 'You're right, of course.' Noticing that Zaim's bottle was nearly empty, he said, 'What are you drinking?'

'Dust,' Alem's father replied. 'That's all there is to drink up here. Dust and ash.'

Bourne went and got him another bottle, set it down on the table. As he was about to fill the glass, Zaim stayed his hand.

'There won't be time,' he muttered under his breath. 'Not when you have brought your enemy with you.'

'I didn't know I had an enemy.' There was no point in telling this man the truth.

'You came from the Site of Death, did you not?' Zaim stared hard at Bourne with watery eyes. 'You climbed into the metal carcasses of the warbirds, you sifted through the bones of the warriors berthed inside. Don't bother to deny it. Anyone who does gathers enemies the same way a rotting corpse gathers flies.' He flicked his free hand. His heavily callused palms and fingers were tattooed with dirt so ingrained, it could never be washed away. 'I can smell it on you.'

'This enemy,' Bourne said, 'is at the moment unknown to me.'

Zaim grinned, showing many dark gaps between what

teeth were left in his mouth. His breath was as rank as the grave. 'Then I have become valuable to you. More valuable, surely, than a bottle of liquor.'

'My enemies were in hiding, watching the Site of Death?'

'How much is it worth to you,' Zaim said, 'to be shown the face of your enemy?'

Bourne slid money across the table.

Zaim took it with a practiced swipe of his clawlike hand. 'Your enemy keeps watch on the Site, day and night. It's like a spiderweb, you see? He wants to see what insects it attracts.'

'What's it to him?'

Zaim shrugged. 'Very little.'

'So there's someone else.'

Zaim leaned closer. 'We are pawns, you see. We are born pawns. What else are we good for? How else are we to scratch out a living?' He shrugged again. 'Even so, one can keep the evil times at bay only so long. Sooner or later, grief comes in whatever guise will be most painful.'

Bourne thought of Zaim's son, buried alive in the landslide. But he could say nothing; he'd promised Alem.

'I'm looking for a friend of mine,' he said softly. 'He was carried onto Ras Dejen by the first warbird. His body is not at the Site of Death. Therefore, I believe he's alive. What do you know of this?'

'I? I know nothing. Except for snatches overheard here and there.' Zaim scratched at his beard with gnarly black nails. 'But there is perhaps someone who could help.'

'Will you bring me to him?'

Zaim smiled. 'That is entirely up to you.'

Bourne pushed another wad of money across the stained table. Zaim took it, grunted, folded it away.

'On the other hand,' he said, 'we can do nothing while your enemy watches.' He pursed his lips reflectively. 'The eye

135

of your enemy sits spread-legged over your left shoulder – a foot soldier, we would say, no one higher up.'

'Now you're involved,' Bourne said, nodding to where the other had put the money.

Alem's father shrugged. 'I am unconcerned. I know this man; I know his people. Nothing evil will come of me talking to you, believe me.'

'I want him off my back,' Bourne said. 'I want the eye to sleep.'

'Of course you do.' Zaim rubbed his chin. 'Anything can be arranged, even such a difficult wish.'

Bourne slid over more money, and Zaim nodded, apparently satisfied, at least for the moment. He reminded Bourne of a Vegas slot machine: He wasn't going to stop taking money from Bourne until Bourne walked away.

'Wait exactly three minutes – no more, no less – then follow me out the front door.' Zaim stood. 'Walk a hundred paces down the main street, then turn left into an alley, then take the first right. Of course, I cannot risk being seen to help you in this. In any event, I trust you'll know what to do. Afterward you'll walk away without retracing your steps. I'll find you.'

'There's a message for you,' Peter Marks said when Soraya returned to Typhon to clean out her desk.

'You take it, Pete,' she said dully. 'I've been bounced out of here.'

'What the hell—?'

'The acting director has spoken.'

'He's gonna kill everything that Lindros wanted Typhon to be.'

'That seems to be the idea.'

As she was about to turn away, he took hold of her arm, swung her back. He was a young man, stocky, with deep-set

136

eyes, hair the color of corn, a faint dry Nebraska twang. 'Soraya, I just want to say for me – well, for all of us, really – no one blames you for what happened to Tim. Shit happens. In this business it's, unfortunately, all really bad.'

Soraya took a breath, let it out slowly. 'Thanks, Pete. I appreciate that.'

'I figured you'd been beating yourself up for letting Bourne run roughshod all over you and Tim.'

She was silent for a moment, unsure what she was feeling. 'It wasn't Bourne,' she said at last, 'and it wasn't me. It just happened, Pete. That's all.'

'Sure, okay. I only meant that, you know, Bourne is another outsider forced on us by the Old Man. Like that sonovabitch Lerner. If you ask me, the Old Man's losing his grip.'

'Not my worry anymore,' Soraya said, beginning to move toward her office.

'But this message—'

'Come on, Pete. Handle it yourself.'

'But it's marked urgent.' He held it out. 'It's from Kim Lovett.'

After Zaim left, Bourne went into the WC, which stank like the inside of a zoo. Using the Thuraya phone, he checked in with Davis.

'I have new intel that the site is being watched,' he said. 'So keep a sharp lookout.'

'You, too,' Davis said. 'There's a weather front moving in.'

'I know. Is our exit strategy going to be compromised?'

'Don't worry,' Davis assured him. 'I'll take care of things on this end.'

Exiting the filthy pit, Bourne paid his bill at the bar. Under cover of the transaction, he caught a glimpse of the 'eye of his enemy,' as Zaim called him, and knew at once that he was

Amhara. The man didn't bother lowering his gaze, instead glowered at Bourne with undisguised enmity. This was his territory, after all. He was confident on his home ground and, under normal circumstances, would have every right to be.

Bourne, who'd started the three-minute clock running in his head the moment Zaim had walked out the door, realized it was time to go. He chose a path that took him directly past the Eye. He was gratified to see the man's muscles bunch up in tension as he neared. His left hand went to his right hip, to whatever weapon he had there out of Bourne's sight. Bourne knew then what was required of him.

He went out of the bar. As he silently measured off the hundred paces, he became aware that the Eye had followed him out onto the street. Quickening the pace so that his tail would have to hurry to catch up, he reached the corner Zaim had described to him and turned left without warning into a narrow alley clogged with snow. Almost immediately he saw the next right, and rounded it at a brisk clip.

He'd only taken two steps when he turned around, flattened himself against the icy wall, and waited until the Eye came into view. Bourne grabbed him, slammed him against the corner of the building so that his teeth clacked together sharply. A blow to the side of the head rendered him unconscious.

A moment later Zaim darted lopsidedly into the alley. 'Quickly now!' he said breathlessly. 'There are two others I hadn't counted on.'

He led Bourne to the nearest intersection of alleys, turned left. At once they found themselves on the outskirts of the village. The snow lay thickly, its crust brittle. Zaim was having difficulty negotiating the terrain, especially at the pace he had set. But quite soon they came to a ramshackle outbuilding behind which three horses stood grazing.

'How are you at bareback riding?' he said.

'I'll manage.'

Bourne put his hand on the muzzle of a gray horse, looked him in the eye, then vaulted up. Leaning over, he grabbed Zaim above the elbow, assisted him onto a brown horse. Together they turned their steeds into the wind and took off at a canter.

The wind was rising. Bourne did not need to be a native to know that a storm was coming in from the northwest, laden with the bitter taste of serious snow. Davis was going to have a hell of a time digging the copter out. He'd have to, though; there was no other way to get off the mountain quickly.

Zaim was making directly for the tree line but, glancing behind him, Bourne saw that it was already too late. The riders – no doubt the two Amhara whom Zaim was worried about – were pounding along behind them, closing the gap.

Bourne, making a quick calculation, discovered that the Amhara would overtake them several hundred meters before they'd have a chance to lose themselves in the forest. Putting his head against the horse's mane, he kicked it hard in the sides. The gray horse leapt forward, racing toward the trees. Startled for an instant, Zaim kneed his mount, taking off after Bourne.

Halfway there, Bourne realized they weren't going to make it. Without another thought, he squeezed his knees against the horse's flanks and jerked its mane to the right. Without breaking stride, the gray wheeled around, and before their pursuers had time to react Bourne was galloping full-out directly at them.

They split apart, as he had foreseen. Leaning to his right, he drew his left leg back and kicked out from the hip. His thick-soled boot slammed into the chest of one of the Amhara, knocking him off his horse. By this time, the other Amhara had had time to wheel around. He'd drawn a handgun – an old but deadly 9mm PM Makarov – and was aiming it at Bourne.

A shot rang out, lifting the Amhara from his blanket saddle. Bourne turned to see Zaim rising up, a gun in his hand. He waved his free hand, and they headed as fast as they could for the outlying stand of firs.

Another shot snipped off branches above their heads as they galloped into the forest. The Amharan whom Bourne had kicked off his horse had remounted and was coming after them.

Zaim threaded them through the fir trees. It had turned markedly colder and wetter. Even here, in the shelter of the forest, the icy wind cut through them, shaking periodic snowfalls from the upper branches. Bourne, thinking of their pursuer, could not rid himself of the itching along his spine, but he kept going in the brown horse's wake.

The ground began to fall away, at first gradually, then more steeply. The horses put their heads down, snorting, as if to more carefully feel the buried stones, their curved surfaces slick with ice, which made the footing alarmingly treacherous.

Bourne heard a cracking behind them, and he urged the gray on. He wanted to ask Zaim where they were headed and how close they were to it, but raising his voice would only serve to reveal their location in the maze of the forest. Just as he was thinking this, he glimpsed a clearing through the trees, then the heavy glitter of a sheet of ice. They were coming to a river that wound steeply from the edge of one alpine meadow to a lower one.

At that moment he heard a shot; an instant later Zaim's horse collapsed from under him. Zaim went tumbling. Urging the gray on, Bourne reached down, dragging Zaim up behind him.

They were almost at the bank of the frozen river. Another shot, snapping nearby branches.

'Your gun!' Bourne said.

'I lost it when my horse was shot,' Zaim replied unhappily.

'We'll be picked off like wooden ducks.'

Bourne handed Zaim down to the snowpack, then slid off the gray. A smart slap to its rump sent it crashing through the forest on a more or less parallel course to the river.

'Now what?' Zaim slapped his bum leg. 'With this, we'll be helpless out here.'

'Let's go.' Grabbing him by his thick wool jacket, Bourne began to run down the bank to the river.

'What are you doing?' Zaim's eyes were wide with fear.

Bourne half lifted him off his feet an instant before they hit the ice on the run. Compensating for the other man's weight, Bourne began the long back-and-forth strides of an ice skater. Using the blades embedded in his boot soles as skates, he built up speed with the natural downward slope of the river.

He took the snaking turns expertly, but he had almost no control over his speed, and he was racing along faster and faster as the rivercourse steepened.

They flashed around another bend and Zaim uttered an inarticulate cry. A moment later Bourne saw why. Not a thousand meters away the river broke sharply downward into a waterfall, now frozen in place like a stop-motion photo.

'How high,' Bourne called over the howling of the wind in his face.

'Too high,' Zaim moaned in terror. 'Oh, too, too high!'

NINE

Bourne tried to veer to the left or right, but he couldn't. He was flying along a fold in the ice that would not allow him to change direction. At any rate, it was too late now. The ruffled top of the waterfall was upon them, so he did the only thing he could think of: He steered for the exact center, where the water was deepest and the ice thinnest.

They hit it at speed, which combined with their weight to shatter the thin crust of ice that had formed over the streaming water. Into the waterfall they plunged, tumbling down and down, the icy water taking their breath away, freezing them from their limbs inward.

As he fell from the heights, Bourne struggled against becoming disoriented, which was his primary concern. If he lost his sense of direction, he'd either freeze to death or drown before he could break through the ice at the base of the waterfall. There was another concern: If he allowed himself to get too far from the base area, the ice would quickly thicken into a layer he'd likely find unbreakable.

Light and shadow, blue-black, gray-opal spun across his vision as he was tossed and tumbled through the churning water. Once, his shoulder smashed into a rock outcropping. Pain leapt through him like a surge of electricity, and as his downward momentum abruptly ceased, he searched for the light in the jumble of darkness. There was none! His head was spinning, his hands almost completely numb. His heart was laboring from both the physical pounding and the lack of oxygen.

He struck out with his arms. At once he realized that Zaim's body was almost against him; as he drew it to one side, he saw pearlescent light shining behind it and knew which way was up. Zaim seemed to be unconscious. Blood plumed from the side of his head, and Bourne guessed that he, too, had struck a rock.

With one arm around the limp form, Bourne kicked out hard for the surface, banging the top of his head sooner than he had anticipated against the ice sheet. It didn't give.

His head was pounding, and the ribbons of blood leaking from Zaim's wound were obscuring his vision. He clawed against the ice, but could find no purchase. He slid along the underside, searching for a crack, a flaw he could exploit. But the ice was thicker than he'd imagined, even here at the waterfall's base. His lungs were burning and the headache caused by the lack of oxygen was fast becoming intolerable. Perhaps Zaim was already dead. Surely he himself would be if he couldn't break through to the surface.

A strong eddy caught him, threatening to send them swirling out to certain death in the darkness where the ice sheet was thickest. As he struggled against it, his nails bit into something – not a crack precisely, but a stress flaw in the sheet. He could see that one side was allowing more light in, and there he concentrated his efforts. But his fists, numbed into clumsy weights, were of no use.

Only one chance now. He let go of Zaim and dove down into the darkness until he felt the river bottom. Reversing himself, he coiled his legs, launching himself upward in a straight line. The top of his head struck the stress flaw and he heard it crack, then splinter apart as his shoulders followed his head into the blessed air. Bourne drew air into his lungs once, twice, three times. Then he dove back down. Zaim wasn't where he had left him. He had been caught in the powerful eddy and was now being launched into the darkness.

Bourne kicked, fighting the current, stretching out full-length to grab Zaim by the ankle. Slowly, surely he drew him back to the light, bringing him up through the ragged hole in the ice, laying him out on the frozen riverbed before he levered himself out of the water.

They had come through just to the east of the falls, at the edge of a thick slice of the fir forest that continued unabated to the north and east.

He spent a moment hunkered down in their shadows of the trees, catching his breath. But that was all the time he could spare. He checked Zaim's vital signs – his pulse, his breathing, his pupils. The man was alive. An examination of the wound showed it to be superficial. Zaim's hard skull had done its job, protecting him from serious injury.

Bourne's problem now, apart from stanching the flow of blood from Zaim's wound, was drying him off so he wouldn't freeze to death. Bourne himself had been partially protected by his extreme-weather jumpsuit, though he saw now that it had been abraded badly in several places during his violent tumble down the falls. Water was already freezing against his skin. Unzipping the suit for a moment, he stripped off a sleeve of his shirt, packed it with snow, and wrapped it around Zaim's wound. Then he hoisted the still-unconscious man over his unbruised shoulder, stumbling up the treacherous bank into the forest. He could feel the cold slowly seeping in at his elbows and shoulder, where the outer layer of his jump-suit had been shredded.

Zaim was becoming heavier and heavier, but Bourne pushed on, angling north and east away from the river. A vague memory surfaced – a flash akin to the one he'd had when he'd first alit on Ras Dejen, but more detailed. If he was right, there was another village – larger than the one where he'd found Zaim – several kilometers ahead.

All at once he was brought up short by a familiar sound: the snorting of a horse. Carefully putting Zaim down against the bole of a tree, he moved cautiously toward the sound. Perhaps five hundred meters ahead, he came upon a small clearing. In it, he saw the gray, its muzzle picking through the snowpack for something to eat. Apparently the animal had followed the course of the river down to this patch of open space. It was just what Bourne needed to carry him and Zaim to safety.

Bourne was about to move into the glade when the gray's head came up and its nostrils dilated. What had it smelled? The wind was swirling, bringing with it the scent of danger.

Bourne thought he understood, and he silently thanked the gray. Moving back into the firs, he began to circle to his left, keeping the clearing in sight as he went, keeping the wind in his face. Perhaps a quarter of the way around, he saw a spot of color, then a slight movement. Heading obliquely toward it, he saw that it was the Amhara whom he had kicked off his horse. This man must have brought the gray down here as bait, to lure them if one or both had survived the waterfall.

Keeping low, Bourne came at him fast, blindsiding him. He went down with a grunt, got his left hand free as Bourne pummeled him, drew out a curving knife. It slashed down, heading straight for Bourne's exposed side just above his kidney. Bourne rolled, his torso flicking out of range. At the same time, he locked his ankles around the tribesman's neck, back and front. With a swift, violent twist Bourne snapped the Amhara's neck.

He rose, took from the corpse the knife, sheath, and 9mm Makarov. Then he loped into the clearing, bringing the gray back to where Zaim lay. Slinging the other over the horse's sturdy back, Bourne swung up and set off through the firs, down the mountainside, heading by memory for the village.

When Soraya Moore strode into the FIU lab, Kim Lovett was still kicking around forensic evidence with Detective Overton.

Kim, having taken care of the introductions, got right down to business by bringing Soraya up to date on their case. Then she handed her the set of two porcelain teeth.

'I found these in the suite's bathtub drain,' she said. 'At first glance, it could easily be mistaken for a dental bridge, but I don't think it is.'

Soraya, looking at the interior hollows, knew that she had seen something very similar in Deron's lab. Examining it more closely, she recognized the high quality of the workmanship. No doubt this was part of a world-class chameleon's arsenal. She had no doubt what she was holding, and to whom it belonged. She'd thought she was through with all this when Lerner kicked her butt out of Typhon, but now she knew the truth. Maybe she'd known it all along. She wasn't through with Fadi, not by a long shot.

'You're right, Kim,' she said. 'It's a prosthetic.'

'Prosthetic?' Overton echoed. 'I'm not following.'

'This is a shell,' Soraya told him, 'used to slip over perfectly good teeth, not as a substitute for nonviable ones, but to alter the shape of the mouth and cheek line.' She slipped the prosthetic on. Though it was too big for her, both Kim and Overton were astonished to see how much it changed the shape of her mouth and lips. 'Which means your Jakob Silver and his brother were using aliases,' she said as she spat out the teeth. To Kim, she said, 'Do you mind if I borrow this?'

'Go on,' Kim said. 'But I'll have to log it out.'

Overton shook his head. 'None of this makes sense.'

'It makes perfect sense if you know all the facts.' Soraya shared with them the incident outside CI headquarters. 'This man who passed as a Cape Town entrepreneur named Hiram Cevik is, in actuality, a Saudi who calls himself Fadi, a terrorist leader with high-level connections to what seems to be an enormous amount of money. What his real name might be we have no idea. He disappeared within blocks of where the

146

Hummer picked him up.' She held up the prosthetic. 'Now we know where he went.'

Kim considered everything Soraya had told them. 'Then the remains we found aren't either brother.'

'I very much doubt it. The fire seems like a diversion for him slipping out of D.C. Out of the country, for that matter.' Soraya went over to the shallow metal pan in which Kim had placed the bones found in the bathtub. 'I do believe we're looking at all that's left of Omar, the Pakistani waiter.'

'Jesus Christ!' *At last we're getting somewhere*, Overton thought. 'Then which brother was Fadi?'

Soraya turned to him. 'Jakob, undoubtedly. It was Lev who checked into the suite. Fadi was in Cape Town, and then in our custody.'

Overton was elated. At last his luck was changing. He'd hit the mother lode with these two. Very soon now, he'd have enough intel to bring to Homeland Security. He'd become their newest recruit and their newest hero in one fell swoop.

Soraya turned back to Kim. 'What else did you find?'

'Very little. Except the accelerant.' Kim picked up a sheaf of computer readouts. 'It was carbon disulfide. I can't remember the last time I encountered it. Arsonists typically use acetone, kerosene, something easily attainable like that.' She shrugged. 'On the other hand, in this case carbon disulfide makes a certain kind of sense. It's more dangerous than the others because of its low flashpoint and the probability of an explosion once it's ignited. Fadi wanted the windows blown out so that the flames could feed on the added oxygen. But you'd have to be a real professional to use it without blowing yourself up.'

Soraya took a look at the printout Kim handed her. 'That's Fadi all over. Where would you get it?'

'You'd have to have access to a manufacturing plant or one of their sources,' Kim said. 'It's used in the manufacture of cellulose, carbon tetrachloride, and other organic sulfur compounds.'

'Can I borrow your computer?'

'Help yourself,' Kim said.

Soraya sat down at Kim's workstation and brought up the Internet browser. Navigating to the Google Web site, she typed in 'carbon disulfide.'

'Cellulose is used in the manufacture of rayon and cellophane,' she called out to them as she read the text on the screen. 'Carbon tet used to be a key ingredient in fire extinguishers and refrigeration, though it's been abandoned because of its toxicity. Dithiocarbamates, dmit, xanthate are flotation agents in mineral processing. It's also used to make metham sodium, a soil fumigant.'

'One thing's for sure,' Kim said. 'You won't find it in your neighborhood hardware store. You've got to go searching for it.'

Soraya nodded. 'And it presupposes prior knowledge of the compound and its specific charactistics.' She made a few quick notes in her PDA, then got up. 'Okay, I'm out of here.'

'Mind if I tag along?' Overton said. 'Until you showed up, this case was a brick wall in my face.'

'I don't think so.' Soraya's glance slid over to Kim. 'I was going to tell you when I came in. I've been fired.'

'What?' Kim was aghast. 'Why?'

'The new acting director doesn't appreciate my streak of rebelliousness. I think he's out to establish his authority. Today I'm the one he decided to piss on.'

Kim came over and hugged her in sympathy. 'If there's anything I can do.'

Soraya smiled. 'I know who to call. Thanks.'

She was too preoccupied to notice the scowl of displeasure that had darkened Detective Overton's face. He wasn't going to be thwarted, not when he was so close to his goal.

*

Snow had begun to fall by the time Bourne and Zaim reached the village. It was there, nestled in a narrow valley like a ball in a cupped palm, just as Bourne remembered it. The clouds, low and heavy, made the mountains seem small and insignificant, as if they were about to be crushed in a clash of titans. The steeple of the church was the most prominent structure, and Bourne made for it.

Zaim stirred and groaned. Some time ago, he had awakened, and Bourne had gotten him off the horse just in time for him to vomit copiously among the whistling firs. Bourne made the Amhara eat some snow in order to hydrate him. He was dizzy and weak, but he understood completely when Bourne filled him in on what had happened. Their destination, he had informed Bourne, was a camp just outside the village in Bourne's memory.

Now they had arrived at the village. Though Bourne was eager to link up with the person Zaim claimed could take him to Lindros, Zaim's clothes had already frozen; unless he could be warmed up reasonably quickly, the cloth would take his skin with it when it was removed.

The gray, which Bourne had urged on at full gallop through knee-high snowbanks, was just about done in by the time they reached the outskirts of the camp. Three Amhara appeared as if out of nowhere, brandishing curved knives similar to the one Bourne had taken off the man whose neck he'd broken.

Bourne had been expecting them. No campsite would be left unguarded. He sat very still atop the panting, snorting gray while the Amhara drew Zaim down. When they saw who it was, one of them ran into a tent at the center of the campsite. He returned within minutes with an Amhara who was quite obviously the tribal chieftain, the *nagus*.

'Zaim,' he said, 'what happened to you?'

'He saved my life,' Zaim muttered.

'And he, mine.' Bourne slid off the horse. 'We were attacked on our way here.'

If the *nagus* was surprised that Bourne spoke Amharic, he gave no outward sign of it. 'Like all Westerners, you brought your enemies with you.'

Bourne shivered. 'You're only half right. We were attacked by three Amhara soldiers.'

'You know who is paying them,' Zaim said weakly.

The *nagus* nodded. 'Take them both inside to my hut, where it is warm. We will build up the fire slowly.'

Abbud ibn Aziz stood squinting up at the noxious sky that swirled around Ras Dejen's north face, listening for the sound of rotors slicing the thin air.

Where was Fadi? His helicopter was late. Abbud ibn Aziz had been monitoring the weather all morning. With the front moving in, he knew the pilot had an extremely narrow window in which to make his landing.

In truth, though, he knew it wasn't the cold or the thin air he silently railed against. It was the fact that he and Fadi were here in the first place. The plan. He knew who was behind it. Only one man could have dreamed up such a high-risk, volatile scheme: Fadi's brother, Karim al-Jamil. Fadi might be the firebrand face of Dujja, but Abbud ibn Aziz, alone of all of Fadi's many followers, knew that Karim al-Jamil was the heart of the cadre. He was the chess master, the patient spider spinning multiple webs into the future. Even thinking about what Karim al-Jamil might be planning sent Abbud ibn Aziz's head spinning. Like Fadi and Karim al-Jamil, he had been educated in the West. He knew the history, politics, and economics of the non-Arab world – a prerequisite, so far as Fadi and Karim al-Jamil were concerned, in stepping up the ladder of command.

The problem for Abbud ibn Aziz was that he didn't altogether trust Karim al-Jamil. For one thing, he was reclusive. For another, so far as he knew Karim al-Jamil spoke only to

Fadi. That this might not be the case at all – that he knew less than he suspected about Karim al-Jamil – made him all the more uneasy.

This was his bias against Karim al-Jamil: that he, Fadi's second in command, his most intimate comrade, was shut out from the inner workings of Dujja. This seemed to him eminently unjust, and though he was utterly loyal to Fadi, still he chafed to be kept on the outside. Of course, he understood that blood was thicker than water – who among the desert tribesmen wouldn't? But Fadi and Karim al-Jamil were only half Arab. Their mother was English. Both had been born in London after their father had moved his company base there from Saudi Arabia.

Abbud ibn Aziz was haunted by several questions that part of him did not want answered. Why had Abu Sarif Hamid ibn Ashef al-Wahhib left Saudi Arabia? Why had he taken up with an infidel? Why had he compounded his error by marrying her? Abbud ibn Aziz could find no earthly reason why a Saudi would do such a thing. In truth, neither Fadi nor Karim al-Jamil was of the desert, as he was. They had grown up in the West, been schooled in the ceaselessly throbbing metropolis of London. What did they know of the profound silence, the severe beauty, the clean scents of the desert? The desert, where the grace and wisdom of Allah could be seen in all things.

Fadi, as befit an older brother, was protective of Karim al-Jamil. This, at least, was something Abbud ibn Aziz could understand. He himself felt the same way about his younger brothers. But in the case of Karim al-Jamil, he had been asking himself for some time into what dark waters he was leading Dujja. Was it a place that Abbud ibn Aziz wanted to go? He had come this far without raising his voice because he was loyal to Fadi. It was Fadi who had indoctrinated him into the terror war they had been forced into by the West's incursions into their lands. It was Fadi who had sent him to Europe to be schooled, a time in his life he had despised but had nevertheless proved of benefit. To know the enemy, Fadi had told him many times, is to defeat him.

He owed Fadi everything; where Fadi led, he would follow. On the other hand, he wasn't deaf, dumb, and blind. If at some future date when he had more information, he felt that Karim al-Jamil was leading Dujja – and, therefore, Fadi – into ruin, he would speak up, no matter the consequences.

A harsh, dry wind broke against his cheek. The whirring of the helicopter's rotors came to him as if from a dream. But it was his own reverie from which he needed to free himself. He looked up, feeling the first snowflakes on his cheeks and lashes.

He picked out the black dot against the roiled grays of the sky. It bloomed quickly. Swinging his arms back and forth over his head, he stepped back from the landing site. Three minutes later, the helicopter had landed. The door swung open, and Muta ibn Aziz jumped out into the snow and ice.

Abbud ibn Aziz waited for Fadi to appear, but only his brother came to where he stood, outside the slowing swing of the rotor blades.

'All went well.' His embrace of his brother was stiff, formal. 'Fadi has contacted me.'

Muta stood silent in the harsh wind.

For some time, a dispute had carved itself into the frontier of their lives. Like the rift created by an earthquake, the issue had separated them more than either of them would admit. Like an earthquake it had spit up, festering sores that now, years later, had turned to scoria – hard, dry, twisted as scar tissue.

Muta squinted. 'Brother, where did Fadi go after he and I parted?'

Abbud could not keep the superior edge out of his voice.

'His business lies elsewhere.'

Muta grunted. A bitter taste, all too familiar, had flooded his mouth. *It is as it has always been. Abbud uses his power to keep me away from Fadi and Karim al-Jamil, the centers of our universe. Thus does he lord it over me. Thus has he sworn me to keep our secret. He is my elder brother. How can I fight him?* His teeth ground together. *As always, I must obey him all things.*

Muta shivered mightily, moved out of the wind, into the lee of a rock formation. 'Tell me, brother, what has been happening here?'

'Bourne arrived on Ras Dejen this morning. He's making progress.'

Muta ibn Aziz nodded. 'Then we must move Lindros to a safe location.'

'It is about to be done,' Abbud said with an icy edge to his voice.

Muta, his heart full of bile, nodded. 'It's almost over now. Within the next few days, Jason Bourne's use to us will be at an end.' He smiled deeply, but it was completely self-contained. 'As Fadi has said, revenge is sweet. How pleasurable it will be for him to see Jason Bourne dead!'

The *nagus*'s hut was surprisingly spacious and comfortable, especially for a structure that was more or less portable. The floor consisted of overlapping rugs. Skins hung on the walls, helping keep in the warmth provided by a fire fueled with dried bricks of dung.

Bourne, wrapped in a rough wool blanket, sat cross-legged by the fire while the *nagus*'s men slowly and gingerly undressed Zaim. When that was done, they wrapped him as well, made him sit beside Bourne. Then they served both men steaming cups of hot, strong tea.

Other men tended to Zaim's wound, cleaning it, packing it with an herbal poultice, rebandaging it. As this was happening, the *nagus* sat down next to Bourne. He was a small man, unprepossessing save for the black eyes that burned like twin lamps in his burnished bronze skull. His body was thin and wiry, but Bourne was not fooled. This man would be skilled in the many ways, offensive and defensive, to keep himself and his men alive.

'My name is Kabur,' the *nagus* said. 'Zaim tells me your name is Bourne.' He pronounced it in two syllables: *Boh-orn*.

Bourne nodded. 'I've come to Ras Dejen to find my friend, who was on one of the warbirds that were shot down nearly a week ago. You know of this?'

'I do,' Kabur said.

His hand moved to his chest, and he held out something silver for Bourne to see. It was the pilot's dog tags.

'He has no more need of them,' Kabur said simply.

Bourne's heart sank. 'He's dead?'

'As close as can be.'

'What about my friend?'

'They took him along with this man.' The *nagus* offered Bourne a wooden bowl of heavily spiced stew into which a rough semicircle of unleavened bread had been stuck. While Bourne ate, using the bread as a spoon, Kabur went on. 'Not by us, you understand. We are nothing in this, though, as you have already witnessed, some have taken money from them in return for service.' He shook his head. 'But it is evil, a form of enslavement for which some have paid the ultimate price.'

'They.' Bourne, having eaten his fill, put the bowl aside. 'Who, precisely, are they?'

Kabur tilted his head. 'I feel surprise. I would have expected you to know far more about them than I. They come to us from across the Gulf of Aden. From Yemen, I imagine. But they aren't Yemeni, no. God alone knows where they make their base. Some are Egyptian, others Saudi, still others Afghani.'

'And the leader?'

'Ah, Fadi. He is Saudi.' The *nagus's* fierce black eyes had gone opaque. 'We are, to a man, afraid of Fadi.'

'Why?'

'Why? Because he is powerful, because he is cruel beyond imagining. Because he carries death in the palm of his hand.'

Bourne thought of the uranium transshipments. 'You have seen evidence of the death he carries.'

The *nagus* nodded. 'With my own eyes. One of Zaim's sons—'

'The boy in the cave?'

Kabur swung toward Zaim, in whose eyes was a sea of pain. 'A wayward son who could not hold advice in his head. Now we cannot touch him, even to bury him.'

'I can do that,' Bourne said. Now he understood why Alem was hiding out in the Chinook closest to the cave: He wanted to be near his brother. 'I can bury him up there, near the summit.'

The *nagus* was silent. But Zaim's eyes had turned liquid as they reengaged Bourne's. 'That would be a true blessing – for him, for me, for my family.'

'It will be done, this I swear,' Bourne said. He turned back to Kabur. 'Will you will help me find my friend?'

The *nagus* hesitated a moment while he studied Zaim. At length, he sighed. 'Will finding your friend hurt Fadi?'

'Yes,' Bourne said. 'It will hurt him badly.'

'This is a very difficult journey you ask us to take with you. But because of my friend, because of his bond to you, because of your promise to him, I am honor-bound to grant your request.'

He raised his right hand and a man brought a device similar to a hookah. 'We will smoke together, to seal the bargain we have made.'

*

Soraya had every intention of going home, but somehow she found herself driving into the Northeast quadrant of D.C. It was only when she turned onto 7th Street that she knew why she had come here. Making one more turn, she arrived outside Deron's house.

For a moment, she sat, listening to the engine ticking. Five or six of the tough-looking crew infested the stoop of the house to the left but, though they observed her with gimlet eyes, they made no move to stop her as she got out of the car and went up the steps to Deron's front door.

She knocked on the front door several times. Waited, then knocked again. There was no answer. Hearing someone coming up the walk, she turned, expecting Deron. Instead she encountered a tall, lean young man, one of the crew.

'Yo, Miss Spook, name's Tyrone. What yo doin' here?'

'Do you know where Deron is?'

Tyrone kept a neutral expression. 'Yo could see me instead, Miss S.'

'I would, Tyrone,' she said carefully, 'if you could instruct me on the uses of carbon disulfide.'

'Huh, yo think I'm a useless nigga, doantcha?'

'To be honest, I don't know anything about you.'

Without a change in expression, he said, 'Walk wid me.'

Soraya nodded. Instinctively she knew that any hesitation on her part would reflect badly on her.

Together they went down the walk and turned right, past the stoop where members of the crew were perched like a murder of crows.

'Deron, he down wid his daddy. Won't be back for coupla days.'

'No lie?'

'True dat.' Tyrone pursed his lips. 'So. What yo want ta know 'bout me? Maybe my druggie mama? Is it my daddy you're interested in, rottin' away in prison? Or my younger sister nursin' a baby when she should be in high school? My older brother makin' shit-per-week working for the man as a motorman in the Metro? Shee-it, yo mustave heard all that sob stuff before, so yo doan need t'hear it again.'

'It's your life,' Soraya said. 'That makes it different from anything I've heard.'

Tyrone snorted, but by his look she knew he was pleased.

'Me, though I was trained for the street, I was born with an engineer's mind. What's that mean?' He shrugged and pointed into the distance. 'Down Florida, they puttin' up a shitload a high-rises. I go there every chance I get, see how it all goin' up, y'know?'

Soraya met his eyes for a moment. 'Will you think me a fool if I say there're ways for you to take advantage of your mind.'

'Fo yo maybe.' A slow smile spread across his face, an expression considerably older than his years. 'We walkin' in my prison, girl.'

Soraya considered answering that, but decided she'd pushed him far enough for the moment. 'I gotta go.'

Tyrone pursed his lips. 'Yo, just so you know, yo. It's about the car that followed you here.'

Soraya stopped in her tracks. 'Tell me you're putting me on.'

His head swiveled, and he looked at her as a cobra stares down its prey. 'Straight dope, like before.'

Soraya was furious with herself. She'd been so wrapped up in her own personal fog, she hadn't even considered that someone might tail her. She had failed to check, which was usually second nature to her. Obviously she was more upset about that sonovabitch Lerner benching her than she'd realized. Now she'd paid the price for her lack of vigilance.

'Tyrone, I owe you one.'

He shrugged. 'It's what Deron pays me t'do. Protection doan come cheap, but loyalty ain't got no price.'

She looked at him, but for the first time seemed to really

see him. 'Where is it? The car that tailed me?'

They began to walk again. 'Up ahead, at the corner of Eighth,' Tyrone said. 'Far side, so the driver get a good look at what yo up to.' He shrugged. 'My crew'll take care a him.'

'Not that I don't appreciate the offer, Tyrone.' She gave him a serious look. 'But I brought him here. It's on me.'

'Yo, I admire that, yo.' He stopped, stood facing her for a minute. His expression was as serious as hers. There was no mistaking the grim determination in it. Around here, he was the immovable object. 'Understand, it's gotta be done 'fore he get any idea 'bout Deron. Afta that, nuthin can save him. Even yo.'

'I'll take care of it right now.' She ducked her head, abruptly shy. 'Thanks.'

Tyrone nodded, headed back to his crew. Taking a deep breath, she kept on the way she had been going, down to the corner of 8th Street, where Detective Overton sat in his car, scribbling on a slip of lined paper.

She rapped her knuckles on the glass. He looked up, hastily jammed the paper into his shirt's breast pocket.

When the window whispered down, she said, 'What the hell d'you think you're doing?'

He put away his pen. 'Making sure you don't get hurt. This a helluva neighborhood.'

'I can take care of myself, thank you very much.'

'Listen, I know you're on to something – something important Homeland Security doesn't have a clue about. I gotta have the info.'

She glared down at him. 'What you have to do is leave. Now.'

All at once his face turned into a granite mask. 'I want what you know soon's you know it.'

Soraya felt the heat of combat in her cheeks. 'Or what?'

Without warning, he swung the door open, catching her

in the stomach. Down she went to her knees, gasping.

Slowly, Overton climbed out of the car and stood over her. 'Don't fuck with me, little lady. I'm older'n you. I don't play by the book. I've forgotten more tricks than you'll ever learn.'

Soraya closed her eyes for a moment, to show him that she was trying to regain both her wind and her composure. Meanwhile her left hand had pulled a compact no-snag ASP pistol from its slim holster at the small of her back, aimed it at Overton. 'This is loaded with nine-by-nineteen-millimeter Parabellum bullets,' she said. 'At this range, one of them will most likely tear you in two.' She took two deep breaths. Her gun hand was steady. 'Get the hell out of here. Now.'

He backed up slowly and deliberately, sitting down behind the wheel without taking his eyes off her. He shook out a cigarette, stuck it between his bloodless lips, lit it with a languid motion, drew down on it.

'Yes, ma'am.' There was nothing in his voice; all the venom was in his eyes. He slammed the door shut.

He watched her regain her feet as the engine roared to life and he pulled out. Glancing in the rearview mirrors, he saw her aiming the ASP squarely at his rear window until the car disappeared into traffic.

When he lost sight of her, he pulled out his cell phone, pressed a speed-dial key. The moment he heard Matthew Lerner's voice, he said, 'You were right, Mr. Lerner. Soraya Moore's still nosing around, and to tell you the truth she's just become a clear and present danger.'

Kabur directed them to the church whose steeple had guided Bourne to the village. It was, like all the churches in the country, part of the Ethiopian Orthodox Tewahedo Church. The religion was old, and with more than thirty-six million members, it was the world's largest Oriental Orthodox church. In fact, it was the only pre-colonial Christian church in its part of Africa.

There was a moment, in the watery light of the church, when Bourne thought Kabur had played him for a fool. That not only Zaim's radiation-eaten son but also the *nagus* himself was in Fadi's employ; that he had been led into a trap. He whipped out the Makarov. Then the shadows and patches of light resolved themselves and he saw a figure beckoning wordlessly to him.

'It's Father Mihret,' Zaim whispered. 'I know him.'

Zaim, though still recovering from his wound, had insisted on coming along. He was attached to Bourne now. They had saved each other's lives.

'My sons,' Father Mihret said softly, 'I fear you've come too late.'

'The pilot,' Bourne said. 'Please take me to him.'

As they hastily made their way through the church, Bourne said, 'Is he still alive?'

'Barely.' The priest was tall and thin as a post. He possessed the large eyes and emaciated look of an ascetic. 'We've done everything we can for him.'

'How did he come to you, Father?' Zaim asked.

'He was found by herders on the outskirts of the village, within a clump of firs near the river. They came to me and I ordered him moved here on a litter, but I fear it did him little good.'

'I have access to a warbird,' Bourne said. 'I can airlift him out.'

Father Mihret shook his head. 'He has fractures of the neck and spinal cord. There is no way to successfully immobilize him. He would never survive another move.'

The pilot, Jaime Cowell, was in Father Mihret's own bed. Two women tended to him, one salving his flayed skin, the other squeezing water from a cloth into his half-open lips. A flicker appeared in Cowell's eyes when Bourne came into his line of sight.

Bourne briefly turned his back to him. 'Can he talk?' he said to the priest.

'Very little,' Father Mihret replied. 'When he moves at all, the pain is excruciating.'

Bourne stood over the bed so that his face was in Cowell's direct line of sight. 'I've come to take you home, Jaime. D'you understand me?'

Cowell's lips moved, a soft hiss emanating from between them.

'Look, I'll make this short,' Bourne said. 'I need to find Martin Lindros. You two were the only ones to survive the attacks. Is Lindros alive?'

Bourne had to bend down, his ear almost touching Cowell's lips.

'Yes. When I . . . last saw him.' Cowell's voice was like sand slithering across a dune.

Though his heart leapt, Bourne was appalled by the stench. The priest wasn't wrong: Death was already in the room, stinking up the place.

'Jaime, this is very important. Do you know where Lindros is?'

Again, the terrible stench as Bourne leaned in.

'Three klicks west by southwest . . . across the . . . river.' Cowell was sweating with the effort and the pain. 'Camp . . . heavily defended.'

Bourne was about to move away when Cowell's rasp began again. His chest, rising and falling with unnatural rapidity, began to shudder, as his already overstressed muscles began to spasm. Cowell's eyes closed, tears leaking out from under the lids.

'Take it easy,' Bourne urged. 'Rest now.'

'No! Oh, God!'

Cowell's eyes flew open, and when he stared up into Bourne's the darkness of the abyss could be seen moving closer.

'This man . . . the leader . . .'

'Fadi.' Bourne supplied his name.

'He's tortur . . . torturing Lindros.'

Bourne's stomach rolled up into a ball of ice. 'Is Lindros holding out? Cowell! Cowell can you answer me?'

'He's beyond all questions now.' Father Mihret stepped forward, put his hand on Cowell's sweat-soaked forehead. 'God has granted him blessed relief from his suffering.'

They were moving him. Martin Lindros knew this because he could hear Abbud ibn Aziz barking out a multitude of orders, all in the service of getting them the hell out of the cave. There came the clangor of booted feet, the clash of metal weapons, the grunting of men lifting heavy loads. Then he heard the rattling engine of the truck as it backed up to the cave mouth.

A moment later, Abbud ibn Aziz himself came to blindfold him.

He squatted down beside Lindros. 'Don't worry,' he said.

'I'm beyond worry,' Lindros said in a cracked voice he barely recognized as his own.

Abbud ibn Aziz fingered the hood he was about to place over Lindros's head. It was sewn of black cloth and had no eyeholes. 'Whatever you know about the mission to murder Hamid ibn Ashef, now would be the time.'

'I've told you repeatedly, I don't know anything. You still don't believe me.'

'No.' Abbud ibn Aziz placed the hood over his head. 'I don't.'

Then, quite unexpectedly, his hand briefly gripped Lindros's shoulder.

What is this, Lindros wondered, *a sign of empathy?* It was amusing in a way that was currently beyond him to appreciate.

He could observe it as he observed everything these days, from behind a sheet of bulletproof glass of his own manufacture. That the pane was figurative made it no less effective. Ever since he'd returned from his private vault, Lindros had found himself in a semi-dissociative state, as if he couldn't fully inhabit his own body. Things his body did – eating, sleeping, eliminating, walking for exercise, even talking occasionally with Abbud ibn Aziz – seemed to be happening to someone else. Lindros could scarcely believe that he had been captured. That the dissociation was an inevitable consequence of being locked up for so long in his mental vault – that the state would slowly dissolve and, finally, vanish – seemed at the moment to be a pure pipe dream. It seemed to him that he would live out the rest of his life in this limbo – alive, but not truly living.

He was pulled roughly to his feet, feeling as if he were in a dream imagined over and over during his time out on the placid lake. Why was he being moved with this kind of haste? Had someone come after him? He doubted that it was CI; from snippets he'd overheard days ago, he knew that Dujja had destroyed the second helicopter of agents sent to find him. No. There was only one person who had the knowledge, tenacity, and sheer skill to get to the summit of Ras Dejen without being killed: Jason Bourne! Jason had come to find him and bring him home!

Matthew Lerner sat in the rear of Golden Duck. Though it was in Chinatown, the small restaurant was featured in many D.C. guidebooks, which meant it was frequented by tourists and shunned by locals, including members of Lerner's peculiar covert fraternity of spies and government agents. This, of course, suited him just fine. He had a good half a dozen meeting places he'd ferreted out around the district, randomizing his rendezvous with conduits and certain other individuals whose services he found useful.

The place, dim and dingy, smelled of sesame oil, five-spice powder, and the bubbling contents of a deep fryer from which egg rolls and breaded chicken parts were periodically lifted.

He was nursing a Tsingtao, drinking it out of the bottle because he found the oily smudges on the water glasses disturbing. Truth to tell, he'd much rather have been swigging Johnnie Walker Black, but not now. Not with this particular rendezvous.

His cell phone buzzed and, opening it, he saw a text message: 'OUT THE BACK ONTO 7 ST. FIVE MINUTES.'

Deleting it at once, he pocketed the phone and returned to polishing off his Tsingtao. When he'd finished, he plunked some bills onto the table, got his coat, and walked to the men's room. He was, of course, familiar with the restaurant's layout, as he was with the sites of all his rendezvous. After urinating, he turned right out of the men's room, went past a kitchen clouded with steam, alive with shouted Cantonese and the angry sizzle of huge iron woks over open flames.

Pulling the rear door open, he slipped through onto 7th Street. The late-model Ford was as anonymous as you could get in D.C., where all government agencies were mandated to buy American when it came to transportation. With a quick look in either direction, he opened the rear door and slid inside. The Ford began to roll.

Lerner settled back into the seat. 'Frank.'

'Hello, Mr. Lerner,' the driver said. 'How's tricks?'

'Tricky,' Lerner replied drily. 'As usual.'

'I hear you,' Frank nodded. He was a beefy, bullnecked man, carrying the air of one who slavishly worked out in the gym.

'How's the secretary this PM?'

'You know.' Frank snapped his fingers. 'What's the word?'

'Angry? Pissed off? Homicidal?'

Frank gave him a glance in the rearview mirror. 'Sounds about right.'

They went over the George Mason Memorial Bridge, then swung southeast onto the Washington Memorial Parkway. Everything in the district, Lerner observed, seemed to have *memorial* attached to it. Pork-barrel politics at its worst. Just the kind of crap to piss off the secretary.

The stretch limousine was waiting for him on the outskirts of Washington National Airport's cargo terminal, its colossal engine purring like an aircraft about to take off. As Frank slid the Ford to a stop, Lerner got out and made the transfer, as he'd done so many times in recent years.

The interior bore no resemblance to any vehicle Lerner had ever heard of, save Air Force One, the president's airplane. Walls of polished burlwood covered the windows when need be – as now. A walnut desk, a state-of-the-art wi-fi communications center, a plush sofa that doubled as a bed, a pair of equally plush swivel chairs, and a half-size refrigerator completed the picture.

A distinguished man pushing seventy, with a halo of close-cut silver hair sat behind the desk, his fingers roving over the keyboard of a laptop. His large, slightly bulging eyes were as alert and intense as they had been in his youth. They belied his sunken cheeks, the paleness of his flesh, the loose wattle beneath his chin.

'Secretary,' Lerner said, with a potent combination of respect and awe.

'Take a pew, Matthew.' Secretary of Defense Halliday's clipped Texas accent marked him as a man born and raised in the urban wilds of Dallas. 'I'll be with you momentarily.'

As Lerner chose one of the chairs, the stretch started up. Bud Halliday grew anxious if he remained in one place for long. What Lerner responded to most about him was that he was a self-made man, having been raised far from the rural oil fields that had spawned many of the men Lerner had come across during his time in the district. The secretary had earned his millions the old-fashioned way, which made him his own man. He was beholden to no one, not even the president. The deals he parlayed on behalf of his constituents and himself were so shrewd and politically deft, they invariably added to his clout, while rarely putting him in any of his colleagues' debt.

Finishing his work, Secretary Halliday looked up, tried to smile, and didn't quite make it. The only evidence of the minor stroke he'd suffered some ten years was the left corner of his mouth, which didn't always work as he wished it to.

'So far, so good, Matthew. When you came to me with the news that the DCI had proposed your transfer, I couldn't believe my good fortune. In one backdoor way or another, I've been trying to get control of CI for several years. The DCI is a dinosaur, the last remaining Old Boy still in service. But he's old now, and getting older by the minute. I've heard the rumors that he's beginning to lose his grip. I want to strike now, while he's beset on all sides. I can't touch him publicly; there are other dinosaurs who still have plenty of muscle inside the Beltway, even though they're retired. That's why I hired you and Mueller. I need to be at arm's length. Plausible deniability when the shit hits the fan.

'Still and all, bottom line, he's got to go; his agency needs a thorough housecleaning. They've always taken the lead in the so-called human intelligence, which is just Beltway-speak for spying. The Pentagon, which I control, and NSA, which the Pentagon controls, have always taken a backseat. We were responsible for the recon satellites, the eavesdropping – preparing the battlefield, as Luther LaValle, my strong right arm in the Pentagon, likes to say.

'But these days we are at war, and it's my firm belief that the Pentagon needs to take control of human intelligence as well. I want to control all of it, so that we become a more efficient machine in destroying every goddamn terrorist network and cell working both outside our borders and inside toward our destruction.'

Lerner watched the secretary's face, though such was the long and intimate nature of their relationship that he could sense what was coming. Anyone else would have been satisfied with his progress, but not Halliday. Lerner mentally braced himself, because whenever he got a compliment from the secretary, it was followed by a demand for the all but impossible. Not that Halliday gave a shit. He was made in the leathery mold of Lyndon Johnson: one tough sonovabitch.

'Mind telling me what you mean by that?'

Halliday eyed him for a moment. 'Now that you've confirmed my suspicion that CI has become newly infested with Arabs and Muslims, your first act after we take care of the DCI is to purge them.'

'Which ones?' Lerner said. 'D'you have a list?'

'List? I don't need a fucking list,' Halliday said sharply. 'When I say purge, I *mean* purge. I want them *all* gone.'

Lerner nearly winced. 'That will take some time, Mr. Secretary. Like it or not, we're living in religiously sensitive times.'

'I don't want to hear that bullshit, Matthew. I've had a pain in my right buttock for close to ten years. You know what's causing that pain?'

'Yessir. Religious sensitivity.'

'Damn right. We're at war with the goddamn Muslims. I won't tolerate any of 'em undermining our security agencies from the inside, got me?'

'I do indeed, sir.'

It was like a stand-up routine between them, though Lerner doubted the secretary would agree. If he had a sense of humor, it was buried as deep as a Neanderthal's bones.

'While we're on the subject of pains in the ass, there's the matter of Anne Held.'

Lerner knew the real show was about to commence. All of this other stuff was part of the secretary's preliminary dance. 'What about her?'

Halliday plucked a manila folder off the desk, spun it into Lerner hands. Lerner opened it and leafed quickly through the sheets. Then he looked up.

Halliday nodded. 'That's right, my friend. Anne Held has started her own personal investigation into your background.'

'That bitch. I thought I had her under control.'

'She's whip-smart, Matthew, and she's intensely loyal to the DCI. Which means she will never tolerate your move up the CI ladder. Now she's become a clear threat to us. QED.'

'I can't just terminate her. Even if I made it look like a break-in or an accident—'

'Forget it. The incident would be investigated so thoroughly, it would tie you up till kingdom come.' Halliday tapped the cap of a fountain pen against his lips 'That's why I propose you find a way to sever her in a manner that will be most embarrassing and painful to her and to him. Another embarrassment in a string of others. Stripped of his loyal right hand, the DCI will be all the more vulnerable. Your star will rise even more quickly, hastening the dinosaur's demise. I'll see to it.'

TEN

Once they crossed the frozen river, heading west by southwest, the darkness of the steeply rising mountain overtook them. Bourne and Zaim were in the company of three of Kabur's foot soldiers, who were more familiar with the terrain than Zaim.

Bourne was uneasy to be traveling in what was, for him, a large pack. His methodology depended on stealth and invisibility – both of which were made extremely difficult in the present circumstances. Still, as they moved briskly along, he had to admit that Kabur's men were silent and concentrated on their mission, which was to get him and Zaim to Fadi's camp alive.

After rising gradually from the western bank of the river, the terrain leveled off for a time, indicating that they had mounted a forested plateau. The mountain loomed up in an ever-more-forbidding formation: an almost sheer wall that, thirty meters up, abruptly jutted out in a massive overhang.

The snow, which had begun to fall in earnest as they set out, had now abated to a gentle shower that did nothing to impede their progress. Thus they covered the first two and a half kilometers without incident. At this point, one of Kabur's men signaled them to halt while he sent his comrade out on a scouting foray. They waited, hunkered down amid the sighing firs, as snow continued to drift down on them. A terrible silence had come down with the vanguard of the storm, which now overstretched the area as if the massive overhanging shelf had sucked all sound out of the mountainside.

The Amhara returned, signaling that all was clear ahead, and they moved out, trudging through the snow, eyes and ears alert. As they drew nearer the overhang, the plateau steadily rose, the way becoming simultaneously rockier and more densely forested. It made perfect sense to Bourne that Fadi would pitch his camp on the high ground.

When they had gone another half a kilometer. Kabur's commander called another halt and once again sent a comrade to scout ahead. He was gone for longer this time, and when he returned he huddled with his superior in a heated conference. Kabur's man broke away and approached Bourne and Zaim.

'We have confirmation of the enemy up ahead. There are two of them to the east of us.'

'We must be close to their camp now,' Bourne said.

'These aren't guards. They're actively searching the forest, and they're coming this way.' The commander frowned. 'I'm wondering if they somehow know we're coming.'

'There's no way to know,' Zaim said. 'In any case, we need to kill them.'

The commander's frown deepened. 'These are Fadi's men. There will be consequences.'

'Forget it,' Bourne said brusquely. 'Zaim and I will go on alone.'

'Do you take me for a coward?' The commander shook his head. 'Our mission is to get you to Fadi's camp. This we will do.'

He signaled to his men, who set out heading due east. 'The three of us will keep to our original course. Let my brothers do their work.'

They were climbing in earnest, the mountain reaching upward as if trying to touch the massive overhang. It had stopped snowing for the moment, and now the sun broke out behind a rent in the streaming clouds.

All at once a flurry of gunshots echoed and reechoed. The three of them stopped, crouching down within the trees. A second flurry came on its heels, then all was silent again.

'We must hurry now,' the commander said, and they rose, resuming their course west-southwest.

Within moments, they heard a bird trill. Soon thereafter, the commander's two soldiers rejoined them. One was wounded, but not badly. They continued on grimly, a tight-knit unit, with the scout in the lead.

Almost immediately the rising ground began to level out, the trees becoming sparser. When the scout went to his knees it seemed as if he'd stumbled over a rock or a tree root. Then blood spattered the snow as the second soldier was shot through the head. The rest of the group took cover. They'd been unprepared, Bourne thought, because the shots had come from the west. The two-man scouting party coming from the east was a feint, part of a hidden pincer movement from both east and west. Bourne now learned something else about Fadi. He had accepted the risk of losing two men in order to ambush the entire party.

More shots were being fired, a veritable fusillade, so that it was impossible to determine how many of Fadi's men opposed them. Bourne broke away from Zaim and the commander, both of whom were firing back from behind whatever makeshift cover they could find. Heading off to his right, he scrambled up a steep slope, rough enough for him to find hand- and footholds through the snow. He knew it had been a mistake to allow Kabur's men to come – he didn't even want Zaim's assistance – but the culture made it impossible to refuse these gifts.

Reaching a high point, he crawled to the far edge where the wave of rock fell sharply away. From the vantage point he saw four men, carrying rifles and handguns. Even at this distance it was impossible to mistake them for Amhara. They had to be part of Fadi's terrorist cadre.

The problem now was one of logistics. Armed only with handguns, Bourne was at a distinct disadvantage opposing an enemy with rifles. The only way to negate that was to move into close quarters. This plan had its own dangers, but there was no help for it.

Circling, Bourne came at them from the rear. Very soon he realized that a simple rear assault was out of the question. The terrorists had posted a man to watch their backs. The guard sat on a rock he'd cleared of snow, holding a German-made sniper rifle – a Mauser SP66. It used 7.62 × 51mm ammo and was equipped with a precision Zeiss Diavari telescopic sight. All of this detail was vital to Bourne's next move. Though the Mauser was an excellent weapon for bringing down a long-range target, it was heavy-barreled and manually bolt-operated. It was a poor weapon if you needed to fire it in a hurry.

He crept within fifteen meters of the man, drew out the curved knife he'd taken off the Amhara soldier. Breaking cover, he stood in full view of the terrorist, who jumped up off the rock, providing Bourne with a maximum target. He was still trying to aim the Mauser when Bourne sent the knife whistling through the air. It struck the man just below the sternum, burying itself to the hilt. The curved blade sliced through tissue and organ alike. Even before the terrorist hit the snow, he was drowning in his own blood.

Bourne retrieved the knife as he stepped over the corpse, wiped the blade in the snow, slipped it into its sheath. Then he took up the Mauser and went in search of a place of concealment.

He heard shots being fired in short and long bursts, like Morse code spelling out the deaths of the combatants. He began to run toward the terrorists' position, but they had begun to move. He threw down the Mauser, drew out the Makarov.

Breaking out along the high ridge, he saw just below him

the commander sprawled in the snow amid a cloud of blood. Then, as he inched forward, two terrorists came into view. He shot one in the heart from the back. The second turned and fired back. Bourne dove behind a rock.

More shots were being fired, ragged bursts, a peppering of sound taken up by the overhang, rocketed back into Bourne's ears. Bourne rose to his knees and three shots spanged off a nearby rock, sending sparks into the air.

He made a show of moving to his right, drawing fire, then slithered on his belly to his left until one shoulder of the terrorist came into view. Bourne fired twice, heard a grunt of pain. He made a show of rising up, coming forward, and when the terrorist popped up, Makarov aimed directly at him, Bourne shot the man cleanly between the eyes.

Moving on, Bourne searched for the third terrorist. He found him writhing in the snow, one hand clutching his stomach. His eyes flashed as he saw Bourne and, curiously, the ghost of a smile crossed his face. Then, in a final spasm, blood erupted from his mouth and his eyes clouded over.

Bourne ran on, then. Not more than thirty meters along he found Zaim. The Amhara was on his knees. He'd been shot twice in the chest. His eyes were crossed in pain. Nevertheless, as Bourne came to him, he said, 'No, leave me. I'm finished.'

'Zaim—'

'Go on. Find your friend. Bring him home.'

'I can't leave you.'

Zaim arranged his lips in a smile. 'You still don't understand. I have no regrets. Because of you my son will be buried. This is all I ask.'

With a long, rattling sigh, he fell sideways and did not move again.

Bourne approached him at last and, kneeling down, closed his companion's eyes. Then he went on toward Fadi's camp. Fifteen minutes later, after wending his way through thickening stands of firs, he saw it: a military array of tents pitched on a patch of flat ground that had been cleared some time ago, judging by the healed-over tree stumps.

Hunkered down beside the bole of a tree, he studied the camp: nine tents, three cook fires, a latrine. The trouble was that he could see no one. The camp appeared deserted.

He rose, then, and began to make his surveillance circuit around the camp's periphery. The moment he left the sanctuary of the fir's low-hanging branches, bullets kicked up snow all around him. He glimpsed at least half a dozen men.

Bourne began to run.

'Up here! This way! Quickly!'

Bourne, looking up, saw Alem lying prone on a shelf of snow-laden rock. He found a foothold, vaulted up onto the ledge. Alem slithered back from the edge beside Bourne, who was on his belly, watching Fadi's men fan out to search for him.

Following Alem's lead, Bourne pushed himself farther back onto the ledge. When they were far enough to gain their feet, Alem said: 'They've moved your friend. There are caves beneath the overhang. This is where they've taken him.'

'What are you doing here?' Bourne said as they began to climb upward.

'Where is my father? Why isn't he with you?'

'I'm sorry, Alem. He was shot to death.'

Bourne reached out to the boy, but Alem flinched away. The boy hung off the rock, his gaze turned inward.

'He gave as good as he got, if that makes a difference.' Bourne crouched next to Alem. 'He was at peace at the end. I promised to bury your brother.'

'You can do that?'

Bourne nodded. 'I think so. Yes.'

Alem's dark eyes roved over Bourne's face. Then he nodded

and, silently, they resumed their ascent. It had begun to snow again – a heavy white curtain coming down, putting them at a remove from the rest of the world. It also muffled all sound, which was both good for them and bad. While it would hide the sounds of their movement, it would do the same for their pursuers.

Nevertheless, Alem led them on fearlessly. He was using a channel that ran diagonally across the bulge of the overhang. He was sure-footed, didn't miss a step. Within fifteen minutes, they had gained the top.

Alem and Bourne crept the irregular surface. 'There are chimneys that go all the way down to the caves,' he said. 'Many times I played hide-and-seek here with my brother. I know which chimney to use to get to your friend.'

Even through the snow, Bourne could see that the overhang was pocked with the holes that marked vertical chimneys, indications of glacial ice powerful enough to excavate through the mountain's granitic material.

Bent over one of these, Bourne wiped away the accumulated snow and peered down. Light didn't quite make it all the way down to the bottom, but the shaft looked to be several hundred meters in height.

Beside him, Alem said, 'Your enemies were watching.'

'Your father told me this.'

Alem nodded. Clearly he was not surprised. 'Your friend was then moved out of the camp so you would not find him.'

Bourne sat back, contemplating the boy. 'Why are you telling me this now? Assuming it is the truth.'

'They killed my father. I think now that was always what they intended. What do they care for us, how many of us are killed or maimed, so long as they gain what they want. But they assured me that he would be safe, that he'd be protected, and I was stupid enough to believe them. So now I say fuck them. I want to help you rescue your friend.'

Bourne said nothing, made no move.

'I know I must prove myself to you, so I'll go first down the chimney. If it is a trap, if your suspicion is right, if they think you'll use the chimney, then they will shoot me dead. You will be safe.'

'No matter what you've done, Alem, I don't want to see you hurt.'

Confusion flitted across the boy's face. Clearly, it was the first time a stranger had expressed interest in his welfare.

'I've told you the truth,' Alem said. 'The terrorists have no knowledge of these chimneys.'

After a moment's hesitation, Bourne said, 'You can prove your loyalty to me and to your father, but not this way.' He dug in his pocket, taking out a small octagonal object made of a dark gray rubbery plastic compound in the center of which were two buttons, one black and one red.

As he put it into Alem's hand, he said, 'I need you to go back down the overhang, heading south. You'll no doubt come across some of Fadi's men. As soon as you see them, press the black button. When you're within a hundred meters of them, press the red button, then throw this at them as hard as you can. Do you have all that?'

The boy looked down at the octagon. 'Is this an explosive?'

'You know it is.'

'You can count on me,' Alem said solemnly.

'Good. I'm not going to make a move until I hear the explosion. Then I'll go down the chimney.'

'The explosion will draw them.' Alem rose to leave. 'Two-thirds of the way down, the chimney branches. Take the right branch. When you reach the end, turn right. You'll be fifty meters from where they're holding your friend.'

Bourne watched as the boy scrambled across the top of the overhang, vanishing into the swirling snow as he went over the south side. At once, he called Davis on the Thuraya satellite phone.

'Your position is compromised,' he said. 'Has there been any activity? Anything at all?'

'Quiet as a tomb,' the pilot said. 'You have an ETA? There's a helluva front forming to the northwest.'

'So I've heard. Listen, I need you to get out of there. I passed through an alpine meadow thirteen or fourteen klicks northwest of your current position. Head for that. But first, I want you to bury the body in the cave. You won't be able to get anywhere with the ground, so use rocks. Make a cairn. Say a prayer over it. Oh, and one other thing – wear the radiation suit I saw in the cockpit.'

Bourne turned back to the job at hand. He had to trust that Alem was now telling him the truth. And yet he needed to take precautions in the event he was wrong. Instead of waiting for the detonation, as he'd told Alem he would, he lowered himself at once into the chimney, slithering his way down. At this moment, the boy might be handing the grenade over to one of Fadi's men. At least Bourne wouldn't be where Alem thought he'd be.

Knees, ankles, and elbows were the means of locomotion as Bourne descended the rock chimney. The pressure he put on them was the only thing stopping him from plummeting the full length of the channel to the rock floor below.

Just as Alem had said, the chimney diverged approximately two-thirds of the way down. Bourne hung for a moment above the crux, pondering the imponderable. Either he believed Alem or he didn't, it was as simple as that. But of course it wasn't simple at all. When it came to human motivations and impulses, nothing was simple.

Bourne took the right fork. Within a short distance, the way narrowed slightly, so that at points he had to force himself through. Once, he had to turn forty-five degrees in order to get his shoulders through. Eventually, though, he emerged onto the cave floor. Makarov in hand, he looked both ways. No terrorist lurked in ambush. But a meter-and-a-half stalagmite rose from the cavern floor, a calcite deposit caused by mineral-rich water washed down the chimney.

Bourne kicked out, snapping the stalagmite a foot above its base. Taking it up in his free hand, he headed right along the cavern. It wasn't long before the passageway curved to the left. Bourne slowed his pace, then dropped down to knee level.

What he saw when he first took a look around the corner was one of Fadi's men standing with a Ruger semiautomatic rifle on his hip. Bourne waited, breathing slowly and deeply. The terrorist moved, and Bourne could see Martin Lindros. Bound and gagged, he was propped up against a canvas pack of some kind. Bourne's heart beat hard in his chest. Martin was alive!

He had no time to fully assess his friend's condition because at that moment the echo of an explosion ricocheted in the cave. Alem had proved himself; he'd lobbed Deron's grenade, just as he'd promised.

The terrorist moved once again, cutting off Bourne's view of Lindros. Now he could see two more terrorists as they huddled with the first, who was speaking in rapid Arabic on a satellite phone, deciding their course of action. So Fadi had left three men to guard his prisoner. Bourne now had a crucial bit of information.

The three terrorists, having come to a decision, arrayed themselves in a triangular defensive formation: one man on point, near the cave mouth, two spread out behind Lindros, near where Bourne crouched.

Bourne put away the Makarov. He couldn't afford to use a firearm. The noise would surely bring the rest of Fadi's men to the cave at a run. He rose, planting his feet. Holding the stalagmite in one hand, he drew out the curved blade knife.

He threw that first, strong and true, so that it buried itself to the hilt in the back of the left-facing rear guard. As the other one turned, Bourne hurled the stalagmite like a spear. It struck the terrorist in the throat, piercing clean through. The man clawed briefly at it as he toppled over. Then he slumped over his comrade.

The terrorist on point had spun around and was aiming his Ruger at Bourne, who immediately raised his hands and came walking toward the other.

The terrorist said, 'Halt!' in Arabic.

But Bourne had already broken into a sprint. He reached the terrorist while the man's eyes were still wide in shock. Shoving the muzzle of the Ruger to the side, Bourne slammed the heel of his hand into the terrorist's nose. Blood and bits of cartilage sprayed outward. Bourne chopped down on the man's clavicle, breaking it. The terrorist was on his knees now, swaying groggily. Jason ripped the Ruger out of his hands and mashed the butt into his temple. The man pitched over, unmoving.

Bourne was already striding away. He slit the ropes that bound Lindros hand and ankle. As he pulled his friend to his feet, he stripped off the gag.

'Easy,' he said. 'Are you okay?'

Lindros nodded.

'Okay. Let's get you the hell out of here.'

As he hustled Lindros back the way he had come, Bourne untied his friend's wrists. Martin's face was puffy and dis-colored, the most easily visible effects of his torture. What agonies of mind and body had Fadi put him through? Bourne had been a victim of articulated torture more than once. He knew that some people stood up to it better than others.

Skirting the stub of the stalagmite Bourne had broken off, they arrived at the chimney.

'We have to go up,' Bourne said. 'It's the only way out.'

'I'll do what I have to do.'

'Don't worry,' Bourne said. 'I'll help you.'

As he was about to hoist himself up into the chimney, Lindros put a hand on his arm.

'Jason, I never lost hope. I knew you'd find me,' he said. 'I owe you a debt I can never adequately repay.'

Bourne squeezed his arm briefly. 'Now come on. Follow me up.'

The ascent took longer than the descent. For one thing, the climb up was far more difficult and tiring. For another, there was Lindros. Several times, Bourne was obliged to stop and move back a meter or two to help his friend get through a particularly rough spot in the chimney. And he had to haul Lindros bodily through one of the narrow places.

At last, after a harrowing thirty minutes, they emerged onto the top of the overhang. While Martin regained his breath, Bourne took a reading of the weather. The wind had swung around. It was now coming out of the south. The light pattering of snow was all that was coming down – and clearly all that would come down: The front had shifted away. The ancient demons of Ras Dejen had been merciful this time.

Bourne pulled Lindros to his feet, and they began the trek to the waiting helicopter.

ELEVEN

Anne Held lived in a two-story Federal redbrick house a stone's throw from Dumbarton Oaks in Georgetown. It had black shutters, a slate roof, and a neat privet hedge out front. The house had belonged to her late sister, Joyce. She and her husband, Peter, had died three years ago when their small plane had gone down in fog as they headed toward Martha's Vineyard. Anne had inherited the house, which she never could have afforded on her own.

Most nights, returning home from CI, Anne didn't miss her Lover. For one thing, the DCI invariably kept her late. He'd always been a tireless worker, but after his wife had walked out on him two years ago, he had absolutely no reason to leave the office. For another, once she was home she kept herself busy up until the moment she took an Ambien, slipped beneath the covers, and snapped off the bedside lamp.

But there were other nights – like this one – when she could not turn her thoughts away from her Lover. She missed the scent of him, the feel of his muscled limbs, the flutter of his flat belly against hers, the exquisite sensation as he took her – or she took him. The emptiness inside her his absence caused was a physical pain, the only anodyne more work or drugged sleep.

Her Lover. He had a name, of course. And a thousand love-names she had given him over the years. But in her mind, in her dreams, he was her Lover. She had met him in London, at a festive consular party – the ambassador of somewhere-or-other was celebrating his seventy-fifth birthday, and all of his six-hundred-odd friends had been invited, she among them. She had been working then for the director of MI6, an old and trusted friend of the DCI.

At once, she had grown dizzy and a little afraid. Dizzy at his proximity, afraid of his profound effect on her. She was, at twenty, not without experience when it came to the opposite sex. However, her experience had been with callow boys. Her Lover was a man. She missed him now with an ache that left a knot in her breast.

Her throat was parched. She crossed the entryway and entered the library, on the other side of which was the hallway to the kitchen. She had taken no more than three or four steps into the room when she stopped dead in her tracks.

Nothing was as she had left it. The sight snapped her out of the emotional pit she'd fallen into. Without taking her eyes from the scene, she opened her handbag and took out her Smith & Wesson J-frame. She was a good shot; she practiced twice a month at the CI firing range. Not that she was a big fan of guns, but the training was mandatory for all office personnel.

Thus armed, she took a closer look around. It wasn't as if a sneak thief had broken in and rifled the place. This job was neat and tidy. In fact, if she hadn't been such an anal retentive she might never have noticed the changes – that's how minute most of them were. Papers on her desk not quite as neatly stacked as they had been, an old-fashioned chrome stapler at more of an angle than she had left it, her colored pencils in a slightly different order, the books on the shelves not precisely aligned as she had ordered them.

The first thing she did was go through every room and closet in the house to make sure she was alone. Then she checked all the doors and windows. None had been broken or damaged in any way. Which meant someone either had a set of keys or had picked the lock. Of the two possibilities, the second seemed far more probable.

Next, she returned to the library and slowly and methodically examined every single item there. It was important to her to get a sense of who had invaded her house. As she moved from shelf to shelf, she imagined him stalking her, poking, prodding in an attempt to ferret out her innermost secrets.

In a sense, considering the business she was in, it seemed inevitable that this would happen. However, that knowledge did not assuage the dread she felt at this rape of her private world. She was defended, of course, heavily so. And as scrupulously careful here as she was at the office. Whoever had been here had found nothing of value, of this she was certain. It was the act itself that gnawed at her. She had been attacked. Why? By whom? Questions without immediate answers.

Forget that glass of water now, she thought. Instead she poured herself a stiff single-malt Scotch and, sipping it, went upstairs to her bedroom. She sat on the bed, kicked off her shoes. But the adrenaline still racing through her body would not allow her respite. She got up, padded over to her dresser, set her old-fashioned glass down. Standing before the mirror, she unbuttoned her blouse, shrugged it off. She went into the closet, swept a line of other blouses out of the way to get to the free hanger. Reaching up, she stopped in midmotion. Her heart beat like a trip-hammer and she felt a wave of nausea wash over her.

There, swinging from the chrome hanger rod, was a miniature hangman's noose. And caught in that noose, pulled tight as if around the condemned's neck, was a pair of her underpants.

'They wanted to know what I knew. They wanted to know why I was following them.' Martin Lindros sat with his head against the specially configured airplane seat's back, eyes half closed. 'I could've kicked myself. They made me in Zambia, my interrogator told me. I never knew it.'

'No use beating yourself up,' Bourne said. 'You aren't used to fieldwork.'

Lindros shook his head. 'No excuse.'

'Martin,' he said gently, 'what's happened to your voice?'

Lindros winced. 'I must have been screaming for days. I don't remember.' He tried to twist away from the memory. 'I never saw what it was.'

His friend was still in a kind of post-rescue shock, that was clear enough to Bourne. He'd asked twice about the fate of Jaime Cowell, his pilot, as if he hadn't heard Bourne the first time or had not been able to absorb the news. Bourne had chosen not to tell him about the second helicopter; time for that later. So much had happened so quickly, they'd hardly been able to say another word to each other, until now. The moment they'd taken off from Ras Dejen, Davis had radioed Ambouli airport in Djibouti for a CI physician. For that choppy flight, Lindros had been lying down on a stretcher, moving in and out of a fitful sleep. He was thinner than Bourne had ever seen him, his face haggard and gray. The beard altered his appearance in an unsettling way: It made him look like one of his captors.

Davis, a hotshot pilot if ever there was one, had wrestled the helicopter into the air, raced through the eye of a needle: a rent in the howling wind at the side edge of the front. He skillfully followed it down the mountain, out into clear weather. Beside him, Lindros lay, white-faced, the mask feeding him oxygen clamped firmly in place.

During the pulse-quickening flight, Bourne tried to keep the ruined, pitted face of Alem's brother out of his mind. He wished he could have buried the boy himself. That had proved impossible, so he'd done the next best thing. Imagining the stone cairn Davis had erected, he said a silent prayer for the dead, as he'd done months ago over Marie's grave.

In Djibouti, the CI physician had clambered aboard the moment they touched down. He was a young man with a stern countenance and prematurely graying hair. After spending close to an hour examining Lindros, he and Bourne stood outside the chopper and spoke.

'Clearly, he's been badly mistreated,' the doctor had said. 'Bruises, contusions, a cracked rib. And of course, dehydration. The good news is there's no sign of internal bleeding. I have him on saline and antibiotic drips, so for the next hour or so he can't be moved. Clean up, get yourself something proteinaceous to eat.'

He had given Bourne the ghost of a smile. 'Physically, he'll be fine. What I can't quantify is what was done to him mentally and emotionally. The official evaluation will have to wait until we get back to D.C., but in the meantime you can do your bit. Engage his mind, when you can, during the trip back. I understand the two of you are good friends. Talk to him about the times you've spent together, see if you can get a sense of what changes – if any – have occurred.'

'Who interrogated you?' Bourne said now to Lindros as they sat side by side in the CI jet.

His friend's eyes closed briefly. 'Their leader: Fadi.'

'So Fadi himself was there on Ras Dejen.'

'Yes.' A slight shudder went through Lindros like a gust of wind. 'This shipment was too important to leave in the hands of a lieutenant.'

'So you found out before they captured you.'

'Uranium, yes. I had taken radiation detectors with me.' Lindros's gaze slid away to the shrieking darkness outside the jet's Perspex window. 'I started out by thinking Dujja was after TSGs. But really, that didn't make sense. I mean, *why* would they want triggered spark gaps unless . . .' His body was racked by another small spasm. 'We have to assume they have it all, Jason. The TSGs and, far worse, the means to enrich the uranium. We have to assume they're constructing a nuclear bomb.'

'That was my conclusion as well.'

'And it's none of this "dirty bomb" crap that would impact a couple of square blocks. This is the real thing, power enough to devastate a major city, irradiate the surrounding areas. For the love of God, we're talking millions of lives!'

Lindros was right. In Djibouti, Bourne had called the Old Man while the doctor was assessing Martin's condition, giving him an abbreviated briefing on Lindros, their current status, and, especially, what they'd discovered about Dujja's threat and its capacity to carry it out. For now, however, all he could do was try to assess his friend's mental condition. 'Tell me about your time in captivity.'

'There's not much to tell, really. Most of the time I had a hood over my head. Believe it or not, I came to dread the times it would be removed, because that was when Fadi interrogated me.'

Bourne knew he was now skating on thin ice. But he had to get at the truth, even if it wasn't what he wanted to hear. 'Did he know you were CI?'

'No.'

'Did you tell him?'

'I told him I was NSA, and he believed me. He had no reason not to. One American spy agency is like another to these people.'

'Did he want information on NSA personnel deployment or mission objectives?'

Lindros shook his head. 'As I said, what interested him was how I came to be following him and how much I knew.'

Bourne hesitated fractionally. 'Did he find that out?'

'I know what you're getting at, Jason. I had a strong conviction that if I broke, he'd kill me.'

Bourne said nothing more for the moment. Lindros's breathing was coming quick and fast, cold sweat breaking out across his forehead. The doctor had warned him that if he went too far, too fast with Lindros, a reaction might set in.

'Should I call the doctor?'

Lindros shook his head. 'Give me a minute. I'll be okay.'

Bourne went back to the galley, made plates of food for them both. There were no attendants on board, just the doctor, a CI pilot, and an armed copilot up front. Returning to his seat, he handed a plate to his friend, sat down with the other. For some time, Bourne ate in silence. Presently, he could see that Lindros had calmed down enough to begin picking at his food.

'Tell me what's been happening while I've been gone.'

'I wish I had some good news. But the fact is your people caught that Cape Town dealer who sold the TSGs to Dujja.'

'Hiram Cevik, yes.'

Bourne produced the PS3, brought up the photo of Cevik, showed it to Lindros.

'This him?'

'No,' Lindros said. 'Why?'

'This is the man picked up in Cape Town and brought to D.C. He escaped, but not before one of his people shot Tim Hytner to death.'

'Dammit all. Hytner was a good man.' Lindros tapped the PS3 screen. 'So who is this?'

'I think it's Fadi.'

Lindros was incredulous. 'We had him, and lost him?'

'I'm afraid so. On the other hand, this is the first lead we have to what Fadi actually might look like.'

'Let me see that.' Lindros stared hard at the photo. After a long time, he said, 'Christ, that *is* Fadi!'

'You're sure?'

Lindros nodded. 'He was there when they took us. He's got a load of makeup on here, but I recognize the shape of the face. And those eyes.' He nodded, handing back the PS3. 'That's Fadi, all right.'

'Can you make a sketch of him for me?'

Lindros nodded. Bourne rose, then came back a moment later with a pad and a fistful of pencils he'd gotten from the copilot.

While Lindros went to work, Bourne spoke of something he had noticed in his friend. 'Martin, you look like there's something else you want to tell me.'

Lindros looked up from the sketch. 'It's probably nothing, but . . .' He shook his head. 'When I was alone with another of my interrogators – a man named Abbud ibn Aziz, who by the way is Fadi's right hand – a name kept coming up. Hamid ibn Ashef.'

'I don't know him.'

'Really? I thought I saw his name in your file.'

'If so, it must have been a mission set up by Alex Conklin. But if it involved me, I have no memory of it.'

'I was just wondering why Abbud ibn Aziz wanted information on that particular mission. I guess now I'll never know.' Lindros took a long drink of water. He was following the doctor's orders to rest and rehydrate. 'Jason, I may still be somewhat out of it, but I'm no longer in shock. I know the powers that be are going to run a complete battery of tests to determine my fitness.'

'You're going to return to duty, Martin.'

'I hope you know you're going to play a major role in that decision. After all, you know me best. CI will have to be guided by your opinion.'

Bourne couldn't help laughing. 'Now, that will be a switch.'

Lindros took a deep breath, let it out, along with a little whistle of pain. 'Irrespective of all this, I want you to promise me something.'

Bourne searched his shadowed face for any sign that he knew what the powers that be would really be looking for: whether he had been brainwashed, turned into a ticking time bomb, a human weapon to be used against CI. It had always been in the back of Bourne's mind as he'd gone after his friend. What would be the worse horror, he'd wondered. To find his friend dead, or to discover that he'd been turned into the enemy?

'Dujja's rigid, almost businesslike, organization, its seemingly unending supply of modern armament, the fact that Fadi is obviously Western-educated – all these factors taken together make this cadre unlike any other terrorist network we've ever been up against,' Lindros continued. 'The construction of a uranium enrichment plant is massively expensive. Who has that kind of money to throw around? My guess is a crime cartel. Drug money from crops in Afghanistan or Colombia. Turn off that spigot – the money men – and you cut off its ability to enrich uranium, to get more up-to-date weapons. There's no surer way of sending it all the way back into the Iron Age.' His voice lowered. 'In Botswana, I unearthed what I believe to be Dujja's money trail, which runs back to Odessa. I have a name: Lemontov. Edor Vladovich Lemontov. The intel I gathered in Uganda is that Lemontov is based there.'

His eyes gleamed, the old excitement returning. 'Think of it, Jason! Up until now, the only realistic way to destroy an Islamic terrorist network was to try to infiltrate it. A tactic that is so difficult, it's never succeeded. Now, for the first time, we have another option. A tangible means to dismantle the world's most lethal terrorist network from the outside in.

'I can take care of that end. But as for this money man, I

don't trust anyone else the way I trust you. I need you to go to Odessa as soon as possible, track down Lemontov, and terminate him.'

The rambling fieldstone house had been built more than a hundred years before. Since then, it'd had ample time to settle into the rolling hills of Virginia. It had dormer windows, slate-tile roof, and a high stone wall around the property, with iron gates that opened electronically. It was said by neighbors that the estate was owned by an old recluse of a writer who, if anyone were to take the trouble to look at a copy of the deed housed in the municipal building fifty kilometers away, had bought the estate twenty-two years ago for the sum of $240,000 after the county had closed the insane asylum. This writer was something of a paranoid, it was said. Why else would his wall be electrified? Why else would the pair of lean and perpetually hungry Dobermans roam the grounds, sniffing and growling ominously?

In fact, the estate was owned by CI. Veteran agents, those in the know, had given it the name of Bleak House, because it was here that CI enacted its formal debriefs. They made macabre jokes about it because its very existence filled them with anxiety. It was to here that Bourne and Lindros were driven, on a joint-cracking winter's morning, upon their arrival at Dulles airport.

'Place your head just there. That's right.'

The CI agent cupped his hand to the back of Martin Lindros's head as, moments before, he had done with Jason Bourne.

'Look straight ahead, please,' the agent continued, 'and try not to blink.'

'I've done this a thousand times before,' Lindros growled.

The agent ignored him, switching on the retinal reader and watching the readout as it scanned the center of Lindros's right eye. Having taken its picture, the reader automatically compared the retinal pattern with the one on file. The match was perfect.

'Welcome home, Deputy Director.' The agent grinned, extending his hand. 'You're cleared to enter Bleak House. Second door on your left. Mr. Bourne, you're the third door on the right.'

He nodded them to the elevator that had been installed when CI bought the estate. Since it was controlled by him, the doors were open, the car waiting patiently for them. Inside the shining stainless-steel cab, there was no need for numbers or buttons to push. This elevator went only to the sub-basement, where the warren of rough concrete corridors, claustrophobic windowless rooms, and mysterious laboratories staffed by a veritable phalanx of medical and psychological experts awaited like a medieval chamber of horrors.

Everybody in CI knew that being taken to Bleak House meant something had gone horribly wrong. It was the temporary home of defectors, double agents, incompetents, and traitors.

After that, these people were never heard from again, their fate a source of endless grisly rumor within the agency.

Bourne and Lindros reached the sub-basement and stepped out into the corridor, which smelled vaguely of cleaning fluid and acid. They stood facing each other for a moment. There was nothing more to say. They gripped each other's hand like gladiators about to enter the bloody arena, and parted.

In the room behind the third door on the right, Bourne sat on a ladder-backed metal chair bolted to the concrete floor. The long fluorescent tubes of an industrial overhead light, covered by a steel grille, buzzed like a horsefly against a windowpane. It revealed a metal table and another metal chair, both also bolted to the floor. There was a stainless-steel toilet in one corner, prison-style, and a tiny sink. The room was otherwise bare save for a mirror on one wall, through which he could be observed by whoever was assigned to his interrogation.

For two hours he waited with only the company of the fluorescent tube's angry buzzing for company. Then abruptly the door opened. An agent walked in, sat down on the other side of the table. He set out a small tape recorder, turned it on, opened a file on the tabletop, and began his questioning.

'Tell me in as much detail as you remember what happened from the moment you arrived on the north face of Ras Dejen to the moment you took off with the subject on board.'

While Bourne spoke, the interrogator never took his eyes off his face. He himself was a man of middle years, of medium height, with a high domed forehead and thin, receding hair. He had a receding chin but the eyes of a fox. He never once looked at Bourne directly, instead he studied him from the corners of his eyes, as if this might give him the advantage of insight, or at least intimidation.

'What was the subject's condition when you found him?'

The interrogator was asking Bourne to repeat what he'd already said. This was standard operating procedure, a way to ferret out the lies from the truth. If a subject was lying, his story would change sooner or later. 'He was bound and gagged. He appeared very thin – much as he does now – as if his captors had fed him minimally.'

'I imagine he had great difficulty managing the ascent back to the helicopter.'

'The beginning was the most difficult for him. I thought

I might have to carry him. His muscles were cramped and his stamina was virtually nil. I fed him a couple of protein bars and that helped. Within an hour, he was walking more steadily.'

'What was the first thing he said?' the interrogator said with a false mildness.

Bourne knew that the more casually a question was asked, the more important it was to the interrogator. '"I'll do what I have to do."'

The interrogator shook his head. 'I mean when he first saw you. When you removed the gag.'

'I asked him if he was okay—'

The interrogator regarded the ceiling as if he was bored. 'And he said what, precisely?'

Bourne remained stone-faced. 'He nodded. He didn't say a word.'

The interrogator looked puzzled, a sure sign that he was trying to trip Bourne up. 'Why not? You'd think after more than a week in captivity, he'd say something.'

'It was insecure. The less we spoke at that moment, the better. He knew that.'

Bourne was in the corners of the interrogator's eyes again. 'So his first words to you were . . .'

'I told him we needed to climb the rock chimney in order to escape and he said "I'll do what I have to do."'

The interrogator appeared unconvinced. 'All right, passing over that. In your opinion, what was his mental state at that time?'

'He seemed okay. Relieved. He wanted out of there.'

'He wasn't disoriented, didn't exhibit any lapses of memory? He didn't say anything odd, out of place?'

'No, none of that.'

'You seem very sure of yourself, Mr. Bourne. Don't you yourself have a memory problem?'

Bourne knew he was being baited, and he relaxed inside.

Baiting was the method of last resort, when every other avenue to break a story apart had been exhausted. 'Of events in the past. My memories of yesterday, last week, last month are crystal clear.'

Without a moment's hesitation the interrogator said, 'Has the subject been brainwashed, has he been turned?'

'The man across the hall is Martin Lindros as he's always been,' Bourne replied. 'On the plane ride home, we talked of things only he and I knew about.'

'Please be more specific.'

'He confirmed the identity of the terrorist Fadi. He made a sketch for me. A huge breakthrough for us. Before that, Fadi was just a cipher. Martin also gave me the name of Fadi's right-hand man, Abbud ibn Aziz.'

The interrogator asked him another dozen questions, many of which he'd asked before with different wording. Bourne patiently answered them all. Nothing was going to ruffle his calm.

As abruptly as it had started, the session came to an end. Without either acknowledgment or explanation, the interrogator turned off the tape recorder, then took it and his notes with him out of the room.

Another period of waiting ensued, interrupted only by another agent, younger, bringing in a tray of food. He left without saying a word.

It was just after six in the evening, according to Bourne's watch – an entire day spent in interrogation – when the door next opened.

Bourne, who thought he was ready for anything, was very much surprised to see the DCI walk in. He stood, regarding Bourne for a long time. In his face, Bourne recognized the conflicting emotions that clogged the Old Man's throat. It had cost him something to come in here at all, and now what he'd come to say stuck in his craw like a fish bone.

At last he said, 'You made good on your promise. You

brought Martin home.'

'Martin's my friend. I wasn't about to fail him.'

'You know, Bourne, it's no secret I wish I'd never met you.' The Old Man shook his head. 'But really, you're a fucking enigma.'

'Even to myself.'

The DCI blinked several times. Then he turned on his heel and strode out, leaving the door open. Bourne rose. He supposed he was free to leave, and so was Martin. That's all that mattered. Martin had passed the exhausting battery of physical and psychological tests. They had both survived Bleak House.

Matthew Lerner, sitting in the Typhon director's chair, behind the Typhon director's desk, knew something was amiss the moment he heard the applause. He turned away from the computer terminal, where he had been devising a new system of cataloging Typhon e-files.

He rose, crossed the director's office, and opened the door. There he was greeted by the sight of Martin Lindros being surrounded by the members of his Typhon cadre, all of whom were smiling, laughing, and pumping his hand enthusiastically when they weren't egging him on with their applause.

Lerner could scarcely believe his eyes. *Here comes Caesar,* he thought bitterly. *And why didn't the DCI see fit to tell me he'd returned?* With a mixture of repulsion and envy, he watched the prodigal general making his slow, triumphal way toward him. *Why are you here? Why aren't you dead?*

With no small pain, he screwed a smile onto his face and held out his hand.

'All hail the returning hero.'

Lindros reflected back the smile in all its steel-clad irony. 'Thanks for keeping my chair warm, Matthew.'

He swept by Lerner and into his office. There he stood

195

stock-still, taking inventory. 'What, no new coat of paint?' As Lerner followed him in, he added: 'A verbal debriefing will do, before you go upstairs.'

Lerner did as he was asked while he went about gathering his personal items. When he was finished, Lindros said, 'I'd appreciate getting the office back as I left it, Matthew.'

Lerner glared at him for a microsecond, then carefully put back all the photos, prints, and memorabilia he had put away, hoping never to see again. As an accomplished commander, he knew when to leave the field of battle. It was with the certain knowledge that this was a war, and it had just begun.

Three minutes after Lerner had left the Typhon offices, Lindros's phone rang. It was the Old Man.

'I bet it feels good to be sitting behind that desk.'

'You have no idea,' Lindros said.

'Welcome back, Martin. And I mean that most sincerely. The confirmation of Dujja's intentions you obtained is invaluable.'

'Yes sir. I've already worked up a step-by-step plan to interdict them.'

'Good man,' the DCI said. 'Assemble your team and press forward with the mission, Martin. Until the crisis has been dealt with, your mission is CI's mission. From this moment, you have unlimited access to all of CI's resources.'

'I'll get the job done, sir.'

'I'm counting on you, Martin,' the DCI said. 'You'll be able to deliver your first briefing at dinner tonight. Eight sharp.'

'I'll look forward to it, sir.'

The DCI cleared his throat. 'Now, what do you propose to do about Bourne?'

'I don't understand, sir.'

'Don't play games with me, Martin. The man's a menace, we both know it.'

'He brought me home, sir. I doubt anyone else could have done it.'

The Old Man shook off Lindros's words. 'We're in the midst of a national crisis of unprecedented proportion and gravity. The last thing we need is a loose cannon. I want you to get rid of him.'

Lindros shifted in his chair, staring out the window at the silver pellets of freezing rain. He made a mental note to check whether Bourne's flight would be delayed. Into the mounting silence, he said: 'I'm going to need clarification on that.'

'Oh, no, no, nothing like that. Anyway, the man is cursed with nine lives.' The DCI paused a moment. 'I know you two have formed some sort of bond, but it's unhealthy. Trust me, I know. Consider that we buried Alex Conklin three years ago. It's dangerous for anyone to get too close to him.'

'Sir—'

'If it helps, I'm giving you one last loyalty test, Martin. Your continuation at Typhon depends on it. I don't have to remind you there's someone snapping at your heels. As of this moment, you are to sever all ties with Jason Bourne. He gets no information – none at all – from your office or any other in the building. Are we clear?'

'Yessir.' Lindros severed the connection.

Carrying the cordless phone, he rose and stood by the window, resting his cheek against the pane, felt the cold wash over him. His bone-deep aches and pains remained, along with a headache he'd neglected to mention to the CI physicians, which never quite left him – all vivid reminders of what had happened to him, how long his journey here had been.

Dialing a number, he held the phone to his ear. 'Is Bourne's flight on time?' He nodded at the reply. 'Good. He's at Washington National? You've made visual contact? Excellent, come on home. That's right.' He severed the connection.

Whatever might transpire here, Bourne was on his way to Odessa.

Returning to his desk, he opened the intercom and told his secretary to set up an immediate phone conference with all of Typhon's overseas agents. When that had been accomplished, he activated the speakerphone in the conference room where he had assembled an emergency meeting of all D.C. Typhon personnel. There he gave them what details he had of the threat, then outlined his plan. Dividing his people into four-man teams, he meted out assignments that, he told them, were to begin immediately.

'As of this moment, all other missions are frozen,' he told them. 'Finding and stopping Dujja is our first and only priority. Until that's accomplished, all leaves are hearby canceled. Get used to these walls, folks. We're going on a day-and-night emergency schedule.'

Once he saw that his orders were being carried out to his satisfaction, he left to go to Soraya's apartment to straighten out whatever it was Matthew Lerner had fucked up with her. In the car, he opened his quad-band GSM cell phone and dialed a number in Odessa.

When the familiar male voice answered, Lindros said, 'It's done. Bourne will be arriving at 4:40 local time tomorrow afternoon, from Munich.' He ran a red light, made a right turn. Soraya's apartment building was three blocks ahead. 'You will keep him on a short leash, as we discussed . . . No, I simply want to make sure you haven't decided to make changes to the plan on the fly. All right, then. He'll find his way to the kiosk because that's where he'll think Lemontov is headquartered. Before he can find out the truth, you'll kill him.'

BOOK TWO

TWELVE

In Odessa, there is a kiosk, one among many on the beach fronting the Black Sea. It is weathered, gray as the water that rolls into the tide line. Bourne picks the lock of a side door in the kiosk, steals his way inside. Where is the person he was carrying? He doesn't remember, but he sees that his hands are covered with blood. He smells violent death on himself. What happened? he wonders. No time, no time! Somewhere a clock is ticking; he has to move on.

The kiosk, which should be filled with life, is as still as a bone-yard. At the back, a windowed kitchen, garishly lit by fluorescent tubes. He sees movement through the glass and, crouching, makes his way between the crates of beer and soda piled up like columns in a cathedral. He sees the silhouette of the man he was sent here to kill, who has done his best to confuse and elude him.

To no avail.

He's about to make the final approach to his target when movement to his left causes him to spin around. A woman comes toward him out of the shadows – Marie! What is she doing in Odessa? How did she know where he was?

'Darling,' she says. 'Come with me, come away from here.'

'Marie.' He feels panic constrict his chest. 'You can't be here. It's too dangerous.'

'Marrying you was dangerous, darling. That didn't stop me.'

A high keening begins, reverberating through the empty space inside him. 'But now you're dead.'

'Dead? Yes, I suppose I am.' A frown momentarily fractures the beauty of her face. 'Why weren't you there, darling? Why weren't

you protecting me and the children? I would be alive now if you hadn't been halfway across the globe, if you hadn't been with her.'

'Her?' Bourne's heart is beating like a trip-hammer, and his panic grows exponentially.

'You're an expert at lying to everyone, except me, darling.'

'What do you mean?'

'Look at your hands.'

He stares down at the blood drying into the crevasses of his palms. 'Whose blood is this?'

Wanting – needing – an answer, he looks up. But Marie is gone. There is nothing but the lurid light spilling out onto the floor like blood from a wound.

'Marie,' he calls softly. 'Marie, don't leave me!'

Martin Lindros and his retinue of captors had been traveling for quite some time. He had flown in a helicopter and, after a short wait, on a small jet, which had stopped at least once for refueling. He wasn't sure because either he had slept or they had given him something to make him sleep. Not that it mattered. He knew he was off Ras Dejen, out of northwest Ethiopia, out of the continent of Africa altogether.

Jason. What had happened to Jason? Was he dead or alive? Clearly Jason had failed to find him in time. He didn't want to think about Jason being dead. He wouldn't believe it even if Fadi himself told him so. He knew Bourne too well. He always had a way of turning over the newly shoveled earth to climb out of his grave. Jason was alive, Lindros knew it.

But he wondered whether it even mattered. Did Jason suspect that Karim al-Jamil had taken Lindros's place? If he'd been fooled, then even if he'd survived the rescue attempt on Ras Dejen he'd have abandoned the rescue. An even worse scenario made him break out into a cold sweat. What if Jason had found Karim al-Jamil, brought him back to CI headquarters. God in heaven, was that what Fadi had planned all along?

His body swayed and juddered as the plane hit a pocket of turbulence. To steady himself, he leaned against the plane's chill concave bulkhead. After a moment, he put his hand over the bandage that covered half his face. Underneath was the excavation where his right eye had been. This had become a habit of his. His head throbbed with an unspeakable pain. It was as if his eye were on fire – only his eye was no longer his. It belonged to Fadi's brother, Karim al-Jamil ibn Hamid ibn Ashef al-Wahhib. At first, this thought had made him sick to his stomach; he would vomit often and rackingly, like a junkie going cold turkey. Now it simply made him sick at heart.

The violation of his body, the harvesting of his organ while he was still alive, was a horror from which he would never recover. At several points, while he was out on the silver lake fishing for rainbow trout, the thought of killing himself crossed his mind, but he had never actually considered it. Suicide was the coward's way out.

Besides, he very much wanted to live, if only to exact his revenge on Fadi and Karim al-Jamil.

Bourne awoke with a violent twitch. He looked around him, momentarily disoriented. Where was he? He saw a bureau, a night table, curtains drawn against the light. Anonymous furniture, heavy, threadbare. A hotel room. Where?

Sliding out of bed, he padded across the mottled carpet, pulled back the thick curtains. A sudden glare struck him a clean blow across his face and chest. He squinted at the tiny scimitars of sunlight, gold against the deep gray of the water. The Black Sea. He was in Odessa.

Had he been dreaming of Odessa, or remembering Odessa?

He turned, his mind still filled with the dream-memory,

stretched like taffy into the blue morning. Marie in Odessa? Never! Then what was she doing in his memory shard of . . .

Odessa!

It was in this city that his memory shard had been born. He'd been here before. He'd been sent to kill . . . someone. Who? He had no idea.

He sat back down on the bed, rubbing the heels of his hands against his eyes. He still heard Marie's voice.

'I would be alive now if you hadn't been halfway across the globe, if you hadn't been with her.' Not accusatory. Sad.

What did it matter where he was, what he was doing? He hadn't been with her. Marie had phoned him. She thought she had a cold, that's all. Then the second call, which had sent him half out of his mind with grief. And guilt.

He should have been there to protect his family, just as he should have been there to protect his first family. History had repeated itself, if not exactly, then tragically close enough. Ironically, this far away in kilometers from the scene of the disaster had brought him closer, to the very brink of the black void inside him. Staring into it, he felt that old, overwhelming despair well up inside him – a need to punish himself, or to punish someone else.

He felt totally, absolutely alone. For him, this was a deeply disturbing state, as if he had stepped outside himself, as one does in a dream. Only this was no dream; this was waking life. Not for the first time he wondered whether his judgment was being impaired by his current emotional turmoil. He could find no other logical explanation for certain anomalies: his bringing Hiram Cevik out of the CI cell; his waking up here and not knowing where he was. For a brief, despairing moment, he wondered if Marie's death had ripped him completely asunder, if the delicate threads that held his multiple identities together had snapped. *Am I losing my mind?*

His cell phone buzzed.

'Jason, where are you?' It was Soraya.

'In Odessa,' he said thickly. His mouth felt wadded with cotton.

There was a quick catch to her breathing. Then: 'What on earth are you doing there?'

'Lindros sent me here. I'm following up a lead he gave me. He thinks a man named Lemontov is funding Dujja. Edor Vladovich Lemontov. Criminal cartel – drugs, most likely. Does the name ring a bell?'

'No. But I'll check the CI database.'

Briefly, she told him about the events at the Hotel Constitution. 'The one true oddity is that a highly unusual accelerant was used – carbon disulfide. According to my friend, she's never encountered it before.'

'What's it used in?'

'Mainly the manufacture of cellulose, carbon tet, all kinds of sulfur compounds. It's also used in soil fumigants, a flotation agent in mineral processing. In the past, it was a component of refrigerants and fire extinguishers. She said she thought it was used because it has a low flashpoint.'

Bourne nodded as he stared at an oil tanker chugging in empty from Istanbul. 'Turning it into an explosive.'

'Very effective. Blew out the suite. A complete firestorm. We were lucky with the prosthesis, which was protected by the bathtub catch basin. Nothing else of value was left, not even enough of a body to ID.'

'Fadi's luck seems to be going down the drain,' Bourne said drily.

Soraya laughed. 'The Lemontov lead interests me, because I thought of the old refrigerants and fire extinguishers that had been banned in the States, but probably not elsewhere, like Eastern Europe, Ukraine, Odessa.'

'That's a thought worth following up on,' Bourne said, breaking the connection.

*

Although it was after 1 AM, Martin Lindros was at his computer terminal entering information. CI was still in Code Mesa. There was a crisis on, all leaves canceled. Sleep was a luxury none of them could afford.

A soft knock on the door, then Soraya poked her head in, gave him a questioning look. He raised a beckoning hand, and she shut the door behind her. Taking a seat in front of the desk, she placed something on the desktop.

'What's this?' Lindros said.

'It's a prosthetic. A friend of mine – an arson expert with the Fire Investigation Unit – called me in.' Soraya had previously filled him in on the events at the Hotel Constitution. 'She found something in the Silvers' suite at the Constitution she couldn't explain. That. It's used in highly sophisticated disguises.'

He picked up the prosthetic. 'Yes. Jason showed me something like this once. It's meant to change your appearance.'

Soraya nodded. 'There's enough evidence to conclude that Jakob Silver was, in fact, Fadi, that his brother was another terrorist, that they were responsible for the fire.'

'Wasn't there a body found in the suite? Wasn't it Silver's?'

'Yes, and no. It seems more than likely that the body was that of a Pakistani waiter. There never were a pair of Mr. Silvers.'

'Ingenious,' Lindros mused as he turned the prosthetic between his fingertips. 'But not of much use to us now.'

'On the contrary.' Soraya took it back. 'I'm going to see if I can find out who manufactured it.'

Lindros was lost in thought for a moment.

'I talked to Bourne less than an hour ago,' Soraya continued.

'Oh?'

'He wanted me to dig up whatever I can on a drug lord by the name of Edor Vladovich Lemontov.'

Lindros set his elbows on his desk, steepled his fingers. This was a situation that could quickly spiral out of control if he let it. Keeping his voice neutral, he said, 'And what have you discovered?'

'Nothing yet. I wanted to bring you up to date on the prosthetic first.'

'You did well.'

'Thanks, boss.' She rose. 'Now I've got hours of eyestrain ahead of me.'

'Forget research. I couldn't find anything on this sonova-bitch. Whoever he is, he's securely shielded. Just the sort Dujja would use as a money man.' Lindros had already turned back to his computer screen. 'I want you on the next plane to Odessa. I want you to back Bourne up.'

Soraya was clearly surprised. 'He won't like that.'

'He's not required to,' Lindros said shortly.

When Soraya reached for the prosthetic, Lindros swept it up in his hand. 'I'll take care of this myself.'

'Sir, if you don't mind my saying, you've got a lot on your plate as it is.'

Lindros searched her face. 'Soraya, I wanted to be the one to tell you this. We've had a mole inside Typhon.' He could hear her sharply indrawn breath and was pleased. Opening a drawer, he spun across a thin dossier he'd prepared.

Soraya picked it up, flipped back the cover. As soon as she started reading, she felt hot tears distorting her vision. It was Tim Hytner. Bourne had been right, after all. Hytner had been working for Dujja.

She looked up at Lindros. 'Why?'

He shrugged. 'Money. It's all in there. The electronic trail back to an account in the Caymans. Hytner was born dirt-poor, wasn't he? His father is in a long-term care medical facility his insurance won't pay for, isn't that right? His mother has no money to speak of. Everyone's got a weakness, Soraya. Even your best friend.'

He took the file from her. 'Forget Hytner, he's yesterday's news. You've got work to do. I want you in Odessa ASAP.'

When he heard the door sigh shut, Lindros stared after her as if he could see her walking away. *Yes, indeed*, he thought. *In Odessa, you'll be killed before you can find out who made this prosthetic.*

THIRTEEN

Bourne was booked into the Samarin Hotel, a rather shambling mammoth of a place on the seaport directly across from the Passenger Sea Terminal, where ferries went to and fro on a regular schedule. The sleek ultramodern Odessa Hotel had risen from the massive sea terminal pier since the last time he'd been here. To him, it seemed as out of place as a Dolce & Gabbana suit on a homeless man.

Shaved, bathed, and dressed, he walked down to the vast somnolent lobby, which was as ornate as an early nineteenth-century Easter bonnet. In fact, everything about the hotel reeked of early nineteenth century, from the massive frayed velvet furniture to the floral-patterned wallpapered walls.

He ate breakfast amid florid-faced businessmen in the sun-filled dining room overlooking the harbor. It smelled vaguely of burned butter and beer. When his waiter brought the check, he said, 'At this time of year, where does one go here to have a good time?'

Bourne spoke in Russian. Though this was Ukraine, Russian was Odessa's official language.

'Ibitza is closed,' the waiter said, 'as are all the clubs in Arkadia.' Arkadia was the beachside district; in summer the strands swarmed with young, affluent Russian women and male tourists on the prowl. 'It depends. What is your preference, female or male?'

'Neither,' Bourne said. He put his fingertip to his nose, inhaled noisily.

'Ah, that trade is open year-round,' the waiter said. He was a thin man, stoop-shouldered, prematurely old. 'How much do you need?'

'More than you can get for me. I'm in wholesale.'

'Another story entirely,' the waiter said warily.

'Here's all you have to know.' Bourne pushed over a roll of American money.

Without hesitation, the waiter vacuumed up the bills. 'You know the Privoz Market?'

'I'll find it.'

'Egg Row, third stall from the east end. Tell Yevgeny Feyodovich you want brown eggs, only brown.'

The Samarin, like all of old Odessa, was built in the neoclassical style, which meant it was Frenchified. This was hardly surprising, since one of the founding fathers of Odessa was the duc de Richelieu, who had been the city's chief architect and designer during the eleven years he was governor in the early 1800s. It was the Russian poet Aleksander Pushkin, living in exile here, who said that he could smell Europe in Odessa's shops and coffeehouses.

On shadowy, linden-lined Primorskaya Street, Bourne was immediately greeted by a chill, damp wind that slapped his face and reddened his skin. To the south, far out on the water, low clouds hung dense and dark, dispensing a sleety rain onto goosefleshed waves.

The salt tang from the sea brought memory back with breathless ferocity. Night in Odessa, blood on his hands, a life hanging in the balance, a desperate search for his target, leading to the kiosk where he'd found his target.

His gaze turned inland, toward the terraced levels that rose into the hills guarding the scimitar-shaped harbor. Consulting a map he'd been given by the hotel's ancient concierge, he leapt onto a slowing tram that would take him to the railway station on Italiansky Boulevard.

The Privoz farmers' market, a stone's throw from the station, was a colossal array of live food and produce under a corrugated tin roof. The stalls were set up behind waist-high concrete slabs that made Bourne think of the antiterrorist blockades in D.C. Makeshift shanties and bedrolls surrounded the market. Farmers came from near and far, and those who were obliged to travel a great distance invariably slept here overnight.

Inside, it was a riot of sounds, smells, cries in different languages – butchered Russian, Ukrainian, Romanian, Yiddish, Georgian, Armenian, Turkish. The scents of cheese mingled with those of fresh meat, root vegetables, pungent herbs, and plucked fowl. Bourne saw huge, linebacker-like women with moth-eaten sweaters and head scarves manning the booths at Turkey Row. For the uninitiated, the market presented a thoroughly bewildering array of stalls against which hordes of stout shoppers pressed their impressive bellies.

After asking directions from several people, Bourne made his way through the clamor and throb to Egg Row. Orienting himself, he moved to the third stall from the east end, which was typically crowded. A red-faced woman and a burly man – presumably Yevgeny Feyodovich – were busily exchanging eggs for money. He waited on the man's side of the stall, and when his turn came he said, 'You are Yevgeny Feyodovich?'

The man squinted at him. 'Who wants to know?'

'I'm looking for brown eggs, only brown. I was told to come here and ask for Yevgeny Feyodovich.'

Yevgeny Feyodovich grunted, leaned over, said something to his female partner. She nodding without breaking her practiced rhythm of packing eggs and shoveling money into the outsize pockets of her faded dress.

'This way,' Yevgeny said with a flick of his head. He pulled on a ratty wool peacoat, came out from behind the concrete barrier, led Bourne out the eastern side of the market. They crossed Srednefontanskaya Street and entered Kulikovo Pole Square. The sky was white now, as if a colossal cloud had come down from the heavens to blanket the city. The light, flat and shadowless, was a photographer's dream. It revealed everything.

'As you can see, this square is very Soviet, very ugly, retro, but not in a good way,' Yevgeny Feyodovich said with a good bit of ironic humor. 'Still, it serves to remind us of the past – of starvation and massacres.'

He kept walking until they arrived at a ten-meter-high statue. 'My favorite place to transact business: at Lenin's feet. In the old days, the communists used to rally here.' His meaty shoulders lifted and fell. 'What better place, eh? Now Lenin watches over me like a bastard patron saint who, I trust, has been banished to the lowest fiery pit of hell.'

His eyes squinted again. He smelled the way a baby smells, of curdled milk and sugar. He had a beetling brow below a halo of brown hair that curled every which way like a wad of used steel wool.

'So it's brown eggs you desire.'

'A large amount,' Bourne said. 'Also, a constant supply.'

'That so?' Yevgeny parked a buttock on the limestone plinth of the Lenin statue, shook out a black Turkish cigarette. He lit it in a slow, almost religious ritual, drawing a goodly amount of smoke into his lungs. Then he held it there like a hippie enjoying a doobie of Acapulco Gold. 'How do I know you're not Interpol?' he said in the soft hiss of an exhale. 'Or an undercover operative of SBU?' He meant the Security Service of Ukraine.

'Because I'm telling you I'm not.'

Yevgeny laughed. 'You know the ironic thing about this city? It's smack up against the Black Sea but has always been short of drinking water. That in itself wouldn't be of much interest, except it's how Odessa got its name. They spoke French in Catherine's imperial court, see, and some wag suggested she name the city Odessa, because that's what it sounds like when you say *assez d'eau* backward. 'Enough water,' see? It's a fucking joke the French played on us.'

'If we're through with the history lesson,' Bourne said, 'I'd like to meet Lemontov.'

Yevgeny squinted up at him through the acrid smoke. 'Who?'

'Edor Vladovich Lemontov. He owns the trade here.'

Yevgeny started, rose from the plinth, his eyes looking past Bourne. He led them around the plinth.

Without turning his head, Bourne could see in the periphery of his vision a man walking a large Doberman pinscher. The dog's long, narrow face swung around, its yellow eyes staring at Yevgeny as if sensing his fear.

When they reached the other side of the statue of Lenin, Yevgeny said, 'Now, where were we?'

'Lemontov,' Bourne says. 'Your boss.'

'Are you telling me he is?'

'If you work for someone else, tell me now,' Bourne said shortly. 'It's Lemontov I want to do business with.'

Bourne sensed another man stealing up behind him but didn't move, giving Yevgeny Feyodovich no sign that he knew until the frigid muzzle of the gun pressed the flesh just behind his right ear.

'Meet Bogdan Illiyanovich.' Stepping forward, Yevgeny Feyodovich unbuttoned Bourne's overcoat. 'Now we'll get at the truth, *tovarich*.' With minimum effort, his fingers lifted the wallet and passport from the inside pocket.

Stepping back, Yevgeny opened the passport first. 'Moldavian, are you? Ilias Voda.' He stared hard at the photo. 'Yes, that's you, all right.' He flipped a page. 'Came here straight from Bucharest.'

'The people I represent are Romanian,' Bourne said.

Bourne watched Yevgeny Feyodovich paw through the wallet, sifting through three different kinds of identification, including a driver's license and an import-export license. That last was a nice touch, Bourne thought. He'd have to thank Deron when he got back.

At length, Yevgeny handed back the wallet and the passport. Keeping his eye on Bourne, he took out a cell phone, punched in a local number.

'New business,' he said laconically. 'Ilias Voda, representing Romanian interests, he says.' He put the cell phone aside for a moment, said to Bourne, 'How much?'

'Is that Lemontov?'

Yevgeny's face darkened. *'How much?'*

'A hundred kilos now.'

Yevgeny stared at him, entranced.

'Twice as much next month if everything pans out.'

Yevgeny walked a bit away, putting his back to Bourne while he spoke again into the phone. A moment later, he came back. The cell was already in his pocket.

Another flick of his head caused Bogdan Illiyanovich to remove the gun from Bourne's head, stow it away beneath the long wool coat that flapped around his ankles. He was a thick-necked man with very black hair that was pomaded across his scalp from right to left in a style vaguely reminiscent of the one Hitler had favored. His eyes were like agates, glimmering darkly at the bottom of a well.

'Tomorrow night.'

Bourne looked at him steadily. He wanted to get on with it; time was of the essence. Every day, every hour brought Fadi and his cadre closer to unleashing their nuclear weapon. But he saw in Yevgeny's face the cold expression of the hardened professional. It was no good trying to see Lemontov sooner. He was being tested to determine if he was as hardened as they were. Bourne knew that Lemontov wanted time to observe him before he allowed him an audience. Protesting that would be more than foolhardy; it would make him seem weak.

'Give me the time and place,' Bourne said.

'After dinner. Be ready. Someone will call your room. The Samarin, yes?'

The waiter who had given him Yevgeny's name, Bourne thought. 'I needn't give you my room number, then.'

'Indeed not.'

Yevgeny Feyodovich held out his hand. As Bourne gripped it, he said, '*Gospadin*, Voda, I wish you good fortune in your quest.' He did not immediately release his ferocious clamp on Bourne's hand. 'Now you are within our orbit. Now you are either friend or enemy. I beg you to remember that if you try to communicate with anyone by any means for any reason whatsoever, you are enemy. There will be no second chance.' His yellow teeth appeared as his lips drew back from them. 'For such a betrayal, you will never leave Odessa alive, you have my assurance on this.'

FOURTEEN

Martin Lindros, dossiers in hand, was on his way to the Old Man's office for a hastily called briefing when his cell buzzed. It was Anne Held.

'Good afternoon, Mr. Lindros. There's been a change of plan. Please meet the DCI down in the Tunnel.'

'Thank you, Anne.'

Lindros disconnected, punched the DOWN button. The Tunnel was the underground parking facility where the pool of agency cars was housed and maintained, and where service people on CI-approved lists came and went under the scrutiny of armed agents wearing body armor.

He rode the elevator down to the Tunnel, where he showed his ID to one of the agents on duty. The place was in effect an enormous reinforced concrete bunker: both bomb- and fireproof. There was only one ramp that led up to the street, which could be sealed on both ends at a moment's notice. The Old Man's armored Lincoln limousine sat purring on the concrete, its rear door open. Lindros ducked as he entered, sitting beside the DCI on the plush leather seats. The door closed without his help, electronically locking itself. The driver and his shotgun nodded to him, then the privacy window slid up, sealing the passengers in the spacious rear compartment. The windows in the rear compartment were specially tinted so no one could see in, but the passengers could see out.

'You've brought both dossiers?'

'Yessir.' Lindros nodded as he handed over the folders.

'That was good work, Martin.' The Old Man scrunched up his face. 'I've been summoned by the POTUS.' *POTUS* was the preferred acronym among security people in the district for the president of the United States. 'Judging by the crises we're in – external and internal – the question is how bad this interview is going to be.'

As it turned out, the meeting was very bad indeed. For one thing, the Old Man was conducted not to the Oval Office, but to the War Room, three floors underground. For another, the president was not alone. There were six people ranged around the oval table in the center of the concrete-reinforced room. It was lit solely by the giant screens that flickered on all four walls, showing shifting scenes of military bases, jet recon missions, digital war simulations in a dizzying array.

The Old Man knew some of the players confronting him; the president introduced him to the others. From left to right, the group started with Luther LaValle, the Pentagon's intelligence czar, a big, boxy man with a creased dome of a forehead and a thin bristle of gunmetal-gray hair. On his left, the president introduced Jon Mueller, a ranking official from the Department of Homeland Security, a gimlet-eyed specimen whose utter stillness spoke to the DCI of his extreme danger. The man to his left needed no introduction: Bud Halliday, secretary of defense. Then came the president himself, a slight, dapper man with silver hair, a forthright face, and a keen mind. To his left was the national security adviser, dark-haired, round-shouldered, with the restless and overly bright eyes, the Old Man had always thought, of a large rodent. The last person on the right was a bespectacled man by the name of Gundarsson, who worked for the International Atomic Energy Agency.

'Now that we're all assembled,' the president began

without the usual protocol or oratory preamble, 'let's get down to it.' His eyes came to rest on the DCI. 'We are in the midst of a crisis of unprecedented proportions. We've all been briefed on the situation, but as it's in a highly fluid state, bring us up to date, would you, Kurt?'

The Old Man nodded, opened the Dujja dossier. 'Having Deputy Director Lindros back with us has brought us added intel on Dujja's movements, as well as significantly boosting morale within the agency. We now have confirmation that Dujja was in the Semien mountain range of northwest Ethiopia, and that they were transporting uranium as well as the TSGs used to trigger a nuclear device. From analysis of the latest translations of Dujja's phone traffic, we're beginning to home in on the place where we believe they're enriching uranium.'

'Excellent,' LaValle said. 'As soon as you confirm actual coordinates, we'll order a surgical air strike that will bomb the sons-of-bitches back into the Stone Age.'

'Director,' Gundarsson said, 'how certain are we that Dujja possesses the capacity to enrich uranium? After all, it takes not only specialized know-how but also a facility stocked with, among other things, thousands of centrifuges to get the form of enriched uranium needed for even a single nuclear weapon.'

'We're not certain at all,' the director said crisply, 'but we now have eyewitness account from both Deputy Director Lindros and the agent who brought him back that Dujja is trafficking in both uranium and TSGs.'

'All well and good,' LaValle said, 'but we all know that yellowcake uranium is both plentiful and inexpensive. It's also a long, long way from weapons grade.'

'I agree. Trouble is, the residual signature leads us to believe Dujja is transshipping uranium dioxide powder,' the DCI said. 'Unlike yellowcake, UO_2 is only one simple step removed from weapons-grade uranium. It can be converted to the metal in any decent lab. As a consequence, we have to take extremely seriously anything Dujja is planning.'

'Unless it's all disinformation,' LaValle said doggedly. He was a man who often used his undeniable power to rub people the wrong way. Worse, he appeared to enjoy it.

Gundarsson cleared his throat portentously. 'I agree with the director. The idea of a terrorist network possessing uranium dioxide is terrifying. When it comes to the direct threat of a nuclear device, we cannot afford to dismiss it as disinformation.' He reached into a briefcase at his side and took out a sheaf of papers, which he distributed to everyone. 'A nuclear device, whether it's a so-called dirty bomb or not, has a certain size, specifications, and unvarying components. I have taken the liberty of drawing up a list, along with detailed drawings showing size, specs, and possible markers for detection. I would suggest getting these out to all law enforcement entities in every large city in America.'

The president nodded. 'Kurt, I want you to coordinate the distribution.'

'Right away, sir,' the DCI said.

'Just a moment, Director,' LaValle said. 'I want to go back to that other agent you mentioned. That would be Jason Bourne. He was the agent involved in the debacle of the escaped terrorist. He was the one who took your prisoner out of his cell without proper authorization, correct?'

'This is strictly an internal matter, Mr. LaValle.'

'In this room, at least, I think the need to be candid outweighs any sense of interagency rivalry,' the Pentagon intelligence czar said. 'Frankly, I question whether anything Bourne says can be believed.'

'You've run into difficulty before with him, haven't you, Director?' This from Secretary Halliday.

The DCI looked as if he was half asleep. In fact, his brain was running at full speed. He knew the moment he'd been waiting for had arrived. He was under a carefully coordinated attack. 'What of it?'

Halliday smiled thinly. 'With all due respect, Director, I'd submit that this man is an embarrassment to your agency, to the administration, to all of us. He allowed a high-level suspect to escape from CI custody and in the process endangered the lives of I don't know how many innocent citizens. I submit that he needs to be dealt with, the sooner the better.'

The DCI swiped the secretary's words away with the back of his hand. 'Can we get back to the issue at hand, Mr. President? Dujja—'

'Secretary Halliday is right,' LaValle persisted. 'We are at war with Dujja. We cannot afford to lose control of one of their assets. That being the case, kindly tell us what steps your agency is taking against Jason Bourne.'

'Mr. LaValle's point is well taken, Director,' Secretary Halliday said in his oiliest Texan imitation of Lyndon Johnson. 'That very public screwup on the Arlington Memorial Bridge gave us all a black eye and our enemy a moral lift just when we can least afford it. Following the collateral death of one of your own—' He snapped his fingers. 'What was his name?'

'Timothy Hytner,' the DCI supplied.

'That's right. Hytner,' the secretary continued as if confirming the DCI's response. 'With all due respect, Director, if I were you, I'd be far more concerned with internal security than you seem to be.'

This was what the DCI had been waiting for. He opened the thinner of the two dossiers that Martin Lindros had turned over to him in the Tunnel. 'In point of fact, we have just concluded our internal investigation into those matters you just brought up, Mr. Secretary. Here is our irrefutable conclusion.' He spun the top sheet across the tabletop, watched Halliday take cautious possession of it.

'While the Defense Secretary is reading, I'll summarize

the conclusions for the rest of you.' The DCI laced his fingers, bent forward like a professor addressing his students. 'We discovered that we had a mole inside CI. His name? Timothy Hytner. It was Hytner who caught Soraya Moore's call informing him that the prisoner was being taken out of his cell. It was Timothy Hytner who called the prisoner's cohorts to effect his escape. Unfortunately for him, a shot meant for Ms. Moore struck him instead, killing him.'

The DCI looked from face to face around the War Room. 'As I said, our internal security is under control. Now we can direct our full attention to where it belongs: stopping Dujja in its tracks and bringing its members to justice.'

His gaze fell upon Secretary Halliday last, lingered there significantly. Here was the origin of the attack, he was certain of it. He'd been warned that Halliday and LaValle wanted to move into the sphere traditionally controlled by CI, which was why he'd concocted the rumors about himself. Over the last six months, during meetings up on Capitol Hill, lunches and dinner with both colleagues and rivals, he'd put in some strenuous acting time, pretending bouts of vagueness, depression, momentary disorientation. His aim was to give the impression that his advanced age was taking its toll on him; that he wasn't the man he'd once been. That he was, at long last, vulnerable to political attack.

In response, as he had hoped, the cabal had come out of the shadows at last. One thing concerned him, however: Why hadn't the president intervened to stop the attack against him? Had he done too good a job? Had the cabal convinced the president that he was on the verge of becoming incompetent to continue as DCI?

The call came at precisely twelve minutes after midnight. Bourne picked up the phone and heard a male voice give him a street corner three blocks from the hotel. He'd had hours to prepare. He grabbed his overcoat and went out the door.

The night was mild, with very little breeze. Now and again, a wisp of cloud scudded across the three-quarter moon. The moon was quite beautiful: very white, very clear, as if seen through a telescope.

He stood at the corner, arms hanging loosely at his side. In the day and a half since his meeting with Yevgeny, he'd done nothing but sightsee. He'd walked endlessly, the activity allowing him the opportunity to check on who was following him, how many there were, how long their shifts were. He'd memorized their faces, could have picked them out of a crowd of a hundred or a thousand, if need be. He'd also had ample time to observe their methodology, as well as their habits. He could imitate any of them. With a different face, he could have been one of them. But that would have taken time, and time was in short supply. One thing disturbed him: There were times when he was certain his followers weren't around – they were between shifts or, as an amusement to pass the time, he'd given them the slip. During those intervals, animal instincts honed on stone and steel told him that he was being observed by someone else. One of Lemontov's bodyguards? He didn't know, since he could never catch a glimpse of him.

The throaty gurgle of a diesel engine rose from behind him. He didn't turn around. With an awful grinding of gears, a *marshrutka* – a routed minibus – pulled up in front of him. Its door opened from the inside, and he climbed in.

He found himself staring into the agate eyes of Bogdan Illiyanovich. He knew better than to ask him where they were going.

The *marshrutka* let them out at the foot of French Boulevard. They walked across the cobblestones beneath towering acacia trees, so familiar to him in memory. At the end of the cobbled street rose the terminus of a cable car that ran down to the beach. He'd been here before, he was certain of it.

Bogdan made his way toward the terminus. Bourne was about to follow him when some sixth sense caused him to turn. He noted that their driver hadn't backed away. He slouched in his seat with his cell phone to his cheek. His eyes flicked left and right, but never lit on either Bourne or Bogdan.

The cable car, like a ride in an amusement park, comprised candy-colored two-person gondolas that hung vertically from the creaking steel cable overhead. The cable was strung high above the green zone, trees and dense shrubbery through which narrow paths and steep steps zigzagged before giving out onto Otrada Beach. In the height of summer, this beach was filled with bronzed bathers and sun worshippers, but at this time of year, this time of day, with an onshore wind whipping up the damp sand, it was nearly deserted. Craning his neck over the iron railing, Bourne could see a large brindled boxer romping in the pale green moonlit foam while its master – a slim man, wide-brimmed hat on his head, hands jammed into the huge pockets of his oversize tweed coat – paced the dog along the beach. A blast of chaotic Russian pop blasted through a pair of tinny speakers, then abruptly was cut off.

'Turn around. Arms at shoulder height.'

Bourne did as Bogdan ordered. He felt the other man's big hands patting him down, searching for weapons or a wire with which to tape the transaction, trap Lemontov. Bogdan grunted, stood back. He lit a cigarette and his eyes went dead.

As they entered the cable car terminus, Bourne saw a black car pull up. Four men got out. Businessmen dressed in cheap Eastern European suits. Except these men looked uncomfortable in their outfits. They looked around, stretched and yawned, then took another look around, during which time they all fastened their gaze on Bourne. Another shock of recognition raced through Bourne. This, too, had happened before.

One of the businessmen took out a digital camera and started snapping photos of the others. Laughter ensued, along with a certain amount of manly banter.

While the businessmen joked and made like sightseers, Bourne and Bogdan waited for the candy-apple-red gondola to reach the concrete terminus. Bourne stood with his back to the fist of men.

'Bodgan Illiyanovich, we're being followed.'

'Of course we're being followed, I'm only surprised you mention it.'

'Why?'

'Do you take me for a fool?' Bogdan took out his Mauser and aimed it casually at Bourne. 'They're your men. You were warned. No second chances. Here is the gondola. Climb in, *tovarich*. When we're out over the green zone, I will kill you.'

At precisely 5:33 PM, the DCI was up in the Library, which was where Lerner found him. The Library was a large, roughly square room with double-height ceilings. It did not, however, contain any books. Not one volume. Every bit of data, history, commentary, strategy, tactic – in sum, the collected wisdom of CI directors and officers past and present – was digitized, housed on the enormous linked hard drives of a special computer server. Sixteen terminals were arrayed around the periphery of the room.

The Old Man had accessed the files on Abu Sarif Hamid ibn Ashef al-Wahhib, the mission instituted by Alex Conklin, the only one in the DCI's knowledge that Bourne had failed to execute. Hamid was owner of a multinational conglomerate refining oil, manufacturing chemicals, iron, copper, silver, steel, and the like. The company, Integrated Vertical Technologies, was based in London, where the Saudi had emigrated when he'd married for the second time, an upper-class

Brit named Holly Cargill, who had borne him two sons and a daughter.

CI – specifically Conklin – had targeted Hamid ibn Ashef. In due course, Conklin had sent Bourne to terminate him. Bourne had run him down in Odessa, but there had been complications. Bourne had shot the Saudi but failed to kill him. With the vast network of operatives at Hamid ibn Ashef's disposal, he'd gone to ground; Bourne had barely made it out of Odessa alive.

Lerner cleared his throat. The Old Man turned around.

'Ah, Matthew, have a seat.'

Lerner dragged over a chair, sat. 'Dredging up old wounds, sir?'

'The Hamid ibn Ashef affair? I was trying to find out what happened to the family. Is the old man alive or dead? If he's alive, where is he? Soon after the Odessa hit cracked open, his younger son, Karim al-Jamil, took over the company. Some time after that, the elder son, Abu Ghazi Nadir al-Jamuh, vanished, possibly to take care of Hamid ibn Ashef. That would be in keeping with Saudi tribal tradition.'

'What about the daughter?' Lerner asked.

'Sarah ibn Ashef. She's the youngest of the siblings. As secular as her mother, so far as we know. For obvious reasons, she's never been on our radar.'

Lerner inched forward. 'Is there a reason you're looking at the family now?'

'It's a loose end that sticks in my craw. It's Bourne's lone failure, and in light of recent events failure is much on my mind these days.' He sat for a moment, his eyes in the middle distance, ruminating. 'I told Lindros to sever all ties with Bourne.'

'That was a wise decision, sir.'

'Was it?' The DCI regarded him darkly. 'I think I made a mistake. One I want you to rectify. Martin is working night and day mobilizing Typhon in tracking down Fadi. You have a different mission. I want you to find Bourne and terminate him.'

'Sir?'

'Don't play coy with me,' the DCI said sharply. 'I've watched you rise up the CI ladder. I know how successful you were in the field. You've done wet work. Even more important, you can get intel out of a stone.'

Lerner said nothing, which was, in its way, an acknowledgment. His silence didn't mean his mind wasn't working a mile a minute. *So this is the real reason he promoted me*, he thought. *The Old Man doesn't care about reorganizing CI. He wants my particular expertise. He wants an outsider to do the one piece of wet work he can't entrust to one of his own.*

'Let's continue then.' The Old Man held up a forefinger. 'I've had a bellyful of this insolent sonovabitch. He's had his own agenda from the moment he first came to us. Sometimes I think we work for him. Witness his taking Cevik out of the cells. He had his reasons, you can bet on it, but he'll never willingly tell us what they were. Just like we know nothing of what happened in Odessa.'

Lerner was taken aback. He was wondering whether he'd underestimated the Old Man.

'You can't mean that Bourne was never fully debriefed.'

The DCI looked aggrieved. 'Of course he was debriefed, along with everyone involved. But he claimed he could remember nothing – not a fucking thing. Martin believed him, but I never did.'

'Give me the word. I can get the truth out of him, sir.'

'Don't fool yourself, Lerner. Bourne will kill himself before he'll give up intel.'

'One thing I learned in the field, anyone can be broken.'

'Not Bourne. Trust me on this. No, I want him dead. That will have to suffice for my pound of flesh.'

'Yessir.'

'Not a word to anyone, including Martin. He's saved

Bourne from the executioner more times than I can count. Not this time, dammit. He said he's severed Bourne. Now go find him.'

'I understand.' Lerner briskly rose.

The DCI lifted his head. 'And Matthew, do yourself a favor. Don't come back without the intel.'

Lerner met his gaze unflinchingly. 'And when I do?'

The Old Man recognized a challenge better than the next man. He sat back, steepled his fingers, tapped the pads together as if in deep contemplation. 'You may not get what you want,' he said. 'But you just might get what you need.'

Bourne climbed into the narrow cabin, and Bogdan followed close behind. The gondola left the terminus and swung out over the steeply dropping limestone cliff.

Bourne said: 'I assumed those men were yours.'

'Don't make me laugh.'

'I'm here alone, Bogdan Illiyanovich. I want only to make a deal with Lemontov.'

The two men's eyes locked for a moment. Between them there was a kind of animus so strong it could actually be felt as a third party. Bogdan's woolen coat stank of mildew and cigarette smoke. There were dandruff flakes on his lapels.

The cable groaned as the steel wheels above the gondola ground along. At the last moment, the four men leapt into the last two gondolas. They continued to make noise, as if they were drunk.

'You wouldn't survive a fall from this height,' Bogdan observed mildly. 'No one would.'

Bourne watched the men behind them.

The sea was restless. Tankers shambled across the harbor, but the ferries, like the gulls, were at rest. Farther out, moonlight frosted the tips of the waves.

On the beach, the boxer was scampering. As it made its way across the gray sand, it lifted its head. Its square muzzle was grizzled with foam and bits of sea kelp. It barked once and was hushed by its master, who patted its flank as they passed under a wooden pier, its greenish pilings creaking in the tide. To the left was a skeletal labyrinth of wooden beams; they held up a part of the green area that at some time in the past had been undermined by the sea. Past that was the line of darkened kiosks, bars, and restaurants that serviced the summer crowds. Down the gentle curve of the beach, perhaps a kilometer to the south, was the yacht club, where lights were burning like the glow from a small village.

The four men from the cable car had arrived on the beach.

Bogdan said, 'Something has to be done.'

The moment he said it, Bourne knew this was another test. A glance told him that the men had disappeared, just like that. But of course he knew they must still be on the beach. Perhaps they were in the wooden framework that held up part of the hillside, or in one of the refreshment kiosks.

He held out his hand. 'Give me the Mauser and I'll go after them.'

'Do you imagine that I'd trust you with a gun? Or trust you to actually shoot them?' Bogdan spat. 'If it's going to be hunting, we'll both do it.'

Bourne nodded. 'I've been here before, I know my way around. Just follow me.' They were crossing the sand, moving diagonally away from the surf. He ducked into the labyrinth, picked up a length of wood, banged it against a pole to judge its sturdiness. He looked at Bogdan to see if the other man would protest, but Bogdan only shrugged. He had the Mauser, after all.

They moved through the shadows in the labyrinth, ducking here and there so as not to hit their heads on low-bolted beams.

'How close are we to our rendezvous with Lemontov?' Bourne whispered.

Bogdan laughed silently. The suspicion hadn't left his eyes.

Bourne had a feeling it was to be on one of the boats anchored in the yacht basin. He returned his attention to peering into the shadows. Ahead of him, he knew, was the first of the kiosks – the place where he'd been before.

They crept ahead, Bourne a pace in front of Bogdan. Moonlight, reflected off the sand, stretched pale fingers into this subterranean world of four-square spars, massive trusses, and crossbeams. They were more or less parallel with the pier, very close to the kiosk now, Bourne knew.

Out of the corner of his eye, he saw a movement, furtive and indistinct. He didn't change direction, didn't turn his head, only moved his eyes. At first, he saw nothing but a jumbled crisscross of shadows. Then, out of the architectural angles, he saw an arc – a curve that could only belong to a human. One, two, three. He identified them all. The men were waiting for them, spread like a spider web in the shadows, placed perfectly.

They knew he was heading here, just as if they could read his mind. But how? Was he going mad? It was as if his memories were leading him into making choices that led to mistakes and danger.

What could he do now? He stopped, started to back up, but at once felt the muzzle of Bogdan's gun in his side, urging him forward. Was Bogdan in on this? Was the Ukrainian part of the conspiracy meant to trap him?

All at once, Bourne broke to his left, toward the beach. He twisted his torso as he ran, threw the length of wood at Bogdan's head. Bogdan dodged it easily, but it delayed his firing, allowing Bourne to dodge behind a spar an instant before a bullet from the Mauser shredded a corner of it.

Bourne feinted right, sprinted left, taking longer strides

with his right leg than with his left in order to keep Bogdan from predicting his pace. Another shot, this one a bit wider of the mark.

A third shot made a ragged hole in his overcoat, which was flared out by his flight. But then he'd reached the pier's first piling and he slipped into shadow.

Bogdan Illiyanovich's breathing increased as he raced after the man calling himself Ilias Voda. His lips were pulled back, baring teeth clenched with the effort of running through sand that became increasingly boggy as he neared the pier. His shoes were coated with sand inside and out, the ends of his overcoat blistered with clumps of it.

The water was frigid. He didn't want to go any deeper, but all at once he caught a glimpse of his prey, and he pressed on. The water rose to his knees, then slapped against his thighs. The tide was coming in, slowing his progress considerably. It was becoming a struggle to—

A sudden sharp noise to his left caused him to wheel around. But the damnable water clawed at his ankle-length woolen coat, slowing him, and at the same time the incoming tide threw him off balance. He stumbled and, in that moment of being physically out of control, he realized why Voda had run this way. It was to deliberately lure him into the water, where his coat would limit his maneuverability.

He began a string of curses, but bit it off as if it were his tongue. In the moonlight, he saw three of the businessmen, guns drawn, sprinting full-tilt toward him.

As he ran on, the lead man aimed and fired.

Bourne saw the men coming before Bogdan did. He was almost upon the Ukrainian when the first shot took a chunk out of the nearest piling. Bogdan was in the process of turning toward him when he slipped. Bourne pulled him back up, swung him around so he was between Bourne and the armed men.

Another of them aimed and fired. A bullet plowed into Bogdan's left shoulder, jerking his body back and to the left. Bourne was ready – he had, in fact, braced himself in the stance of a martial artist: feet at hip width, knees slightly flexed, torso loose and, therefore, ready for the next move. His strength fountained up from his lower belly. He hauled Bogdan's body back around, keeping him as a shield. The three men were quite close now, almost in the surf, spread out in a triangle. Bourne could see them very clearly in the cool moonlight.

Another bullet struck the Ukrainian in the abdomen, almost doubling him over. Bourne brought him back up, aiming Bogdan's Mauser with his own arm, his own hand. He pulled the trigger, his forefinger over Bogdan's. The man on the right, the one closest to him, buckled and went down headfirst. A third bullet struck Bogdan in the thigh, but by that time Bourne had squeezed off another shot. The man in the middle flew backward, his arms spread wide.

Bourne dragged Bogdan to the right. Two more bullets missed the Ukrainian's head by centimeters. Then Bourne squeezed off another shot, missed. The third man came on in a wild zigzag pattern, firing as he neared, but he was in the increasingly rough surf now and his balance was off. Bourne shot him between the eyes.

In the ringing aftermath, Bourne became aware of an animal stirring, a faint wriggling as Bogdan drew a second gun strapped beneath his overcoat. He'd lost the first one somewhere in the water, which was black and full of the sea-weedy plumes of his own blood. Bourne chopped down with the edge of his hand, and the gun flew from the Ukrainian's hand, vanishing into the restless sea.

He reached up and with the strength of the damned closed

his hands around Bourne's neck. An incoming wave brought Bourne to his knees. Bogdan groped with his thumbs to crush the cartilage of Bourne's throat. Bourne jammed the heel of his hand into one of the bullet wounds. Bogdan's head went back as he screamed.

Bourne rose, staggering, delivered a final blow that took Bogdan off his feet, hurled him backward. The side of his head slammed against a piling, and blood spewed out of his mouth.

He looked at Bourne for a moment. A little smile curled the corners of his mouth.

'Lemontov,' he said.

There was now no other sound on the beach save for the waves running hard at the pilings. No thrum of a ship's engine, no other earthly noise, until the boxer gave a whining bark, as if in distress.

Then Bogdan began a gurgling laugh.

Bourne grabbed him. 'What's so damn funny, Bogdan Illiyanovich?'

'Lemontov.' The Ukrainian's voice was thin, insubstantial, like air being released from a balloon. His eyes were rolling up, yet still he fought to say this one last thing. 'There is no Lemontov.'

Bourne, letting the corpse sink into the water, sensed someone coming at him fast out of the shadows. He whirled to his left. The fourth man!

Too late. He felt a searing pain in his side, then a gush of warmth. His assailant began to twist the knife. He shoved the man away with both his hands and the knife the man had buried in his side released, spewing a line of blood.

'He was right, you know,' the man said. 'Lemontov is a ghost we conjured up for you to chase.'

'We?'

His assailant came forward. Moonlight, creeping between the planks of the pier, revealed a face, strangely familiar.

'You don't recognize me, Bourne.' His grin was as feral as it was venomous.

But with a shock, recalling the face Martin Lindros had sketched for him, Bourne did.

'Fadi,' he said.

FIFTEEN

'I've waited a long time for this moment,' Fadi said. He held a Makarov in one hand, a bloody snake-bladed knife in the other.

'A long time to look you in the face again.'

Bourne felt the tide sucking and drawing around his thighs. He held his left arm hard against his side in an effort to stanch the bleeding.

'A long time to exact my revenge.'

'Revenge,' Bourne echoed. There was a metallic taste in his mouth, and all at once he was possessed with a burning thirst. 'For what?'

'Don't pretend you don't know. You couldn't have forgotten – not that.'

The tide was strengthening as it came in, bringing with it larger clumps of kelp and seaweed. Without taking his eyes off Fadi's, Bourne's right hand dipped beneath the water, scooped up a fistful of the floating morass. Giving no warning at all, he threw the soaked ball directly at Fadi's head. Fadi fired blindly at almost the same instant the seaweed-kelp mass struck him in the face.

Bourne was already moving, but the tide that had been his ally against Bogdan and Fadi's men now betrayed him as a strong wave struck him obliquely. He stumbled, pain lanced through him, his left arm came away from his wound, and the blood began to flow again.

By this time, Fadi had recovered. As he held Bourne

square in the Makarov's sights, he loped toward him through the waves, flicking the serpent-bladed knife with which he clearly meant to carve Bourne up.

Bourne struggled to recover, to keep moving to his right, away from Fadi's attack, but another wave struck him full in the back, pitching him directly toward the oncoming blade.

At that moment he heard a guttural animal growl close by. The brindled boxer leapt through the water, slamming its muscular body into Fadi's right side. Taken completely by surprise, Fadi went down, pitched into the water, the boxer on top of him, snapping its jaws, raking him under with its forepaws.

'Come on, come on!'

Bourne heard the whispered voice in the darkness beneath that pier. Then he felt an arm, slim but strong, come around him, urging him off to his left, a winding, shadowy path between the mossy pilings, out into the moonlight.

He gasped. 'I have to go back and—'

'Not now.' The whispered voice was firm. It came from the slender man with the wide-brimmed hat he'd seen on the beach – the boxer's master. The man gave a whistle and the dog came bounding out from under the pier, paddling through the water toward them.

And then Bourne heard the wail of sirens. Someone from the nearby yacht club must have heard the repeated sound of gunfire and called the police.

So he lumbered on, the helping arm around him, the pain throbbing hotly and agonizingly with every step he took, as if the blade were still being twisted inside him. And with every beat of his heart, he lost more blood.

When Fadi, choking and sputtering, broke the surface, the first thing he saw through reddened eyes was Abbud ibn Aziz, who was leaning over the low rail of a sailboat running without lights. The boat, heeled over slightly, had taken advantage of the onshore breeze to move in closer to land than many powerboats could without running aground.

Abbud ibn Aziz held out a strong, browned arm. His forehead was furrowed in concern. As Fadi clambered onto the deck, Abbud ibn Aziz called out. The mate, who was already at the sheets, hauled the yardarm, causing the sailboat to tack away from the shore.

Just in time. As they turned, Fadi could see what had caused Abbud ibn Aziz's concern. Three police launches had just turned the headland to the north and were speeding toward the area surrounding the pier.

'We'll make for the yacht club,' Abbud ibn Aziz said in Fadi's ear. 'By the time they're close enough to scrutinize the area, we'll be safely berthed.' He said nothing of the three men. They weren't here, clearly they weren't coming. They were dead.

'Bourne?' he asked.

'Wounded, but still alive.'

'How bad?'

Fadi lay on his back, wiping blood off his face. That damn dog had bitten him in three places, including his right biceps, which felt as if it were on fire. His eyes glowed like a wolf's in the moonlight. 'Bad enough, perhaps, that he'll end up as damaged as my father.'

'A just fate.'

The lights from the yacht club were coming up fast on the bow. 'The documents.'

Abbud ibn Aziz handed over a packet wrapped in waterproof oilskin.

Fadi took possession of the packet, turned on his side, spat into the water. 'But is it a just revenge?' His head moved from side to side as he answered his own question. 'I don't think so, no. Not yet.'

*

This way, this way!' the urgent voice said in Bourne's ear. 'Don't slacken now, it's not far.'

Not far? he thought. Every three steps he took felt like a kilometer. His breathing was labored and his legs felt like stone columns. It was becoming more and more difficult to keep them moving. Waves of exhaustion swept over him and from time to time he lost his balance, pitching forward. The first time took his companion by surprise. He was facedown in the water before he was hauled back into the humid Odessa night. Thereafter, he was saved from the same watery fate.

He tried to lift his head, to see where they were, where they were headed. But keeping himself moving through the water was struggle enough. He was aware of his companion, aware of a peculiar familiarity that spread across the surface of his mind like an oil slick. Yet like an oil slick he couldn't see beneath it, couldn't decide who this person was. Someone from his past. Someone . . .

'Who are you?' he gasped.

'Come on now!' the whispered voice urged him. 'We must keep on. The police are behind us.'

All at once he became aware of lights dancing in the water. He blinked. No, not in the water, *on* the water. The wave-smeared reflections of electric lights. Somewhere in the back of his head a bell rang, and he thought, *Yacht club.*

But his curiously familiar companion turned them toward land before they got to the northern end of the network of piers, berths, and slatted walkways. With immense effort, they staggered into the surf. Once, Bourne went to his knees. Furious, he was about to hurl himself to his feet when his companion kept him in position. He felt something soft being wrapped around his torso so tight it nearly took his breath away. Around and around until he lost count. The pressure did its job. He stopped bleeding, but the moment he got to his feet and they continued up the sideline and onto the sand, a small stain appeared, spreading slowly, soaking into the material. Still, he wouldn't leave a bloody trail on dry land. Whoever his companion was, he was both clever and brave.

On the beach, he became aware of the boxer, a huge brindled male with the magnificent face of royalty. They had passed the end of the line of kiosks. At the land side of the beach, bare rock towered over them, silent, frowning. Directly in front of them he saw a waist-high wooden shed, painted dark green, closed and padlocked, where beach umbrellas were stored.

The boxer emitted a short, sharp whine, and his rear end began to twitch anxiously.

'Quickly now! Quickly!'

Half bent over, they scrambled forward. From the water rose the thrumming of powerful marine engines, and all at once the beach to their right was ablaze with the intense glare of spotlights, directed from the police launches. The beams swept the beach, coming directly toward them. In a moment, they'd be revealed.

They tumbled to the landward side of the umbrella lockbox, crouched, pressing their bodies against it. Here came the beams, swiping back and forth across the sand. For a nerve-racking moment, the lockbox was caught square in the nexus of the spotlights. Then they had moved on.

But there was shouting from the police launches, and now Bourne could see that another police unit had begun to infiltrate the yacht club. The men wore steel helmets, flak vests. They carried semiautomatic rifles.

His companion pulled urgently on him, and they ran on toward the base of the cliff. Bourne felt naked and vulnerable as they crossed the upper portion of the beach. He knew he lacked the strength to defend himself, let alone both of them.

Then a push on his back took him off his feet. Facedown

in the sand, his companion beside him, he saw more beams of light bobbing through the night, perpendicular to the searchlights from seaside. Several policemen at the yacht club were scanning the beach with their flashlights. The beams passed over the two prone bodies with scarcely twenty centimeters to spare. There was movement in the periphery of his vision. A contingent of policemen were jumping down from the wharves onto the sand. They were coming this way.

Acting on a silent signal from his companion, Bourne crawled painfully into the shadow of the naked cliff face where the dog crouched, waiting. Turning back, he saw that his companion had taken off his overcoat and was using its skirt behind him to cover the tracks they had made in the sand.

He stood, panting, weaving on his feet like a wrestler who'd gone one too many rounds against a superior opponent.

He saw his companion on his knees, gripping the thick iron bars of what appeared to be a sewage outlet. The shouting increased in volume. The police were moving closer.

He bent over to help and together they pulled out the grille. He saw that someone had already removed the bolts.

His companion shoved him inside, the boxer loping excitedly at his side. He watched his companion follow. As the man ducked down, his wide-brimmed hat came off. He twisted to retrieve it and moonlight shone on the face.

Bourne sucked in a sharp breath, which caused an explosion of pain.

'You!'

For the person who'd saved him, whose manner was so familiar to him, wasn't a man at all.

It was Soraya Moore.

SIXTEEN

At 6:46 pm, Anne Held's PDA began to vibrate. This was her personal PDA, a gift from her Lover, not the one issued to her by CI. When she grabbed it, the black housing was warm from the outside of her thigh, where she had it strapped. On its screen appeared this message, like the writing of a genie: TWENTY MINUTES. HIS APARTMENT.

Her heart raced, her blood sang, because the message was from a genie of sorts: her Lover. Her Lover had returned.

She told the Old Man she had an appointment with her gynecologist, which made her laugh inside. In any event, he took it in stride. HQ was like a hospital ER: They'd all been working nonstop for hours, ever since Lindros had placed them on emergency status.

She exited the building, called for a taxi, took it to within six blocks of Dupont Circle. From there, she walked. The high moonlit sky, without any clouds to speak of, brought with it a knifing wind that intensified the cold. Anne, hands jammed in her pockets, felt warm inside, despite the weather.

The apartment was on 20th Street, in a historic four-story nineteenth-century house in the Colonial Revival style, designed by Stanford White. She was buzzed through a wood-framed beveled-glass door. Beyond was a wainscoted hallway that ran straight through the center of the building, ending in a rear glass-and-wood-framed door that looked out onto a narrow, minimally landscaped area between buildings used as a private parking lot.

She stopped at the bank of mailboxes, her fingertips running over the vertically hinged brass door with 401: MARTIN LINDROS stenciled on it.

On the fourth landing, in front of the cream-colored door, she paused, one hand on the thick wood. It seemed to her that she could feel a subtle vibration, as if the apartment, so long vacant, was humming with newfound life. Her Lover's body, warm and electric, inhabited the rooms beyond the door, flooding them with energy and a magnified heat, like sunlight through glass.

Into her mind came the moment of their last parting. It carried with it the same pain, sharp as an indrawn breath on a freezing night that shot between her ribs, inflicting another wound to her heart. And yet this time the pain had also been different, because she'd been certain not to see him for a minimum of nine months. In fact, today would make it just shy of eleven. Yet it wasn't only the matter of time – bad enough – but also the knowledge of the changes that would be effected.

Of course she had put that fear away in a cupboard in the far recesses of her mind, but now, here in front of the apartment door, she understood that it was a weight she had been carrying like an unwanted child for all these months.

She leaned forward, pressing her forehead against the painted wood, remembering their parting.

'*You look so troubled,*' he had said. '*I've told you not to worry.*'

'*How can I not?*' she'd replied. '*It's never been done before.*'

'*I've always thought of myself as something of a pioneer.*' He smiled encouragement. Then, seeing that fail, he enfolded her in his arms. '*Extreme times require extreme measures. Who better than you to understand this.*'

'*Yes, yes. Of course.*' She had shuddered. '*Still, I can't help but wonder what will happen to us on . . . the other side.'*

'Why should anything change?'

She had pushed away from him just enough so that she could look into his eyes. *'You know why,'* she had whispered.

'No, I don't. I will be the same, just the same inside. You must trust me, Anne.'

Now here she was – here they both were – on the other side. This was the moment of truth, when she would discover what changes had been wrought in him by those eleven months. She did trust him, she did. Yet the fear she'd been living with now unleashed itself, slithered in her lower belly. She was about to enter the great unknown. There was no precedent, and she was genuinely frightened that she would find him so altered, he would no longer be her Lover.

With a low growl of self-disgust, she turned the brass knob of the door and pushed it open. He'd left it unlatched for her. Walking into the entryway, she felt like a Hindu, as if her path had been set for her long ago and she lived in the grip of a destiny that outstripped her, that outstripped even him. How far she was from the privileged upbringing her parents had foisted upon her. She had her Lover to thank for that. She had come partway, it was true, but her rebelliousness had been reckless. He had tamed that, turned it into a focused beam of light. She had nothing to fear.

She was about to call out when she heard his voice, the ululating song she had come to know so well floating to her as if on a personal current of air. She found him in the master bedroom on one of Lindros's carpets because of course he could not carry one of his own.

He was on his knees, feet bare, head covered with a white skullcap, his torso bent over so that his forehead pressed against the low nap of the carpet. He was facing toward Mecca, praying.

She stood very still, as if any movement would disturb

him, and let the Arabic flow over her like a gentle rain. She was fluent in the language – in a number of the many dialects, a fact that had intrigued him when they'd first met.

At length, the prayer came to an end. He rose and, seeing her, smiled with Martin Lindros's face.

'I know what you want to see first,' he said softly in Arabic, pulling his shirt over his head.

'Yes, show me all of it,' she answered in the same language.

There was the body she knew so well. Her eyes took in his abdomen, his chest. Traveling up, they met his eyes – his altered right eye with its new retina. Martin Lindros's face, complete with Lindros's right retina. It was she who had provided the photos and retinal scans that had made the transformation possible. Now she studied the face in a way she hadn't been able to at work on those two occasions when he'd passed by her on his way in and out of the Old Man's office. Then they had acknowledged each other with a brief nod, exchanging hellos, as she would have done with the real Martin Lindros.

She marveled. The face was perfect – Dr. Andursky had done a magnificent job. The transformation was everything he'd promised, and then some.

He put his hands up to his face, laughing softly as he touched the bruises, abrasions, and cuts. He was very pleased with himself. 'You see, the "rough treatment" I received from my "captors" was calculated to conceal what little remains of the scars Andursky's scalpel made.'

'Jamil,' she whispered.

His name was Karim al-Jamil ibn Hamid ibn Ashraf al-Wahhib. *Karim al-Jamil* meant 'Karim the beautiful.' He allowed Anne to call him Jamil because it gave her so much pleasure. No one else would even think of such a thing, let alone dare to say it.

Without ever taking her eyes off his face, she shrugged off

her coat and jacket, unbuttoned her shirt, unzipped her skirt. In the same slow, deliberate manner, she unhooked her bra, rolled down her underpants. She stood in high heels, shimmering stockings, lacy garter belt, her heart thrilling to see his eyes drinking her in.

She stepped out of the soft puddle her clothes made and walked toward him.

'I've missed you,' he said.

She came into his arms, fit her bare flesh against him, moaned low in her throat as her breasts flattened against his chest. She ran the palms of her hands along the largest of his muscles, her fingertips tracing the small hillocks and hollows she had memorized the first night they'd spent together in London. She was a long time at it. He didn't rush her, knowing she was like a blind person assuring herself that she had entered familiar territory.

'Tell me what happened. What did it feel like?'

Karim al-Jamil closed his eyes. 'For six weeks it was terribly painful. Dr. Andursky's biggest fear was infection while the grafted skin and muscles healed. No one could see me, except him and his team. They wore rubber gloves, a mask over their mouths and noses. They fed me one antibiotic after another.

'After the retinal replacement, I couldn't open my right eye for many days. A cotton ball was taped over the lowered lid, and then a patch over that. I was immobilized for a day, my movements severely limited for ten days after that. I couldn't sleep, so they had to sedate me. I lost track of time. No matter what they injected into my veins, the pain wouldn't stop. It was like a second heart, beating with mine. My face felt like it was on fire. Behind my right eye was an ice pick I couldn't remove.

'That's what happened. That's what it felt like.'

She was already climbing him, as if he were a tree. His hands came down to grasp her buttocks. He backed her against the wall, pressing her against it, her legs wrapped tightly, resting on his hipbones. Fumbling at his belt, he pushed down his pants. He was so hard it hurt. She cried out as he bit her, cried out again as his pelvis tilted, thrust upward.

In the kitchen, Anne, her bare skin pleasantly raised in goose bumps, poured champagne into a pair of crystal flutes. Then she dropped a strawberry into each, watching the drizzle of fizz as they bobbed. The kitchen was on the western side of the building. Its windows looked out onto a courtyard between buildings.

She handed him one of the flutes. 'I can still see your mother in the coloring of your skin.'

'Allah be praised. Without her English blood I would never have been able to pass for Martin Lindros. His great-grandfather came from a town in Cornwall not eighty kilometers from my mother's family estate.'

Anne laughed. 'Now, that's irony.' It felt as if, so long deprived of the feel of his flesh, her hands could caress him for all eternity. Putting her flute on the granite counter, she grabbed him, pushed him playfully backward until he was against the window. 'I can't believe we're both here together. I can't believe you're safe.'

Karim al-Jamil kissed her forehead. 'You had doubts about my plan.'

'You know I did. Doubts and fears. It seemed to be so . . . reckless, so difficult to pull off.'

'It's all a matter or perception. You must think of it as a clock. A clock performs a simple function, measuring off the seconds and minutes. And when the hour strikes, it lets forth a chime. Simple, yet reliable. That's because inside are a set of carefully conceived parts, honed and polished, so that when they are set in motion, they mesh perfectly.'

It was at this moment that he saw her gaze shift beyond him. A terrible light came into her eyes.

He turned, stared out the window at the parking lot between the buildings. Two late-model American cars were side by side, headed in opposite directions. The north-facing car was idling. Both drivers' windows were rolled down. It was clear two men were talking.

'What is it?'

'The two cars,' she whispered. 'That's a cop formation.'

'Or any two drivers who want to chat.'

'No, there's something—'

Anne bit off her words. One of the men was leaning out of the window enough for her to recognize him.

'That's Matthew Lerner. Dammit!' She shivered. 'I haven't had a chance to tell you, but he broke into my house, went through it, and left a noose in my closet strangling a pair of my underpants.'

Karim al-Jamil choked off a bitter laugh. 'He's got a sense of humor, I'll give him that. Does he suspect?'

'No. He would have gone to the DCI if he had even an inkling. What he wants is me out of the way. I strongly suspect it's so he can take an uncontested shot at the Old Man's job.'

Down in the parking lot, whatever had needed to be said between the two men was finished. Lerner, in the north-facing car, drove away, leaving the other man sitting behind the wheel of his vehicle. He made no move to turn on his engine. Instead, he lit a cigarette.

Karim al-Jamil said, 'In either case, he's having you followed. Our security has been compromised.' He turned away from the window. 'Get dressed. We have work to do.'

The moment the sailboat pulled into the yacht club, police jumped aboard and, as was typical of them, began to swarm.

The captain and mates, including Abbud ibn Aziz, looking suitably cowed, produced their identity documents for the officious lieutenant. Then he turned to Fadi.

Without a word, without looking in the least bit intimidated, Fadi handed over the documents Abbud ibn Aziz had given him. They identified him as Major General Viktor Leonidovich Romanchenko, counterintelligence SBU. His orders, attached, were signed by Colonel General Igor P. Smeshko, chief of SBU.

It amused Fadi to see this smug police lieutenant come so smartly to attention, all the blood draining from his face. It was an instant transformation: The overlord had become the servant.

'I'm here to track down a murderer, a high-priority fugitive from justice,' Fadi said, repossessing his cunningly forged papers. 'The four men on the sideline were murdered by him, so you see for yourself how dangerous, how highly skilled he is.'

'I am Lieutenant Kove. We are at your full command, Major General.'

Fadi led the lieutenant and his men off the sailboat at a fast trot. 'A word of caution,' he said over his shoulder. 'I will personally execute anyone who kills the fugitive. Inform all your men. This criminal is mine.'

Detective Bill Overton sat in his car, smoking. He was relaxed, happier than he'd been in a year. This off-the-books job he'd taken on for Lerner had been a godsend. When it was over, Lerner had guaranteed him he'd have that position in Homeland Security he so desperately wanted. Overton knew Lerner wasn't yanking his chain. This was a man of devious power. He said what he meant and he meant what he said. All that the detective had to do was whatever Lerner ordered without asking the whys and wherefores. Easy for him; he didn't give a rat's ass what Lerner was up to. He cared only that the man was his ticket to HS.

Overton chewed on his cigarette. HS meant everything to him. What else did he have? A wife he was indifferent to, a mother with Alzheimer's, an ex-wife he hated, and a couple of kids poisoned by her into disrespecting him. If he didn't have his work, he had nothing of value.

Which, he supposed, was the way it worked best in law enforcement.

He might be smoking and musing, but he hadn't forgotten his training. He had been checking the environment every fifteen seconds like clockwork. He was positioned so that he had a clear view of the building's hallway through the re-inforced glass-and-wood rear door, all the way to the front entrance. It was a beautiful setup, which he'd exploited to the max.

Now he saw Anne Held coming out of the elevator. She turned, heading down the hall toward the rear door. She was hurrying, a frown of concern on her face. He watched as she swept out of the rear door. She looked as if she'd been crying. As she neared, he noticed that her face was red and puffy looking. What had happened to her?

Not that it mattered to him. His mandate was to follow her wherever she went, at some point give her a scare – sideswiping her car, a quick mugging on an otherwise deserted street. Something she wouldn't soon forget, Lerner had told him. Cold bastard, Overton thought. He admired that.

As Anne strode past, he got out of his car, ditched his cigarette, and with hands jammed into the pockets of his overcoat followed her at a safe distance. Between the build-ings, there was no one about. Just the woman and him. He couldn't possibly lose her.

Up ahead, his target had reached the end of the area between the buildings. She turned the corner onto

Massachusetts Avenue NW, and Overton lengthened his stride so as not to lose her.

Just then something knocked him sideways so hard he was taken off his feet. His head slammed into the brick wall of the neighboring building. He saw stars. Even so, instinct made him reach for his service revolver. But his right wrist was struck with such a blow that the hand was rendered useless. Blood covered one side of his face. One ear was half torn off. He turned, saw a male figure looming over him. On hands and knees, he tried to reach his revolver. But a powerful kick to his ribs turned him over like a tortoise in the dust.

'What . . . what . . . ?'

It was all a blur. An instant later his assailant was pointing a gun, affixed with an air-baffled silencer.

'No.' He blinked up into the pitiless face of his killer. He was ashamed to discover he wasn't above begging. 'No, please.'

A sound filled his ears, as if his head had been submerged in water. To anyone else it was as soft as a discreet cough; to him it was loud enough to make him believe that the world had been torn apart. Then the bullet entered his brain and there was nothing but a terrible, all-encompassing silence.

The problem now,' Soraya said as she and Bourne fit the grille back into place, 'is how to get you to a doctor.'

On the beach, they could hear the shouts of the policemen. There were more of them now. Possibly the police launches had tied up at the yacht club so their personnel could join in the hunt. Powerful searchlights crisscrossed the area visible to them through the grille. In that rather poor illumination, Soraya took her first close look at the wound.

'It's deep, but seems clean enough,' she told him. 'Clearly, it hasn't punctured an organ. Otherwise you'd be flat on your back.' The question that plagued her, that she couldn't answer, was how much blood he had lost, therefore how much his stamina might be affected. On the other hand, she'd seen him go full-out for thirty-six hours with a bullet lodged in his shoulder.

'It was Fadi,' he said.

'What? He's here?'

'Fadi was the one who stabbed me. The boxer—'

'Oleksandr.' At the sound of his name, the dog's ears pricked up.

'Fadi was the one you sicced him on.'

They were alone, isolated in a hostile environment, Soraya thought. Not only was the beach crawling with Ukrainian police, but now Fadi was stalking them as well. 'What is Fadi doing here?'

'He said something about revenge. For what, I don't know. He didn't believe me when I told him I couldn't remember.'

Bourne was white-faced and sweating. But she had witnessed the depth of his inner strength, his determination not only to survive but to succeed at all costs. She gathered strength from him, leading him away from the grille. With only the fast-diminishing cone of pale moonlight to guide them, they hurried, stumbling down the tunnel.

The air was gritty. It smelled as lifeless as a snake's shed skin. All around them were little creaks and moans, as if spirits in distress were trying to make themselves heard. Packed earth filled in spots where the sandstone had been partially quarried or had split beneath the crushing weight from above. Massive six-by-six rough-hewn beams, bound with iron, black with mold, here and there sporting a dark reddish crust, rose at intervals, bolted to joists and headers. The passageways smelled of rot and decomposition, as if the earth through which they wound were in the process of slowly dying.

Soraya's stomach clenched painfully. What had the police found? What had she forgotten? Dear God, let it be nothing.

Odessa was the site of her worst mistake, a nightmare that had haunted her day and night. Now fate had put her and Bourne here together again. She was bound and determined to make up for what had gone before.

Oleksandr roamed ahead of them, muzzle to the ground, as if following his nose. Bourne followed without complaint. His entire torso felt as if it had burst into flame. He had to reach back for his training, maintain slow deep breaths even when it seemed most painful. He had assumed Soraya had found an outlet of the city's sewer, but there was neither the stench nor the seepage associated with such a system. Besides, they were moving steeply downward. Then he remembered that much of Odessa had been built with blocks of the underlying sandstone, resulting in an immense network of catacombs. During World War II, partisans used the catacombs as a base when launching guerrilla raids against the invading German and Romanian armies.

Soraya had come prepared: She now switched on a strong battery-powered xenon light strapped to her wrist. Bourne was not reassured at what he saw. The catacombs were very old. Worse, they were in disrepair, in desperate need of shoring up. Here and there, the two of them were obliged to climb over a fall of rock and debris, which slowed their progress considerably.

From behind them they heard a grinding sound of metal against metal, as if an enormous rusted wheel was being forced into use. They stopped in their tracks, half turned.

'They've found the grate,' Soraya whispered. 'There was no way to replace the screws that fastened it in place. The police are in the tunnel.'

'He's a cop.' Karim al-Jamil was holding Overton's open wallet in his hand. 'A detective, no less, in the Metro Police.'

Anne had driven Overton's car to where he lay slumped

253

against the wall of the building. The pallid brick was discolored with his blood.

'Clearly he was on Lerner's payroll,' she said. 'He might've been the one who broke into my house.' She regarded his crude, horsey face. 'I'll bet he got off on it.'

'The question we need to answer,' Karim al-Jamil said as he rose, 'is how many more individuals does Matthew Lerner have on his payroll?'

He gestured with his head, and Anne popped the trunk. Stooping down, Karim al-Jamil picked Overton up, grunting. 'Too many doughnuts and Big Macs.'

'Like all Americans,' Anne said, watching him dump the body into the trunk, slam down the lid. She slid out from behind the wheel, went over to the garden hose on its reel bolted to the brick. Turning on the spigot, she played the stream of water over the wall, sluicing it free of Overton's blood. She had felt no remorse at his death. On the contrary, the spilling of his blood made her feel inside her chest the beating of a second heart, filled with hatred for Western society: the waste, the selfishness of the moneyed, the privileged, the American celebristocracy so self-involved in reproducing themselves they were deaf, dumb, and blind to the world's poorest. This feeling, she supposed, had always been with her. Her mother had, after all, been first a model, then an editor for *Town & Country*. Her father had been born into money and aristocracy. No surprise that Anne had been embedded in a life filled with chauffeurs, butlers, personal assistants, private jets, skiing in Chamonix, clubbing in Ibiza, all within the boundaries set by her parents' bodyguards. Someone to do everything for you that you ought to be doing for yourself. It was all so artificial, so out of touch with reality. Life as a prison she couldn't wait to flee. Her pointed rebelliousness had been her way of expressing that hatred. But it had taken Jamil to make her brain understand what her emotions had been telling her. The clothes she wore here –

expensive designer fashions – were part of her cover. Inside them, her skin itched as if she were covered in fire ants. At night, she threw them off as quickly as she could, never looked at them again until she donned them in the morning.

With these thoughts boiling in her head, she got back into the car. Karim al-Jamil slid in beside her. Without hesitation, she pulled out onto Massachusetts Avenue.

'Where to?' she asked.

'You ought to go back to CI,' Karim al-Jamil said.

'So should you,' she pointed out. Then she looked him in the eye. 'Jamil, when you recruited me I was no starry-eyed idealist, wanting to wage war on inequality and injustice. That's what you thought of me at first, I know. I doubt you realized then that I had a brain that could think for itself. Now I hope you know better.'

'You have doubts.'

'Jamil, orthodox Islam works against women. Men like you are brought up believing that woman should cover their heads, their faces. That they shouldn't be educated, shouldn't think for themselves, and Allah help them if they begin to think of themselves as independent.'

'I wasn't brought up that way.'

'Thank your mother, Jamil. I mean it. It was she who saved you from believing that it was all right to stone a woman to death for imagined sins.'

'The sin of adultery is not imagined.'

'It is for men.'

He was silent, and she laughed softly. But it was a sad laugh, tinged with disappointments and disillusionment dredged up from the core of her. 'There is more than a continent that separates us, Jamil. Is it any wonder I'm terrified when the two of us are apart?'

Karim al-Jamil eyed her judiciously. For some reason he found it impossible to be angry with her. 'This is not the first time we've had this discussion.'

'And it won't be the last.'

'Yet you say you love me.'

'I *do* love you.'

'Despite what you see as my sins.'

'Not sins, Jamil. We all have our blind spots, even you.'

'You're dangerous,' he said, meaning it.

Anne shrugged. 'I'm not any different from your Islamic women, except I recognize the strength inside me.'

'This is precisely what makes you dangerous.'

'Only to the status quo.'

There was silence for a moment. She had pushed him farther than anyone else would dare. But that was all right. She'd never fed him bullshit like most of the others circling him to gain a measure of his influence and power. It was times like these that she wished she could crawl inside his mind, because he'd never willingly tell her what he was thinking, even by his expression or body language. He was something of an enigma, which in part was why she had been drawn to him in the first place. Men were usually so transparent. Not Jamil.

At length, she put a hand lightly over his. 'You see how much like a marriage this is? For better or for worse, we're in it together. All the way to the end.'

He contemplated her for a moment. 'Drive east by southeast. Eighth Street, Northeast, between L and West Virginia Avenue.'

Fadi would have been happy to put a bullet through Lieutenant Kove's head, but that would have led to all manner of complications he couldn't afford. Instead he contented himself with playing his part to the hilt.

This was hardly difficult; he was a born actor. His mother, recognizing his talent with a mother's unerring instinct, had enrolled him in the Royal Theatrical Academy when he was seven. By nine, he was an accomplished performer, which stood him in good stead when he became radicalized. Gathering followers – winning the hearts and minds of the poor, the downtrodden, the marginalized, the desperate – was, at bedrock, a matter of charisma. Fadi understood the essential nature of being a successful leader: It didn't matter what your philosophy was; all you needed to concern yourself with was how well you sold it. That was not to say Fadi was a cynic – no radical worth his salt could be. It simply meant he had learned the crucial lesson of market manipulation.

These thoughts brought the ghost of a smile to his full lips as he followed the bobbing police searchlights.

'These catacombs are two thousand kilometers long,' Lieutenant Kove said, trying to be helpful. 'A honeycomb all the way to the village of Nerubaiskoye, half an hour's drive from here.'

'Surely not all of the catacombs are passable.' Fadi had taken in the cracked and rotting wooden beams, walls that bulged alarmingly in places, offshoots blocked by debris falls.

'No, sir,' Lieutenant Kove said. 'They run short tours out of the museum in Nerubaiskoye, but of those who venture down here on their own the percentage of dead and missing is exceedingly high.'

Fadi could feel the anxiety mounting in the contingent of three policemen Lieutenant Kove had chosen to accompany them. He realized that Kove continued to talk in order to damp down on his own nervousness.

Anyone else would have picked up this agitation from his companions, but Fadi was incapable of feeling fear. He approached new and perilous situations with the steely confidence of a mountain climber. The possibility of failure never entered his mind. It wasn't that he didn't value life; it wasn't only that he didn't fear death. In order to feel alive, it was necessary to drive himself to extremes.

'If the man is wounded, as you told me, he can't get far,' Lieutenant Kove said – though whether this was for Fadi's benefit or that of his jumpy men wasn't entirely clear. 'I have some expertise in this place. This close to the water, the catacombs are particularly susceptible to falls and cave-ins. We must also watch out for slurry pits. The seepage in some spots is so bad that it has undermined the integrity of the floor. These pits are particularly dangerous because they act like quicksand. A man can be pulled under in less than a minute.'

The lieutenant broke off abruptly. Everyone in their contingent was standing stock-still. The point man was half turned toward them. He made a gesture indicating that he'd heard something from up ahead. They waited, sweating.

Then it came again: a soft scraping sound as of leather against stone. A boot heel?

The lieutenant's expression had changed. It now resembled a hunting dog that had scented its prey. He nodded, and silently they moved forward.

Anne drove Detective Overton's car through increasingly destitute neighborhoods, cruising past intersections with burned-out traffic lights and lewdly defaced street signs. It was fully dark now, winter's ashy twilight having fallen by the wayside, along with neat row houses, clean streets, museums, and monuments. This was another city on another planet, but it was one with which Karim al-Jamil was all too familiar and in which he felt comfortable.

They drifted down 8th Street until Karim al-Jamil pointed out a double-width cement block building on which a faded sign was still affixed: M&N BODYWORK. At his direction, Anne swung onto a cracked cement apron, stopping in front of the metal doors.

He jumped out. As they walked up the apron, he took a long, lingering look around. The shadows were deep here where few streetlights remained. Illumination came in fits and starts from the headlights of cars passing on L Street NE, to the north and West Virginia Avenue to the south. There were only two or three cars parked on this block, none of them near where they stood. The sidewalks were clear; the windows of the houses dark and blank.

He opened a large padlock with a key taken from beneath a small section of cracked concrete. Then he rolled up the door and signaled Anne.

She put the car in gear. When she was abreast of him, she rolled down her window.

'Last chance,' he said. 'You can walk away now.'

She said nothing, didn't budge from behind the wheel.

He searched her eyes in the firefly light of the passing cars, looking for the truth. Then he waved her into the abandoned body shop. 'Roll up your sleeves, then. Let's get to work.'

'I hear them,' Soraya whispered. 'But I can't see their lights yet. That's a good sign.'

'Fadi knows I'm wounded,' Bourne said. 'He knows I can't outrun them.'

'He doesn't know about me,' Soraya said.

'Just what do you intend?'

She rubbed Oleksandr's brindled coat, and he nuzzled her knee. They had come to a division, where the passable cata-comb branched into a Y. Without hesitation, she led them into the left-hand tunnel.

'How did you find me?'

'The way I'd shadow any target.'

So it was Soraya he'd sensed following him, even when Yevgeny Feyodovich's men were off duty.

'Besides,' she went on, 'I know this city inside and out.'

'How?'

'I was chief of station here when you arrived.'

'When I . . . ?'

Instantly his mind filled with memory . . .

. . . Marie comes to him, in a place of mature acacia trees and cobbled streets. There is a sharp mineral tang in the air, as of a restless sea. A humid breeze lifts her hair off her ears, and it streams behind her like a banner.

He speaks to her. 'You can get me what I want. I have faith in you.'

There is fear in her eyes, but also courage, and determination. 'I'll be back soon,' she says. 'I won't let you down.' . . .

Bourne staggered under the assault of the memory. The acacia trees, the cobbled street: It was the approach to the cable car terminal. The face, the voice: It wasn't Marie he was speaking with. It was . . .

'Soraya!'

She gripped him now, fearing he'd lost so much blood that he couldn't continue.

'It was you! When I was in Odessa years ago, I was here with you!'

'I was the agent in place. You wanted nothing to do with me, but in the end you had no choice. It was my conduit who was funneling the intel you needed to get to your target.'

'I remember talking to you under the acacia trees on French Boulevard. Why was I here? What the hell happened? It's driving me crazy.'

'I'll fill in the blanks.'

He stumbled. With a strong hand, she pulled him upright.

'Why didn't you tell me we'd worked together when I first walked into the Typhon ops center?'

'I wanted to—'

'That look on your face—'

'We're almost there,' Soraya said.

'Where?'

'The place where you and I holed up before.'

They were now perhaps a thousand meters down the left-hand fork. Conditions looked particularly bad here. Cracked beams and seeping water were everywhere. The catacomb itself seemed to emit a terrible groaning sound, as if forces were threatening to pull it apart.

He saw that she had led him toward a gap in the left wall. It wasn't an offshoot at all, but a section that had been worn away by seepage, as the tide will create a cove over time. But quickly they were confronted by a debris fall that filled the space almost to the top.

He watched as Soraya climbed the mound, slithering on her belly through the space between the top of the fall and the ceiling. He followed her, each step, each reach upward bringing a fresh stabbing pain to his side. By the time he wormed through, his entire body seemed to throb with the beat of his heart.

Soraya led him on, down a dogleg to the right, where they came upon what could only be called a room, with a raised plank platform for a bed, a thin blanket. Opposite were three smaller planks nailed between two wooden pillars on which several bottles of water and tins of food were arrayed.

'From the last time,' Soraya said as she helped him onto the plank bed.

'I can't stay here,' Bourne protested.

'Yes, you can. We have no antibiotics and you need a full dose, the sooner the better. I'm going to get some from the CI doctor. I know and trust her.'

'Don't expect me to just lie here.'

'Oleksandr will stay with you.' She rubbed the boxer's shiny muzzle. 'He'll guard you with his life, won't you, my little man?' The dog seemed to understand. He came and sat by Bourne, the tiny pink tip of his tongue showing between his incisors.

'This is crazy.' Bourne swung his legs over the side of the makeshift bed. 'We'll go together.'

She watched him for a moment. 'All right. Come on.'

He pushed himself off the planks, and got to his feet. Or rather he tried to, his knees buckling as soon as he let go his grip on the plank. Soraya caught him, pushed him back onto the bed.

'Let's can that idea, okay?' She rubbed her knuckles absently between Oleksandr's triangular ears. 'I'm going back to the fork in the catacombs. I need to take the right fork to get to the doctor, but I'll do it with just enough noise that they'll follow me, assuming it's the two of us. I'll lead them away from you.'

'It's too dangerous.'

She waited a moment. 'Any other ideas?'

He shook his head.

'Okay, I won't be long, I promise. I won't leave you behind.'

'Soraya?'

She faced him in profile, her body already half turned to go.

'Why didn't you tell me?'

She hesitated for a split second. 'I figured it was better all around that you couldn't remember how badly I'd fucked up.'

He watched her leave, her words echoing in his head.

A rugged fifteen-minute march brought them to a cross-roads.

'We're at a major juncture,' Lieutenant Kove said as their searchlights probed the beginnings of the Y.

Fadi didn't like hesitation. To him, indecision was a sign of weakness. 'Then we need an educated guess, Kove, as to which fork he took.' His eyes bored into the policeman's.

'You're the expert. You tell me.'

In Fadi's presence, it was nearly impossible either to disagree or to remain inactive. Kove said, 'The right fork. That's the one I'd choose if I were in his position.'

'Very well,' Fadi said.

They entered the right fork. It was then that they heard the sound again, the scrape of leather on stone, more distinct this time and repeated at regular intervals. There could be no doubt that they were hearing footfalls echoing down the shaft. They were gaining on their quarry.

With a grim determination, Kove urged his men on. 'Quickly, now! In a moment we'll overtake him.'

'One moment.'

They were brought up short by the cold voice of authority.

'Sir?'

Fadi thought for a moment. 'I need one of those searchlights. You continue on the course you laid out. I'm going to see what I can find down the left fork.'

'Sir, I hardly think that wise. As I told you—'

'I never need to be told anything twice,' Fadi said shortly. 'This criminal is devilishly clever. The sounds might be a feint, a way to throw us off their scent. In all probability, with the man having lost so much blood, you'll overtake him in the right fork. But I can't leave this other possibility unexplored.'

Without another word, he took the light one of Kove's men offered and, backtracking several paces to the juncture of the Y, headed down the left-hand fork. A moment later, his snake-bladed knife was in his hand.

SEVENTEEN

Karim al-Jamil, in thick rubber apron and heavy work gloves, pulled the cord that started the chain saw. Under cover of its horrific noise, he said, 'Our objective to detonate a nuclear device in a major American city has been a decade in conception and planning.' Not that he suspected there to be a microphone in sight, but his training would not allow him to relax his strict code of security.

He approached the corpse of Detective Overton, which lay on a zinc-topped table inside the eerie hollow interior of M&N Bodywork. A trio of purplish fluorescent lights sizzled above their heads.

'But to ensure that we'd have the highest percentage for success,' Anne Held said, 'you needed Jason Bourne to be able to vouch for you when you became Martin Lindros. Of course, he'd never do that willingly, so we needed to find a way to manipulate and use him. Since I had access to Bourne's file, we were able to exploit his one weakness – his memory – as well as his many strengths, like loyalty, tenacity, and a highly intelligent, paranoid mind.'

Anne was also bound into an apron. She gripped a hammer in one gloved hand, a wide-headed chisel in the other. As Karim al-Jamil went to work on Overton's feet and legs, she placed the chisel into the crease on the inner side of the left elbow, then brought the hammer down in a quick, accurate strike onto the chisel's head. The body shop was once again alive with industry, as it had been in its happy heyday.

'But what was the trigger mechanism that would allow you access to Bourne's weakness?' she asked.

He gave her a thin smile as he concentrated on his grisly work. 'My research on the subject of amnesiacs provided the answer: Amnesiacs react most strongly to emotionally charged situations. We needed to give Bourne a nasty shock, one that would jar his memory.'

'Is that what you did when I told you that Bourne's wife had died suddenly and unexpectedly?'

With his forearm, Karim al-Jamil wiped a thick squirt of blood off his face. 'What do we Bedouins say. Life is but Allah's will.' He nodded. 'In his grief, Bourne's sickness of memory threatened to overwhelm him. So I instructed you to present him with a cure.'

'Now I see.' She turned away momentarily from an eruption of gas. 'Naturally, it had to come from his friend Martin Lindros. I gave Lindros the name and address of Dr. Allen Sunderland.

'But in fact the phone call came to us,' Karim said. 'We set up Bourne's appointment for a Tuesday, the day of the week when Sunderland and his staff aren't there. We substituted our own Dr. Costin Veintrop, who posed as Sunderland.'

'Brilliant, my darling!' Anne's eyes were shining with her admiration.

There was a large oval tub made of galvanized steel into which the body parts were dropped, one by one, like the beginnings of an experiment in Dr. Frankenstein's laboratory. Karim al-Jamil kept one eye on Anne, but she neither flinched nor blanched at what she was doing. She was going about her business in a matter-of-fact manner that both pleased and surprised him. One thing she was right about: He had underestimated her right down the line. The fact was, he was unprepared for a woman who exhibited the attributes of a man. He had been used to his sister, meek and subservient.

Sarah had been a good girl, a credit to the family; in her slim form, all their honor had resided. She had not deserved to die young. Now revenge was the only way to win back the family honor that had been buried with her.

In the culture of his father, women were excluded from anything a man had to do. Of course, Karim al-Jamil's mother was an exception. But she hadn't converted to Islam. Mysteriously to Karim al-Jamil, his father had neither cared nor forced her to convert. He seemed to take great pleasure in his secular wife, though she had made for him a great many enemies among the imams and the faithful. Even more mysteriously to Karim al-Jamil, he didn't care about that, either. His mother mourned for their lost daughter, and he, the crippled old man, engulfed every day by her grief, was forced to mourn, too.

'What exactly did Veintrop do to Bourne?' Anne asked.

Happily bisecting a knee joint, Karim replied, 'Veintrop is an unheralded genius in memory loss. It was he whom I consulted regarding Bourne's amnesiac state. He used an injection of certain chemically engineered proteins he designed to stimulate synapses in parts of Bourne's brain, subtly altering their makeup and function. The stimulation acts as a trauma, which Veintrop's research revealed can alter memories. Veintrop's protein injection is able to affect *specific* synapses, thus creating *new* memories. Each individual memory is designed to be triggered in Bourne's head by certain outside stimuli.'

'I'd call that brainwashing,' Anne said.

Karim nodded. 'In a sense, yes. But in a whole new sphere that doesn't involve physical coercion, weeks of sensory deprivation, and articulated torture.'

The oval basin was almost full. Karim signaled to Anne. Together they laid their tools on Overton's chest – which, other than his head, was about all that was left whole.

'Give me an example,' she said.

Together they hoisted the basin by its oversize handles and moved it over to a large dry well that in earlier times had been used to illegally dump used motor oil.

'The sight of Hiram Cevik triggered an "added" memory in Bourne – the tactic of showing a prisoner the freedom he'd lost as a means of getting him to talk. Otherwise he would never have taken Fadi out of the cells for any reason whatsoever. His action accomplished two things at once: It allowed Fadi to escape, and it put Bourne under suspicion by his own organization.'

They tipped the basin. Out tumbled the contents, vanishing down the dry well.

'But I didn't feel that a single added memory was enough to slow Bourne down,' Karim said, 'so I had Veintrop add an element of physical discomfort – a debilitating headache whenever an added memory is triggered.'

As they were carrying the receptacle back to the table, Anne said, 'This much is clear. But wasn't it unconscionably dangerous for Fadi to allow himself to be captured in Cape Town?'

'Everything I design and do is by default dangerous,' said Karim al-Jamil. 'We're in a war for the hearts, minds, and future of our people. There's no action too perilous for us. As for Fadi, first of all he was posing as the arms dealer Hiram Cevik. Second of all, he knew that we had arranged for Bourne to unwittingly rescue him.'

'And what if Dr. Veintrop's procedure hadn't worked, or hadn't worked properly?'

'Well, then, we always had you, my darling. I would have provided you with instructions that would have extracted my brother.'

He switched on the chain saw, made short shrift of the remains. Into the dry well they went. 'Fortunately, we never had to implement that part of the plan.'

'We assumed Soraya Moore would call the DCI to clear

267

Bourne's request to release Fadi,' Anne said. 'Instead she called Tim Hytner to inform him that he should meet her outside on the grounds. She told him exactly where Fadi would be. Since I was monitoring all her calls, you were able to set the rest of the escape plan in motion.'

Karim picked up a can of gasoline, unscrewed the cap, poured a third of the contents into the dry well. 'Allah even provided us with the perfect scapegoat: Hytner.'

Pulling off the car's gas cap, he splashed most of what was left in the can into the car's interior. No forensics team was going to get anything out of what would be left. Pointing to the rear entrance, he backed away from the car, pouring a trail from the can as he went.

They both bellied up to the oversize soapstone sink, stripped off their gloves, and washed the blood off their arms and cheeks. Then they untied their aprons and dropped them onto the floor.

When they were at the door, Anne said, 'There's still Lerner to consider.'

Karim al-Jamil nodded. 'You'll have to watch your back until I decide how to handle him. We can't deal with him the way we did Overton.'

He lit a match and dropped it at his feet. With a whoosh, blue flame sprang up, rushed headlong toward the car.

Anne opened the door, and they walked out into ghetto darkness.

Way before M&N Bodywork burst into flames, Tyrone had the man and woman in his sights. He'd been crouched on a stone wall, deep in the shadows of an old oak that spread its gnarled branches in a domed Medusa's nest. He had on black sweats, and his hoodie was up over the back of his head. He'd been hanging, waiting for DJ Tank to bring a pair of gloves because, damn, it was cold.

He'd been blowing on his hands when the car had drawn up in front of the ruins of M&N Bodywork. For months, he'd had his eye on the place: He was hoping it had been abandoned, and he coveted it as a base for his crew. But six weeks ago, he'd been told of some activity there, late at night when any legitimate business was shut down, and he'd taken DJ Tank over for a look-see.

Sure enough, people were inside. Two bearded men. Even more interestingly, there was another bearded man posted outside. When he'd turned, Tyrone had clearly seen the glint of a gun at the man's waist. He knew who wore beards like that: either Orthodox Jews or Arab extremists.

When he and DJ Tank had sneaked around to the side and peered in through a grimy window, the men were outfitting the place with canisters, tools, and some kind of machinery. Though the electricity had been restored, clearly no renovations were being contemplated, and when the men left, they'd locked the front door with an immense padlock that Tyrone's expert eye knew was unbreakable.

On the other hand, there was the back door, hidden in a narrow back alley, which hardly anyone knew about. Tyrone did, though. There wasn't hardly anything in his turf he didn't know about or could get info on at a moment's notice.

After the men had left, Tyrone had picked the lock on the back door, and they went in. What did he find? A mess of power tools, which told him nothing about the men and their intentions. But the canisters, now they were another story entirely. He inspected them one by one: trinitrotoluene, penthrite, carbon disulfide, octogen. He knew what TNT was, of course, but he'd never heard of the others. He'd called Deron, who'd told him. Except for carbon disulfide, they were all high-level explosives. Penthrite, also known as PETN, was used as the core in detonator fuses. Octogen, also known as HMX, was a polymer-bonded explosive, a solid like

C-4. Unlike TNT, it wasn't sensitive to motion or vibration.

From that night on the incident had sat in his mind like a squalling baby. Tyrone wanted to understand what that baby was saying, so he'd staked out M&N Bodyworks, and tonight his vigilance was rewarded.

Lookee here: a body on the zinc-topped table in the center of the floor. And a man and a woman in aprons and work gloves were cutting the damn thing up as if it were the carcass of a steer. What some people got up to! Tyrone shook his head as he and DJ Tank peered through the smeared glass of the side window. And then he felt a small shock ping the back of his neck. He recognized the face of the corpse on the table! It was the man who had followed Miss S a couple of days ago, the one she said she'd take care of.

He watched the man and the woman at their work, but after the shock of recognition he paid no attention to what they were doing. Instead he spent his time more advantageously memorizing their faces. He had a feeling Miss S would be very interested in what these two were up to.

Then the night lit up, he felt an intense heat on his cheek, and flames gushed out of the building.

Fire – or more accurately arson – was no stranger to Tyrone, so he couldn't say he was shocked, merely saddened. He'd lost the use of M&N Bodywork for sure. But then a thought occurred to him, and he whispered something to DJ Tank.

When they'd snuck into the place the first time, the interior had been stocked with all manner of explosives and accelerants. If the chemicals had still been inside, the explosion would have taken out the entire block, him and DJ Tank with it.

Now he asked himself: If the explosives weren't inside, where the fuck were they?

*

Secretary of Defense E. R. 'Bud' Halliday took his meals at no fixed time of the day or night. But unless summoned by the president for a policy skull session or to take the current temperature of the Senate, unless jawboning with the vice president or the Joint Chiefs, he took his meals in his limousine. Save for certain necessary pit stops of various sorts, the limousine, like a shark, was never at rest, but continued to roll through the streets and avenues of D.C. undisturbed.

Matthew Lerner enjoyed certain privileges in the secretary's company, not the least of which was to break bread with Bud, as he was about to do this evening. In the world outside the tinted-glass windows, the hour was early for dinner. But this was the secretary's world; dinner was bang on time.

After a short prayer, they dug into their plates of Texas barbeque – massive beef ribs, a deep, glossy red; baked beans with bits of fiery chile peppers in them; and, in the lone concession to the vegetable kingdom, steak fries. All of this was washed down with bottles of Shiner Blonde, proudly brewed, as Bud would say, in Fort Worth.

Finished in jig time, the secretary wiped his hands and mouth, then grabbed another bottle of Blonde and sat back. 'So the DCI hired you to be his personal assassin.'

'Looks that way,' Lerner said.

The secretary's cheeks were flushed, gleaming with a lovely sheen of beef fat. 'Any thoughts about that?'

'I've never backed down from either a job or a dare,' Lerner said.

Bud glanced down at the sheet of paper Lerner had handed him as he'd climbed into the limo. He'd already read it, of course; he did it for effect, something at which the secretary was very good.

'It took some doing, but I found out where Bourne is. His face came up on the closed-circuit security cameras at Kennedy International.' Bud looked up, sucked a shred of charred beef from between his molars. 'This assignment's going to take you to Odessa. That's quite a far piece from CI headquarters.'

Lerner knew the secretary meant it was going to take him away from the mission Bud had sent him on in the first place. 'Not necessarily,' he said. 'I do this for the Old Man and he owes me big time. He'll know it and I'll know it. I can leverage that.'

'What about Held?'

'I've put someone I can trust on Anne Held.' Lerner mopped the last of the thick, spicy sauce with a slice of Wonder Bread. 'He's a dogged sonovabitch. You'd have to kill him to get him to let go.'

Bourne dreamed again. Only this time, he knew it was no dream. He was reliving a shard of memory, another piece of the puzzle clicking into place: *In a filthy Odessa alleyway, Soraya is kneeling over him. He hears the bitter regret in her voice. 'That bastard Tariq ibn Said had me fooled from the outset,' she says. 'He was Hamid ibn Ashef's son, Nadir al-Jamuh. He gave me the information that led us into this trap. Jason, I fucked up.'*

Bourne sits up. Hamid ibn Ashef. He had to find his target, shoot him dead. Orders from Conklin. 'Do you know where Hamid ibn Ashef is now?'

'Yes, and this time the intel's straight,' Soraya says. 'He's at Otrada Beach.'

Oleksandr stirred, nudging Bourne's thigh with his blunt black muzzle. Bourne, blinking the memory from in front of his eyes, struggled to concentrate on the present. He must have fallen asleep, even though he'd meant to stay vigilant. Oleksandr had been vigilant for him.

Propped up on the planks in the tiny underground cell, he saw the ominous pearling of the darkness. The boxer's neck fur bristled. Someone was coming!

Ignoring the flood of pain, Bourne swung his legs over the side. It was too soon for Soraya to be coming back. Leaning against the wall, he levered himself to his feet, stood for a moment, feeling Oleksandr's warm, muscular form against him. He was still weak, but he'd spent his time productively, going into energizing meditation and deep breathing. His forces might be weakened by blood loss, but he was still able to marshal them.

The change in the light was still faint, but now he could confirm that it wasn't coming from a fixed source. It was bobbing up and down, which meant that it was being held by someone coming toward him down the tunnel.

Beside him, Oleksandr, the fur at the ruff of his neck standing straight up, licked his lips in anticipation. Bourne rubbed the place between his ears, as he'd seen Soraya do. Who was she, really? he asked himself. What had she meant to him? The little reactions to him she'd had when he'd first come into the Typhon offices, seeming odd then, now made sense. She'd expected him to remember her, to remember their time here. What had they done? Why had it taken her out of the field?

The light was no longer formless. He had no more time to ponder his fractured memory. It was time to act. But as he began to move, a wave of vertigo caused him to stagger. He grasped the stone wall as his knees buckled. The light brightened and there was nothing he could do.

Fadi, moving along the left-hand branch, kept his ears open for even the smallest sound. Each time he heard something, he swung the light in its direction. All he saw were rats, red-eyed, skittering away with a flick of their tails. There was an acute sense in him of unfinished business. The thought of his father – his brilliant, robust, powerful father – reduced to a drooling shell, bound into a wheelchair, staring at a gray infinity, was like a fire in his gut. Bourne had done that, Bourne and the woman. Not so far from here, and so close to being shot to death by him. He had no illusions when it came to Jason Bourne. The man was a magician – changing his appearance, materializing as if out of nowhere, vanishing just as mysteriously. In fact, it was Bourne who had inspired his own chameleon-like changes of identity.

His life's work had changed the moment the shot Bourne had fired lodged in his father's spine. The bullet had caused instant paralysis. Worse, the trauma had brought on a stroke, robbing his father of the ability to speak, or to think coherently.

Fadi had internalized his radical philosophy. As far as his followers were concerned, nothing had changed. But inside, he knew it had. Since his father's maiming at the hands of Jason Bourne, he had his own personal agenda, which was to inflict the worst possible damage on Bourne and Soraya Moore before he killed them. A quick death for them was intolerable. He knew that, and so did his brother, Karim al-Jamil. The living death of their father had bonded them in a way nothing else could. They became one mind in two bodies, dedicated to the revenge they would wreak. And so they had applied their prodigious minds to the task.

Fadi – born Abu Ghazi Nadir al-Jamuh ibn Hamid ibn Ashef al-Wahhib – passed a hole in the passageway on his left. Up ahead, his light picked out passageways left and right. He went several meters down each of them without finding a sign of anyone.

Deciding he'd been wrong after all, he turned back, heading toward the fork. He was hurrying now to catch up with Lieutenant Kove and his men. He desperately needed to be in on the kill. There was always the chance that in the heat of battle, his express orders to keep Bourne alive would be forgotten.

He'd just passed the hole in the passageway when he paused. Turning, he probed the darkness with his light. He saw nothing out of the ordinary, but he ventured in anyway. Quite soon, he came to the debris fall. He saw the bulging walls, the substantial cracks in the stone, the groaning wooden beams. The place was a mess, undoubtedly unsafe.

Playing the beam of light over the debris, he saw that there was a small gap between the top of it and the ceiling of the chamber. He was just contemplating whether it was wide enough for a man to slither through when he heard the gunfire echoing through the catacombs.

They've found him! he thought. Turning on his heel, he emerged into the main passageway, heading for the fork at a dead run.

EIGHTEEN

Soraya, flying down the passageway, felt stone fragments from the ricochets whiz by her. One struck her shoulder, almost made her cry out. She pulled it out of her on the run, dropped it for her pursuers to find. She was determined to protect Bourne, to atone for the dreadful mistake in judgment she'd made the last time they'd been in Odessa.

She had switched off her light and was traveling by memory alone, which was far from the ideal way to make her way through these catacombs. Still, she knew she had no choice. She had been counting her strides. By her calculations, rough though they might be, she was five kilometers from the fork. Another two klicks to the access nearest Dr. Pavlyna's house.

But first she'd have to negotiate three turns, another branching. She heard something. An instant later the catacombs behind her were briefly, though dimly, lit. Someone had picked up her trail! Taking advantage of the light to orient herself, she dashed into a tunnel on her right. Blackness, the sounds of pursuit for the moment muted.

Then the toe of her right shoe struck something. She stumbled, pitched forward onto hands and knees. She could feel the ground rise irregularly just in front of her, and her heart clenched. It could only mean a new debris fall. But how extensive was it? She'd have to risk turning on her light, if only for a second or two.

This she did, clambering up and over the new fall, continuing on. She heard no more sounds of pursuit. It was entirely possible that she'd eluded the police, but she couldn't count on it.

She kept going, pushing herself. Around the second turn to the left she went, then the third. Approximately a kilometer ahead, she knew, was the second branching. After that, she was home free.

Fadi discovered that the police had not only caught sight of Bourne but fired at him. Without asking Kove's permission, he struck the offending officer a terrible blow that nearly cracked his skull. Kove stood red-faced, biting his lip. He said nothing, even when Fadi ordered them on. Several hundred meters farther, Fadi spotted a stone shard, shiny with blood in the floodlights. He picked it up, closed his fist around it, and was heartened.

But now, this far into the catacombs, he knew that following in a pack made no sense. He turned to Kove and said, 'The longer he stays in the catacombs, the greater his chance of eluding us. Split up the men, let them fan out singly as they would in a forest in enemy territory.'

He could see that Kove's men were rapidly losing their nerve – and that their anxiety was spreading to their commander. He had to get them moving now or it would happen not at all.

He drew close to Kove, whispering in the lieutenant's ear: 'We're losing the race against time. Give the order now, or I will.'

Kove jerked as if coming in contact with a live wire. He retreated a pace, licked his lips. For a moment, he seemed mesmerized by Fadi. Then, with a minute shiver, he turned to his men and delivered the order for them to fan out, one man to a passageway or arm.

*

Soraya sensed the branching up ahead. A wisp of fresh air brushed her cheek like a lover's caress: the access point. Darkness behind her. It was very damp. She could smell the rot as the underground water worked on the earth and wood, decomposing it bit by bit. She risked another flicker of light. She ignored the weeping walls, because she saw the Y juncture less than twenty meters directly ahead. Here she needed to take the left branch.

At that moment a splinter of light probed the passage behind her. At once she extinguished her light. Her pulse throbbed in her temples; her heart raced. Had her pursuer seen the light up ahead and realized she was here? Though she needed to continue, she nevertheless could not allow Dr. Pavlyna to be compromised. The doctor was CI, under deep cover.

She stood still, turned so that she could see the way she had come. The light was gone. No, there it was again, a tiny beacon in the pitch blackness, less diffuse now. Someone was, indeed, coming down this part of the catacombs.

Slowly, she began to back up, edging away from her pursuer, moving cautiously toward the Y juncture, never taking her eyes from the bobbing stab of light. She kept moving, trying to decide what to do. Then it was too late.

Her back foot broke the soft surface of the catacomb floor. She tried to shift her weight forward, but the suck of the disintegrated floor pulled her backward, and down. She flung out her arms for balance, but it wasn't enough. She had already sunk into the ooze to the level of her thighs. She began to struggle.

A sharp brightening brought the passageway into sudden focus. A black blob resolved itself into a familiar shape: a Ukrainian policeman, massive-looking in the confided space.

He saw her, his eyes widened, and he drew his gun.

*

At precisely 10:45 PM Karim al-Jamil's computer terminal chimed softly, reminding him that the second of his twice-daily briefings with the DCI was fifteen minutes away. This concerned him less than the mysterious disappearance of Matthew Lerner. He'd asked the Old Man, but the bastard had only said that Lerner was 'on assignment.' That could mean anything. Like all the best schemers, Karim al-Jamil hated loose ends, which was precisely what Matthew Lerner had become. Even Anne didn't know where the man was, an oddity in itself. Normally, she would have booked Lerner's itinerary personally. The DCI was up to something. Karim al-Jamil could not discount the possibility that Lerner's sudden disappearance had something to do with Anne. He'd have to find out, as quickly as possible. That meant dealing directly with the DCI.

The monitor chimed again: time to go. He scooped up the translations of the latest Dujja chatter the Typhon team had compiled, picking up a couple more as he stepped out of his office. He read them on his way up to the DCI's suite.

Anne was waiting for him, sitting behind her desk in her usual formal pose. Her eyes lit up for a tenth of a second when he appeared. Then she said, 'He's ready for you.'

Karim al-Jamil nodded, strode past her. She buzzed him into the enormous office. The DCI was on the phone, but he waved Karim al-Jamil in.

'That's right. All stations to remain on highest alert.'

It seemed clear he was talking to the chief of Operations Directorate.

'The director of the IAEA was briefed yesterday morning,' the DCI continued, after listening for a moment to the voice on the other end. 'Their personnel have been mobilized and are temporarily under our aegis. Yes. The chief problem now is keeping Homeland Security from screwing up the works. No, as of now we're maintaining a strict news blackout on all of this. The last thing we need is the media instigating a panic among the civilian population.' He nodded. 'All right. Keep me informed, night or day.'

He put down the receiver, motioned for Karim al-Jamil to take a seat. 'What d'you have for me?'

'A break, finally.' Karim al-Jamil handed over one of the sheets he'd been given on exiting his office. 'There's unusual activity with Dujja's signature coming out of Yemen.'

The DCI nodded as he studied the intel. 'Specifically Shabwah, in the south, I see.'

'Shabwah is mountainous, sparsely populated,' Karim al-Jamil said. 'Perfect for building an underground nuclear facility.'

'I agree,' the Old Man said. 'Let's get Skorpion units there ASAP. But this time I want ground assist.' He grabbed the phone. 'There are two battalions of Marine Rangers stationed in Djibouti. I'll get them to send in a full company to coordinate with our personnel.' His eyes were alight. 'Good work, Martin. Your people may have provided us with the means to nip this nightmare in the bud.'

'Thank you, sir.'

Karim al-Jamil smiled. The Old Man would have been right, had the intel not been disinformation his people at Dujja had put out into the airwaves. Though the wilds of Shabwah did indeed make an excellent hiding place – one that he and his brother had once considered – the actual location of Dujja's underground nuclear facility was, in fact, nowhere near South Yemen.

Soraya was lucky in one sense, though at first blush it failed to impress her: Veins of metal in the walls of the catacombs made it impossible for the policeman to contact the rest of his contingent. He was on his own.

Regaining her composure, she ceased to move. Her struggling had only served to work her body deeper into the slurry pit in the catacombs' floor. She was up to her crotch in muck, and the Ukrainian policeman was strutting toward her.

It was only when he neared her that she realized just how frightened he was. Maybe he'd lost a brother or a daughter to the catacombs, who knew? In any event, it was clear that he was all too aware of the multiple dangers that lurked in every corner of the tunnels. He saw her now where he'd been imagining himself ever since he'd been ordered inside.

'For the love of God, please help me!'

The policeman, as he approached the edge of the pit, played the beam of light over her. She had one arm in front of her, the other behind her back.

'Who are you? What are you doing here?'

'I'm a tourist. I got lost down here.' She began to cry. 'I'm afraid. I'm afraid I'll drown.'

'A tourist, no. I've been told who you are.' He shook his head. 'For you and your friend, it's too late. You're both in too deep.' He drew his gun, leveled it at her. 'Anyway, you're both going to die tonight.'

'Don't be so sure,' Soraya said, shooting him through the heart with the ASP pistol.

The policeman's eyes opened wide, and he fell backward as if he were a cardboard target on a firing range. He dropped the light, which rang onto the floor and immediately went out.

'Shit,' she said under her breath.

She stowed the ASP back in its shoulder holster. She'd drawn it the moment she'd regained her equilibrium, had been holding it behind her back as the policeman approached. Now her first order of business was to reach his feet. She lowered her upper torso into the muck, trying to splay herself out horizontally. This maneuver also had the effect of moving her closer to her objective.

Float, she thought. *Float, dammit!*

She let her legs go slack, using the strength in her upper body only to inch forward, arms stretched out in front of her to their farthest extent. She could feel the muck sucking at her, reluctant to release her legs and hips. She fought down another wave of panic, set her mind firmly on moving one inch at a time. In the darkness, it was more difficult. Once or twice she thought she was already under, already dead.

Then her fingers encountered rubber: boot soles! Squirming another centimeter or two brought her enough purchase to grasp the policeman's boots. She took a deep breath, hauled with all her might. She didn't move, but he did. His feet and legs angled down into the pit. That was it, though; his huge body wouldn't budge another millimeter.

It was all she needed. Using his corpse as a makeshift ramp, she slowly but surely pulled herself hand over hand up his legs until she could grasp his wide belt with both her palms. In this way, she slowly pulled herself the rest of the way out of the slurry pit.

For a moment, she lay atop him, feeling the thunder of her heart, hearing the breath sigh in and out of her lungs. At length, she rolled away, onto the damp floor of the catacombs, and regained her feet.

As she feared, his light was beyond repair. Wiping off her own, she prayed that it still worked. A feeble beam flickered on, off, on again. Now that she had more leverage, she was able to roll the policeman into the pit. She scuffed at the floor, kicking dirt and debris over whatever blood had leaked from him.

Knowing the light's batteries were running down, she hurried into the left-hand fork, heading toward the access point nearest Dr. Pavlyna's house.

At the second refueling stop, the plane carrying Martin Lindros took on a new passenger. This individual sat down next to Lindros and said something in the Bedouin-inflected Arabic of Abbud ibn Aziz.

'But you are not Abbud ibn Aziz,' Lindros said, turning his head in the way of a blind man. He still wore the black cloth hood.

'No, indeed. I am his brother, Muta ibn Aziz.'

'Are you as good at maiming human beings as your brother is?'

'I leave such things to my brother,' Muta ibn Aziz said rather sharply.

Lindros, whose sense of hearing had been honed by his lack of sight, heard the note; he thought he could exploit the emotion behind it. 'Your hands are clean, I imagine.' He sensed the other studying him, as if he'd just stumbled upon a new species of mammal.

'My conscience is clear.'

Lindros shrugged. 'It doesn't matter to me that you're lying.'

Muta ibn Aziz struck him across the face.

Lindros tasted his own blood. He wondered dimly if his lip could swell any more than it already had. 'You have more in common with your brother than you seem to think,' he said thickly.

'My brother and I could not be more different.'

There was an awkward silence. Lindros realized that Muta had revealed something he regretted. He wondered what dispute lay between Abbud and Muta, and whether there was a way to exploit it.

'I've spent some weeks with Abbud ibn Aziz,' Lindros said. 'He has tortured me then, when that didn't work, he tried to become my friend.'

'Hah!'

'That was my response also,' Lindros said. 'All he wanted was how much I knew about the shooting of Hamid ibn Ashef.'

He could hear Muta's body shift, could feel him moving closer. When Muta spoke again, his voice was barely audible over the drone of the engines. 'Why would he want to know about *that*? Did he tell you?'

'That would have been stupid.' Lindros's internal antenna was focused now on what had just happened. The mention of the Hamid ibn Ashef incident was obviously of extreme importance to both brothers. Why? 'Abbud ibn Aziz may be many things, but stupid isn't one of them.'

'No, he's not stupid.' Muta's voice had hardened into steel. 'But a liar and a deceiver, now that is another matter.'

Karim al-Jamil bin Hamid ibn Ashraf al-Wahhib, the man who for the past few days had passed for Martin Lindros, was in the process of worming his way into the CI mainframe, where every iota of sensitive data was stored. The problem was, he didn't know the access code that would unlock the digital gateway. The real Martin Lindros had failed to cough up his access code. No surprise there. He'd devised an alternative that was as elegant as it was efficient. Trying to hack into the CI mainframe was useless. People more talented than he was at geek-logic had tried and failed. The CI firewall – known as Sentinel – was notorious for its vault-like properties.

The problem was then how to get into a hackproof computer for which you lacked an access code. Karim knew that if he could shut down the CI mainframe, the CI tech people would issue everyone – including him – new access codes. The only way to do that was to introduce a computer virus into the system. Since that couldn't be done from the outside – because of Sentinel – it had to be done from the inside.

Therefore, he had needed an absolutely foolproof way to

get the computer virus into the CI building. Far too dangerous for him or Anne to smuggle it in; and there were too many safeguards for it to be done another way. No. It could not even be brought into the building by a CI agent. This was the problem he and Fadi had spent months trying to solve.

Here was what they had come up with: The cipher on the button the CI agents had found on Fadi's shirt wasn't a cipher at all, which was why Tim Hytner had gotten nowhere in trying to break it. It was step-by-step instructions on how to reconstruct the virus using ordinary computer binary code – a string of root-level commands that worked in the background, totally invisible. Once reconstructed on a CI computer, the root-level commands attacked the operating system – in this case, UNIX – corrupting its basic commands. The process would create wholesale havoc, rendering the CI terminals inoperative in the space of six minutes.

There was a safeguard, too, so that even if by some fluke of luck Hytner tumbled to the fact that it wasn't a cipher, he couldn't inadvertently begin the chain of instructions – because they were reversed.

He brought up the computer file Hytner was working on, typed in the binary string in reverse, saved it to a file. Then he exited the Linux OS and went into C++ computer language. Pasting the chain of instructions into this set up the steps he needed to build the virus in C++.

Karim al-Jamil, staring at the virus, needed only to depress one key to activate it. In a tenth of a second it would insinuate itself into the operating system – not simply the main pathways, but also the byways and cross-connections. In other words, it would clog and then corrupt the data streams as they entered and exited the CI mainframe, thus bypassing Sentinel altogether. This could only be accomplished on a networked computer *inside* CI, because Sentinel would stop any extra-network attack, no matter how sophisticated, dead in its tracks.

First, however, there was one more matter that required his attention. On another screen, he brought up a personnel file and began affixing to it a string of irrefutable artifacts, including the cipher he was using to create the virus.

This done, he made hard copies of the file, put the pages in a CI dossier, locked it away. With one fingertip, he cleared the screen, brought up the program that had been patiently awaiting its birth. Exhaling a small sigh of satisfaction, he depressed the key.

The virus was activated.

NINETEEN

Abbud ibn Aziz, alone with the waves and his darkening thoughts, was the first to see Fadi emerge from the hole where the grate had been. It had been more than three hours since he and the police contingent had gone in. Attuned to the facial expressions and body language of his leader, he knew at once that Bourne hadn't been found. This was very bad for him, because it was very bad for Fadi. Then the policemen stumbled out, gasping for breath.

Abbud ibn Aziz heard Lieutenant Kove's plaintive voice. 'I've lost a man in this operation, Major General Romanchenko.'

'I've lost far more than that, Lieutenant,' Fadi snapped. 'Your man failed to detain my objective. He was killed for his incompetence, a just punishment, I should say. Instead of whining to me, you should use this incident as a learning experience. Your men are not hard enough – not by a long shot.'

Before Kove could respond, Fadi turned on his heel and strode down the beach to the jetty at which the sailboat was tied up.

'Get under way,' he snapped as he came aboard.

He was in such a foul mood, sparks seemed to fly off him. At such times, Fadi was at his most volatile, as Abbud ibn Aziz knew better than anyone, save perhaps Karim al-Jamil. It was about Karim al-Jamil that he needed to talk to his leader now.

He waited until they had cast off, the sails trimmed. Gradually, they left the police contingent behind, plowing through the Black Sea night on their way to a dockage where Abbud ibn Aziz had a car waiting to take them to the airport. Sitting with Fadi in the bow, away from the two-man crew, he offered food and drink. For some time, they ate together with only the whooshing of the water purling in a symmetrical bow wave and the occasional hoot of a ship's horn, mournful as the cry of a lost child.

'While you were gone, I had a disturbing communication from Dr. Senarz,' Abbud ibn Aziz said. 'It is his contention that Dr. Veintrop is ready for the final series of procedures to complete the nuclear device, even though Veintrop denies this.'

'Dr. Veintrop is stalling,' Fadi said.

Abbud ibn Aziz nodded. 'That's Dr. Senarz's contention, and I'm inclined to believe him. He's the nuclear physicist, after all. Anyway, it wouldn't be the first time we had a problem with Veintrop.'

Fadi considered a moment. 'All right. Call your brother. Have him fetch Katya Veintrop and bring her to Miran Shah, where we will meet him. I think once Dr. Veintrop gets a look at what we can do to his wife, he'll become compliant again.'

Abbud ibn Aziz looked pointedly at his watch. 'The last flight took off hours ago. The next one isn't scheduled until this evening.'

Fadi sat rigid, his gaze unmoving. Once again, his consciousness had removed itself, Abbud ibn Aziz knew, back to the time when his father had been shot. His guilt over the incident was enormous. Many times, Abbud ibn Aziz had tried to counsel his leader and friend to keep his mind and energies in the present. But the incident had been complicated with the deep pain of betrayal, of murder. Fadi's mother had never forgiven him for the death of her only daughter.

Abbud ibn Aziz's mother would never have placed such a terrible burden on him. But then she was Islamic; Fadi's mother was Christian, and this made all the difference. He himself had met Sarah ibn Ashef innumerable times, but he'd never given her a second thought until that night in Odessa. Fadi, on the other hand, was half English; who could fathom what he thought or felt about his sister, or why?

Abbud ibn Aziz felt the muscles of his abdomen tighten. He licked his lips and began the speech he'd been practicing.

'Fadi, this plan of Karim al-Jamil's has begun to worry me.' Fadi still said nothing; his gaze never wavered. Had he even heard Abbud ibn Aziz's words? Abbud ibn Aziz had to assume so. He continued: 'First, the secretiveness. I ask you questions, you refuse to answer. I try to check security, but I am obstructed by you and your brother. Second, there is the extreme danger of it. If we are thwarted, the entire Dujja network will be threatened, the major source of our funding exposed.'

'Why bring this up now?' Fadi had not moved, had not removed his gaze from the past. He sounded like a ghost, making Abbud ibn Aziz shudder.

'It has been in my mind from the start. But now, I have discovered the identity of the woman Karim al-Jamil is seeing.'

'His mistress,' Fadi said. 'What of it?'

'Your father took an infidel as a mistress, Fadi. She became his wife.'

Fadi's head swung around. His dark eyes were like those of a mongoose that has set its sights on a cobra. 'You go too far, Abbud ibn Aziz. You speak now of my mother.'

Abbud ibn Aziz had no choice but to shudder again. 'I speak of Islam and of Christianity. Fadi, my friend, we live with the Christian occupation of our countries, the threat to our way of life. This is the battle we have vowed to fight, and to win. It is our cultural identity, our very essence that hangs in the balance.

'Now Karim al-Jamil sleeps with an infidel, plants his seed in her, confides in her – who knows? If this were to become known among our people, they would rise up in anger, they would demand her death.'

Fadi's face darkened. 'Is this a threat I hear from your lips?'

'How could you think that? I would never say a word.'

Fadi rose, his feet planted wide against the rocking of the sailboat, and looked down at his second. 'Yet you sneak around, spying on my brother. Now you speak to me of this, you hold it over my head.'

'My friend, I seek only to protect you from the influence of the infidel. I know, though the others do not, that this plan was conceived by Karim al-Jamil. Your brother consorts with the enemy. I know, because you yourself placed me in the enemy citadel. I know how many distractions and corruptions Western culture provides. The stink of them turned my stomach. But there are others for whom that may not be so.'

'My brother?'

'It may be so, Fadi. For myself, I cannot say, since there is an impenetrable wall between him and me.'

Fadi shook his fists. 'Ah, now the truth comes out. You resent being kept in the dark, even though this is my brother's wish.' Leaning over, he landed a stinging blow to his second's face. 'I know what this is about. You want to be elevated above the others. You crave knowledge, Abbud ibn Aziz, because knowledge is power, and more power is what you're after.'

Abbud ibn Aziz, quaking inside, did not move, did not dare raise a hand to his inflamed cheek. He knew only too well that Fadi was quite capable of kicking him overboard, leaving him to drown without an ounce of remorse. Still, he had embarked on a course. If he failed to see it through, he would never forgive himself.

'Fadi, if I show you a fistful of sand, what do you see?'

'You ask me riddles now?'

'I see the world. I see the hand of Allah,' Abbud ibn Aziz hurried on. 'This is the tribal Arab in me. I was born and raised in the desert. The pure and magnificent desert. You and Karim al-Jamil were born and raised in a Western metropolis. Yes, you must know your enemy in order to defeat him, as you have rightly told me. But Fadi, answer me this: What happens when you begin to identify with the enemy? Isn't it possible that you *become* the enemy?'

Fadi rocked from side to side on the balls of his feet. He was close to erupting entirely. 'You dare imply—'

'I imply nothing, Fadi. Believe me. This is a matter of trust – of faith. If you do not trust me, if you do not have faith in me, turn me out now. I will go without another word. But we have known each other all our lives. I owe everything to you. As you strive to protect Karim al-Jamil, my wish is to protect you from all dangers, both within and without Dujja.'

'Then your obsession has made you mad.'

'That possibility exists, certainly.' Abbud ibn Aziz sat as he had before, without cowering or wincing, which would surely induce Fadi to kick him into the water. 'I say only that Karim al-Jamil's self-imposed isolation has made him a force unto himself. You cannot argue with the point. Perhaps this is solely to your advantage, as you both believe. But I submit that the relationship has a serious drawback. You feed off each other. There is no intermediary, no third party to provide balance.'

Abbud ibn Aziz risked gaining his feet, slowly and carefully. 'Now I give you a case in point. I beg you to ask yourself: Are your motives and Karim al-Jamil's motives pure? You know the answer: They are not. They have been clouded, corrupted by your obsession with revenge. I say to you that you and Karim al-Jamil must forget Jason Bourne, forget what your father has become. He was a great man, no question. But his day is gone; yours has dawned. This is the way of life. To stand in its path is pure arrogance; you risk getting plowed under.

'The future must be your focus, not the past. You must think of your people now. You are our father, our protector, our savior. Without you, we are dust in the wind, we are nothing. You are our shining star. But only if your motives are once again pure.'

For a long time, then, no sound issued from either of them. For his part, Abbud ibn Aziz felt as if an enormous weight had been lifted off his shoulders. He believed in his argument, every word of it. If this was to be the end of him, so be it. He would die knowing that he had fulfilled his duty to his leader and his friend.

Fadi, however, was no longer glaring at him, no longer aware of the sea or the lights of Odessa twinkling in the darkness. His gaze had turned inward again, his essence fleeing down into the depths, where, Abbud ibn Aziz suspected – no, hoped with all his might – not even Karim al-Jamil was allowed entry.

With all of CI's computers down, all hell had broken loose within its headquarters complex. Every available member of the Signals and Codes Directorate had been ordered to tackle the problem of the computer virus. A third of them had taken Sentinel – the CI firewall – offline in order to run a series of level-three diagnostics. The rest of the agents were using hunt-and-destroy software to stalk through every vein and artery of the CI intranet. This software, designed by DARPA for CI, used an advanced heuristic algorithm, which meant that it was a problem-solving code. It changed, continually adapting depending on which form of virus it encountered.

The premises were in full lockdown mode – no one in or out. In the soundproof oval conference room across from the Old Man's suite of offices, nine men sat around a burnished burlwood table. At each seat was a computer terminal, sunk into the tabletop, plus bottles of chilled water. The man to the DCI's immediate left, the director of the Signals and Codes Directorate, was being continually updated on the progress of his feverish legions. These updates appeared on his own terminal, were cleaned up – made intelligible to the nongeeks in the room – and bloomed on one of half a dozen flat-panel screens affixed to the matte-black felt-clad walls.

'Nothing leaks outside these walls,' the DCI said. Today he was feeling all of his sixty-eight years. 'What's happened here today remains here.' History pressed down on him with the weight of Atlas's burden. One of these days, he knew, it was going to break his back. But not today. Not today, dammit!

'Nothing has been compromised.' This from the director of S&C, scanning the raw data scrolling across his terminal. 'This virus, it appears, did not come from outside. The diagnostics on Sentinel have been completed. The firewall was doing its job, just as it was programmed to do. It was not breached. I say again, it was not breached.'

'Then what the hell happened?' the DCI barked. He was already thanking his lucky stars that the defense secretary would never know anything about this unmitigated disaster.

The S&C director lifted his shining, bald head. 'As far as we can determine at this stage, we were attacked from inside.'

'*Inside?*' Karim al-Jamil said, incredulously. He was sitting at the Old Man's right hand. 'Are you saying we have a traitor inside CI?'

'It would seem that way,' said Rob Batt, the chief of operations, most influential of the Seven – as the directors were known internally.

'Rob, I want you all over this angle ASAP,' the Old Man said. 'Confirm it, or assure us we're clean.'

'I can handle that,' Karim said, and immediately regretted it.

Rob Batt's snakelike gaze was turned in his direction. 'Don't you have enough on your plate as it is, Martin?' he said softly.

The DCI cleared his throat. 'Martin, I need you to concentrate all your resources on stopping Dujja.' The last thing he needed now, he thought sourly, was an interdirectorate turf war. He turned to the director of S&C. 'I need an ETA for the computers to be restored.'

'Could be a day or more.'

'Unacceptable,' the Old Man snapped. 'I need a solution so we'll be up and running within two hours.'

The S&C director scratched his bald dome. 'Well, we could switch to the backup net. But that would entail distributing new access codes to everyone in the build—'

'Do it!' the DCI said sharply. He slapped the table with the flat of his hand. 'All right, gentlemen. We all know what we have to do. Let's get this shit off our shoes before it starts to stink!'

Bourne, slipping in and out of consciousness, was revisited by the events from his past that had been haunting him ever since Marie's death.

. . . *He is in Odessa, running. It is night; a chill mineral wind coming in off the Black Sea skids him along the cobbled street. She is in his arms – the young woman leaking blood at a terrific rate. He sees the gunshot wound, knows she is going to die. Even as this thought comes to him, her eyes open. They are pale, the pupils dilated in pain. She is trying to see him in the darkness at the end of her life.*

He can do nothing, nothing but carry her from the square where she was gunned down. Her mouth moves. She cannot project her voice. His ear is bloodied as he presses it to her open mouth.

Her voice, fragile as glass, reverberates against his eardrum, but what he hears is the sound of the sea rushing in, pulling back. Breath fails her. All that remains is the unsteady beat of his shoes against the cobbles . . .

He falters, falls. He crawls until his back is against a slimy brick wall. He cannot relinquish his hold on the woman. Who is she? He stares down at her, trying to concentrate. If he can bring her back to life, he can ask her who she is. I could have saved her, *he thinks in despair.*

And now, in a flash, it is Marie he's holding in his arms. The blood is gone, but life has not returned. Marie is dead. I could have saved her, *he thinks in despair . . .*

He woke, crying for his lost love, for his lost life. 'I should have saved you!' And all at once he knew why the fragment of his past returned at the moment of Marie's death.

Guilt was crippling him. Guilt at not being there to save Marie. Then it must follow that he'd had a chance to save the bloody woman, and didn't.

'Martin, a word.'

Karim al-Jamil turned to see Rob Batt watching him. The director of operations had not risen like everyone else in the conference room. Now only he and Karim remained in the darkened space.

Karim regarded him with a deliberately neutral expression. 'As you said, Rob, I have a great deal on my plate.'

Batt had hands like meat cleavers. The palms were unnaturally dark, as if they had been permanently stained by blood. He spread them, normally a conciliatory gesture – but now there was something distinctly menacing in the display of raw animal power, as if he were a silverback gorilla preparing to charge.

'Indulge me. This won't take but a minute.'

Karim went back, sat down at the table across from him. Batt was one of those people for whom an office environment was almost intolerable. He wore his suit as if it had bristles on the inside. His leathery, deeply scored, sun-crisped face could have come from either skiing in Gstaad or taking lives in the Afghani mountains. Karim found all this interesting, as he had spent so much time in fine tailor shops being fitted in fine Western clothes that a Savile Row suit felt as natural to him as a burnoose.

He steepled his fingers, stitched the ghost of a smile onto his face. 'What can I do for you, Rob?'

'Frankly, I'm a little concerned.' Batt apparently did not care to beat around the bush, but perhaps conversation wasn't his forte.

Karim, his heart beating fast, kept his tone polite. 'In what way?'

'Well, you've had a helluva difficult time. To be honest, I felt strongly that you should take a few weeks off – relax, be evaluated by other doctors.'

'Shrinks, you mean.'

Batt went on as if the other hadn't responded. 'I was over-ruled by the DCI. He said your work was too valuable – especially in this crisis.' His lips pulled back in what in someone else might have been a smile.

'But then, just now, you wanted in on my investigation into whoever the hell it was set the virus loose on us.' Those snakelike eyes, black as volcanic soil, ran over Karim as if he were mentally frisking the DDCI. 'You've never poached on my territory before. In fact, we made a pact never to poach.'

Karim said nothing. What if the statement was a trap? What if Lindros and Batt had never made such a pact?

'I'd like to know why you've reneged,' Batt said. 'I'd like to know why, in your current state, you'd want to take on even more work.' His voice had dropped in volume and, at the same time, had slowed like cooling honey. If he were an animal, he'd be circling Karim now, waiting for a moment to his advantage.

'Apologies, Rob. I just wanted to help, that's all. There was no—'

Batt's head lunged forward so sharply that Karim had to keep himself in check, lest he recoil.

'See, I'm concerned about you, Martin.' Batt's lips, already thin, were compressed into bloodless lines. 'But unlike our peerless leader, who loves you like a son, who forgives you anything, my concern is more like that of an older brother for his younger sibling.'

Batt spread his enormous clublike hands on the table between them. 'You lived with the enemy, Martin. The enemy tried to fuck you up. I know it and you know it. You know how I know it? Do you?'

'I'm sure my test results—'

'Fuck the test results,' Batt said shortly. 'Test results are for academics, which you and I most certainly are not. Those boys are still debating the results; they'll be in that hole till hell freezes over. To boot, we've been forced to take the opinion of Jason Bourne, a man who is at best unstable, at worst a menace to CI protocol and discipline. But he's the one person who knows you best. Ironic, no?' He cocked his head. 'Why the hell do you maintain your relationship with him?'

'Take a look at his file,' Karim said. 'Bourne is more valuable to me – to *us* – than a handful of your Ways and Means agents.' *Me singing Jason Bourne's praises, now that's irony,* he thought.

Batt would not be deterred. 'See, it's your *behavior* I'm worried about, Martin. In some ways it's fine – just as it always was. But in other, smaller, more subtle ways . . .' He shook his head. 'Well, let's just say it doesn't track. God knows you were always a reclusive sonovabitch. "Too good for the rest of us," the other directorate chiefs said. Not me. I had you pegged. You're an idea tank; you have no need for the idle chitchat that passes for friendship in these hallways.'

Karim wondered whether the time had come – a possibility he had, of course, factored into his plan – when one of Lindros's colleagues would become suspicious. But he'd calculated that the probability of this was low – his time at CI was a matter of days, no more. And as Batt himself had said, Lindros had always been something of a loner. Despite the odds, here he was on the precipice of having to decide how to neutralize a directorate chief.

'If you've noticed anything erratic in my behavior, I'm quite certain it's due to the stress of the current situation. One thing I'm a master of is compartmentalizing my life. I assure you that the past isn't an issue.'

There was silence for a moment. Karim had the impression of a very dangerous beast passing him by, so close he could smell its rank musk.

Batt nodded. 'Then we're done here, Martin.' He rose, extended his hand. 'I'm glad we had this little heart-to-heart.'

As Karim walked out, he was grateful that he had planted convincing evidence as to the identity of the 'traitor.' Otherwise Batt's teeth would be sinking into the back of his neck.

'Hello, Oleksandr. Good boy.'

Soraya, a heavily laden satchel slung over one shoulder, returned with a terrible intimation of death to the hidey-hole where she had left Bourne. In the light of the oil lamp she lit, she found Bourne, not dead, but unconscious from blood loss. The boxer sat steadfastly by his side. His liquid brown eyes sought hers, as if pleading for help.

'Don't worry,' she said both to Bourne and the dog. 'I'm

here now.'

She produced from the satchel the bulk of the paraphernalia she had obtained from Dr. Pavlyna: plastic bags filled with a variety of fluids. She felt Bourne's forehead to assure herself he wasn't running a fever, recited to herself the protocol Dr. Pavlyna had made her memorize.

Tearing open a plastic envelope, she took out a needle and inserted it into a vein on the back of his left hand. She attached a port and fit the end of the tube leading to the first bag of fluid into the open end of the port, beginning the drip of two wide-spectrum antibiotics. Next, she removed the blood-soaked makeshift bandage and irrigated the wound with a large amount of sterile saline solution. An antiseptic, the doctor told her, would only retard the healing process.

Bringing the lamp closer, she probed for foreign bodies – threads, bits of cloth, whatever. She found none, much to her relief. But there was some devitalized tissue at the edges that she had to snip away with surgical scissors.

Taking up the tiny curved needle by its holder, she pierced the skin, pulling the nylon suture material through. Very carefully, she drew the two sides of the wound together, using a rectangular stitch, just as Dr. Pavlyna had showed her. Gently, gently, making sure she didn't pull the skin too tightly, which would increase the risk of infection. When she was done, she tied off the last suture and cut away the rest of the nylon still attached to the needle. Lastly, she placed a sterile gauze pad over her handiwork, then wound a bandage around and around, fixing the pad in place.

By this time, the bag of antibiotics was empty. She unhooked it, replacing the tube with the one from the bag of hydrating and nourishing fluids.

Within an hour, Bourne was sleeping normally. An hour after that, he began to come around.

His eyes opened.

She smiled down at him. 'Do you know where you are?'

'You came back,' he whispered.

'I said I would, didn't I?'

'Fadi?'

'I don't know. I killed one of the policemen, but I never saw anyone else. I think they've all given up.'

His eyes closed for a moment. 'I remember, Soraya. I remember.'

She shook her head. 'Rest now, we'll talk later.'

'No.' His expression was one of grim concentration. 'We need to talk. Now.'

What had happened to him? He woke up and felt immediately different, as if his mind had been removed from a vise. It was as if he had been freed from the endless defile in which he had been existing, filled with the smoke of voices, compulsions. The pounding headaches were gone, the repeating phrases. With perfect clarity, he recalled what Dr. Sunderland had told him about how memories were formed, how abnormal brain activity brought on by trauma or extreme conditions could affect their creation and resurrection.

'For the first time, I realize how stupid I was to even contemplate taking Cevik out of the Typhon cells,' he said. 'And there have been other odd things. For instance, a blinding headache paralyzed me while Fadi was making his escape.'

'When Tim was shot.'

'Yes.' He tried to sit up, winced in pain.

Soraya moved toward him. 'No, you don't.'

He would not be deterred. 'Help me sit up.'

'Jason—'

'Just do it,' he said sharply.

She reached around him, pushing as he rose, scooting him so that his back pressed against the wall.

'These odd compulsions have led me into dangerous situations,' he continued. 'In every case, the compulsions have led to behavior that has benefited Fadi.'

'But surely that's a coincidence,' she said.

His smile was almost painful. 'Soraya, if my life has taught me anything it's that coincidence is most often a symptom of a conspiracy.'

Soraya laughed softly. 'Spoken like a true paranoid.'

'There's a case to be made that it's my paranoia that's kept me alive.' Bourne stirred. 'What if I'm on to something?'

Soraya crossed her arms over her breast. 'Like what?'

'Okay, let's start with the premise that these coincidences, as you call them, have their roots in a conspiracy. As I said, all of them have way benefited Fadi in a material way.'

'Go on.'

'The headaches began after I saw Dr. Sunderland, the memory expert Martin recommended.'

Soraya frowned. All of a sudden, there was nothing funny in what Bourne was saying. 'Why did you go see him?'

'I was being driven crazy by the memory fragments of my first visit here, to Odessa. But at the time, I didn't even know it was Odessa, let alone what I was doing there.'

'But how could that memory be part of this conspiracy you're constructing?'

'I don't know,' Bourne conceded.

'It *can't* be part of it.' Soraya realized that she was pleading a case against him.

Bourne waved a hand. 'Let's leave that aside for the moment. When I was bringing Martin home, he told me that I needed to come here – *no matter what* – to find a man named Lemontov who, he said, was Dujja's banker. His reasoning was that if I got Lemontov, Dujja's money flow would dry up.'

Soraya nodded. 'Acute thinking.'

'It would have been if Lemontov existed. He doesn't.' Bourne's expression was perfectly unreadable. 'Not only that, but Fadi *knew* about Lemontov. *He knew Lemontov was fiction!*'

'So?'

Bourne pushed off the wall, faced her squarely. 'So by what possible means could Fadi know about Lemontov?'

'You forget that Lindros was interrogated by Dujja. Maybe they fed him disinformation.'

'That would presuppose they knew he was going to be rescued.'

Soraya considered for a moment. 'This Lemontov thing interests me. Lindros told me about him as well. He's the reason I'm here. But why? Why did he send us both here?'

'To chase a ghost,' Bourne said. 'Chasing Lemontov was just a ruse. Fadi was waiting for us. He *knew* we were coming. He was prepared to kill me – in fact, if I'm any judge, he *needed* to. I could see it in his eyes, hear it in his voice. He'd been waiting a long time to catch up to me.'

Soraya looked shaken.

'One other thing,' Bourne pressed on. 'On the plane ride home, Martin said that his interrogators kept asking about a mission targeting Hamid ibn Ashef. A mission of mine. He kept asking if I'd remembered it.'

'Jason, why would Lindros want to know about a mission dreamed up by Alex Conklin?'

'You know why,' Bourne said. 'Fadi and Martin are some-how connected.'

'*What?*'

'As is Dr. Sunderland.' There was a relentless logic to his theory. 'Sunderland's treatment did something to me, some-thing that caused me to make mistakes at crucial moments.'

'How is that possible?'

'A technique in brainwashing is to use a color, a sound, a key word or phrase to trigger a certain response in the subject at a later date.'

Nothing to burn in the hole. The words had bounced around in Bourne's head until he thought he'd go mad.

Bourne repeated the phrase to Soraya. 'Fadi used it. That phrase is what set off the headache. Fadi had the trigger phrase Sunderland set up in my brain.'

'I remember the look on your face when he said it,' Soraya said. 'But do you also remember that he said he'd spent time in Odessa?'

'The Odessa mission to kill Hamid ibn Ashef is the key, Soraya. Everything points back to it.' His skin was gray; he seemed abruptly weary. 'The conspiracy is in place. But what's its ultimate purpose?'

'Just as impossible to fathom is how they coerced Lindros into helping them.'

'They didn't. I know Martin better than anyone. He couldn't be coerced to turn traitor.'

She spread her hands. 'What other explanation is there?'

'What if the man I saved from Dujja, the man I brought back to CI, the man I vouched for, isn't Martin Lindros?'

'Okay, stop right there.' Her hands came up, palms outward. 'You've just crossed the line from paranoia into full-blown psychosis.'

He ignored her outburst. 'What if the man I brought back, the man who is right now running Typhon, is an impostor?'

'Jason, that's impossible. He looks like Lindros, talks like Lindros. For God's sake, he passed the retinal scanner test.'

'The retinal scanner can be fooled,' Bourne pointed out. 'It's extremely rare and difficult to do – it requires a retinal or a full eye implant. But then if this impostor went to the trouble of having his face remade, the retinal implant would have been a piece of cake.'

Soraya shook her head. 'Do you have any idea of the ramifications of what you're saying? An impostor in the center of CI, controlling more than a thousand agents worldwide. I say again it's impossible, utterly insane.'

'That's precisely why it's worked. You, me, everyone in Typhon and CI – all of us are being manipulated, misdirected. That was the plan all along. While we trot all around the globe, Fadi has been free to smuggle his people into the

United States, to ship the nuclear device – in pieces, no doubt – to the location where they mean to detonate it.'

'What you're saying is monstrous.' Soraya was near shock. 'No one's going to believe you. I can't even get my head around it.'

She sank onto the edge of the planks. 'Look, you've lost a lot of blood. You're exhausted, not thinking clearly. You need to sleep and then—'

'There's one sure way to verify whether or not the Martin Lindros I brought back is real or an impostor,' Bourne continued, ignoring her. 'I need to find the real Martin Lindros. If I'm right about all this, it means he's still alive. The impostor needs him alive.' He began to slide off the bed. 'We've got to—'

A powerful wave of dizziness forced him to stop and slump back against the wall. Soraya levered him back down to a prone position. His eyelids grew heavy with fatigue.

'Whatever we decide to do, right now you must get some rest,' she said with newfound firmness. 'We're both exhausted, and you need to heal.'

A moment later, sleep overtook him. Soraya rose and settled herself on the floor next to the planks. She opened her arms; Oleksandr curled up against her breasts. She was filled with foreboding. What if Bourne was right? The consequences of such a scheme were unthinkable. And yet she found herself thinking about nothing else.

'Oh, Oleksandr,' she whispered. 'What are we to do?'

The boxer turned his muzzle up to her, licked her face.

She closed her eyes, deepened her breathing. Gradually, feeling the comforting *thump-thump* of Oleksandr's heartbeat, she gave in to the stealthy approach of sleep.

TWENTY

Matthew Lerner and Jon Mueller had met ten years ago by fortuitous accident in a whorehouse in Bangkok. The two men had a lot in common besides whoring, drinking, and killing. Like Lerner, Mueller was a loner, a self-taught genius at tactical operation and strategic analysis. The moment they met, they recognized something in each other that drew them, even though Lerner was CI and Mueller, at the time, NSA.

Lerner, walking through the air terminal in Odessa, moving closer to his target, had cause to think of Jon Mueller and all Mueller had taught him when his cell phone rang. It was Weller at D.C. Metro Police, where Lerner had a number of men on his payroll.

'What's up?' Lerner asked as soon as he'd recognized the desk sergeant's voice.

'I thought you'd want to know. Overton's missing.'

Lerner stood still, jostled as other arriving and departing passengers strode by him. 'What?'

'Didn't show for his shift. Not answering his cell. Hasn't been home. He's dead gone, Matt.'

Lerner, his mind churning, watched a pair of policemen pass. They stopped for a moment to talk to a comrade who was coming in the opposite direction, then moved on, their eyes alert.

Into the significant silence, Weller ventured a postscript. 'Overton was working on a case for you, wasn't he?'

'That was awhile ago,' Lerner lied. What Overton was doing for him was none of Weller's business. 'Hey, thanks for the heads-up.'

'It's what you pay me for,' Weller said before hanging up.

Lerner grabbed his small suitcase and moved to the side of the terminal passageway. Instinct told him that Overton was more than missing – he was dead. The question he asked himself now was: How had Anne Held had him killed? Because he knew as sure as he was standing in the Odessa air terminal that Held was behind Overton's death.

Perhaps he'd seriously underestimated the bitch. Clearly she hadn't been intimidated by Overton's house break-in. Just as clearly, she had decided to fight back. Too bad he was so far away. He'd relish butting heads with her. But at the moment, he had bigger fish to fillet.

He opened his cell, dialed an unlisted Washington number. He waited while the call went through the usual security switching. Then a familiar voice answered.

'Hey, Matt.'

'Hey, Jon. I've got an interesting one for you.'

Jon Mueller laughed. 'All your jobs are interesting, Matt.'

That was true. Briefly, Lerner described Anne Held, bringing Mueller up to date on the situation.

'The escalation caught you by surprise, didn't it?'

'I underestimated her,' Lerner admitted. He and Jon had no secrets from each other. 'Don't you do the same.'

'Gotcha. I'll take her out.'

'I mean it, Jon. This is one serious bitch. She's got resources I know nothing about. I never imagined she could have Overton offed. But don't make a move before you talk to the secretary. This is his game, it's his decision whether or not to roll the dice.'

*

Dr. Pavlyna was waiting for him just past the line of Customs and Immigration kiosks. Lerner hadn't thought about it, but with a name like that he should've realized she'd be a woman. She was now CI chief of station in Odessa. A woman. Lerner made a mental note to do something about that as soon as he got back to D.C.

Dr. Pavlyna was a rather handsome woman, tall, deep-breasted, imposing, her thick, dark hair streaked with gray, though to look at her face she couldn't be past forty.

They walked through the terminal, out into an afternoon warmer than he'd imagined. He'd never been to Odessa before. He'd been expecting Moscow weather, which he'd unhappily endured several times.

'You're in luck, Mr. Lerner,' Dr. Pavlyna said as they crossed a road on the way to the parking lot. 'I've had contact with this man Bourne you need to find. Not direct contact, mind you. It seems he's been injured. A knife wound to the side. No vital organs pierced, but a deep wound nonetheless. He's lost a lot of blood.'

'How d'you know all this if you've had no direct contact with him?'

'Fortunately, he's not alone. He's with one of us. Soraya Moore. She appeared at my door last night. Bourne was too badly hurt to accompany her, she said. I gave her antibiotics, sutures, and the like.'

'Where are they?'

'She didn't say, and I didn't ask. SOP.'

'That's a pity,' Lerner said, meaning it. He wondered what the hell Soraya was doing here. How had she known Bourne was here unless Martin Lindros had sent her? But why would he do that – Bourne notoriously worked alone . . . the assignment made no sense. Lerner would dearly have liked to call Lindros on his decision, but of course he couldn't. His own presence here was a secret, a point made clear to Dr. Pavlyna when the Old Man had called her.

They'd stopped at a new silver Skoda Octavia RS, a small but neat sports wagon. Dr. Pavlyna opened the doors, and they got in.

'The DCI himself told me to give you all the assistance I could organize.' Dr. Pavlyna drove through the lot, paid her ticket. 'There have been some newer developments. It seems Bourne is wanted by the police for the killing of four men.'

'That means he's going to have to get out of Odessa as quickly and as stealthily as possible.'

'That's certainly what I would do.' She waited for an opening in the traffic flow and pulled out.

Lerner's practiced eye took in everything around him. 'This is a relatively big city. I'm sure there are a number of ways to get out.'

'Naturally.' Dr. Pavlyna nodded. 'But very few of them will be open to him. For instance, the heightened police presence at the airport. He can't get out that way.'

'Don't be so sure. The guy's a fucking chameleon.'

Dr. Pavlyna, moved left, accelerating into the passing lane. 'You forget that he's badly wounded. Somehow the police know this. It would be too much of a risk.'

'What then?' Lerner said. 'Train, car?'

'Neither. The railway system won't get him out of Ukraine; driving would take too long and prove too hazardous – roadblocks and the like. Especially in his condition.'

'That leaves boat.'

Dr. Pavlyna nodded. 'There's a passenger ferry from Odessa to Istanbul, but it only runs once a week. He'd have to hole up for four days before the next one sails.' She considered for a moment as she put on more speed. 'Odessa's lifeblood is commerce. Freight and rail ferries run several times a day between here and a number of destinations: Bulgaria, Georgia, Turkey, Cyprus, Egypt. Security is relatively slack. In my opinion, that's far and away his best bet.'

'Then you'd better get us there first,' Lerner said, 'or we'll lose him for sure.'

Yevgeny Feyodovich strode purposely into the Privoz farmers' market. He headed directly toward Egg Row without his usual stops to smoke and gab with his circle of buddies. This morning, he had no time for them, no time for anything but getting the hell out of Odessa.

Magda, the partner with whom he owned the kiosk, was already there. It was Magda's farm from which the eggs came. He was the one with the capital.

'Had anyone come around asking for me?' he said as he came around behind the counter.

She was uncrating the eggs, separating the colors and sizes. 'Quiet as a churchyard.'

'Why did you use that phrase?'

Something in the tone of his voice made her stop what she was doing, look up. 'Yevgeny Feyodovich, whatever is the matter?'

'Nothing.' He was busy gathering up personal items.

'Huh. You look like you've seen the sun at midnight.' She put her fists on her ample hips. 'And where d'you think you're going? We'll be swamped here morning till sunset today.'

'I have a business matter to attend to,' he said hurriedly.

She barred his way. 'Don't think you can leave me like this. We have an agreement.'

'Get your brother to help you.'

Magda puffed her chest out. 'My brother's an idiot.'

'Then he's tailor-made for the job.'

He shouldered her roughly out of the way while her face was filling with blood. Putting his back to the whole scene, he strode quickly away, ignoring her indignant screeches, the stares of nearby vendors.

This morning on his way to the market, he'd received a call with the chilling news that Bogdan Illiyanovich had been shot to death on his way to leading the Moldavian Ilias Voda into the trap set for him by Fadi, the terrorist. Yevgeny had been paid well to be the roper, the one who brought the mark – in this case Voda – to the access point. Until he'd received a call from one of his friends in the police, he'd had no idea what Fadi wanted with Ilias Voda or that it would involve multiple murders. Now Bogdan Illiyanovich was dead, along with three of Fadi's men and, worst of all, a police officer.

Yevgeny knew that if anyone got caught, his name would be the first one to pop up. He was about the last person in Odessa able to withstand a full-on police investigation. His livelihood – his very life – depended on him being anonymous, clinging to the shadows. Once the spotlight was shone on him, he was a dead man.

That was why he was on the run, why he was obliged in the most urgent terms to leave his past behind and relocate, hopefully outside Ukraine altogether. He was thinking Istanbul, of course. The man who had hired him for this godforsaken job was in Istanbul. Since Yevgeny was the only one who'd come out of this fiasco alive, perhaps the man would give him a job. Going to one of Yevgeny's current drug sources was out of the question. That entire chain of custody was in jeopardy now. Best to sever his ties to them completely, start over. In Yevgeny's chosen field, Istanbul was a more hospitable base than many he could think of, especially those closer to hand.

He hurried through the crowds that had begun to clog the access points. He was impelled by an uncomfortable prickling at the back of his neck, as if he was already in the crosshairs of an unknown assassin.

He was just passing a stack of crates in which beakless chickens were roiling as though they'd already lost their heads when he saw a pair of policemen threading their way through the pedestrian traffic. He didn't have to ask anyone why they were there.

Just as he was shying away, a woman stepped out from between two stacks of crates. Already on edge, he took an involuntary step back, his fingers curled around the grip of his gun.

'The police are here, they've set a trap,' the woman said.

She looked slightly Arabian to him, but that could mean anything. Half of his world was part Arabian.

She gestured urgently. 'Come with me. I can get you out of here.'

'Don't make me laugh. For all I know you're working for the SBU.'

He started to move away from her, away from the two policemen he'd seen. Soraya shook her head. 'They're waiting for you that way.'

He continued on. 'I don't believe you.'

She went with him, shouldering her way through the thick stream of people until she was slightly ahead of him. All at once she stopped, indicated with her head. An unpleasant ball of ice formed in Yevgeny's lower belly.

'I told you it was a trap, Yevgeny Feyodovich.'

'How do you know my name? How do you know the police are after me?'

'Please. There's no time.' She plucked at his sleeve. 'This way, quickly! It's your only hope of evading them.'

He nodded. What else could he do? She took him back to the city of chicken crates, then through them. They had to walk sideways to make it through the narrow lanes. On the other hand, the crate stacks, rising above their heads, kept them invisible to the police moving through the market.

At last, they broke out onto a street, hurried across it against traffic. He could see that they were heading toward a battered old Skoda.

'Please get in back,' she said curtly as she slid behind the wheel.

In something of a blind panic, Yevgeny Feyodovich did as she ordered, wrenching open the door, climbing in. He slammed the door shut, and she pulled out from the curb. That was when he became aware of someone sitting unmoving on the seat next to him.

'Ilias Voda!' His voice sounded bleak.

'You've stepped in it this time.' Jason Bourne relieved him of gun and knife.

'What?' Yevgeny Feyodovich, shocked to be unarmed, was even more so to see how white and drawn Voda was.

Bourne turned to him. 'In this town you're thoroughly fucked, *tovarich*.'

Deron had often said that Tyrone could be like a dog with a bone. He'd get certain ideas stuck in his head and he couldn't – or wouldn't – let them go until they were resolved. He was like this with the two people he'd seen chopping up the cop's body then burning down M&N Bodywork. He followed the inevitable aftermath like the most rabid fan of *American Idol*. The fire department came, and then the cops. But nothing remained inside the concrete-block building except ash and cinders. Moreover, it was District NE, which meant nobody really gave a shit. Inside an hour, Five-O had given up and, with a collective sigh of relief, had hightailed it to safety in the white parts of the city.

But Tyrone knew what had happened. Not that anyone had asked him. Not that he would have told them shit had they bothered to interview him. In fact, he didn't even call his friend Deron in Florida to tell him.

In his world, you took the knife off your hoop enemy when you beat him to a pulp for dissing you, or your sister, or your girlfriend, whatever. So at ten or eleven, you gained

312

a measure of respect, which increased exponentially when your Masta Blasta slipped you a Saturday-night special with a taped butt and the serial numbers filed off.

Then, of course, you had to use it, because you didn't want to be a hop-along, a wannabe nobody would hang with or, worse, a mentard. It wasn't so difficult, really, because you already had some experience blowing people's heads off playing Postal 2 and Soldier of Fortune. As it turned out, the real thing wasn't much different. Just that you had to be careful afterward so the kill wouldn't turn into a career-ending move.

And yet there was something inside him, some nagging sense that this was not the only way it could be. There was Deron, of course, who'd been born and raised in the hood. But he'd had a momma who was straight and a father who'd loved him. In some way Tyrone couldn't understand, let alone articulate, he suspected those things counted for something. Then Deron had gone away to be educated in the white world and everyone in the hood – including Tyrone – had instantly hated his guts. But when he'd returned they forgave him everything because they saw he hadn't abandoned them, as they'd feared. For that, they loved him all the more, and rallied 'round to protect him.

Now Tyrone, sitting under the tree opposite the burned-out hulk of M&N Bodywork, faced both the destruction of his dream to make it his crew's crib, and the terrible notion that the dream was not what he'd wanted after all. He stared at the blank, blackened wall of cinder block, and it looked not much different than his life.

He drew out his cellie. He didn't have Miss S's number. How to contact her, how to let her know he had the 411 – what did Deron call it? intel, yeah – for her? Him and only him. If she'd meet him, if she'd walk with him again. He forced himself to believe that's all he wanted from her. The real truth he couldn't face yet.

He called 411. The only listed number for CI was the so-called public relations office. Tyrone knew what a joke that was, but he dialed it anyway. Once again, his life had refused to allow him a choice.

'Yes? How can I help?' a young white male voice said in clipped fashion.

'I'm tryin' t'reach a agent I spoke to coupla days ago,' Tyrone said, for once self-conscious about his ghetto slur.

'The agent's name?'

'Soraya Moore.'

'Just a moment, please.'

Tyrone heard some clicking, all at once became paranoid. He got up from his perch, began to walk down the street.

'Sir? May I have your name and number, please?'

Paranoia in full flower. He began to walk faster, as if he could outrun the inquiry. 'I just want to speak to—'

'If you give me your name and number, I'll see that Agent Moore gets the message.'

At this, Tyrone felt completely boxed in by a world he knew nothing about. 'Just tell her I know who put the salt on her tail.'

'Pardon me, sir, you know *what*?'

Tyrone felt that his own ignorance was being used as a weapon against which he was powerless. By design, his world was hidden within the larger one. Once, he'd been proud of that. Now, all at once, he knew it was a failing.

He repeated what he'd said, disconnected. Disgusted, he threw the cellie into the gutter, made a mental note to have DJ Tank get him another burner. His old one had just gotten too hot.

'So who are you, really?' Yevgeny Feyodovich asked with world weariness.

'Does it matter?' Bourne said.

'I suppose not.' Yevgeny stared out the window as they passed through the city. Every time he saw a police car or a policeman on foot, his muscles tensed. 'You're not even Moldavian, are you?'

'Your pal, Bogdan Illiyanovich, tried to kill me.' Bourne, watching the other's face carefully, said: 'You don't seem surprised.'

'Today,' Yevgeny Feyodovich replied, 'nothing surprises me.'

'Who hired you?' Bourne said sharply.

Yevgeny's head swung around. 'You don't expect me to tell you.'

'Was it the Saudi, Fadi?'

'I don't know a Fadi.'

'But you knew Edor Vladovich Lemontov, a fictitious drug lord.'

'I never actually said I knew him.' Yevgeny Feyodovich looked around. Judging by the sun, they were heading southwest. 'Where are we going?'

'A killing field.'

Yevgeny affected nonchalance. 'I should say my prayers then.'

'By all means.'

Soraya drove hard and fast, always staying within the speed limit. The last thing any of them needed was to attract the attention of a cruising police car. At length, they left the urban sprawl of Odessa behind, only to be confronted by rows of huge factories, transfer depots, and rail yards.

A bit farther on, there was a break of perhaps three or four kilometers where a village had sprung up, stores and houses looking tiny and incongruous amid the gargantuan structures on either side. Near the far end, Soraya turned down a side street that was soon fleshed out with foliage, both natural and artificial.

Oleksandr was waiting for them in the front yard of his owner and trainer – a friend of Soraya – who was, at the moment, nowhere to be seen. The boxer lifted his head as the battered Skoda turned into the driveway. The dacha behind him was of moderate size, set in a shallow dell, protected from its neighbors by thick stands of fir and cypress.

As Soraya rolled to a halt, Oleksandr rose, trotting toward them. He barked in greeting as he saw Soraya emerge from the car.

'My God, that's a huge beast,' Yevgeny Feyodovich said under his breath.

Bourne smiled at him. 'Welcome to the killing ground.' He grabbed the Ukrainian by his collar and dragged him off the backseat, out into the yard.

Oleksandr, seeing an unfamiliar face, raised his ears, sat back on his haunches, growled low in his throat. He bared his teeth.

'Let me introduce you to your executioner.' Bourne shoved Yevgeny toward the dog.

The Ukrainian appeared thunderstruck. 'The dog?'

'Oleksandr chewed Fadi's face off,' Bourne said. 'And hasn't eaten since then.'

Yevgeny Feyodovich shuddered. He closed his eyes. 'All I want is to be somewhere else.'

'Don't we all,' Bourne said, meaning it. 'Just tell me who hired you.'

Yevgeny Feyodovich wiped his sweating face. 'He'll kill me, no doubt.'

Bourne swept his hand toward the boxer. 'At least that way you'll have a head start.'

At that moment, just as they'd planned, Soraya gave Oleksandr a hand command. The dog leapt forward directly toward Yevgeny, who let out with a high, almost comical yelp.

At the last instant Bourne reached down and grabbed the

dog's collar, pulling him up short. The maneuver took more out of Bourne than it should have, sending shock waves of pain radiating from the wound in his side. He gave no outward sign of his distress. Nevertheless, he was aware of Soraya's eyes reading his face as if it were today's newspaper.

'Yevgeny Feyodovich,' Bourne said, straightening up, 'as you can plainly see, Oleksandr is big and powerful. My hand is getting tired. You have five seconds before I let go.'

Yevgeny, his mind functioning off the adrenaline of terror, made up his mind in three. 'All right, keep that dog away from me.'

Bourne began to walk toward him, a straining Oleksandr in tow. He saw Yevgeny's eyes open wide enough to see the whites all around.

'Who hired you, Yevgeny Feyodovich?'

'A man named Nesim Hatun.' The Ukrainian could not take his eyes off the boxer. 'He works out of Istanbul – the Sultanahmet District.'

'Where in Sultanahmet?' Bourne said.

Yevgeny cringed away from Oleksandr, whom Bourne had allowed to rise up on his hind legs. He was as tall as the Ukrainian. 'I don't know,' Yevgeny said. 'I swear. I've told you everything.'

The moment Bourne let go of Oleksandr's collar, the dog sprang forward like an arrow from a drawn bow. Yevgeny Feyodovich screamed. A stain appeared at the crotch of his trousers as he was plowed under.

A moment later, Oleksandr was sitting on his chest, licking his face.

'As far as freight ports are concerned, you basically have two choices,' Dr. Pavlyna said. 'Odessa and Ilyichevsk, some seven kilometers to the southwest.'

'What's your take?' Matthew Lerner said. They were in her car, heading toward the northern end of Odessa, where the shipyards were located.

'Odessa is, of course, closer,' she said. 'But the police are sure to have at least some surveillance there. On the other hand, Ilyichevsk is appealing simply because it's farther away from the center of the manhunt; there's sure to be less of a police presence – if any. Also, it's a larger, busier facility, with ferries on more frequent schedules.'

'Ilyichevsk it is, then.'

She changed lanes, preparing to make a turn, so that they could head south. 'The only problem for them will be road-blocks.'

Leaving the main road behind, Soraya drove through back streets, even some alleys she could squeeze the Skoda through.

'Even so,' Bourne said, 'I wouldn't rule out hitting one roadblock between here and Ilyichevsk.'

They had left Yevgeny Feyodovich in the front yard of Soraya's friend, guarded for the time being by Oleksandr. Three hours from now, when his release would be meaning-less to them, Soraya's friend would let him go.

'How are you feeling?' Soraya drove through narrow streets lined with warehouses. Here and there in the distance, they could see the portal and floating cranes at the port of Ilyichevsk rising like the necks of dinosaurs. It was slower going along this route, but it was also safer than taking the main road.

'I'm fine,' he said, but she could tell he was lying. His face was still pale, stitched with pain, his breathing ragged, not as deep as it ought to be.

'Glad to hear it,' she said with heavy irony. 'Because like it or not, we're going to come up against that roadblock in about three minutes.'

He looked up ahead. There were several cars and trucks stopped, lined up to be funneled through a gap between two armored police vehicles parked perpendicular to the street, so that their formidable tanklike sides were presented to the oncoming traffic. Two policemen in riot gear were questioning the cars' occupants, peering into their trunks or – in the case of the trucks – checking the rear and underneath the carriage. With faces clamped tight, they worked slowly, methodically, thoroughly. Clearly, they were leaving nothing to chance.

Soraya shook her head. 'There's no way out of this, no alternate route I can take. The water's on our right, the main highway on our left.' She glanced in her side mirror, at the traffic building behind her, another police car. 'I can't even turn around without the risk of being stopped.'

'Time for Plan B,' Bourne said grimly. 'You watch the cops in back of us; I'll keep my eye on the ones in front.'

Valery Petrovich, having just emptied his bladder against the brick side of a building, walked back to his position. He and his partner had been assigned to check that no vehicle lined up for the roadblock tried to turn around. He was thinking with some disgust about this bottom-of-the-barrel assignment, worrying that he'd been hit with it because he'd pissed off his sergeant, because, true, he'd beaten him at dice and at cards, taking six hundred rubles off him each time. Also true, the man was a vindictive bastard. Look what he'd done to poor Mikhail Arkanovich for mistakenly eating the sergeant's pierogi, vile though they'd been, so he'd heard from a very bitter Mikhail Arkanovich.

He was considering methods for remedying his deteriorating situation when he saw someone slip out of a battered Skoda seven cars from the front of the queue. His curiosity piqued, Valery Petrovich walked forward along the fronts of the warehouses, keeping his eye on the figure. He had just made out that it was a man when the figure slipped into a refuse-strewn alley between two buildings. Glancing front and back, the officer realized that no one else had noticed the man.

For half a second, he thought about using his walkie-talkie to alert his partner to the suspicious figure. That's all the time it took for him to realize that this was his ticket to returning to his sergeant's good graces. He sure as hell wasn't going to let the opportunity slip through his fingers by allowing someone else to capture what might very possibly be the fugitive they'd been sent to capture. He had no intention of becoming the next Mikhail Arkanovich, so, pistol drawn, licking his chops like a wolf about to rend its unsuspecting prey, he hurried eagerly on.

Taking a quick visual survey behind the line of warehouses, Bourne had already determined the best route to work his way around the roadblock. Under normal circumstances, there would have been no problem. Trouble was, he now found himself in anything but normal circumstances. Certainly he'd been injured before in the field – many times, in fact. But rarely this severely. On the car ride out to the dog handler's, he'd begun to feel feverish. Now he felt chills running through him. His forehead was hot, his mouth dry. He was in need not only of rest but also of more antibiotics – a full course – to fully pull himself out of the weakness inflicted by the knife wound.

Rest was, of course, out of the question. Where he was going to get antibiotics was problematic. If he didn't have an urgent reason to get out of Odessa immediately, he could have gone to the CI doctor. But that, too, was now out of the question.

He was in the open area behind the warehouses. A wide paved road gave access to the row of loading docks. Here and there were scattered refrigerated trucks and semis, either backed up to the docks or pulled to the far side of the road, where they sat idle, waiting for their drivers to return.

As he moved toward the area parallel to the roadblock on the other side of the buildings on his left, he passed a couple of forklifts, dodging several others loaded with large crates that scooted from one loading dock to another.

He saw his pursuer – a policemen – as a reflection in a forklift. Without breaking stride, he clambered painfully onto a loading dock and passed between two stacks of boxes into the warehouse interior. All the men, he noticed, were wearing port ID tags.

He found his way to the locker room. It was past the beginning of the shift, and the tiled room was deserted. He went along the lines of lockers, picking the locks at random. The third locker provided what he was looking for: a maintenance uniform. He donned it, not without a series of hot stitches of pain radiating out from his side. A thorough search turned up no ID tag. He knew how to take care of that. On the way out, he brushed against a man coming in, mumbling a hasty apology. As he hurried back onto the loading dock, he clipped on the tag he'd lifted.

Checking the immediate environment, he could find no sign of his pursuer. He set out on foot, skirting the empty steel cabs of the trucks whose cargo was being unloaded onto the concrete docks, where each crate, barrel, or container was checked against a manifest or bill of lading.

'Halt!' came a voice behind him. 'Stop right there!' He saw the policeman behind the wheel of one of the empty forklifts. The policeman put the vehicle in gear and drove it straight at him.

Though the forklift wasn't fast, Bourne nevertheless found himself at a distinct disadvantage. Because of the path the forklift was taking, he was imprisoned within a relatively narrow space, bordered on one side by the parked trucks, on the other by a strip of bunkerlike raw concrete buildings that housed the offices of the warehouse companies.

For the moment, the traffic was dense, and everyone was too busy at their jobs to notice the wayward forklift and its prey, but that might change at any moment.

Bourne turned and ran. With every stride the forklift gained on him, not only because it was in high gear but also because Bourne was in crippling agony. He dodged the machine once, twice, the tips of its forks releasing a shower of sparks as they scraped along a concrete wall.

He was near the end of the loading docks closest to the roadblock. There was an enormous semi backed into the last bay. Bourne's only chance was to run directly at the side of the cab, ducking under it at the last minute. He would have made it, too, but at almost the last instant, the overworked muscles of his left leg buckled under the pain.

He stumbled, slamming his side against the cab. A heartbeat later the ends of the forks punctured the painted steel on either side of Bourne, pinning him in place. He tried to duck down but he couldn't; he was held fast on either side by the forks.

He struggled to recover, to disengage himself from a pain so debilitating it made all thought difficult. Then the policeman crashed the gears, and the forklift ground forward. The tines buried themselves deeper into the side of the semi, thrusting him forward toward the truck.

A moment more and he would be crushed between the forklift and the semi.

TWENTY-ONE

Bourne exhaled and twisted his body. At the same time, he jammed his hands against the tops of the horizontal forks, levering his torso, then his legs up above the level of the tines. He spread his feet on the metal sill in front of the cab and levered himself onto the windshield.

The policeman threw the forklift into reverse in an attempt to dislodge Bourne, but the forks had pierced into the core of the cab and now something there was holding them fast.

Seeing his opening, Bourne swung around to the open side. The policemen drew his gun, aimed it at Bourne, but before he could pull the trigger Bourne kicked out, the toe of his shoe colliding with the side of the policeman's face. The jawbone dislocated, cracking apart.

Bourne grabbed the policeman's pistol and drove another fist into the man's solar plexus, doubling him over. He turned, jumped to the ground, the jarring force running right up into his left side like a spear thrust.

Then Bourne was off and running, past the line of the roadblock into a small woods, then out again on the other side. By the time he reached the side of the road several thousand meters beyond the police presence, he was winded and spent. But there was the battered Skoda, its passenger door open, Soraya's face, drawn and anxious, peering across the car's interior, watching him all the way as he climbed aboard. He slammed the door shut, and the Skoda lurched forward as she put it in gear.

'Are you all right?' she said, her eyes flicking from him to the road ahead. 'What the hell happened?'

'I had to go to Plan C,' Bourne said. 'And then to Plan D.'

'There were no Plans C and D.'

Bourne put his head against the seat. 'That's what I mean.'

Arriving at Ilyichevsk under gathering clouds, Lerner said, 'Take me to the ferry slips. I want to check the first outgoing ferry, because that's where he's headed.'

'I disagree.' Dr. Pavlyna drove the car through the byways of the port with the assurance of someone who'd done it many times before. 'The facility maintains its own Polyclinic. Believe me when I tell you that by now Bourne is going to need what only the clinic has got.'

Lerner, who'd never taken an order from a woman in his life, disliked the idea of taking Dr. Pavlyna's suggestion. In fact, he disliked having her driving him around. But for the time being, it served its purpose. That didn't mean her competence didn't put him in a surly mood.

Ilyichevsk was vast, a cityscape of low, flat, ugly buildings, vast warehouses and silos, cold storage facilities, container terminals, and monstrously tall TAKRAF cranes floating on barges. To the west, fishing trawlers lay at berth being off-loaded or refitted. The port, built in a kind of arc around a natural inlet to the Black Sea, comprised seven cargo-handling complexes. Six specialized in areas such as steel and pig iron, tropical oils, timber, vegetables and liquid oils, fertilizer. One was an immense grain silo reloader. The seventh was for ferries and ro-ro vessels. *Ro-ro* was short for 'roll on–roll off,' meaning that the central space housed enormous containers from both rail lines and tractor-trailers that were driven onto the ferry and stacked in its bowels. Above this space was the area housing the passengers, captain, and much of the crew. The main drawback to the design was its inherent instability. With only a centimeter or two of water penetrating the cargo deck, the ferry would start to roll over and sink. Nevertheless, no other craft could serve its purpose as efficiently, so ro-ros continued to be used all over Asia and the Middle East.

The Polyclinic lay more or less midway between Terminals Three and Six. It was in an unremarkable three-story building with strictly utilitarian lines. Dr. Pavlyna drew her car up to the side of the Polyclinic and switched off the engine.

She turned to Lerner. 'I'll go in myself. That way, there won't be any questions with security.'

As she moved to open her door, Lerner grasped her arm. 'I think it would be better if I went with you.'

She glanced down at his hand for a moment before saying, 'You're making things difficult. Let me take the lead in this; I know the people here.'

Lerner tightened his grip. His grin revealed a set of very large teeth. 'If you know the people, Doctor, there won't be any questions with security, will there?'

She gave him a long appraising look, as if seeing him for the first time. 'Is there a problem?'

'Not from my end.'

Dr. Pavlyna wrested her arm from his grasp. 'Because if there is, we should settle it now. We're in the field—'

'I know precisely where we are, Doctor.'

'—where misconceptions and misunderstandings can lead to fatal errors.'

Lerner got out of the car and began walking toward the front door of the Polyclinic. A moment later, he heard Dr. Pavlyna's boots crunch against the gravel before she caught up with him on the tarmac.

'You may have been sent by the DCI, but I'm the COS here.'

'For the time being,' he said blithely.

'Is that a threat?' Dr. Pavlyna didn't hesitate. Men of one sort or another had been trying to intimidate her ever since she was a little girl. She'd taken her early knocks before learning how to fight back with her arsenal of weapons. 'You're under my command. You understand that.'

He paused for a moment in front of the door. 'I understand that I have to deal with you while I'm here.'

'Lerner, have you ever been married?'

'Married, and divorced. Happily.'

'Why am I not surprised.' As she tried to brush past him, he grabbed her again.

Dr. Pavlyna said, 'You don't like women much, do you?'

'Not the ones who think they're men, I don't.'

Having made his point, he dropped his hand from her arm.

She opened the door, but for the moment barred his entry with her body. 'For God's sake keep your mouth shut, otherwise you'll compromise my security.' She stepped aside. 'Even someone as crude as you can understand that.'

Under the pretext of a mission briefing update, Karim al-Jamil wangled himself an invitation to breakfast with the Old Man. Not that he didn't have an update, but the mission was bullshit, so anything he had to say about it was bullshit. On the other hand, it felt fine to feed the DCI bullshit for breakfast. Anyway, he had his own intel update to digest. The memories Dr. Veintrop implanted had led Bourne to the ambush point. Somehow the man had recovered enough to shoot four men to death and escape Fadi. But not before Fadi had knifed him in the side. Was Bourne dead or alive? If Karim al-Jamil were allowed to bet, he'd put his money on alive.

But now that he had reached the top floor of CI headquarters, he forced his mind back into its role of Martin Lindros.

Even during a crisis, the Old Man took his meals where he always did.

'Being chained to the same desk, staring at the same monitor day in, day out, is enough to drive a man mad,' he said as Karim al-Jamil sat down opposite him. The floor was divided in two. The west wing was devoted to a world-class gym and Olympic-size swimming pool. The walled-off east wing, where they were now, housed quarters off limits to everyone except the Old Man.

This was the room to which the seven heads of directorates had from time to time been invited. It had the look and feel of a greenhouse, with a thick terracotta tile floor and a high humidity level, the better to accommodate a wide variety of tropical greenery and orchids. Who tended them was the stuff of much speculation and fanciful urban legends. The bottom line was that no one knew, just as no one knew who – if anyone – occupied the east wing's ten or twelve securely locked off-limits offices.

This was, of course, Karim al-Jamil's first time in the Gerbil Circuit, as it was referred to internally. Why? Because the DCI kept three gerbils in side-by-side cages. In each cage, one gerbil was confined to a wheel on which it ran endlessly. Much like the agents of CI.

Those few directorate heads who spoke of their breakfasts with the Old Man claimed he found watching the gerbils at their labor relaxing – like staring at fish in a tank. Speculation among the agents, however, was that the DCI perversely enjoyed being reminded that, like the ancient Greek Sisyphus, CI's task was without either praise or end.

'On the other hand,' the Old Man was saying now, 'the job itself can drive a man mad.'

The table was set with a starched white cloth, two bone-china settings, a basket of croissants and muffins, and two carafes, one of strong, freshly brewed coffee, the other of Earl Grey tea, the Old Man's favorite.

Karim al-Jamil helped himself to coffee, which he sipped black. The DCI liked his tea milky and sweet. There was no sign of a waiter, but a metal cart stood tableside, keeping its contents warm for the diners.

Digging out his papers, Karim al-Jamil said, 'Should I start the briefing now or wait for Lerner?'

'Lerner won't be joining us,' the DCI said enigmatically.

Karim al-Jamil began. 'The Skorpion units are three-quarters of the way to their destination in the Shabwah region of South Yemen. The marines have been mobilized out of Djibouti.' He glanced at his watch. 'As of twenty minutes ago, they were on the ground in Shabwah, awaiting orders from our Skorpion commanders.'

'Excellent.' The DCI refilled his teacup, stirred in cream and sugar. 'What progress on pinning down the specific location of the transmissions?'

'I put two separate Typhon teams onto parsing different packets of data. Right now we're reasonably certain the Dujja facility is somewhere within the eighty-kilometer target radius.'

The DCI was staring into the cages at the busy gerbils. 'Can't we pin it down more accurately?'

'The chief problem is the mountains. They tend to distort and reflect the signals. But we're working on it.'

The Old Man nodded absently.

'Sir, if I might ask, what's on your mind?'

For a moment it appeared as if the older man hadn't heard. Then the DCI's head swung around, his canny eyes engaging those of Karim al-Jamil. 'I don't know, but I feel as if I'm missing something . . . something important.'

Karim al-Jamil kept his breathing even, arranged his expression into one of mild concern. 'Is there anything I can help you with, sir? Perhaps it's Lerner—'

'Why d'you mention him in particular?' the DCI said a trifle too sharply.

'We've never spoken about his taking over my position in Typhon.'

'You were gone; Typhon was leaderless.'

'And you put an outsider into the breach?'

The DCI set down his cup with an ungainly clatter. 'Are you second-guessing my judgment, Martin?'

'Of course not.' *Be careful*, Karim al-Jamil thought. 'But it was damn strange to see him in my chair when I got back.'

The Old Man frowned. 'Yes, I can see that.'

'And now in the middle of this ultimate crisis, he's nowhere to be found.'

'Get us our breakfast, would you, Martin,' the DCI said. 'I'm hungry.'

Karim al-Jamil opened the food cart, taking out two plates of fried eggs and bacon. It was all he could do not to gag. He'd never gotten used to pork products or, for that matter, eggs fried in butter. As he set a plate down in front of the DCI, he said, 'If there's still a bit of distrust after my ordeal, I certainly understand.'

'It's not that,' the Old Man said, again a bit too sharply.

Karim al-Jamil set his own plate down. 'Then what is it? I'd appreciate knowing. These mysterious incidents with Matthew Lerner make me feel as if I've been cut out of the loop.'

'Seeing how much it means to you, Martin, I'll make you a proposition.'

The Old Man paused to chew a mouthful of bacon and eggs, swallow, and wipe his glistening lips in a fair imitation of gentlemanly fashion.

Karim al-Jamil almost felt sorry for the real Martin Lindros, who'd had to put up with this insulting behavior. *And they call us barbarians.*

'I know you have a great deal on your plate at the moment,' the DCI finally continued. 'But if you could find your way to make some discreet inquiries for me—'

'Who or what?'

The DCI sliced into his eggs and neatly piled a third of a strip of bacon on top. 'It has lately come to my attention through certain back channels that I have an enemy inside the Beltway.'

'After all these years,' Karim al-Jamil observed, 'there has to be a list of some size.'

'Of course there is. But this one's special. I ought to warn you to be exceedingly careful; he's as powerful as they come.'

'I trust it's not the president,' Karim al-Jamil said, joking.

'No, but damn close.' The Old Man was perfectly serious. 'Secretary of Defense Ervin Reynolds Halliday, known as Bud to everyone who kisses his ass. I very much doubt he has anything approaching real friends.'

'Who does, in this town?'

The DCI emitted a rare chuckle. 'Just so.' He stuffed the forkful of food into his mouth, transferred it to one cheek in order to continue talking. 'But you and I, Martin, we're friends. Close as, anyway. So this little deal is between us.'

'You can count on me, sir.'

'I know I can, Martin. The best thing I've done in the past decade is bring you along to the top of the CI ladder.'

'I appreciate your trust in me, sir.'

The DCI gave no indication he'd heard the other's remark. 'After Halliday and his faithful pit bull, LaValle, tried to ambush me in the War Room, I made some inquiries. What I've discovered is that the two of them have been quietly setting up parallel intelligence units. They're moving into our turf.'

'Which means we have to stop them.'

The Old Man's eyes narrowed. 'Yes, it does, Martin. And unfortunately they're making their overt move at the worst possible time: when Dujja is attempting a major attack.'

'Maybe that's deliberate, sir.'

The DCI thought about the ambush in the War Room. There was no doubt that both Halliday and LaValle were trying to embarrass him in front of the president. He thought again of the president sitting back, watching the thrust and parry unfold. Was he already on the defense secretary's side? Did he want CI taken over by the Pentagon? The Old Man shuddered at the thought of the military in control of human intelligence. There was no telling what liberties LaValle and Halliday would take with their newfound power. There was a good reason for the separation of power of the Pentagon and CI. Without it, a police state was just a shot away.

'What are you looking for?'

'Dirt.' The DCI swallowed. 'The more the merrier.'

Karim al-Jamil nodded. 'I'll need someone—'

'Anyone. Just say the name.'

'Anne Held.'

The DCI was taken aback. 'My Anne Held?' He shook his head. 'Choose someone else.'

'You said discreet. I can't use an agent. It's Anne or nothing.'

The DCI eyed him to see if he could spot the hint of a bluff. Apparently, he couldn't. 'Done,' he conceded.

'Now tell me about Matthew Lerner.'

The Old Man looked him in the eye. 'It's Bourne.'

After a long, awkward moment during which all that could be heard was the whirring of wheels propelled by twelve tiny gerbil feet, Karim al-Jamil said quietly, 'What does Jason Bourne have to do with Matthew Lerner?'

The DCI put down his knife and fork. 'I know what Bourne has meant to you, Martin. You have a certain, though inexplicable, rapport with him. But the simple fact is that he's the worst kind of poison for CI. Consequently, I've dispatched Matthew Lerner to terminate him.'

For a moment, Karim al-Jamil could not believe what he

331

was hearing. The DCI had sent an assassin to kill Bourne? To take from him and his brother the satisfaction of a long-held and meticulously plotted revenge? No. He wouldn't have it.

The killing rage – what his father had called the Desert Wind – took possession of his heart, heated it, beat it down until it was like a forged blade. All that could be discerned of this grave inner turmoil was the briefest flare of his nostrils – which in any event his companion, having taken up his cutlery, failed to notice.

Karim al-Jamil cut into his eggs, watched the yolks run. One of them had a blood spot on its glassy surface.

'That was a radical move,' he said when he was in full control of his emotions. 'I told you I'd severed him.'

'I thought about it and decided it wasn't the proper solution.'

'You should have come to me.'

'You'd only have tried to talk me out of it,' the DCI said briskly. Clearly he was pleased with how well he'd handled a tricky situation. 'Now it's too late. You can't stop it, Martin, so don't even try.' He wiped his lips. 'The good of the group supersedes the desires of the individual. You know that as well as anyone.'

Karim al-Jamil considered the extreme danger of what the DCI had set in motion. In addition to being a threat to their personal revenge, Lerner's presence in the field was a wild card, one that he and Fadi hadn't taken into consideration. The altered scenario menaced the execution of their plan. He had learned from Fadi – via a scrambled channel piggybacked onto CI's own overseas communications – that he had knifed Bourne. If not dealt with, Lerner could become aware of this, and he'd quite naturally become interested in finding out the identity of who had done it. Alternatively, if he discovered that Bourne had already been killed, he'd want to know who the killer was. Either way, it would lead to dangerous complications.

Pushing back from the table, Karim al-Jamil said, 'Have you considered the possibility of Bourne killing Lerner?'

'I brought Lerner aboard because of his rep.' The Old Man picked up his cup, saw that the tea had gone cold, set it back down. 'They don't make men like him anymore. He's a born killer.'

So is Bourne, Karim al-Jamil thought with a bitterness that burned like acid.

Soraya, noticing the drip of fresh blood on the car seat, said, 'It looks as if you popped a stitch or two. You're never going to make it without immediate medical attention.'

'Forget it,' Bourne said. 'We both need to get out of here now. The police cordon is only going to draw tighter.' He looked around the port. 'Besides, where am I going to get medical attention here?'

'The port maintains a Polyclinic.'

Soraya drove through Ilyichevsk and parked at the side of a three-story building, next to the late-model Skoda Octavia RS. She was aware of how badly Bourne winced as he got out of the car. 'We'd better use the side entrance.'

'That's not going to take care of security,' he said. Opening up the lining of his coat, he took out a small packet sealed in plastic. Ripping it open, he produced another set of ID documents. He leafed through them briefly, though on the plane ride he'd memorized all the documents Deron had forged for him. 'My name is Mykola Petrovich Tuz. I'm a lieutenant general in DZND, the SBU's Department for National Statehood Protection and Combating Terrorism.' He came up to her, took her arm. 'Here's the drill. You're my prisoner. A Chechnyan terrorist.'

'In that case,' Soraya said, 'I'd better put this cloth over my head.'

'No one will even look at you, let alone ask you questions,' Bourne said. 'They'll be dead afraid of you.'

He opened the door and pushed her rudely ahead of him. Almost at once an orderly called for a security guard.

Bourne held out his DZND credentials. 'Lieutenant General Tuz,' he said brusquely. 'I've been knifed, and am in need of a doctor.' He saw the guard's eyes slide toward Soraya. 'She's my prisoner. A Chechnyan suicide bomber.'

The security guard, his face drained of color, nodded. 'This way, Lieutenant General.'

He spoke into his walkie-talkie, then led them down several corridors into a spare examination room typical of hospital ERs.

He indicated the examination table. 'I've contacted the Polyclinic's administrator. Make yourself comfortable, Lieutenant General.' Clearly unnerved by both Bourne's status and Soraya's presence, he drew his pistol. Aimed it at Soraya. 'Stand over there, so the lieutenant general can be seen to.'

Bourne let go of Soraya's arm, giving her an almost imperceptible nod. She went to the corner of the room and sat on a metal-legged chair as the guard tried to keep an eye on her without actually looking at her face.

'A lieutenant general in SBU,' the Polyclinic administrator said from behind his desk. 'This can't be your man.'

'We'll be the judge of that,' Matthew Lerner said in passable Russian.

Dr. Pavlyna shot him a wicked look before turning to the administrator. 'You did say he's suffering from a knife wound.'

The administrator nodded. 'That's what I've been told.'

Dr. Pavlyna rose. 'Then I think I should see him.'

'We'll both go,' Lerner said. He'd been standing near the door, a kind of invisible electricity coming off him in waves, like a racehorse in the starting gate.

'That wouldn't be wise.' The deliberateness with which Dr. Pavlyna said this held significant emphasis for Lerner.

'I agree.' The administrator got up and came around his desk. 'If the patient really is who he says he is, I'll take the brunt of the breach in protocol.'

'Nevertheless,' Lerner said. 'I'm going to accompany the doctor.'

'You'll force me to call security,' the administrator said sternly. 'The lieutenant general won't know who you are or why you're there. In fact, he could order you held or even shot. I won't have anything like that in my facility.'

'Stay here,' Dr. Pavlyna said. 'I'll call you as soon as I've determined his identity.'

Lerner said nothing as Dr. Pavlyna and the administrator left the office, but he had no intention of cooling his heels while the doctor took charge. She had no idea why he was in Odessa, why he was after Jason Bourne. He didn't for a minute believe that the patient was anyone but Bourne. A lieutenant general of the Ukrainian secret police here with a knife wound in his side? No chance.

He wasn't going to allow Dr. Pavlyna to fuck things up. The first thing she would tell Bourne was that Lerner had been dispatched from D.C. to find him. That would set off instant alarm bells in Bourne's head. He'd be gone before Lerner could get to him. And this time, he'd be far more difficult to locate.

The immediate problem was that he didn't know where the patient was. He went out the door, accosted the first person he saw, asked where the lieutenant general was being treated. The young woman pointed the way. He thanked her and walked on down the corridor with such concentration that he failed to see her pick up the receiver of an intraclinic phone on the wall, asking to speak to the administrator.

'Good afternoon, Lieutenant General. I'm Dr. Pavlyna,' she said the moment she entered the examination room. To the administrator, she added, 'This is not our man.'

Bourne, sitting on the examination table, saw nothing in her eye to tell him she was lying, but when he saw her glance over at Soraya, he said, 'Stay away from my prisoner, Doctor. She's dangerous.'

'Please lie back, Lieutenant General.' As Bourne complied, Dr. Pavlyna donned surgeon's gloves, slit open Bourne's bloody shirt, and began to peel back the bloody bandage. 'Is she the one who gave you the knife wound?'

'Yes,' Bourne said.

She palpated around the wound, judging Bourne's pain level. 'Whoever sutured you did a first-rate job.' She looked into Bourne's eyes. 'Unfortunately, you've been a bit too active. I'll have to resuture the part that's torn open.'

On cue, the administrator showed her where the paraphernalia was, opening the locked cupboard where the drugs were stored. She selected a box from the second shelf, counted out fourteen pills, wrapped them in a twist of sturdy paper. 'Also, I want you to take this. One twice a day for a week. It's a powerful wide-spectrum antibiotic to guard against infection. Please take them all.'

Bourne accepted the packet, stowed it away.

Dr. Pavlyna brought a bottle of liquid disinfectant, gauze pads, a needle, and suture material to the table. Then she loaded up a syringe.

'What's that?' Bourne said warily.

'Anesthesia.' She inserted the needle into his side, depressed the plunger. Once again, her eyes caught Bourne's.

'Don't worry, Lieutenant General, it's just a local. It'll take the pain away but will in no way impair your physical or mental acuity.'

As she began the procedure, the phone on the wall burred discreetly. The administrator picked up the receiver and listened for a moment. 'All right, I understand. Thank you, Nurse.' He put back the receiver.

'Dr. Pavlyna,' he said. 'It seems your friend couldn't contain his impatience. He's on his way here.' He went to the door. 'I'll take care of him.' Then he slipped out.

'What friend?' Bourne said.

'Nothing to worry about, Lieutenant General,' Dr. Pavlyna said. She gave him another significant look. 'A friend of yours from headquarters.'

On his way to the room where the patient was being treated, Lerner passed three examination rooms. He took the time to peer into each one. Having determined that they were identical, he memorized the layout: where the examining table was, chairs, cabinets, sink . . . Knowing Bourne's reputation, he didn't think he'd get more than one chance to blow his brains out.

He took out his Glock, screwing the silencer onto the end of the barrel. He would have preferred not to use it, because it cut down on both the range and the accuracy of the gun. But in this environment he didn't have a choice. If he was to accomplish his mission and get out of the building alive, he had to kill Bourne in the quietest way possible. From the moment the DCI had given him his assignment, he knew he'd never be able to torture intel out of him – not in a hostile environment, and possibly not at all. Besides, the best way to take Bourne out was to kill him as quickly and efficiently as possible, giving him no possibility of a counterattack.

At that moment, the administrator rounded the corner up

ahead, carrying a disapproving look on his face.

'Excuse me, but you were asked to stay in my office until called,' he said as he confronted Lerner. 'I must ask you to return to—'

The heavy blow from the end of the silencer struck him square on the left temple, sending him to the floor in a heap, insensate. Lerner took him by the back of his collar, dragged him back to one of the empty examination rooms, and stowed him behind the door.

Without another thought, he returned to the corridor and walked the rest of the way to his destination without further interference. Standing outside the closed door, he settled his mind into the clear quiet of the kill. Grasping the doorknob with his free hand, he slowly turned it as far as he could, held it in place. The kill-state surrounded him, entered him.

Simultaneously, he let go of the knob, kicked the door open and, taking a long stride across the threshold, squeezed off three shots into the figure on the examination table.

TWENTY-TWO

Lerner's brain took a moment to make sense of what his eyes saw. It recognized the rolls of material on the examination table; as a result, he began to turn.

But that lag between action and reaction was just enough to allow Bourne, standing to one side, to drive the syringe loaded with a general anesthetic into Lerner's neck. Still, Lerner was far from finished. He had the constitution of a bull, the determination of the damned. Breaking the syringe before Bourne had a chance to deliver the full dose, he drove his body against Bourne's.

As Bourne delivered two blows, Lerner squeezed off a shot that ripped open the security guard's chest.

'What are you doing?' Dr. Pavlyna screamed. 'You told me—'

Lerner, driving an elbow into Bourne's bloody wound, shot her in the head. Her body flew backward into Soraya's arms.

Bourne dropped to his knees, pain weakening every muscle, firing every nerve ending. As Lerner grabbed him by the neck, Soraya threw the chair she'd been sitting on into his face. His death grip on Bourne broken, he staggered back, firing still, though wildly. She saw the guard's gun across the room, thought momentarily of making a run for it, but Lerner, recovering with frightening speed, made that impossible.

Instead she lunged for Bourne, dragged him to his feet, and got both of them out of there. She heard the *phut! phut!*

of silenced bullets splinter the wall at her elbow, and then they were racing around a corner, down the corridor, retracing their route to the side door.

Outside, she half threw, half stuffed Bourne into the passenger seat of the battered Skoda, slid behind the wheel, fired the ignition, and in a squeal of tires and spray of gravel reversed them out of there.

Lerner, half leaning against the examination table, staggered to his feet. He shook his head, trying to clear it, failed. Reaching up, he pulled the needle from the broken syringe out of his neck. What the hell had Bourne injected him with?

He stood for a moment, weaving like a landlubber on a boat in heavy weather. He gripped the countertop to steady himself. Groggily, he went over to the sink and splashed cold water on his face. The only thing that did was blur his vision even further. He found he had trouble breathing.

Moving his hand along the counter, he discovered a small glass container with one of the rubber tops that allows needles through. He picked it up, put it in front of his face. It took him a moment for his eyes to focus on the small print. Midazolam. That's what this was. A short-term anesthetic meant to induce twilight sleep. Knowing that, he knew what he needed to counteract its effects. He went through the cabinets until he found a vial of epinephrine, the main chemical in adrenaline. Locating the syringes, he loaded one up, zipped a little of the liquid out the end of the needle to get rid of any air bubbles that might have formed, then injected himself.

That was the end of the midazolam. The cotton-wool haziness went up in a blaze of mental fire. He could breathe again. He knelt over the corpse of the late unlamented Dr. Pavlyna and fished out her ring of keys.

Minutes later, finding his way to the side door, he was out

of the Polyclinic. As he approached Dr. Pavlyna's car, he saw fresh skid marks in the gravel by a vehicle that had been parked beside it. The driver had been in a hurry. He piled into the Skoda Octavia. The skid marks led in the direction of the ferry terminal.

Having been thoroughly briefed on Ilyichevsk's workings by Dr. Pavlyna, Lerner knew precisely where Bourne was headed. Up ahead, he saw a huge ro-ro loading. He squinted. What was its name? *Itkursk*.

He grinned fiercely. It looked as if he was going to get a second shot at Bourne after all.

The captain of the ro-ro *Itkursk* was more than happy to accommodate Lieutenant General M. P. Tuz of the DZND and his assistant. In fact, he gave them the stateroom reserved for VIPs, a cabin with windows and its own bathroom. The walls were white, curved inward like the hull of the ship. The floor was much-scuffed wooden boards. There was a bed, a slim desk, two chairs, doors that revealed a narrow clothes closet and the bathroom.

Shaking off his coat, Bourne sat on the bed. 'Are you all right?'

'Lie down.' Soraya threw her overcoat onto a chair, held up a curved needle and a string of suture material. 'I've got work to do.'

Bourne, grateful, did as she asked. His entire body was on fire. With a professional sadist's expertise, Lerner had landed the blow to his side so as to inflict maximum pain. He gasped as she began the resuturing process.

'Lerner really did a number on you,' Soraya said as she worked. 'What is he doing here? And what the hell does he think he's doing coming after you?'

Bourne stared at the low ceiling. By now he was used to CI betrayals, its attempts to terminate him. In some ways, he had made himself numb to the agency's calculated inhumanity. But another part of him found it difficult to fathom the depth of its hypocrisy. The DCI was all too ready to use him when he had no other recourse, but his enmity toward Bourne was unshakable.

'Lerner is the Old Man's personal pit bull,' Bourne said. 'I can only guess he's been sent to fulfill a termination order.'

Soraya stared down at him. 'How can you say that so calmly?'

Bourne winced as the needle went in, the suture pulled through. 'Calmly is the only way to assess the situation.'

'But your own agency—'

'Soraya, what you have to understand is that CI was never my agency. I was brought in through a black-ops group. I worked with my handler, not the Old Man, not anyone else in CI. The same goes for Martin. By CI's strict code, I'm a maverick, a loose end.'

She left him for a moment to go into the bathroom. A moment later, she returned with a washcloth she'd soaked in hot water. She pressed this over the newly restitched wound and held it there, waiting for the bleeding to stop.

'Jason,' she said. 'Look at me. Why don't you look at me?'

'Because,' he said, directing his gaze into her beautiful uptilted eyes, 'when I look at you I don't see you at all. I see Marie.'

Soraya, abruptly deflated, sat down on the edge of the bed. 'Are we so alike, then?'

He resumed his study of the stateroom ceiling. 'On the contrary. You're nothing like her.'

'Then why—'

The deep booming of the ro-ro's horn filled the stateroom. A moment later, they felt a small lurch, then a gentle rocking. They were moving out of the port, on their journey across the Black Sea to Istanbul.

'I think you owe me an explanation,' she said softly.

'Did we . . . I mean before?'

'No. I would never have asked that of you.'

'And me? Did I ask it of you?'

'Oh, Jason, you know yourself better than that.'

'I wouldn't have taken Fadi out of his cell, either. I wouldn't have been led into a trap on the beach.' His gaze slid down to her patiently waiting face. 'It's bad enough not being able to remember.' He remembered the confetti of memories – his and . . . someone else's. 'But having memories that lead you astray . . .'

'But how? Why?'

'Dr. Sunderland introduced certain proteins into the synapses of the brain.' Bourne struggled to sit up, waving off her help. 'Sunderland is in league with Fadi. The procedure was part of Fadi's plan.'

'Jason, we've talked about this. It's insane. For one thing, how could Fadi possibly know you'd need a memory specialist? For another, how would he know which one you'd go to?'

'Both good questions. Unfortunately, I still don't have any answers. But consider: Fadi had enough information about CI to know who Lindros was. He knew about Typhon. His information was so extensive, so detailed, it allowed him to create an impostor who fooled everyone, even me, even the sophisticated CI retinal scan.'

'Could he be part of the conspiracy?' she said. 'Fadi's conspiracy?'

'It sound like a paranoid's dream. But I'm beginning to believe that all these incidents – Sunderland's treatment, Martin's kidnapping and replacement, Fadi's revenge against me – are related, parts of a brilliantly designed and executed conspiracy to bring me down, along with all of CI.'

'How do we discover whether or not you're right? How do we make sense of it all?'

He regarded Soraya for a moment. 'We need to go back to the beginning. Back to the first time I came to Odessa, when you were COS. But in order to do that, I need you to fill in the missing parts of my memory.'

Soraya stood and moved to the window, staring out at the widening swatch of water, the curving haze-smeared coastline of Odessa they were leaving behind.

Painful as it was, he swung his legs around and got gingerly to his feet. The local anesthetic was wearing off; a deeper pain pulsed through him as the full extent of the damage from Lerner's calculated blow hit him like a freight train. He staggered, almost fell back in the bed, but caught himself. He deepened his breathing, slowing it. Gradually, the pain receded to a tolerable level. Then he walked across the stateroom to stand beside her.

'You should be back in bed,' she said in a distant voice.

'Soraya, why is it so difficult to tell me what happened?'

For a moment, she said nothing. Then: 'I thought I'd put it all behind me. That I'd never have to think of it again.'

He gripped her shoulders and spun her around. 'For the love of God, what happened?'

Her eyes, dark and luminous, brimmed with tears. 'We killed someone, Jason. You and I. A civilian, an innocent. A young woman barely out of her teens.'

He is running down the street carrying someone in his arms. His hands are covered in blood. Her blood . . .

'Who?' he said sharply. 'Who did we kill?'

Soraya was trembling as if with a terrible chill. 'Her name was Sarah.'

'Sarah who?'

'That's all I know.' Tears overflowed her eyes. 'I know that because you told me. You told me that before she died, her last words were, "My name is Sarah. Remember me."'

*

Where am I now? Martin Lindros wondered. He had felt the heat, the gritty dust against his skin as he was led off the plane, still blinded by the hood. But he'd been exposed to neither the heat nor the dust for very long. A vehicle – a jeep or possibly a light truck – had rumbled him down a peculiarly smooth incline. Greeted by an air-cooled environment, he had walked for perhaps a thousand meters. He heard a bolt being thrown, a door opened, and then he was shoved in. After he heard the door slam, the lock bolted into place, he stood for a moment, trying to do nothing more than breathe deeply and evenly. Then he reached up and plucked the hood from his head.

He stood in more or less the center of a room, perhaps five meters on a side, constructed solidly but rather crudely of reinforced concrete. It contained a rather dated doctor's examining table, a small stainless-steel sink, a row of low cabinets on top of which were neatly lined boxes of latex gloves, cotton swabs, bottles of disinfectant, various liquids and implements.

The infirmary was windowless, which did not surprise him, since he surmised that they were underground. But where? Certainly he was in a desertlike climate, but not an actual desert – building anything underground in the desert was impossible. So, a hot, mountainous country. From the echoes that had reached him as he and his guards had made their way here, the facility was quite large. Therefore, it had to be situated in a place hidden from prying eyes. He could think of half a dozen such areas – such as Somalia – but he dismissed most of them as too close to Ras Dejen. He moved around the room in a counterclockwise motion, the better to see out of his left eye. If he had to guess, he'd say he was somewhere on the border between Afghanistan and Pakistan. A rugged, utterly lawless swath of real estate controlled from top to bottom by ethnic tribes whose patrons were legions of the world's most deadly terrorists.

He would have enjoyed asking Muta ibn Aziz about that, but Abbud's brother had debarked some hours before the plane had arrived here.

Hearing the bolt slide back, the door open, he turned and saw a slim, bespectacled man with bad skin and a shocking pompadour of sandy gray hair walk in. With a guttural growl, he rushed at the man, who stepped neatly aside, revealing the two guards behind him. Their presence hardly deterred his rage-filled heart, but the butts of their semiautomatics put him on the floor.

'I don't blame you for wanting to do me harm,' Dr. Andursky said from his vantage point safely standing over Lindros's prone body. 'I might feel the same way if I were in your shoes.'

'If only you were.'

This response produced in Dr. Andursky a smile that fairly radiated insincerity. 'I came here to see to your health.'

'Is that what you were doing when you took out my right eye?' Lindros shouted.

One of the guards pressed the muzzle of his semi-automatic to Lindros's chest, to make his point.

Dr. Andursky appeared unruffled. 'As you well know, I needed your eye; I needed the retina to transplant into Karim al-Jamil's. Without that part of you, he never would have fooled the CI retinal scanner. He never would have passed for you, no matter how good a job I did on his face.'

Lindros brushed away the gun muzzle as he sat up. 'You make it sound so cut and dried.'

'Science *is* cut and dried,' Dr. Andursky pointed out. 'Now, why don't you go over to the examining table so I can take a look at how your eye is healing.'

Lindros rose, walked back, lay down on the table. Dr. Andursky, flanked by his guards, used a pair of surgeon's scissors to cut through the filthy bandages over Lindros's right eye. He clucked to himself as he peered into the still-raw pit where Martin's eye used to be.

'They could have done better than this.' Dr. Andursky was clearly miffed. 'All my good work . . .'

He washed up at the sink, snapped on a pair of the latex gloves, and got to work cleaning the excavation. Lindros felt nothing more than the dull ache he'd become accustomed to. It was like a houseguest who showed up unexpectedly one night and never left. Now, like it or not, the pain was a permanent fixture.

'I imagine you've already adjusted to your monovision.' As was his wont, Dr. Andursky worked quickly and efficiently. He knew what he needed to do, and how he wanted to do it.

'I have an idea,' Lindros said. 'Why don't you take Fadi's right eye and give it to me?'

'How very Old Testament of you.' Dr. Andursky rebandaged the excavation. 'But you're alone, Lindros. There's no one here to help you.'

Finished, he snapped off his gloves. 'For you, there is no escape from this hell-pit.'

Jon Mueller caught up with Defense Secretary Halliday as he was coming out of the Pentagon. Halliday was, of course, not alone. He had with him two aides, a bodyguard, and several pilot fish – lieutenant generals eager to ingratiate themselves with the great man.

Halliday, seeing Mueller out of the corner of his eye, made a hand gesture Mueller knew well. He hung back, at the bottom of the stairs, at the last minute allowing himself to be swept up into the secretary's retinue as he ducked into his limo. They said nothing to each another until the two aides had been dropped off near the secretary's office. Then the privacy wall came down between passengers in the rear, and driver and bodyguard in front. Mueller brought Halliday up to date.

Storm clouds of displeasure raced across the secretary's broad forehead. 'Lerner assured me everything was under control.'

'Matt made the mistake of farming out the job. I'll take care of the Held woman myself.'

The secretary nodded. 'All right. But be warned, Jon. Nothing can be traced back to me, you understand? If something goes wrong, I won't lift a finger. In fact, I may be the one to prosecute you. From this moment on, you're on your own.'

Mueller grinned like a savage. 'No worries, Mr. Secretary, I've been on my own for as long as I can remember. It's bred in the bone.'

'Sarah. Just Sarah. You never followed it up?'

'There was nothing to follow up. I couldn't even remember her face clearly. It was night, everything happened so fast. And then you were shot. We were on the run, pursued. We holed up in the catacombs, then got out. Afterward, all I had was a name. There was no official record of her body; it was as if we'd never been in Odessa.' Soraya put her head down. 'But even if there had been some way, the truth is I . . . couldn't. I wanted to forget her, forget her death ever happened.'

'But I remember running down a cobbled street, holding her in my arms, her blood everywhere.'

Soraya nodded. Her face was heavy with sorrow. 'You saw her moving. You picked her up. That's when you were shot. I returned fire and suddenly there was a hail of bullets. We got separated. You went to find the target, Hamid ibn Ashef. From what you told me later, when we rendezvoused in the catacombs, you found him and shot him, but were unsure whether you'd killed him.'

'And Sarah?'

'By then she was long dead. You left her on the way to kill Hamid ibn Ashef.'

For a long time, there was silence in the stateroom. Bourne turned, went to the water jug, poured himself half a glass. He opened the twist of paper Dr. Pavlyna had given him, swallowed one of the antibiotic pills. The water tasted flat, slightly bitter.

'How did it happen?' He had his back to her. He didn't want to see her face when she told him.

'She appeared at the spot where we met my conduit. He told us where Hamid ibn Ashef was. In return, we gave him the money he'd asked for. We were finishing the transaction when we saw her. She was running. I don't know why. Also, she had her mouth open as if shouting something. But the conduit was shouting, too. We thought he'd betrayed us – which, it turned out, he had. We shot at her. Both of us. And she fell.'

Bourne, abruptly tired, sat down in the bed.

Soraya took a step toward him. 'Are you all right?'

He nodded, took a deep breath. 'It was a mistake,' he said.

'Do you think that makes any difference to her?'

'You may not even have hit her.'

'And then again I may have. In any event, would that absolve me?'

'You're drowning in your own guilt.'

She gave a sad little laugh. 'Then I guess we both are.'

They regarded each other across the small space of the stateroom. The *Itkursk*'s horn sounded again, muffled, mournful. The ro-ro rocked them as it plowed south across the Black Sea, but it was so quiet in the stateroom that she imagined she could hear the sound of his mind working through a deep and tangled mystery.

He said, 'Soraya, listen to me, I think Sarah's death is the key to everything that's happened, everything that's happening now.'

'You can't be serious.' But by the expression on his face she knew he was, and she was sorry for her response. 'Go on,' she said.

'I think Sarah is central. I think her death set everything in motion.'

'Dujja's plan to detonate a nuclear bomb in a major American city? That's a stretch.'

'Not the plan per se. I have no doubt that was already being discussed,' Bourne said. 'But I think the timing of it changed. I think Sarah's death lit the fuse.'

'That would mean that Sarah is connected with your original mission to terminate Hamid ibn Ashef.'

He nodded. 'That would be my guess. I don't think she was at the rendezvous point by accident.'

'Why would she be there? How would she have known?'

'She could have found out from your conduit. He betrayed us to Hamid ibn Ashef's people,' Bourne said. 'As to why she was there, I have no idea.'

Soraya frowned. 'But where's the link between Hamid ibn Ashef and Fadi?'

'I've been thinking about that bit of intel you got from your forensics friend at the Fire Investigation Unit.'

'Carbon disulfide – the accelerant Fadi used at the Hotel Constitution.'

'Right. One of things you told me carbon disulfide is used for is flotation – a method for the separation of mixtures. Flotation was developed in the late twentieth century on a commercial scale mainly for the processing of silver.'

Soraya's eyes lit up. 'One of Integrated Vertical Technologies' businesses is silver processing. IVT is owned by Hamid ibn Ashef.'

Bourne nodded. 'I think IVT is the legitimate entity that's been bankrolling Dujja all these years.'

'But Sarah—'

'As for Sarah, or anything else, for that matter, we're dead in the water until we reach Istanbul and can connect to the Internet. Right now, our cell phones are useless.'

Soraya rose. 'In that event, I'm going to get us something to eat. I don't know about you, but I'm starving.'

'We'll go together.'

Bourne began to rise, but she pushed him back onto the bed. 'You need your rest, Jason. I'll get food for both of us.'

She smiled at him before turning and going out the door.

Bourne lay back for a moment, trying to recall more of the abortive mission to terminate Hamid ibn Ashef. He imagined the young woman Sarah as she ran into the square, mouth open. What was she shouting? Who was she shouting at? He felt her in his arms, strained to hear her failing voice.

But it was Fadi's voice he heard, echoing beneath the pier in Odessa:

'I've waited a long time for this moment. A long time to look you in the face again. A long time to exact my revenge.'

So there was a significant personal element to Fadi's plan. Because Fadi had come after him, leading him carefully, craftily into the web of a conspiracy of unprecedented proportions. It was he who had come after the man posing as Lindros; he who had vouched for the impostor at Bleak House. That, too, was part of the plan. Fadi had used him to infiltrate CI on the highest level.

No longer able to lie still, Bourne levered himself off the bed, not without some pain and stiffness. He stretched as much as he could, then padded into the bathroom: a sheet-metal shower, tiny metal sink, porcelain toilet, hexagonal mirror. On a rack were a pair of thin, almost threadbare towels, two large oblong cakes of soap, probably mostly lye.

Reaching up, he turned on the shower, waited for the spray of water to run hot, stepped in.

The afternoon, waning, had turned gray, the sun having lowered beneath dark clouds holding what would soon be a deluge. With the premature darkness a humid wind had sprung up from the southwest, bringing with it imagined hints of the pungent scents of sumac and oregano from the Turkish shore.

Matthew Lerner, standing amidships at the *Itkursk*'s starboard rail, was smoking a cigarette when he saw Soraya Moore emerge from one of the two VIP staterooms on the flagship deck.

He watched her moving away from the stateroom, down a metal stairway to one of the lower decks. He felt the impulse to go after her, to bury the ice pick he carried into the nape of her neck. That would have made him personally happy, but professionally it was suicide – just as it would be to use his gun in the enclosed environment of the ship. He was after Bourne. Killing Soraya Moore would complicate a situation that had already jumped the tracks. He was having to improvise, not the best of scenarios, though in the field improvisation was almost inevitable.

Swiveling adroitly, he faced the rolling waves as she came to the midway landing, for a moment facing in his direction. He pulled on the harsh Turkish cigarette then spun the butt over the side.

He turned back. Soraya Moore had disappeared. There were no colors here. The sea was gunmetal gray, the ship itself painted black and white. Moving quickly across the deck, he climbed the staircase to the flagship deck and the door to the VIP stateroom.

*

Bourne, careful of his wound, soaped up. Aches and muscle tightness sluiced away, along with the layers of sweat and grime. He wished he could stay under the hot water, but this was a working ship, not a luxury liner. The cold water came too quickly, and then the spray stopped altogether, with his skin still partially soap-slicked.

At almost the same moment he saw a blur of movement out of the corner of his eye. Turning, he went into a crouch. His reflexes and the slickness of his skin saved him from having the ice pick wielded by Lerner puncture his neck. As it was, he lurched hard against the back wall of the shower as Lerner rushed him.

Using the heavily callused edge of his hand, Lerner delivered two quick blows to Bourne's midsection. Designed to incapacitate him so that Lerner could strike again with the ice pick, they landed hard, but not hard enough. Bourne countered a third blow, using the added leverage of the stall back to slam the heel of his left foot into Lerner's chest just as Lerner was stepping into the shower. Instead of hemming Bourne in, Lerner shot backward, skidding across the tile of the bathroom floor.

Bourne was out of the stall in an instant. He grabbed a new bar of soap, placed it squarely in the center of the towel. Holding the towel at either end, he spun it around, securely embedding the cake. With the two ends of the towel in his right hand, he swung it back and forth. He blocked a vicious edge-hand strike with his left forearm, lifting Lerner's right arm up and away, creating an opening. He lashed his home-made weapon into Lerner's midsection.

The towel-wrapped bar of soap delivered a surprisingly wicked blow for which Lerner was unprepared. He staggered backward into the stateroom. Nevertheless, with his body in peak condition, it slowed him only momentarily. Set back on his heels, he waited for Bourne's attempt to maneuver inside his defense. Instead Bourne whipped his weapon in low, forcing Lerner to take a swipe at it with the ice pick.

At once Bourne stamped down with his left foot on Lerner's right wrist, trapping it against the stateroom carpet. But Bourne was barefoot; moreover, his foot was still wet and somewhat slick, and Lerner was able to wrench his wrist free. Lerner slashed upward with the ice pick, barely missed impaling Bourne's foot. He feinted right, drove his right knee into the left side of Bourne's rib cage.

The pain reverberated through Bourne, his teeth bared in a grimace. The iron-hard knuckles of Lerner's fist struck him on the opposite shoulder. He sagged and, as he did so, Lerner hooked his heel behind Bourne's ankle, then jerked him off his feet.

He fell on Bourne, who struck upward. Blood spattered them both as Bourne landed a direct hit on Lerner's nose, breaking it. As Lerner wiped the blood out of his eyes, Bourne upended him, jamming his fingertips into the spot just at the bottom of Lerner's rib cage. Lerner grunted in surprise and pain as he felt two of his ribs give.

He roared, letting go with such a flurry of powerful blows that even with both hands free Bourne couldn't protect himself from all of them. Only a third got through his defenses, but those were enough to seriously weaken his already compromised stamina.

Without knowing how it happened, he found Lerner's ham-like hand around his throat. Pinned to the floor, he saw the point of the ice pick sweep down toward his right eye.

Only one chance now. He ceded all conscious control to the killer instinct of the Bourne identity. No thought, no fear. He slammed the palms of his hands against Lerner's ears. The twin blows not only disoriented Lerner but also created a semiairtight seal, so that when Bourne swung his hands apart the resulting pressure ruptured Lerner's eardrums.

The ice pick stopped in midstrike, trembling in Lerner's suddenly palsied hand. Bourne swept it aside, grabbed Lerner by the front of his shirt, jerked him down as he brought his head up. The bone of his forehead impacted Lerner's face just where the bridge of his nose met his forehead.

Lerner reared back, his eyes rolling up. Still he grasped the ice pick. Half unconscious, his superbly developed survival instinct kicked in. His right hand swept down, passing through the skin on the outside of Bourne's right arm as Bourne twisted away.

Then Bourne delivered a two-handed blow to the carotid artery in the right side of Lerner's neck. Lerner, on his knees, fell back, swaying. Forming his fingers into a tight wedge, Bourne drove his fingertips into the soft spot beneath Lerner's jaw. He felt the shredding of skin, muscle, viscera.

The stateroom turned red.

Bourne felt a sudden blackness imposing itself on his vision. All at once, he felt his strength desert him, ebbing like the tide. He shivered, toppled over, unconscious.

TWENTY-THREE

Muta ibn Aziz, his fingers gripping Katya Veintrop's shapely upper arm, rode the stainless-steel elevator down to Dujja's Miran Shah nuclear facility.

'Will I see my husband now?' Katya asked.

'You will,' Muta ibn Aziz said, 'but the reunion won't make either of you happy, this I promise.'

The elevator door slid open. Katya shuddered as they stepped out.

'I feel like I'm in the bowels of hell,' she said, looking around at the bare concrete corridors.

The infernal lighting did nothing to disfigure her beauty, which Muta ibn Aziz, like any good Arab, had done his best to cover with the utmost modesty. She was tall, slender, full-breasted, blond, light-eyed. Her skin, free of blemishes, seemed to glow, as if she'd recently buffed it. A small constellation of freckles rode the bridge of her nose. None of this mattered to Muta ibn Aziz, who ignored her with a absoluteness born and bred in the desert.

During the dusty, monotonous eight-hour trip by Land Rover to Miran Shah, he had turned his mind to other matters. He had been to this spot once before, three years ago. He had come with his brother Abbud ibn Aziz; with them was the brilliant and reluctant Dr. Costin Veintrop. They had been sent by Fadi to escort Veintrop from his laboratory in Bucharest to Miran Shah because the good doctor appeared incapable of making the trip on his own.

Veintrop had been in a depressed and bitter mood, having been summarily severed from Integrated Vertical Technologies for crimes he claimed he'd never committed. He was right, but that was beside the point. The charges themselves had been enough to blackball him from any legitimate corporation, university, or grant program to which he applied.

Along had come Fadi with his seductive offer. He hadn't bothered to sugarcoat the goal of what he was proposing; what would be the point? The doctor would realize it soon enough. Veintrop was, naturally, dazzled by the money. But as it happened, he possessed scruples as well as brilliance. So Fadi had abandoned the carrot for the stick. This particular stick being Katya. Fadi had learned quickly enough that Veintrop would do virtually anything to keep Katya safe.

'Your wife is safe with me, Doctor,' Fadi had said when Muta ibn Aziz and his brother had appeared at Miran Shah with Veintrop in tow. 'Safer than she'd be anywhere else on the planet.' And to prove it, he'd shown Veintrop a video of Katya made just days before. Katya weeping, imploring her husband to come for her. Veintrop, too, had wept. Then, wiping his eyes, he had accepted Fadi's offer. But in his eyes they all recognized the shadow of trouble.

After Dr. Senarz had taken Veintrop away to begin his work at the Miran Shah labs, Fadi had turned to Muta ibn Aziz and Abbud ibn Aziz. 'Will he do what we want? What is your opinion?'

The two brothers spoke up at once, agreeing. 'He'll do everything asked of him as long as we beat him with the stick.'

But it was the last thing they agreed on during that four-day sojourn in the concrete city deep below the wild, bare-knuckled mountains that formed the border between western Pakistan and Afghanistan. A man could get killed in those mountain passes – many men, in fact, no matter how well trained, how heavily armed. Miran Shah was the lethal badlands into which no representative of the Pakistani government or army dared venture. Taliban, al-Qaeda, World Jihad, Muslim fundamentalists of every stripe and flavor – Miran Shah was crawling with terrorists, many of whom were hostile to one another, for it was one of the more successful American lies that all terrorist groups were coordinated and controlled by one or two men, or even a handful. This was ludicrous: There were so many ancient enmities among sects, so many different objectives that interfered with one another. Still, the myth remained. Fadi, schooled in the West, master of the principles of mass communication, used the American lie against them, to build Dujja's reputation, along with his own.

As Muta ibn Aziz marched Katya along the corridors for her interview with Fadi and with her husband, he could not help but reflect on the fundamental splinter that had driven him and his brother apart. They had disagreed on it three years ago, and time had only hardened their respective positions. The splinter had a name: Sarah ibn Ashef, Fadi and Karim al-Jamil's only sister. Her murder had changed all their lives, spawning secrets, lies, and enmity where none had existed before. Her death had destroyed two families, in ways both obvious and obscure. After that night in Odessa when her arms had flung out and she had pitched to the cobbles of the square, Muta ibn Aziz and his brother were finished. Outwardly they acted as if nothing had happened, but inside their thoughts never again ran down parallel tracks. They were lost to each other.

Turning a corner, Muta ibn Aziz saw his brother step out of an open doorway, beckon to him. Muta hated when he did that. It was the gesture of a professor to a pupil, one who was due for a reprimand.

'Ah, you're here,' Abbud ibn Aziz said, as if his brother had taken a wrong turn and was now late.

Muta ibn Aziz contrived to ignore Abbud ibn Aziz, brushing

past him as he manhandled Katya over the threshold.

The room was spacious, though by necessity low-ceilinged. It was furnished in strictly utilitarian fashion: six chairs made of molded plastic, a zinc-topped table, cabinets along the left-hand wall, with a sink and a single electric burner.

Fadi was standing, facing them. His hands were on the shoulders of Dr. Veintrop, who was sitting, clearly not of his own volition, on one of the chairs.

'Katya!' he cried when he saw her. His face lit up, but the light in his eyes was quickly extinguished as he tried, and failed, to go to her.

Fadi, exerting the requisite pressure on Veintrop to keep him from moving, nodded to Muta ibn Aziz, who released the young woman. With an inarticulate cry, she ran to her husband, knelt in front of him.

Veintrop caressed her hair, her face, his fingers moving over every contour as if he needed to reassure himself that she wasn't a mirage or a doppelgänger. He'd seen what Dr. Andursky had done with Karim al-Jamil's face. What would prevent him from doing the same with some other Russian woman, turning her into a Katya who would lie to him, do their bidding?

Ever since Fadi had 'recruited' him, his paranoia threshold was exceedingly low. Everything revolved around the plot to enslave him. In this, he wasn't far wrong.

'Now that you've been reunited, more or less,' Fadi said to Dr. Veintrop, 'I'd like you to stop procrastinating. We have a specific timetable, and your foot-dragging is doing us no good.'

'I'm not procrastinating,' Veintrop said. 'The microcircuits—' He broke off, wincing, as Fadi applied more pressure to his shoulders.

Fadi nodded to Abbud ibn Aziz, who stepped out of the room. When he returned, it was with Dr. Senarz, the nuclear physicist.

'Dr. Senarz,' Fadi said, 'please tell me why the nuclear device I ordered you to construct is not yet complete.'

Dr. Senarz stared directly at Veintrop. He had trained under the notorious Pakistani nuclear scientist Abdul Qadeer Khan. 'My work is complete,' he said. 'The uranium dioxide powder you delivered to me has been converted to HEU, the metal form needed for the warhead. In other words, we have the fissionable material. The casing is also complete. We are now only waiting on Dr. Veintrop. His work is crucial, as you know. Without it, you won't have the device you requested.'

'So Costin, here we come to the crux of the matter at hand.' Fadi's voice was calm, soft, neutral. 'With your help my plan succeeds, without your help my plan is doomed. An equation as simple as it is elegant, to put it in scientific terms. Why aren't you helping me?'

'The process is more difficult than I had anticipated.' Veintrop could not keep his eyes off his wife.

Fadi said, 'Dr. Senarz?'

'Dr. Veintrop's miniaturization work has been complete for days now.'

'What does he know of miniaturization?' Veintrop said sharply. 'It simply isn't true.'

'I don't want opinions, Dr. Senarz,' Fadi said with equal sharpness.

When Senarz produced the small notebook with a dark red leather cover, Veintrop let out an involuntary moan. Katya, alarmed, gripped him tighter.

Dr. Senarz held out the notebook. 'Here we have Dr. Veintrop's private notes.'

'You have no right!' Veintrop shouted.

'Ah, but he has every right.' Fadi accepted the notebook from Dr. Senarz. 'You belong to me, Veintrop. Everything you do, everything you think, write, or dream of is mine.'

Katya groaned. 'Costin, what did you do?'

'I sold my soul to the devil,' Veintrop muttered.

Abbud ibn Aziz must have received a silent signal from Fadi, because he tapped Dr. Senarz on the shoulder and led him out of the room. The sound of the door closing behind them made Veintrop jump.

'All right,' Fadi said in his gentlest voice.

At once, Muta ibn Aziz grabbed Katya's clothes at the nape of her neck and at her waist, wrenching her away from her husband. At the same time, Fadi resumed his two-handed grip on the doctor, slamming him back down onto the chair, from which he struggled to rise.

'I won't ask you again,' Fadi said in that same gentle tone, a father to a beloved child who has misbehaved.

Muta ibn Aziz struck Katya a tremendous blow on the back of her head.

'No!' Veintrop screamed as she sprawled face-first on the floor.

No one paid him the slightest attention. Muta ibn Aziz hauled her up to a sitting position, came around, punched her so hard he broke her perfect nose. Blood gushed forth, spattering them both.

'No!' Veintrop screamed.

Gripping the back of her blond hair, Muta ibn Aziz drove his knuckles into Katya's beautiful left cheek. Tears rolled down Katya's bloated face as she sobbed.

'Stop!' Veintrop shouted. 'For the love of God, stop! I beg you!'

Muta ibn Aziz drew back his bloody fist.

'Don't make me ask you again,' Fadi said in the doctor's ear. 'Don't make me distrust you, Costin.'

'No, all right.' Veintrop was himself sobbing. His heart was breaking into ten thousand pieces he would never be able to fit back together. 'I'll do what you want. I'll have the miniaturization finished in two days.'

'Two days, Costin.' Fadi grabbed his hair, jerked his head

back so that his eyes looked up directly into his captor's. 'Not a moment more. Understood?'

'Yes.'

'Otherwise, what will be done to Katya not even Dr. Andursky will be able to fix.'

Muta ibn Aziz found his brother in Dr. Andursky's operating theater. It was here that Karim al-Jamil had been given Martin Lindros's face. It was here that Karim al-Jamil had been given a new iris, a new pupil, and, most important, a retina that would prove to CI's scanners that Karim al-Jamil was Lindros.

To Muta ibn Aziz's relief, the theater was currently empty save for his brother.

'Now surely we must tell Fadi the truth.' Muta ibn Aziz's voice was low, urgent.

Abbud ibn Aziz, staring at the battery of gleaming equipment, said, 'Don't you think of anything else? This is precisely what you said to me three years ago.'

'Circumstances have changed, radically. It's our duty to tell him.'

'I disagree, in the strongest possible terms, just as I did then,' Abbud ibn Aziz replied. 'In fact, it's our duty to keep the truth from Fadi and Karim al-Jamil.'

'There's no logic to your argument now.'

'Really? The central issue now is the same at it was in the beginning. With Sarah ibn Ashef's death, they have suffered an unsupportable loss. Should there be more? Sarah ibn Ashef was Allah's flower, the repository of the family's honor, the beautiful innocent destined for a life of happiness. It is vital that her memory be kept sacrosanct. Our duty is to insulate Fadi and Karim al-Jamil from outside distractions.'

'Distraction,' Muta ibn Aziz cried. 'You call the truth about their sister a distraction?'

'What would you call it?'

'A full-scale disaster, a disgrace beyond anything—'

'And you would be the one to deliver this terrible truth to Fadi? Toward what end? What would you seek to accomplish?'

'Three years ago, I answered that question by saying I wanted simply to tell the truth,' Muta ibn Aziz said. 'Now their plan includes taking revenge on Jason Bourne.'

'I see no reason to stop them. Bourne is a menace to us – you included. You were there that night, as was I.'

'Their obsession with revenging their sister's death has warped both of them. What if they've overreached?'

'With one man?' Abbud ibn Aziz laughed.

'You were with Fadi both times in Odessa. Tell me, brother, was he successful in killing Bourne?'

Abbud ibn Aziz reacted to his brother's icy tone. 'Bourne was wounded, very badly. Fadi hounded him into the catacombs beneath the city. I very much doubt he survived. But really, it's of no consequence. He's incapacitated; he cannot harm us now. It's Allah's will. Whatever happened, happened. Whatever happens, will happen.'

'And I say that as long as there's the slightest possibility of Bourne being alive, neither of them will rest. The distraction will continue. Whereas if we tell them—'

'Silence! It is Allah's will!'

Abbud ibn Aziz had never before spoken to his younger brother with such venom. Between them, Muta ibn Aziz knew, lay the death of Sarah ibn Ashef, a topic about which both thought but never, ever spoke. The silence was an evil thing, Muta ibn Aziz knew, a poisoning of the well of their fraternal bond. He harbored a strong conviction that one day, the deliberately invoked silence would destroy him and his older brother.

Not for the first time he felt a wave of despair roll over him. In these moments, it seemed to him that he was trapped;

that no matter which way he turned, no matter what action he took now, he and his brother were condemned to the hellfire reserved for the wicked. *La ilaha ill allah! May Allah forbid the Fire from touching us!*

As if to underscore Muta's dark thoughts, Abbud reiterated the stance he had taken from the night of her death: 'In the matter of Sarah ibn Ashef, we keep our own counsel,' he said flatly. 'You will obey me without question, just as you've always done. Just as you must do. We are not individuals, brother, we are links in the family chain. *La ilaha ill allah!* The fate of one is the fate of all.'

The man sitting cross-legged at the head of a low wooden table laden with paraphernalia regarded Fadi with a jaundiced eye. Doubtless, this was because he had the use of only one eye – his left. The other, beneath its white Egyptian cotton patch, was a blackened crater.

Kicking off his shoes, Fadi padded across the poured concrete floor. Every floor, wall, and ceiling in Miran Shah was of poured concrete, looked identical. He sat at a ninety-degree angle from the other.

From a glass jar, he shook out a fistful of coffee beans that had been roasted hours ago. He dropped them into a brass mortar, took up the pestle, ground them to a fine powder. A copper pot sat atop the ring of a portable gas burner. Fadi poured water from a pitcher into the pot, then lit the burner. A circle of blue flame licked at the bottom of the pot.

'It's been some time,' Fadi said.

'Do you actually expect me to drink with you?' said the real Martin Lindros.

'I expect you to behave like a civilized human being.'

Lindros laughed bitterly, touched the center of his eye patch with the tip of his forefinger. 'That would make one of us.'

'Have a date,' Fadi said, pushing an oval plate piled high with the dried fruit in front of Lindros. 'They're best dipped in this goat butter.'

The moment the water began to boil, Fadi upended the mortar, spilling the coffee powder into the pot. He drew to him a small cup, whose contents were fragrant with the scent of freshly crushed cardamom seeds. Now all his concentration was on the roiling coffee. An instant before it would have foamed up, he took the pot off the burner, with the fingers of his right hand he dropped a few crushed cardamom seeds into the coffee, then poured it into what looked like a small teapot. A fragment of palm fiber stuffed into the spout served to keep the grounds out of the liquid. Setting the pot aside, Fadi poured the *qahwah 'Arabiyah* – the Arabic coffee – into a pair of tiny cups without handles. He served Lindros first, as any Bedouin would his honored guest, though never before had a Bedouin sat cross-legged in such a tent – immense, subterranean, fashioned of concrete half a meter thick.

'How's your brother doing? I hope seeing with my eye will give him a different perspective. Perhaps he won't be so hellbent on the destruction of the West.'

'Do you really wish to speak of destruction, Martin? We shall speak then of America's forced exportation of a culture riddled with the decadence of a jaded populace that wants everything immediately, that no longer understands the meaning of the word *sacrifice*. We shall speak of America's occupation of the Middle East, of its willful destruction of ancient traditions.'

'Then those traditions must include the blowing up of religious statues, as the Taliban did in Afghanistan. Those traditions must include the stoning of women who commit adultery, while their lovers go without punishment.'

'I – a Saudi Bedouin – have as much to do with the Taliban as you do. And as for adulterous women, there is Islamic law to consider. We are not individuals, Martin, but part of a family unit. The honor of the family resides in its daughters. If our sisters are shamed, that shame reflects on all in the family until the woman is excised.'

'To kill your own flesh and blood? It's inhuman.'

'Because it's not your way?' Fadi made a gesture with his head. 'Drink.'

Lindros raised his cup to his lips, downed the coffee in one gulp.

'You must sip it, Martin.' Fadi refilled Lindros's cup, then drank his coffee in three small, savory sips. With his right hand, he took up a date, dipped it in the fragrant butter, then popped it into his mouth. He chewed slowly, thoughtfully, and spat out the long, flat pit. 'It will do you good to try one. Dates are delicious, and ever so nutritious. Do you know that Muhammad would invariably break his fast with dates? So do we, because it brings us closer to his ideals.'

Lindros stared at him, stiff and silent, as if on vigil.

Fadi wiped his right hand on a small towel. 'You know, my father made coffee from morning to night. That's the highest compliment I could pay him – or any Bedouin. It means he's a generous man.' He refilled his coffee cup. 'However, my father can no longer make coffee. In fact, he can do nothing at all but stare into space. My mother speaks to him, but he cannot answer. Do you know why, Martin?' He drained his cup in three more sips. 'Because his name is Abu Sarif Hamid ibn Ashef al-Wahhib.'

At this, Lindros's good eye gave a slight twitch.

'Yes, that's right,' Fadi said. 'Hamid ibn Ashef. The man you sent Jason Bourne to kill.'

'So that's why you captured me.'

'You think so?'

'That wasn't my mission, you fool. I didn't even know Jason Bourne then. His handler was Alex Conklin, and Conklin's dead.' Lindros began to laugh.

Without any warning Fadi lunged across the table and

grabbed Lindros by his shirtfront. He shook him so violently that Lindros's teeth chattered.

'You think you're so clever, Martin. But now you're going to pay for it. You and Bourne.'

Fadi gripped Lindros's throat as if he wanted to rip out his windpipe. He took visible pleasure in the man's gasps.

'Bourne is still alive, I'm told, though just barely. Still and all, I know he'll move heaven and earth to find you, especially if he thinks I'll be here as well.'

'What . . . what are you going to do?' Lindros could barely spit the words through his labored breathing.

'I'm going to give him the information he needs, Martin, to find you here in Miran Shah. And when he does, I'll disembowel you in front of his eyes. Then I'll go to work on him.'

Fadi put his face against Lindros's, peering into his left eye as if to find all the things Lindros was hiding from him. 'In the end, Bourne will want to die, Martin. Of this there is no question. But for him, death will be a long time coming. Before he dies, I'll make certain he witnesses the nuclear destruction of the American capital.'

BOOK THREE

TWENTY-FOUR

The coffin is being lowered into the ground. Dull reflections spin off the handles, the inscribed panel set into its lid creating tiny dizzying whorls of light. In response to an emphatic gesture from the minister, the coffin hangs motionless in midair. The minister, dapper and trim in his European-cut suit, leans over the grave so far that Bourne is certain he'll fall in. But he does not. Instead, with an astonishing burst of superhuman strength, he wrenches off the coffin lid.

'What are you doing?' Bourne asks.

The minister turns to him, beckons as he drops the heavy mahogany lid into the grave, and Bourne sees that it isn't the minister at all. It's Fadi.

'Come on,' Fadi says in Saudi Arabic. He lights up a cigarette, hands Bourne the matchbook. 'Take a look.'

Bourne takes a step forward, peers into the open coffin . . .

. . . and finds himself sitting in the backseat of a car. He looks out the window and sees a familiar landscape that he nevertheless cannot identify. He shakes the driver's shoulder.

'Where are we going?'

The driver turns around. It's Lindros. But there's something wrong with his face. It's shadowed, or scarred: It's the Lindros he brought back to CI headquarters. 'Where do you think?' the Lindros impostor says, increasing their speed.

Leaning forward, Bourne sees a figure standing by the side of the road. They come up on it fast. A young woman, a hitchhiker with her thumb out: Sarah. They're almost abreast of her when she

371

takes a step into the path of the speeding car.

Bourne tries to shout a warning, but he is mute. He feels the car lurch and buck, sees Sarah's body flung into the air, blood streaming from her. In a rage, he reaches for the driver . . .

. . . and finds himself aboard a bus. The passengers, blank-faced, ignore him completely. Bourne moves forward along the aisle between the sets of seats. The driver is wearing a neat suit of European manufacture. He is Dr. Sunderland, the D.C. memory specialist.

'Where are we going?' Bourne asks him.

'I already told you.' Dr. Sunderland points.

Through the huge pane of the windshield, Bourne sees the beach at Odessa. He sees Fadi smoking a cigarette, smiling, waiting for him.

'It's all been arranged,' Dr. Sunderland says, 'from the beginning.'

The bus slows. There is a gun in Fadi's hand. Dr. Sunderland opens the door for him; he swings aboard, aims the gun at Bourne, then pulls the trigger . . .

Bourne awoke to the sound of a reverberating gunshot. Someone stood over him. A man with a blue stubble of beard, deeply embedded eyes, and a low, simian hairline. Gauzy light slanted in through the window, illuminating the man's long, somber face. Behind him, the sky was striped blue and white.

'Ah, Lieutenant General Mykola Petrovich Tuz. You're awake at last.' His atrocious Russian was further slurred by heavy drinking. 'I'm Dr. Korovin.'

For a moment Bourne couldn't remember where he was. The bed rocking gently beneath him made his heart skip a beat. He'd been here before – had he lost his memory again?

Then everything came flooding back. He took in the tiny

medical infirmary, realized he was on the *Itkursk*, that he was Lieutenant General Mykola Petrovich Tuz, and said in a voice thick with cotton wool, 'I require my assistant.'

'Of course.' Dr. Korovin took a step back. 'She's right here.'

His face was replaced by that of Soraya Moore's. 'Lieutenant General,' she said crisply. 'You're feeling better.'

He could clearly see the concern in her eyes. 'We need to talk,' he whispered.

She turned to the doctor. 'Please leave us,' she said curtly.

'Certainly,' Dr. Korovin said. 'In the meantime, I'll inform the captain that the lieutenant general is on his way to recovery.'

As soon as the door closed behind him, Soraya sat on the edge of the bed. 'Lerner has been deep-sixed,' she said softly. 'When I identified him as a foreign spy, the captain was only too happy to oblige. In fact, he's relieved. He doesn't want any adverse publicity, and that goes double for the freight company, so over the side Lerner went.'

'Where are we?' Bourne said.

'About forty minutes from Istanbul.' Soraya gripped his arm gently as he sought to sit up. 'As for Lerner being aboard ship, we both missed that.'

'I think I missed something else, something even more important,' Borne said. 'Hand me my trousers.'

They were hanging neatly over the back of a chair. Soraya passed them to Bourne. 'We need to get some food into you. The doctor pumped you full of fluids while he fixed you up. He tells me you should be feeling much better in a couple of hours.'

'In a minute.' He could feel the dull ache of the knife wound and the place where Lerner had kicked him. There was a bandage around his right biceps where the ice pick had pierced him, but he felt no pain there. He closed his eyes, but that only brought back his dream of Fadi, the impostor, Sarah, and Dr. Sunderland.

'Jason, what is it?'

He opened his eyes. 'Soraya, it isn't only Dr. Sunderland who's been playing around inside my head.'

'What do you mean?'

Rummaging through his pockets, he found a matchbook. *Fadi lights up a cigarette, hands Bourne the matchbook.* That image had been in Bourne's dream, but it had happened in real life. Bourne, under the influence of Sunderland's implanted memories, had taken Fadi out of the Typhon cell. Outside, Fadi had lit a cigarette with a matchbook—'*Nothing to burn in the hole so they let me keep it,*' he'd said. Then he'd handed Bourne the matchbook.

Why had he done that? It had been such a simple gesture, barely noticed or recorded in memory, especially with what had come after. Fadi had been counting on that.

'A matchbook?' Soraya said.

'The matchbook Fadi handed me outside CI headquarters.' Bourne opened it. It was all but ruined, creased, the corners bent, the writing nearly unintelligible from the soaking Bourne had endured in the Black Sea.

Virtually the only thing left intact were the bottom layers, from which the matches themselves were torn off. Using a thumbnail, Bourne pried off the metal staples that had held the matches in place. Underneath he found a tiny oblong of metal and ceramic.

'My God, he bugged you.'

Bourne examined it closely. 'It's a tracer.' He handed it to her. 'I want you to throw it overboard. Right now.'

Soraya took it, left the cabin. In a moment she was back.

'Now to other matters.' He looked at her. 'It's clear that Tim Hytner provided Fadi with all the inside knowledge.'

'Tim wasn't the mole,' Soraya said firmly.

'I know he was your friend—'

'That's not it, Jason. Lindros's impostor went out of his way to show me documented evidence that Tim was the mole.'

Bourne took a deep breath and, ignoring the pain it caused him, slid his feet onto the floor. 'Then the odds are good that Hytner wasn't the mole after all.'

Soraya nodded. 'Which means it's likely a mole is still at work inside CI.'

They sat in the Kaktüs Café, half a block south of Istiklal Caddesi – Independence Avenue – in the chicly modern Beyoglu District of Istanbul. Their table was piled with small *meze* plates, tiny cups of thick, strong Turkish coffee. The interior was filled with chatter in many different languages, which suited their purpose.

Bourne had eaten his fill and, on his third cup of coffee, had begun to feel halfway human again. At length, he said, 'It's clear we can't trust anyone at CI. If you get on a computer here can you hack past the Sentinel firewall?'

Soraya shook her head. 'Even Tim couldn't get through it.'

Bourne nodded. 'Then you have to go back to D.C. We've got to ID the mole. With him still in place, nothing inside CI is secure, including the investigation into Dujja's plan. You'll need to keep an eye on the impostor. Since they're both working for Fadi, he might lead you to the mole.'

'I'll go to the Old Man.'

'That's precisely what you *won't* do. We have no concrete evidence. It would be your word against the impostor's. You're already tainted by your association with me. And the Old Man loves Lindros, trusts him completely. It's what makes Fadi's plan so damn brilliant.' He shook his head. 'No, you'll never get anywhere accusing Lindros. The best course is to keep your eyes and ears open and your mouth shut. I don't want the impostor to get the idea you're on to him. He's already going to be suspicious of you. He sent you to keep an eye on me, after all.'

A grim smile came over Bourne's battered face. 'We'll give him what he wants. You'll tell him that you witnessed the struggle between me and Lerner on this ferry, during which we killed each other.'

'That's why you had me throw the tracer overboard.'

Bourne nodded. 'Fadi will confirm that it's at the bottom of the Black Sea.'

Soraya laughed. 'Now we're getting somewhere.'

Down the block from the Kaktüs was an Internet café. Soraya paid for their time while Bourne took a seat in front of a terminal in the back. He was already looking up Dr. Allen Sunderland when Soraya dragged over a chair. It seemed Sunderland had been the recipient of a number of awards and books. One of the sites Bourne pulled up contained a photo of the eminent memory specialist.

'This isn't the man who treated me,' Bourne said, staring at the photo. 'Fadi used a substitute. A doctor he had bought or coerced to screw with the synapses of my brain introduced neurotransmitters. They suppressed certain memories, but they also created false ones. Memories meant to help me accept Martin's impostor, memories meant to lead me to my death.'

'It's horrible, Jason. Like someone has crawled inside your head.' Soraya put a hand on his shoulder. 'How do you fight something like that?'

'The fact is I can't. Not unless I find the man who did this to me.'

His mind went back to his conversation with the false Sunderland. The photo on the desk of the beautiful blonde

Sunderland had called Katya. Was that part of the cover? Bourne opened his mind, listened to the tone of Sunderland's voice. No, he was being sincere about the woman. She, at least, was real to the man who had passed himself off as Allen Sunderland.

And then there was the doctor's accent. Bourne remembered he'd pinned it as Romanian. So this much was legitimate: The man was a doctor – a specialist in memory reconstruction; he was Romanian; he was married to a woman named Katya. Katya, who was so relaxed in front of a camera that she might be a model or an ex-model. These bits and pieces didn't amount to much, he thought, but a little knowledge was better than none at all.

'Now let's go back to our beginning.' His fingers flew over the keyboard. A moment later, he brought up information on Abu Sarif Hamid ibn Ashef al-Wahhib, founder of Integrated Vertical Technologies. 'He was married thirty-three years ago to Holly Cargill, youngest daughter of Simon and Jacqui Cargill of Cargill and Denison, top-tier solicitors. The Cargills are an important part of London society. They claim to trace their lineage back to the time of Henry the Eighth.' His fingers continued their dance; the screen continued to spew out information. 'Holly gave Hamid ibn Ashef three children. The first was Abu Ghazi Nadir al-Jamuh bin Hamid bin Ashef al Wahhib. Then his younger brother, Jamil bin Hamid bin Ashef al Wahhib – who, by the way, assumed the presidency of IVT the same year you and I were first in Odessa.'

'Two weeks after you shot Hamid ibn Ashef,' Soraya said from over his shoulder. 'What about the third child?'

'I'm coming to that.' Bourne scrolled down the page. 'Here we go. The youngest sibling is a daughter.' He stopped, his heart pounding in his throat. He said her name in a strangled voice. 'Sarah ibn Ashef. Deceased.'

'Our Sarah,' Soraya breathed in his ear.

'It would seem so.' All at once, everything fell into place. 'My God, Fadi is one of Hamid ibn Ashef's sons.'

Soraya looked stunned. 'The elder, I'd surmise, since Karim assumed the presidency of IVT.'

Bourne recalled his violent encounter with Fadi in the Black Sea surf. *I've waited a long time for this moment,*' Fadi had said. *'A long time to look you in the face again. A long time to exact my revenge.'* When Bourne had asked him what he meant, Fadi had snarled, *'You couldn't have forgotten – not that.'* He could only have been talking about one thing.

'I killed their sister,' Bourne said, sitting back. 'That's why they wove me into their plan for destruction.'

'We're still no closer to finding out the identity of the man impersonating Martin Lindros,' Soraya said.

'Or to whether they've kept Martin alive.' Bourne returned his attention to the computer terminal. 'But maybe we can find out something about the other impostor.' Bourne had brought up the International Vertical Technologies Web site. On it was listed the conglomerate's personnel, including its R&D staff, far-flung over a dozen countries.

'If you're searching for the man who impersonated Dr. Sunderland, it'll be like looking for a needle in a haystack.'

'Not necessarily,' Bourne said. 'Don't forget, this man was a specialist.'

'In memory restoration.'

'That's right.' Then Bourne remembered another part of his conversation with Sunderland. 'Also miniaturization.'

There were ten doctors in fields that were related or seemed likely. Bourne looked them up on the Net, one by one. None was the man who had performed the procedure on him.

'Now what?' Soraya said.

He quit the IVT site and switched to historical news listings for the conglomerate. Fifteen minutes of wading through articles on announcements of mergers, spin-offs, quarterly

P&L reports, personnel hirings and firings finally led him to an item on Dr. Costin Veintrop, a specialist in biopharmaceutical nanoscience, scanning force microscopy, and molecular medicine.

'It seems that Dr. Veintrop was summarily sacked from IVT for alleged intellectual property theft.'

'Wouldn't that strike him off the list?' Soraya said.

'Just the opposite. Consider. A public sacking like that got Veintrop blackballed from every legitimate laboratory job, every university professorship. He went from the top of the heap to oblivion.'

'Just the kind of situation Fadi's brother could fabricate. Then it was work for Fadi or nothing.'

Bourne nodded. 'It's a theory that bears checking out.' He typed in Dr. Costin Veintrop's name, and out popped a curriculum vitae. All very interesting, but conclusive it was not. The photo link was, however. It showed the doctor posing at an awards ceremony. By his side was his trophy wife: the tall beautiful blonde whose photo he'd seen at Sunderland's office. She was a former Perfect Ten model. Her name was Katya Stepanova Vdova.

Marlin Dorph, CI field commander in charge of Skorpion units Five and Six, had been given a legitimate military rank of captain, which held him in good stead when, just before dawn, he and his team had rendezvoused with the marine detachment just outside the town of al-Ghaydah, in the Shabwah region of South Yemen.

Dorph was the man for the job. He knew the Shabwah like the back of his hand. Its bloody history was tattooed into his flesh both by numerous victories and by defeats. Despite the assurances of Yemen's government, Shabwah was still infested with an unsavory stew of Islamic terrorist militant groups. During the Cold War, the Soviet Union, East Germany, and

Cuba had developed a network of training facilities tucked away in this inhospitable mountainous region. During that time, al-Ghaydah, staffed by Cuban terrorist instructors, had become notorious for training and arming the People's Front for the Liberation of Oman. In a nearby town, East Germans were busy preparing key members of the Saudi Communist Party and the Bahrain Liberation Front for destabilizing activities, including the manipulation of the mass media for the purpose of spreading the groups' ideologies into every corner of their respective countries, thus undermining the spiritual lives of their peoples. Though the Soviets and their satellites left South Yemen in 1987, the terrorist cells did not, finding renewed vigor in the leadership of the venomous al-Qaeda.

'Anything yet?'

Dorph turned to find Captain Lowrie, commander of the marine forces who would be accompanying Skorpions Five and Six to the Dujja nuclear facility. Lowrie was tall, fair-haired, big as a bear, and twice as nasty-looking.

Dorph, who had seen his kind perform heroics and die in battle, hefted his Thuraya satellite phone. 'Waiting for confirmation now.'

They had rendezvoused on a sun-blasted plateau east of al-Ghaydah. The town shimmered in the dawn light, scoured by the restless wind, surrounded by mountains and desert. High clouds, shredded by winds aloft, streamed across the deep blue bowl of the sky. The mud-plastered buildings, ten and twelve stories high, were boxlike with oblong windows that lent the facades the appearance of ancient temples. Time seemed to have stopped here, as if history had never progressed.

On the plateau, the two military groups were silent, tense, spring-loaded, ready for the deployment they knew was imminent. They understood what was at stake; every man there was ready to lay down his life to ensure the safety of his country.

While they waited, Dorph pulled out his GPS, showing his marine counterpart the tentative target site. It was less than a hundred kilometers south-southwest of their present position.

The Thuraya buzzed. Dorph put it to his ear and listened while the man he believed to be Martin Lindros confirmed the coordinates he had marked out on his GPS.

'Yessir,' he said softly into the Thuraya's mouthpiece. 'ETA twenty minutes. You can count on us, sir.'

Breaking the connection, he nodded to Lowrie. Together they gave orders to their men, who silently climbed into the four Chinook helicopters. A moment later the rotors swung into motion, revolving faster and faster. The Chinook war machines took off two at a time, lifting massive clouds of dirt and sand that whirled upward in a fine mist, partially obscuring the aircraft until they reached altitude. Then they tipped forward slightly and shot ahead on a south by southwest course.

The War Room, forty-five meters beneath the ground floor of the White House, was a hive of activity. The flat-panel plasma screens showed satellite photos of South Yemen in differing degrees of detail, from an overview to specific topographic landmarks, details of the terrain around al-Ghaydah. Others presented 3-D-rendered displays of the target area and the progress of the four Chinook helicopters.

Those present were more or less the same contingent that had convened for the Old Man's skewering: the president; Luther LaValle, the Pentagon intelligence czar, plus two lower-ranking generals; Defense Secretary Halliday; the national security adviser; and Gundarsson from the IAEA. The only missing member was Jon Mueller.

'Ten minutes to contact,' the Old Man said. He had a headphone on, patched in to Commander Dorph's scrambled communication net.

'Remind me again what weaponry the strike force is carrying,' Secretary Halliday drawled from his seat on the president's left.

'These Chinooks are specially designed for us by McDonnell Douglas,' the Old Man said evenly. 'In fact, they have more in common with the Apache attack helis McD makes than regulation Chinooks. Like the Apache, they're equipped with target acquisition designation sights and laser range finder/designators. Our Chinooks have the capacity to withstand hits from rounds up to twenty-three millimeters. As for offensive weaponry, they're carrying a full complement of Hellfire antitank missiles, three M230 thirty-millimeter chain guns, and twelve Hydra 70 rockets, which are fired from the M261 nineteen-tube rocket launcher. The rockets are fitted with unitary warheads with impact-detonating fuzes or remote-set multi-option fuzes.'

The president laughed somewhat too loudly. 'That kind of detail should satisfy even you, Bud.'

'Pardon my confusion, Director,' Halliday persisted, 'but I'm baffled. You haven't mentioned the severe breach of CI security at your headquarters.'

'What breach?' The president looked bewildered, then, his face filling with blood, angry. 'What's Bud talking about?'

'We were hit with a computer virus,' the DCI said smoothly. *How in hell did he find out about the virus?* 'Our IT people assure us the integrity of the core mainframe wasn't breached. Our Sentinel firewall ensured that. They're purging the system even as we speak.'

'If I were in your shoes, Director,' Secretary Halliday pressed on, 'I sure as shootin' wouldn't be downplaying any electronic breach of agency security. Not with these goddamn terrorists breathing down our necks.'

As any loyal vassal would, LaValle picked up the interrogation. 'Director, you're telling us that your people are purging the virus. But the fact remains that your agency was electronically attacked.'

'It isn't the first time,' the DCI said. 'Believe me, it won't be the last.'

'Still,' LaValle continued, 'an attack from the outside—'

'It wasn't from the outside.' The DCI fixed the Pentagon intelligence czar in his formidable gaze. 'Due to the alert sleuthing of my deputy, Martin Lindros, we discovered an electronic trail that led back to the mole – the late Tim Hytner. His last action was to insert the virus into the system under the guise of "decrypting" a Dujja cipher that turned out to be the binary code culprit.'

The Old Man's gaze swung to the president. 'Now please, let's return to the grave matter at hand.' *How many more unsuccessful attacks must I endure from these two before the president puts an end to it?* he wondered sourly.

The atmosphere in the War Room was tense as the images flickered across multiple screens. Every mouth was dry, every eye glued to the plasma screen that showed the progress of the four CI Chinooks over the mountainous terrain. The graphics were the same as those of a video game, but once the engagement began all similarities to a game would end.

'They've overflown the westernmost wadi,' the DCI reported. 'Now all that separates them from the Dujja facility is a minor mountain chain. They're taking the gap just to the southwest of their current position. They'll go in two by two.'

'We've got RF,' Marlin Dorph reported to the DCI. He meant radiation fog, an odd phenomenon that sometimes occurred at dawn or during the night, arising from the radiational cooling of the earth's surface, when a layer of relatively moist air was trapped just above surface level by drier air aloft.

'Do you have visual on the target?' the DCI's voice, thin

and metallicized, buzzed in his ear.

'Negative, sir. We're heading in for a closer look, but two of the Chinooks are holding back in perimeter formation.' He turned to Lowrie, who nodded. 'Norris,' he said to the pilot in the heli on their left wing, 'take 'er down.'

He watched as the accompanying Chinook dove down, its rotors beating the RF, dissipating it.

'There!' Lowrie yelled.

Dorph could see a group of perhaps six armed men. Startled, they looked up. He allowed his eyes to follow the path they were taking, saw a cluster of low, bunkerlike buildings. They looked like structures typical of the terrorist training camps, but that's just how Dujja would camouflage its base.

The low-flying Chinook was loosing its M230 chains: The ground erupted with a hail of 30mm rounds. The men fell, fired back, scattered, fired again, were mowed down.

'Let's go!' Dorph spoke into his mike. 'The complex is half a klick dead ahead.' The Chinook began its dive. Dorph could hear the racket increase as the other two helis left their perimeter patrol, heading in after him.

'Hellfires up!' he called. 'I want one missile from each ship launched on my signal.' The different angles would cause even the most heavily reinforced walls to collapse.

He could see the other three helis as they converged on the target. 'On my mark,' Dorph barked. 'Now!'

Four Hellfire missiles were loosed from the undercarriages of the Chinooks. They homed in on the building complex, detonating within seconds of one another. A ball of flame erupted. The shock wave juddered through the heli as great gouts of oily black smoke rose from the target.

Then all hell broke loose.

Soraya Moore, waiting in line to board at Atatürk International Airport for her flight to D.C., took out her cell phone. Ever since she'd left Bourne, she'd been thinking about the situation at headquarters. Bourne was right: The false Lindros had set himself up in a perfect position. But why had he taken all this trouble to infiltrate CI? For its intel? Soraya didn't think so. Fadi was smart enough to know that there was no way his man could smuggle the data past CI's watertight security. He could only be there to deter Typhon's efforts to stop Dujja. To her, that meant an offensive plan. Active disinformation. Because if CI personnel were off on a wild goose chase, Fadi and his team could sneak into the United States under the radar. It was classic misdirection, the conjuror's oldest trick. But it was often the most effective.

She knew that Bourne had said they couldn't approach the DCI, but she could do the next best thing: contact Anne Held. She could tell Anne anything; Anne would find a way to approach the Old Man without anyone else knowing. That effectively cut out the mole, whoever he might be.

Soraya moved forward in the line. The flight was boarding. She thought through her idea again, then dialed Anne's private number. It rang and rang, and she found herself praying that Anne would answer. She didn't dare leave a voicemail message, not even for Anne to call her back. On the seventh ring Anne answered.

'Anne, thank God.' The line was moving in earnest now. 'It's Soraya. Listen, I have very little time. I'm on my way back to D.C. Don't say anything until I've finished. I've discovered that the Martin Lindros whom Bourne brought back from Ethiopia is an impostor.'

'An impostor?'

'That's what I said.'

'But that's impossible!'

'I know it sounds crazy.'

'Soraya, I don't know what's happened to you over there, but believe me, Lindros is who he says he is. He even passed the retinal scan.'

'Please, let me finish. This man – whoever he is – is working for Fadi. He's been planted to throw us off Dujja's trail. Anne, I need you to tell the Old Man.'

'Now I know you've gone crackers. I tell the Old Man that Lindros is a plant and he'll have me institutionalized.'

Soraya was almost up to the boarding gate. She'd run out of time. 'Anne, you've got to believe me. You have to find a way to convince him.'

'Not without some proof,' Anne said. 'Anything of substance will do.'

'But I don't—'

'I've got a pen. Give me your flight info. I'll meet you at the airport myself. We'll figure something out before we get to HQ.'

Soraya gave Anne her flight number and arrival time. She nodded to the attendant at the head of the gate as she handed over her boarding pass.

'Thanks, Anne, I knew I could count on you.'

The Sidewinder missiles came out of nowhere.

'Our right flank!' Dorph yelled, but the alarms were shrieking through the interior of the Chinook. He saw a missile make a direct hit on the lowest-flying heli. The Chinook burst into a fireball, at once engulfed in the fierce stream of smoke rising from the ruined buildings. A second heli, in the process of taking evasive maneuvers, was struck in its tail. The entire rear section flew apart; the rest lurched over on its side and spiraled down into the raging inferno.

Dorph forgot about the remaining heli; he needed to concentrate on his own. He staggered over to the pilot just as the Chinook heeled over in the first of its evasive maneuvers.

'Incoming locked, Skip,' the pilot said. 'It's right on our tail.' As he twisted and turned the joystick, the Chinook made a series of stomach-churning loops and dives.

'Keep on it,' Dorph said. He signed to the ordnance officer. 'I need you to remote-set a multi-option fuze for five seconds.'

The officer's eyes opened. 'That's cutting it mighty close, Skip. We could be caught up in the blast.'

'That's what I'm hoping for,' Dorph said. 'Sort of.'

He glanced out the window as the officer went to work. Not a hundred meters from him another Sidewinder missile found its target, detonating amidships. The third Chinook dropped like a stone. That left only them.

'Skip, ordnance closing on us,' the pilot said. 'I can't keep this up for much longer.'

Hopefully you won't have to, Dorph thought. He slapped the pilot on the shoulder. 'On my mark, veer to the left and down, steep as you can make it. Got it?'

The pilot nodded. 'Roger that, Skip.'

'Keep a firm hand,' Dorph told him. He could hear the shrill scream as the Sidewinder tore up the air in its attempt to get to them. They were running out of time.

The ordnance officer nodded to Dorph. 'All set, Skip.'

'Let 'er rip,' Dorph said.

There was a small chirrup as the Hydra 70 rocket was fired. Dorph counted: 'One-two.' He slapped the pilot. 'Now!'

At once the heli dove sharply to its left, then down. The ground was coming up fast when the Hydra detonated. The blast threw everyone forward and to their right. Dorph could feel the heat even through the armored skin of the Chinook. That was the bait, and the Sidewinder – an air-to-air weapon guided by a heat-seeking mechanism – headed straight into the heart of it, blowing itself to smithereens.

The Chinook shuddered, hesitated as the pilot struggled to pull it out of the dive, then – swinging like a pendulum – righted itself.

'Nicely done.' Dorph squeezed the pilot's shoulder. 'Everyone okay?' He saw the nods and uptilted thumbs out of the corner of his eye. 'Okay, now we go after the hostile aircraft that shot our guys down.'

After Soraya left for the airport, Bourne began to make his plans to find and interrogate Nesim Hatun, the man who had hired Yevgeny Feyodovich. According to Yevgeny, Hatun worked out of the Sultanahmet District, which was some distance from where he was now.

He was almost dead on his feet. He hadn't let himself think about it, but the knife wound Fadi had inflicted was seriously sapping his strength. His fight with Matthew Lerner had done more damage to his body. He knew it would be foolish, possibly suicidal, to seek out Nesim Hatun in his present condition.

Therefore, he went looking for an El Achab. Strictly speaking, these traditional herbalists were centered in Morocco. However, Turkey's many microclimates nurtured more than eleven thousand plant species, so it was hardly surprising that there should be among the many shops in Istanbul an apothecary overseen by a Moroccan expert in phytochemistry.

After forty-five minutes of wandering and asking passers-by and shopkeepers, he found just such a place. It was in the middle of a bustling market, a tiny storefront with narrow, dusty windows and a certain flyblown air.

Inside, El Achab sat on a stool grinding herbs into powder with a mortar and pestle. He looked up as Bourne came toward him, his eyes watery and myopic.

The atmosphere was dense, almost suffocatingly so, with the sharp, unfamiliar odors of dried herbs, grasses, stalks, mushrooms, leaves, spoors, flower petals, and more. The walls were lined from floor to ceiling with wooden drawers and cubbyholes that held the herbalist's vast stock. What light penetrated the dusty windows was defeated by the aromatic dust accumulated by years of grinding.

'Yes?' El Achab said in Moroccan-inflected Turkish. 'How may I help?'

By way of reply, Bourne stripped to the waist, revealing his bandaged wounds, his livid bruises, his cuts etched in dried blood.

El Achab crooked a long forefinger. He was a small man, thin to the point of emaciation, with the dark, leathery skin of a desert dweller. 'Closer, please.'

Bourne did as he asked.

The herbalist's watery eyes blinked heavily. 'What do you require?'

'To keep going,' Bourne said in Moroccan Arabic.

El Achab rose, went to a drawer, and took out what looked like a handful of goat hair. '*Huperzia serrata*. A rare moss found in northern China.' He sat down at his stool, set aside his mortar and pestle, began to tear the dried moss into small bits. 'Believe it or not, everything you need is in here. The moss will counteract the inflammation that is draining your body of energy. At the same time, it will vastly heighten your mental acuity.'

He turned, took a kettle off a hot plate, poured some water just under the boiling point into a copper teapot. Then he dropped the tufts of moss into the pot, poured more water in, set the lid on the teapot, and placed the kettle beside the mortar and pestle.

Bourne, rebuttoning his shirt, sat on a wooden stool.

They waited in companionable silence for the herbal 'tea' to steep. El Achab's eyes might have been watery and myopic, but they nevertheless took in every feature of Bourne's face. 'Who are you?'

Bourne replied, 'I don't know.'

'Perhaps one day you will.'

The steeping was done. El Achab used his long fingers to pour a precise amount into a glass. It was thick, dark, impenetrable, and from it issued the odor of a bog.

'Now drink.' He held out the glass. 'All of it. At once, please.'

The taste was unspeakable. Nevertheless, Bourne swallowed every last drop.

'Within an hour your body will feel stronger, your mind more vibrant,' El Achab said. 'The process will continue for several days.'

Bourne rose, thanking the man as he paid. Back outside in the market, he went first into a clothing store and bought himself a traditional Turkish outfit, right down to the thin-soled shoes. The proprietor directed him back to Istiklal Caddesi, across the Golden Horn from Sultanahmet. There he entered a theatrical supply shop where he chose a beard, along with a small metal can of spirit gum. In front of the shop's mirror, he affixed the beard.

He then rummaged through the shop's other offerings, buying what he needed, stuffing everything into a small, battered secondhand leather satchel. All the while he shopped, he was filled with an implacable rage. He couldn't get out of his mind what Veintrop and Fadi had done to him. His enemy had insinuated himself inside his head, subtly influencing Bourne's thoughts, destabilizing his decisions. How had Fadi planted Veintrop in the real Sunderland's office?

Taking out his cell, he scrolled down to Sunderland's number and punched in the overseas codes, then the eleven-digit number. The office wasn't open at this hour, but a recorded voice asked if he wanted to make an appointment, wanted Dr. Sunderland's office hours, wanted directions from Washington, Maryland, or Virginia. He wanted the second option, definitely. The recorded voice told him the doctor's hours were from 10 AM to 6 PM Monday, and Wednesday through Friday. The office was closed on Tuesday. Tuesday was the day he'd seen Sunderland. Who had made the appointment for him?

Sweat broke out along his hairline as his heart beat faster. How had Fadi's people known that he was taking Fadi out of the cage? Soraya had made the call to Tim Hytner, which was why Bourne had suspected him of being the mole. But Hytner wasn't. Who had access to CI-net cell calls? Who could possibly be eavesdropping except the mole? That would be the same person who had made his appointment with Sunderland on the day the doctor wouldn't be at his office.

Anne Held!

Oh, Christ, he thought. The Old Man's right hand. It couldn't be. And yet it was the only explanation that made sense of the recent history. Who better for Fadi, for anyone wanting to know what took place in the center of the CI web?

His fingers worked his cell phone. He needed to warn Soraya before she boarded the plane. But her voice mail picked up immediately, which meant her phone was already off. She'd boarded, was on her way to D.C., to disaster.

He left a message, telling her that Anne Held must be the mole inside CI.

TWENTY-FIVE

'Come in, Martin.' The DCI waved to Karim, who stood in the doorway to his inner sanctum. 'I'm glad Anne caught you.'

Karim took the long walk to the chair in front of the DCI's immense desk. The walk reminded him of the gauntlet of rock throwers a Bedouin traitor was forced to tread. If he made it to the end alive, he received a swift, merciful death. If not, he was left in the desert for the vultures to feed on.

Sounds came to him. Throughout the building, a strange atmosphere of celebration and mourning had gripped CI following the news that the Dujja nuclear facility in South Yemen had been obliterated, though men were killed in the raid. The DCI had been in contact with Commander Dorph. He and his complement of Skorpions and marines had been the only ones to survive the attack. There had been many casualties – three Chinooks filled with marines and CI Skorpions. The facility had been heavily protected by two Soviet MiGs armed with Sidewinder missiles. Dorph's heli had taken them both down following the destruction of the target.

Karim sat. His nerves were always on edge when he sat in this chair. 'Sir, I know we paid a heavy price, but you seem peculiarly gloomy given the success of our mission against Dujja.'

'I've done my grieving for my people, Martin.' The Old Man grunted as if in pain. 'It's not that I don't feel relief – and no little vindication after the grilling I got in the War Room.' His heavy brows knitted together. 'But between you and me, something doesn't feel right.'

Karim felt a jolt of anxiety travel down his spine. Unconsciously, he moved to the edge of the chair. 'I don't follow, sir. Dorph confirmed that the facility suffered four direct hits, all from different angles. There's no doubt that it was completely destroyed, as were the two hostile jet fighters defending it.'

'True enough.' The DCI nodded. 'Still . . .'

Karim's mind was racing, extrapolating possibilities. The DCI's instincts were well known. He hadn't kept his job for so long solely because he'd learned to be a good politician, and Karim knew it would be unwise simply to placate him. 'If you could be more specific . . .'

The Old Man shook his head. 'I wish I could be.'

'Our intel was right on the money, sir.'

The DCI sat back, rubbed at his chin. 'Here's what sticks in my craw. Why did the MiGs wait to launch the missiles until after the facility was destroyed?'

'Perhaps they were late in scrambling.' Karim was on delicate ground, and he knew it. 'You heard Dorph – there was radiation fog.'

'The fog was low to the ground. The MiGs came in from above; the RF wouldn't have affected them. What if they *deliberately* waited until the facility had been destroyed?'

Karim tried to ignore the buzzing in his ears. 'Sir, that makes no sense.'

'It would if the facility was a dummy,' the Old Man said.

This line of inquiry was one that Karim could not allow the DCI – or anyone in CI – to pursue. 'You may be right, sir, now that I think of it.' He stood. 'I'll look into it right away.'

The Old Man's keen eyes peered up at him from beneath heavy brows. 'Sit down, Martin.'

Silence engulfed the office. Even the dim sounds of cele-bration had faded as the CI personnel got back to their grim work.

'What if Dujja wanted us to believe we'd destroyed their nuclear facility?'

Of course that was exactly what had happened. Karim struggled to keep his heart rate under control.

'I know I sold Secretary Halliday on Tim Hytner being the mole,' the DCI went on doggedly. 'That doesn't mean I believe it. If my hunch on the signal disinformation proves correct, here's another set of theories: Either Hytner was framed by the real mole, or he wasn't the only rotten apple in our barrel.'

'Those are all big ifs, sir.'

'Then eliminate them, Martin. Make it a priority. Use all necessary resources.'

The Old Man put his hands on his desk, levered himself up. His face was pale and pasty-looking. 'Christ on a crutch, Martin, if Dujja's misdirected us, it means we haven't stopped them. To the contrary, they're close to launching their attack.'

Muta ibn Aziz arrived in Istanbul just after noon and went immediately to see Nesim Hatun. Hatun ran the Miraj Ham-mam, a Turkish bath, in the Sultanahmet District. It was in an old building, large and rambling, on a side street not five blocks from the Hagia Sophia, the great church created by Justinian in AD 532. As such, the *hammam* was always well attended, its prices higher than those in less touristed sec-tions of the city. It had been a *hammam* for many years – since well before Hatun had been born, in fact.

Hatun was proud of the fact that he'd bribed the right people so that his business was well written up in all the best guidebooks. The *hammam* made him a good living, especially by Turkish standards. But what had made him a millionaire many times over was his work for Fadi.

Hatun, a man of immense appetites, had a roly-poly body and the cruel face of a vulture. Looking into his black eyes, it was clear there was venom in his soul – a venom that Fadi had identified, coaxed out, and lovingly fed. Hatun had had many wives, all of them either dead or exiled to the countryside. On the other hand, his twelve children, whom he loved and trusted, happily ran the *hammam* for him. Hatun, his heart like a closed fist, preferred it that way. So did Fadi.

'*Merhaba, habibi!*' Hatun said by way of greeting when Muta ibn Aziz crossed his threshold. He kissed his guest on both cheeks and led him through the heavily mosaiced public rooms of the *hammam* into the rear section, which surrounded a small garden in the center of which grew Hatun's prized date palm. He'd brought it all the way from a caravanserai in the Sahara, though at the time it was only a seedling, hardly bigger than his forefinger. He lavished more attention on that one tree than he had on any of his wives.

They sat on cool stone benches in filtered sunlight while they were served sweet tea and tiny cakes by two of Hatun's daughters. Afterward, one of them brought an ornate *nargilah* – a traditional water pipe – which the two men shared.

These rituals and the time it took to perform them were a necessary part of life in the East. They served to cement friendship by showing the proper politeness and respect as observed by civilized people. Even today there were men like Nesim Hatun who observed the old ways, dedicated as they were to keeping the lamp of tradition burning through the neon glare of the electronic age.

At length, Hatun pushed the *nargilah* away. 'You have come a long way, my friend.'

'Sometimes, as you know only too well, the oldest forms of communication are the most secure.'

'I understand completely.' Hatun nodded. 'I myself use a new cell phone each day, and then speak only in the most general terms.'

'We have heard nothing from Yevgeny Feyodovich.'

Hatun's eyebrows knit together. 'Bourne survived Odessa?'

'This we do not know. But Feyodovich's silence is disturbing. Understandably, Fadi is unhappy.'

Hatun spread his hands. They were surprisingly small, the fingers delicate as a girl's. 'As am I. Please be assured that I will see to Yevgeny Feyodovich myself.'

Muta ibn Aziz nodded his acceptance. 'In the meantime, we must assume that he has been compromised.'

Nesim Hatun considered for a moment. 'This man Bourne, they say that he is like a chameleon. If he is still alive, if he does find his way here, how will I know?'

'Fadi knifed him in the left side. Badly. His body will be battered. If he does come, it will be shortly, possibly even later today.'

Nesim Hatun sensed the messenger's nervousness. *The fruition of Fadi's plan must be terribly close*, he surmised.

They rose, passed through the private rooms, silent, lush as the garden outside.

'I will stay here for the remainder of the day and night. If, by then Bourne hasn't shown, he won't. And even if he does, it will be too late.'

Hatun nodded. He was right, then. Fadi's attack against the United States was imminent.

Muta ibn Aziz pointed. 'There is a screen at the far end of the garden, just there. This is where I will wait. If it happens that Bourne comes, he will want to see you. That you will allow, but in the middle of the interview I will send one of your sons to fetch you, and you and I will have a conversation.'

'So Bourne can overhear it. I understand.'

Muta ibn Aziz took a step closer, his voice reduced to a papery whisper. 'I want Bourne to know who I am. I want him to know that I am returning to Fadi.'

Nesim Hatun nodded. 'He will follow you.'

'Precisely.'

Right from the outset, Jon Mueller could see where Lerner's man, Overton, had gotten himself into trouble. Shadowing Anne Held, he discovered her surveillance without too much difficulty. There was a difference between surveillance and shadowing: He was looking not to follow Held but to unearth the people who were protecting her from outside surveillance. As such, he was far back and high up. In the beginning, he used his own eyes rather than binoculars because he needed to see Held's immediate environment in the widest range possible. Binoculars would home in on only narrow sections of it. They were useful, however, once he had IDed the man surveilling her.

In fact, there were three men, working in eight-hour shifts. That they were on twenty-four-hour alert hardly surprised him. Overton's botched surveillance had surely made them both more fearful and more wary. Mueller had anticipated all this, and had a plan for countering it.

For twenty-four hours, he had observed Held's complement of protectors. He noted their habits, quirks, predilections, methods of operation, all of which varied slightly. The one on the night shift needed a constant supply of coffee to keep him alert, while the one on the early-morning shift used his cell phone constantly. The one on the late-afternoon shift smoked like a fiend. Mueller chose him because his innate nervousness made him the most vulnerable.

He knew he would only get one shot, so he made the most of the opportunity he knew would sooner or later come his way. Hours ago, he'd stolen a utility truck off the back of the

Potomac Electric Power Company lot on Pennsylvania Avenue. He drove this now, as Anne Held got into a waiting taxi outside CI headquarters.

As the cab pulled out into traffic, Mueller waited, patient as death. Quite soon, he heard an engine cough into life. A white Ford sedan edged out from its spot across the street as the afternoon man took up his position two vehicles behind the taxi. Mueller followed in the heavy traffic.

Within ten minutes, the Held woman had exited the taxi and had begun to walk. Mueller knew this MO well. She was on her way to a rendezvous. The traffic was such that the afternoon man couldn't follow her in the car. Mueller had deduced this before her protector did, and so he'd pulled the truck over and parked on 17th Street NW, in a no-parking zone, knowing that no one would question someone in a public service utility truck.

Swinging out of the truck, he walked quickly to where the afternoon man had pulled over to the curb. Striding up, he tapped on the driver's-side window. When the man slid down the glass, Mueller said, 'Hey, buddy,' then sucker-punched him just below his left ear.

The traumatic disruption to the nerve bundle put him down for the count. Mueller set the unconscious man upright behind the wheel, then stepped up onto the sidewalk, keeping the Held woman in sight as she walked up the street.

Anne Held and Karim were strolling through the Corcoran Gallery on 17th Street, NW. The impressive collection of artwork was housed in a magnificent white Georgian marble structure that Frank Lloyd Wright had once called the best-designed building in Washington. Karim paused in front of a large canvas of the San Francisco painter Robert Bechtel, a photorealist whose artistic worth he could not fathom.

'The DCI suspects that the raid target was bogus,' Karim

was saying, 'which means he suspects that the Dujja intel Typhon intercepted and decoded is disinformation.'

Anne was shocked. 'Where are these suspicions coming from?'

'The MiG pilots made a crucial mistake. They waited until *after* the American Chinooks leveled the abandoned complex before firing their missiles. Their orders were to allow the bombing so the Americans would believe the raid had been successful, but they were to come on the scene minutes later than they did. They thought the fog would hide them from the Chinooks, but the Americans found a way to dissipate it with their rotors. Now the Old Man wants me to look for a leak inside CI.'

'I thought you sold everyone on Hytner being the mole.'

'Everyone, it appears, except him.'

'What are we going to do?' Anne said.

'Move up the timetable.'

Anne looked around covertly, but nervously.

'Not to worry,' Karim said. 'After we incinerated Overton, I put safeguards in place.' He looked at his watch and headed for the entrance. 'Come. Soraya Moore is due to land in three hours.'

Jon Mueller, behind the wheel of the Potomac Electric truck, was just down the block from the Corcoran. He was now certain that Anne Held was making a rendezvous. That would have occupied Lerner, but not him. It wouldn't matter who she was meeting after he took her out.

As soon as he saw Held come out the front entrance, he pulled out into traffic. Up ahead was the light at the junction of Pennsylvania Avenue. It was still green as she came down the stairs, but as he approached, it changed to amber. There was one car ahead of him. With a crash of gears and a roar of the truck's engine, he pulled out, sideswiping the car as he barreled past it and jumped the red light, driving straight through the intersection to a chorus of curses, angry shouts, and horn blasts.

Mueller stamped the accelerator to the floor as he bore down on Anne Held.

The high-velocity bullet breaking the glass of the truck's side window sounded like a far-off chime. Mueller had no time to consider that it might be anything else because the bullet tore into one side of his head and blew out the opposite, taking half his skull with it.

A moment before the Potomac Electric truck went out of control, Karim took Anne's arm and dragged her back onto the curb. As the truck slammed into the two cars ahead of it, he began to walk with her very fast away from the scene of the deadly pileup.

'What happened?' she said.

'The man driving the truck was intent on making you the victim of a hit-and-run.'

'What?'

He had to squeeze her arm hard to get her not to look back. 'Keep walking,' he said. 'Let's get away from this place.'

Three blocks down, a black Lincoln Aviator with diplomatic plates was idling at the curb. With a single fluid motion, Karim opened the rear door and urged Anne inside. He followed after her, slamming the door, and the Aviator took off.

'Are you all right?' he asked.

Anne nodded. 'Just a bit shaken up. What happened?'

'I made arrangements to have you covertly watched.'

Up front were a driver and his sidekick. Both appeared to be Arab diplomatic officials. For all Anne knew they *were*

Arab diplomatic officials. She didn't know, didn't want to know. Just as she didn't want to know where they were going. In her business, too much information, just like curiosity about the wrong things, could get you killed.

'I had read up on Lerner, so the moment the Old Man told me he'd sent him to Odessa, I suspected that someone even higher up on the intelligence food chain would be put on you. I was right. A man named Jon Mueller from Homeland Security. Mueller and Lerner were whoring buddies. The interesting thing is that Mueller is on the payroll of Defense Secretary Halliday.'

'Which means, chances are that Lerner's also under the defense secretary's control.'

Karim nodded, leaned forward, and told the driver to slow down as the wail of the sirens from police, EMTs, and fire department vehicles rose, then fell away. 'Halliday seems intent on increasing the Pentagon's power. Taking over CI, remaking it in its own image. We can use the chaos caused by this interagency warfare to our advantage.'

By this time, the Aviator had reached the far northern precincts of the city. Skirting the northeastern edge of Rock Creek Park, they at last came to the rear of a large mortuary run by a Pakistani family.

The family also owned the building, courtesy of money from International Vertical Technologies, funneled through one of the independent companies in the Bahamas and the Caymans that Karim had set up over the years since he'd taken over the corporation from his father. As a result, they had gutted the structure, rebuilding it to the specifications Karim had provided.

One of those specs had provided for what appeared to be the hall's own loading bay in the rear. In fact, it *was* a loading bay as far as the hall's suppliers were concerned. As the driver of the Aviator turned into the bay, the concrete 'wall' at the rear slid into a niche in the floor, revealing a ramp down which the vehicle rolled. It stopped in the vast sub-basement, and they all got out.

Barrels and crates lined the wall closest to them, the former contents of M&N Bodywork. To the left of the explosives stood a black Lincoln limousine with familiar plates.

Anne walked over to it, running her fingertips across its gleaming surface. She turned to Jamil. 'Where did you get the Old Man's car?'

'It's an exact replica, down to the armor plating and special bulletproof glass.' He opened a rear door. 'Except for one thing.'

The courtesy light had gone on when the door was opened. Peering in, Anne marveled that the interior was a perfect match, down to the plush royal-blue carpet. She watched as he pulled up a corner of the carpet that hadn't yet been glued down. Using the blade of a pocketknife, he pried up the floorboard far enough for her to see what was underneath.

The entire bottom of the replica was packed tight with neat rectangles of a light gray clay-like substance.

'That's right,' he said, reacting to her sharply indrawn breath. 'There's enough C-Four explosive here to take out the entire reinforced foundation of CI headquarters.'

TWENTY-SIX

The district where Nesim Hatun plied a trade as yet unknown to Bourne was named after Sultan Ahmet I who, during the first decade of the seventeenth century, built the Blue Mosque in the heart of what nineteenth-century Europeans called Stamboul. This was the center of the once immense Byzantine Empire that, at its height, extended from southern Spain to Bulgaria to Egypt.

Modern-day Sultanahmet had lost neither its spectacular architecture nor its power to awe. The center was a hillock called the Hippodrome, with the Blue Mosque on one side and the Hagia Sophia, built a century earlier, on the other. The two were linked by a small park. Nowadays the social center of the district was nearby Akbiyik Caddesi, the Avenue of the White Mustache, whose northernmost end gave out onto Topkapi Palace. This wide thoroughfare was lined with shops, bars, cafés, groceries, restaurants, and, on Wednesday mornings, a street market.

Bourne, appearing among the loudly chattering hordes packing Akbiyik Caddesi, was barely recognizable. He wore the traditional Turkish outfit, his jaw hidden behind the full beard.

He stopped at a street cart to buy *simit* – sesame bread – and pale yellow yogurt, eating them as he took in his surroundings. Hustlers plied their shady trade, merchants shouted out the prices of their wares, locals haggled over prices, tourists were systematically fleeced by clever Turks.

Businessmen on cell phones, kids taking pictures of one another with cell phones, teens playing raucous music they'd just downloaded into their cell phones. Laughter and tears, lovers' smiles, combatants' angry shouts. The boiling stew of human emotion and life lit up the avenue like a neon sign, blazing through the clouds of aromatic smoke billowing from braziers over which sizzling lamb and vegetable kebabs browned.

After finishing his makeshift meal, he headed straight for a rug shop, where he picked out a prayer rug, haggling good-naturedly with the owner on the price. When he left, both were satisfied with the bargain they had made.

The Blue Mosque to which Bourne now walked, his prayer rug tucked under one arm, was surrounded by six slender minarets. These had come from a mistake. Sultan Ahmet I had told his architect he wanted the mosque to have a gold minaret. *Altin* is the Turkish word for 'gold,' but the architect misheard him and instead built *alti* – six – minarets. Still, Ahmet I was pleased with the result, because at that time no other sultan had a mosque with so many minarets.

As befit such a magnificent edifice, the mosque had multiple doors. Most visitors went in through the north side, but Muslims entered from the west. It was through this door that Bourne walked. Just inside, he stopped, took off his shoes, and set them aside in a plastic bag handed to him by a young boy. He covered his head, then at a stone basin washed his feet, face, neck, and forearms. Padding into the mosque proper, he set out his prayer rug on the rug-strewn marble floor and knelt on it.

The interior of the mosque was, in true Byzantine fashion, covered with intricate artwork, filigreed carvings, halos of metalwork lamps, immense columns painted blue and gold, four stories of magnificent stained-glass windows reaching up into the heavens of the central dome. The power of it all was as moving as it was undeniable.

Bourne said the Muslim prayers, his forehead pressed to the carpet he had just bought. He was perfectly sincere in his prayers, feeling the centuries of history etched into the stone, marble, gold leaf, and lapis from which the mosque had been constructed and fervently embellished. Spirituality came in many guises, was called by many names, but they all spoke directly to the heart in a language as old as time.

When he was finished, he rose and rolled up his rug. He lingered in the mosque, allowing the reverberating near silence to wash over him. The sibilant rustle of silk and cotton, the soft hum of muttered prayers, the undercurrent of whispered voices, every human sound and movement gathered up into the mosque's great dome, swirled like granules of sugar in rich coffee, subtly altering the taste.

In fact, all the while he seemed lost in holy contemplation he was covertly watching those finishing their prayers. He spotted an older man, his beard shot through with white, roll up his rug and walk slowly over to the lines of shoes. Bourne arrived at his shoes at the same time the older man was putting on his.

The old man, who had one withered arm, regarded Bourne as he stepped into his shoes. 'You're new here, sir,' he said in Turkish. 'I haven't seen your face before.'

'I just arrived, sir,' Bourne replied with a deferential smile.

'And what brings you to Istanbul, my son?'

They moved out through the western door.

'I'm searching for a relative,' Bourne said. 'A man by the name of Nesim Hatun.'

'Not so uncommon a name,' the old man said. 'Do you know anything about him?'

'Only that he runs his business, whatever that may be, here in Sultanahmet,' Bourne said.

'Ah, then perhaps I can be of help.' The old man squinted in the sunlight. 'There is a Nesim Hatun who, along with his twelve children, runs the Miraj Hammam on Bayramfirini Sokak, a street not so far from here. The directions are simple enough.'

Bayramfirini Sokak – the Street of the Festival Oven, midway along Akbiyik Caddesi – was a shade calmer than the frantic avenues of Istanbul. Nevertheless, the sharp, raised calls of merchants, the chanting of itinerant food sellers, the particular bleat-and-squeal, a product of negotiating a sale, collected in the narrow street like a dense fog. Bayramfirini Sokak, as severely pitched as a mountainside, ran all the way down to the Sea of Marmara. It was home to a number of small guesthouses and the *hammam* of Nesim Hatun, the man who had hired Yevgeny Feyodovich at the behest of Fadi to help lead Bourne to the killing ground on the Odessa beach.

The *hammam*'s door was a thick, dark wooden affair, carved with Byzantine designs. It was flanked by a pair of colossal stone urns, originally used to store oil for lamps. The whole made for an impressive entrance.

Bourne stashed his leather satchel behind the left-hand urn. Then he opened the door and entered the dimly lit forecourt. At once the constant bawling of the city vanished, and Bourne was enfolded in the silence of a snow-cloaked forest. It took a moment for the ringing in his ears to settle. He found himself in a hexagonal space in the center of which was a marble fountain gracefully spewing water. There were graven arches held up by fluted columns on four sides, beyond which were a combination of lush enclosed gardens and hushed, lamplit corridors.

This could have been the vestibule of a mosque or a medieval monastery. As in all important Islamic buildings, the architecture was paramount. Because Islam forbade the use of images of Allah or, indeed, of any living thing, the Islamic artisan's desire to carve was channeled into the building itself and its many embellishments.

It was no coincidence that the *hammam* was reminiscent of a mosque. Both were places of reverence as well as of community. Since much of the religion was based on the purification of the body, a special place was reserved for the *hammam* in the lives of Muslims.

Bourne was met by a *tellak* – a masseur – a slim young man with the face of a wolf. 'I would very much like to meet Nesim Hatun. He and I have a mutual business associate. Yevgeny Feyodovich.'

The *tellak* did not react to the name. 'I will see if my father is available.'

Soraya, striding past the security area of Washington National Airport, was about to thumb on her cell phone when she saw Anne Held wave to her. Soraya felt a flood of relief when she embraced the other woman.

'It's so good to have you back,' Anne said.

Soraya craned her neck, looked around. 'Were you followed?'

'Of course not. I made certain of that.'

Soraya fell into step with Anne as they headed out of the terminal. Her nerves were twanging unpleasantly. It was one thing to be in the field working against the enemy, quite another to be coming home to a viper in your nest. She began to work her emotions as any good actor would, thinking of a tragedy long ago: the day her dog, Ranger, got run over in front of her. *Ah, good,* she thought, *here come the tears.*

Anne's face clouded with concern. 'What is it?'

'Jason Bourne is dead.'

'What?' Anne was so shocked she stopped them in the midst of the bustling concourse. 'What happened?'

'The Old Man sent Lerner after Bourne, like a personal assassin. The two fought. They ended up killing each other.' Soraya shook her head. 'The reason I came back was to keep an eye on the man posing as Martin Lindros. Sooner or later, he's bound to make a mistake.'

Anne held her at arm's length. 'Are you certain about your intel about Lindros? He just masterminded an all-out attack on the Dujja nuclear facility in South Yemen. It's been totally destroyed.'

Blood flushed Soraya's face. 'My God, I was right! It's why Dujja went to all this trouble to infiltrate CI. If Lindros spearheaded it, you can be damn sure the facility was a decoy. CI is dead wrong if they believe they've averted the threat.'

'In that case, the sooner we get back to headquarters, the better, don't you think?' Anne threw an arm around Soraya's shoulders, hurrying her through the electric doors into the damp chill of the Washington winter. Glow from the floodlit monuments engraved a majestic pattern on the dark, low clouds. Anne guided Soraya into a CI-issue Pontiac sedan, then slid behind the wheel.

They joined the long line of vehicles circling like fish around a reef, heading toward the exit. On the way into Washington, Soraya, leaning slightly forward, glanced in the side mirror. It was habit, long ago ingrained in her. She did it as a matter of course, whether or not she was on a field mission. She saw the black Ford behind them, thought nothing of it, until her second glance. It was now one car behind them, but keeping pace in the right-hand lane. Not enough to say anything yet, but when it was still in place on her third look, she felt under the circumstances she had enough evidence to consider that they were being followed.

She turned to Anne to tell her, then saw her glance in the rearview mirror. No doubt she'd seen the black Ford as well. But when she didn't mention it or execute any evasive maneuvers, Soraya felt her stomach slowly clench. She tried to calm down by telling herself that after all Anne was the Old Man's assistant. She was office-trained, unaccustomed to even the rudiments of fieldwork.

She cleared her throat. 'Anne, I think we're being followed.'

Anne signaled, moving them into the right-hand lane. 'I'd better slow down.'

'What? No. What are you doing?'

'If they slow down, then we'll know—'

'No, you've got to speed up,' Soraya said. 'Get away from them as quickly as possible.'

'I want to see who's in that car,' Anne said, slowing even more as she steered toward the shoulder.

'You're crazy.'

Soraya reached for the wheel, abruptly reared back as she saw the Smith & Wesson J-frame compact gun in Anne's hand.

'What the hell d'you think you're doing?'

They were rolling across the shoulder, toward the low metal fence. 'After everything you told me, I didn't want to leave headquarters unarmed.'

'Do you even know how to use that?'

The black Ford followed them off the road, pulling up behind them. Two men with dark complexions got out, came toward them.

'I take shooting practice twice a month,' Anne said, pressing the muzzle of the S&W against Soraya's temple. 'Now get out of the car.'

'Anne, what are you—?'

'Just do as I say.'

Soraya nodded. 'All right.' Edging away, she pushed down on the door handle. As she saw Anne's eyes move toward the door, she struck upward with her left arm, deflecting Anne's right arm upward. The gun exploded, the bullet tearing a hole in the Pontiac's roof.

Soraya slammed her cocked elbow into the side of Anne's face. Galvanized by the gunshot, the men ran toward the Pontiac. Soraya, seeing them coming, quickly leaned across Anne's slumped torso, opened the door, pushed her out.

Just as the men, guns drawn, reached the rear of the Pontiac, Soraya slid behind the wheel, threw it into gear, and stepped on the accelerator. She bounced along the shoulder for a moment then, finding a potential gap in the traffic, pulled out, tires squealing and smoking. Her last glimpse of the men was of them running back to the black Ford, but what made her hands tremble on the wheel was the sight of Anne Held supported between them, helped into the back of their car.

Nesim Hatun was reclining on a carved wooden bench softened by a marshmallow mound of silk pillows beneath the clattering green fronds of his beloved date palm. He was popping fresh dates into his mouth, one by one, chewing thoughtfully, swallowing the sweet flesh, spitting out the white spear-point pits into a shallow dish. Beside his right elbow was a small octagonal table on which stood a chased silver tray filled with a teapot and a pair of small glass tumblers.

As his son brought Bourne – who had peeled off his beard before entering the Turkish bath – into the shade of the date palm, Hatun's head swung around, his vulture's face impassive. His olive eyes did not hide his curiosity, however.

'*Merhaba*, my friend.'

'*Merhaba*, Nesim Hatun. My name is Abu Bakr.'

Hatun scratched at his tiny, pointed beard. 'Named after the companion of our Prophet Muhammad.'

'A thousand apologies for disturbing the tranquility of your magnificent garden.'

Nesim Hatun nodded at his guest's good manners. 'My garden is but a miserable patch of earth.' Dismissing his son, he gestured. 'Please join me, my friend.'

Bourne rolled out the prayer rug so that its silk threads shimmered in the golden shots of sunlight that found their way between the palm fronds.

Hatun slipped off one slipperlike shoe and placed his bare foot on the rug. 'A beautiful example of the weaver's art. I thank you, my friend, for this unexpected largesse.'

'A token altogether unworthy of you, Nesim Hatun.'

'Ah, well, Yevgeny Feyodovich never presented me with such a gift.' His eyes rose to impale Bourne's. 'And how is our mutual friend?'

'When I left him,' Bourne said, 'he'd made rather a mess of things.'

Hatun's face froze into stone. 'I have no idea what you're talking about.'

'Then let me enlighten you,' Bourne said softly. 'Yevgeny Feyodovich did precisely what you paid him to do. How do I know? Because I took Bourne to Otrada Beach, I led him into the trap Fadi had prepared for him. I did what Yevgeny Feyodovich hired me to do.'

'Here is my problem, Abu Bakr.' Hatun pitched his torso forward. 'Yevgeny Feyodovich never would have hired a Turk for this particular piece of work.'

'Of course not. Bourne would have been suspicious of such a man.'

Hatun scrutinized Bourne with his vulture's face. 'So. The question remains: Who are you?'

'My name is Bogdan Illiyanovich,' he said, identifying himself as the man he'd killed at Otrada Beach. He had inserted the prosthetics he'd purchased in the theatrical supply store in Beyoglu. As a result, the shapes of jawline and cheeks were significantly altered. His front teeth slightly splayed.

'You speak excellent Turkish, for a Ukrainian.' Hatun said this with a certain amount of contempt. 'And now I suppose your boss wants the second half of his payment.'

'Yevgeny Feyodovich isn't in any condition to receive anything. As for me, I want what I have earned.'

Some unnamed emotion seemed to come over Nesim Hatun. He poured them both hot sweet tea, handing one of the glasses to Bourne.

When they had both sipped, he said, 'Perhaps that wound on your left side should be looked after.'

Bourne glanced down at the specks of blood on his clothes. 'A scratch. It's nothing.'

Nesim Hatun was about to reply when the son who had brought Bourne to see him appeared, gave a silent signal.

He rose. 'Please excuse me for a moment. I have a bit of unfinished business to attend to. I assure you I won't be long.' Following his son through an archway, he disappeared behind a filigreed wooden screen.

After a short interval, Bourne rose, strolling through the garden as if admiring it. In this fashion, he made his way through the same archway, stood on the garden side of the screen. He could hear two men speaking in hushed voices. One was Nesim Hatun. The other . . .

'—using a messenger, Muta ibn Aziz,' Nesim Hatun said. 'As you have said, this late in the plan it would not do to have any cell phone communication intercepted. And yet now you tell me that just such a thing has happened.'

'The news was vital to both of us,' Muta ibn Aziz said. 'Fadi has been in communication with his brother. Jason Bourne is dead.' Muta ibn Aziz took a step toward the other. 'That being the case, your role in this matter is now ended.'

Muta ibn Aziz embraced Hatun, kissed him on both cheeks. 'I leave tonight at twenty hundred hours. I go straight to Fadi. With Bourne dead, there will be no further delay. The endgame has begun.'

'*La ilaha ill allah!*' Hatun breathed. 'Now come, my friend, I will lead you out.'

412

Bourne turned, went silently back through the garden, swiftly down the side corridor and out of the *hammam*.

Soraya, her foot pressed against the accelerator, knew she was in trouble. Keeping one eye in the rearview mirror for the Ford, she pulled out her cell phone and thumbed it on. There was a soft chime. She had a message. She dialed in, got Bourne's message about Anne.

There was a bitter taste in her mouth. So Anne was the mole after all. *The bitch! How could she?* Soraya pounded her fist against the steering wheel. *Goddamn her to hell.*

As she was putting the phone away, she heard the crunch of metal against metal, felt a sickening jar, had to struggle to keep the Pontiac from screeching over into a truck in the next lane.

'What the—!'

A Lincoln Aviator, looking as big and menacing as an M1 Abrams tank, had sideswiped her. Now it was ahead of her. Without warning, it decelerated and she banged into it. Its brake lights weren't working – or they had been deliberately disconnected.

She swerved, switching lanes, then came abreast of the Aviator. She tried to peer in, to see who was driving, but the windows were tinted so darkly she couldn't even make out a silhouette.

The Aviator lurched toward her, its side smashing the Pontiac's passenger doors. Pressing the window buttons repeatedly, Soraya found them stuck fast. Replacing her right foot on the gas pedal with her left, she kicked at the ruined door with the heel of her right foot. It didn't budge; it, too, was jammed shut. With a burst of anxiety, she returned to her normal driving position. Her heart was racing, her pulse pounding in her ears.

Now the Aviator sprinted ahead, weaving as she had through the traffic until she lost sight of it. She had to get off the highway. She began to look for signs for the next exit. It was three kilometers away. Sweating profusely, she moved over into the right-hand lane so she'd be in position to take the upcoming exit ramp.

That was when the Aviator roared up on her left and swerved hard into her, crumpling the doors on that side. Clearly it had dropped back in the traffic flow so that it could come up on her from behind. She hit the window button, tried to turn the inside handle, but this window and door were jammed shut as well. Now none of them would open. She was effectively trapped, a prisoner inside the speeding Pontiac.

TWENTY-SEVEN

Bourne retrieved his satchel from behind the urn then walked quickly, silently around the side of the *hammam*, searching for the street onto which the rear door to Nesim Hatun's establishment opened. He found it without difficulty, saw a man walking away from the *hammam*'s rear door.

The messenger Muta ibn Aziz, who would lead him back to Fadi.

As he walked, Bourne opened the satchel, found the can of spirit gum, and reapplied his beard. Returned to his Semitic disguise, he followed Muta ibn Aziz out of the alley into the clamorous bustle of Sultanahmet. For close to forty minutes, he kept pace with his quarry, who neither paused nor looked around him. It was clear he knew where he was headed. In the overcrowded heart of the district, with the flow of pedestrians moving toward all points of the compass, it was not easy keeping Muta ibn Aziz in sight. On the other hand, the relentless crowds also worked to Bourne's benefit, for it was easy to keep himself anonymous. Even if his target was using the reflective surfaces of vehicle and shop windows, he'd never spot his tail. They crossed from Sultanahmet into Eminonu.

At length, the domed mass of Sirkeci Station loomed up in front of him. Was Muta ibn Aziz taking a train to where Fadi was located? But no, Bourne saw him bypass the main entrance, walk briskly on, as he threaded his way through the throng.

He and Bourne skirted a huge knot of tourists that had formed a semicircle around three *Mevlevi*, Whirling Dervishes, their long white dresses unfurled around them as they spun in their ecstatic *sema* to the drone of ancient Islamic hymns. As they whirled, the *Mevlevi* threw off sprays of saffron- and myrrh-scented sweat. The air around them seemed alive with the mystic unknown, another world glimpsed in the blink of an eye before vanishing again.

Opposite the station was the Adalar Iskelesi dock. Bourne loitered inconspicuously with a clutch of German tourists while he watched Muta ibn Aziz purchase a one-way ticket to Büyükada. He must be leaving from there, Bourne thought, most likely by boat. But to where? It didn't matter, because Bourne was determined to be on whatever mode of transport Muta ibn Aziz chose to take him to Fadi.

For the time being, exiting her mashed Pontiac was the least of Soraya's problems. Topping the list was the Aviator hard on her tail. The sign for the next exit blurred by overhead, and she prepared herself. She saw the two-lane off-ramp, took the left-hand lane. The Aviator, half a car length away, followed her. There were cars ahead of her in both lanes, but a quick check in her rearview mirror showed her the break in the exiting traffic she was hoping for. Now if only the Pontiac's transmission wouldn't fall out from the punishment she was about to give it.

She swung the wheel hard over. The Pontiac veered into the right-hand lane of the off-ramp. Before the Aviator's driver could fully react, Soraya slammed the Pontiac into reverse and stepped on the gas pedal.

She shot past the Aviator, which was just now swinging into her lane. Its rear end took out the headlight on her side. Then she was accelerating away, back up the off-ramp. There was a dissonant clamor of horns, shouts, along with the squeal of tires as the cars behind her got out of her way.

With an insistent warning from its horn, the Aviator itself reversed, following her. Near the top of the ramp a motorist in a gray Toyota panicked, slamming into the car behind it. Chrome and plastic hanging from its front, it slewed around blocking both lanes, effectively cutting off the Aviator.

Soraya backed onto the breakdown lane of the highway, then shifted the Pontiac into drive and took off, heading into Washington proper.

'It will be easy to ram the Toyota out of the way,' the driver of the Aviator said.

'Don't bother,' the man in the backseat replied. 'Let her go.'

Though they were diplomats stationed at the Saudi embassy, they also belonged to Karim's Washington sleeper cell. As the Aviator reached the city streets, the man in the backseat activated a GPS. At once, a grid of downtown D.C. appeared, along with a moving pinpoint of light. He punched a number into his cell phone.

'The subject slipped the noose,' the man in the backseat said. 'She's driving the Pontiac we fitted with the electronic tracking device. It's heading in your direction. Judging from the speed, it should be in range within thirty seconds.'

He waited patiently until the driver of the black Ford said, 'Got her. It looks like she's heading toward the northeast.'

'Follow her,' the man in the backseat said. 'You know what to do.'

During the ferry ride to the island of Büyükada, Bourne stayed with a family of Chinese tourists with whom he struck up a conversation. He talked with them in Mandarin, joking with the children, pointing out the important buildings as they left Istanbul behind, recounting the city's storied history. All the while, he kept Muta ibn Aziz in view.

Fadi's messenger stood by himself, leaning against the ferry's railing, staring out across the water toward the smudge of land toward which they were headed. He neither moved nor looked around.

When Muta ibn Aziz turned and walked inside, Bourne excused himself from the Chinese family and followed. He saw the messenger ordering tea at the onboard café. Bourne wandered over, poring through a rack of picture postcards and maps. Choosing a map of Büyükada and vicinity, he managed to reach the cashier just ahead of Muta ibn Aziz. He spoke to the cashier in Arabic. The mustachioed man with a gold cross hanging from a chain around his neck shook his head, replying in Turkish. Bourne gestured that he didn't understand.

Muta ibn Aziz leaned over, said, 'Pardon me, friend, but the filthy infidel is asking for payment.'

Bourne showed a handful of coins. Muta ibn Aziz plucked up the right change and gave it to the cashier. Bourne waited until he had paid for his own tea, then said, 'Thank you, friend. I'm afraid Turkish sounds like pig grunts to me.'

Muta ibn Aziz laughed. 'An apt phrase.' He gestured, and together they walked out onto the deck.

Bourne followed the messenger to his spot at the rail. The sun was strong, counteracting the chill of the wind coming in off the Sea of Marmara. The feathery fingertips of cirrus clouds dotted the deep blue of the winter sky.

'The Christians are the swine of the world,' Muta ibn Aziz said.

'And the Jews are the apes,' Bourne replied.

'Peace be upon you, brother. I see we read the same schoolbooks.'

'Jihad in the path of God is the summit of Islam,' Bourne said. 'I needed no schoolmaster to explain this to me. It seems to me that I was born knowing it.'

'Like me, you are Wahhabi.' Muta ibn Aziz gave him a considered sidelong glance. 'Just as we were successful in the past when we came together with the Muslims to evict the Christian crusaders from Palestine, so will we emerge victorious against the latter-day crusaders who occupy our lands.'

Bourne nodded. 'We think alike, brother.'

Muta ibn Aziz sipped his tea. 'Do these righteous beliefs move you to act, brother? Or are they the philosophy of the café and coffeehouse?'

'In Sharm el-Sheikh and in Gaza I have drawn the blood of the infidel.'

'Individual endeavors are to be applauded,' Muta ibn Aziz mused, 'but the greater the organization, the more damage can be inflicted on our enemies.'

'Just so.' *Time to bait the hook*, Bourne thought. 'Again and again I have thought of joining Dujja, but always the same consideration has stopped me.'

The paper cup of tea paused halfway to Muta ibn Aziz's lips. 'And what is that?'

Slowly, slowly, Bourne cautioned himself. 'I don't know whether I can say, brother. After all, we have just met. Your intentions—'

'Are the same as yours,' Muta ibn Aziz said with a new-found quickness. 'Of this I assure you.'

Still Bourne held back, appearing undecided.

'Brother, is it not true that we have spoken of a like philosophy? Is it not true that we share a certain outlook on the world, on its future?'

'Indeed, yes.' Bourne pursed his lips. 'All right then, brother. But I warn you, if you have been untrue about your intentions, then I swear I will find out, and I will mete out the proper punishment.'

'*La ilaha ill allah*. Every word I have spoken is the truth.'

Bourne said: 'I went to school in London with Dujja's leader.'

419

'I don't know—'

'Please, I have no intention of mentioning Fadi's real name. But knowing it myself gives me knowledge of the family others do not have.'

Muta ibn Aziz's curiosity, once feigned, now became real. 'Why is that a deterrent to becoming one with Dujja?'

'Ah, well, it's the father, you see. Or, more specifically, his second wife. She is English. Worse, she is Christian.' Bourne shook his head, his fierce expression reinforcing the edge to his words. 'It is forbidden for a true Muslim to be a loyal friend to someone who does not believe in God and His Prophet. Yet this man married the infidel, mated with her. Fadi is the spawn. Tell me, brother, how can I follow such a creature? How can I believe a word he says, when the devil lurks inside him?'

Muta ibn Aziz was taken aback. 'And yet Fadi has done so much for our cause.'

'This can hardly be denied,' Bourne said. 'But it seems to me, speaking in terms of blood – which, as we know, can be neither ignored nor disowned – Fadi is like the tiger taken from the jungle, brought into a new environment, lovingly domesticated by a foster family. It's merely a matter of time before the tiger reverts to his true nature, turns on those who have adopted him and destroys them.' He shook his head again, this time in perfectly believable sorrow. 'It is a mistake to try to change the tiger's nature, brother. Of this there can be no doubt.'

Muta ibn Aziz turned his head to stare morosely out to sea, where the image of Büyükada rose from the sea like Atlantis or the island of a long-forgotten caliph, stuck in time. He wanted to say something that would refute the other's contention, but somehow he couldn't find it in him to do so. *Doubly depressing*, he thought, *to have the truth come from the mouth of this man.*

*

Soraya's mind was reeling, not only from the violence of her flight from the Lincoln Aviator but also from Anne Held's betrayal. Her blood ran cold. My God, what had she and everyone else told her over the years? How many secrets had they given away to Dujja?

She drove her rolling coffin without conscious thought. The colors of the day seemed supersaturated, vibrating with a strange pulse that made the passing cars, the streets, the buildings, even the roiling clouds overhead seem unfamiliar, menacing, venomous. Her entire being was trapped within the horror of the ugly truth.

Her head ached with the doomsday possibilities, her body trembled in the aftermath of her adrenaline rush.

She needed to go to ground until she could regroup, figure out her next step. She needed an ally here in D.C. She immediately thought of her friend Kim Lovett, but almost as quickly dismissed the notion. For one thing, her situation was too precarious, too dangerous to get Kim involved. For another, people within CI, most especially Anne, knew of the friendship.

She needed someone unknown to anyone at CI. She activated her phone, punched in Deron's number. She prayed that he was back from visiting his father in Florida, but her heart sank as she heard his recorded voice-mail message come on.

Where to now? she asked herself in desperation. She needed a port in this gathering storm, and she needed it now. Then, just before the panic set in, she remembered Tyrone. He was only a teenager, of course, but Deron had enough faith in him to use him for protection. Tyrone had also been the one to tell her that she'd been followed to Deron's house. Still, even if Tyrone might consent to help her, even if she took the chance to trust him, how on earth would she get in touch with him?

Then she remembered him telling her that he hung out at

a construction site. Where was it? She racked her brain.

'Down Florida, they puttin' up a shitload a high-rises. I go there every chance I get, see how it all goin' up, y'know?'

For the first time, she actually looked at where she was. In the Northeast quadrant, right where she needed to be.

Büyükada was the largest of the Princes' Islands, so called because in ancient times the Byzantine emperors exiled the princes who had displeased or offended them to this chain of islands off Istanbul's coast. For three years, Büyükada had been home to Leon Trotsky, who wrote *The History of the Russian Revolution* there.

Because of their unsavory history, the islands remained deserted for years, one of the many boneyards of the Ottoman Empire's bloody history. Nowadays, however, Büyükada had been turned into a lushly landscaped playground for the wealthy, strewn with masses of flowers, tree-shaded lanes, and villas in the ornamentally baroque Byzantine style.

Bourne and Muta ibn Aziz walked off the ferry together. On the dock they embraced, wished each other Allah's grace and protection.

'La ilaha ill allah,' Bourne.

'La ilaha ill allah,' said Fadi's messenger as they parted.

Bourne waited to see which way he went, then opened his map of the island. Turning his head a bit, he could see his target out of the corner of his eye. He had just rented a bicycle. Because no automotive traffic was allowed on the island, there were three modes of transportation: bicycles, horse and carriage, one's own feet. The island was large enough that walking all the time was prohibitive.

Now that Bourne knew which mode Muta ibn Aziz had chosen, he returned his attention to the map. He knew that the messenger was leaving here at eight o'clock this evening, but the exact location and the means were still a mystery.

Entering the bike rental shop, he chose a model with a basket in front. It wouldn't be as fast as the one Muta ibn Aziz had, but he needed the basket to hold his satchel. Paying the proprietor in advance, he set off in the direction the messenger had taken, ascending toward the interior of the island.

When he was out of sight of the dock, he pulled over and, beneath the shade of a palm, rummaged in the satchel for the transponder that went with the NET, the nano-electronic tag that Soraya had planted on him to track his movements. He'd transferred the NET itself to Muta ibn Aziz when they had embraced on the dock. In a place like this without cars, it would be impossible to shadow the messenger on a bicycle without being seen.

Switching on the transponder, he keyed in his location, saw the blip that represented his position appear on the screen. He pressed another key and, soon enough, located the signal. He got back on the bike and set off, ignoring the pain in his side, building speed until he was going at a fairly rapid clip, even though the road ahead of him wound steeply uphill.

Soraya rolled along the southern edge of the immense construction site bounded by 9th Street and Florida Avenue. The housing project that would replace the neighborhood's rotten teeth with towering steel-and-glass implants was well under way. The metal skeletons of two of the towers were almost complete. The site was filled with gigantic cranes swinging steel beams through the air as if they were lollipop sticks. Bulldozers shoved rubble; semis were being unloaded next to a line of trailer offices to which a fistful of electrical lines ran.

Soraya drove her heap slowly along the periphery of the site. She was looking for Tyrone. In her desperation, she had remembered that this was his favorite spot. He came here every day, he'd told her.

The Pontiac's engine wheezed like an asthmatic in Bangkok, then returned to normal. For the past ten minutes, the noises emanating from the engine had been getting louder and more frequent. She was praying that it wouldn't give out before she found Tyrone.

Having traveled the length of the southern perimeter, she now turned north, heading toward Florida Avenue. She was looking for likely vantage points where Tyrone might hide himself in shadow so as not to be seen by the several hundred workmen at the site. She found a couple, but at this time of the morning none were in shadow. No Tyrone. She realized that she'd have to get to the northern border before she might find him.

Florida Avenue was five hundred meters ahead when she heard a loud clank. The wounded Pontiac lurched, then shuddered pathetically. It had ended not with a roar, but with a whimper. The engine was dead. Soraya swore and slammed the dash with the heel of her hand, as if the car were a television whose reception required clearing.

It was when she unstrapped her seat belt that she saw the black Ford. It had turned the corner and was now headed directly toward her.

'God help me,' she whispered to herself.

Putting her back onto the seat, she rolled herself into a ball and slammed both feet into her side window. It was made of safety glass, of course, difficult to shatter. She drew her legs, uncoiled them again. Her soles struck the glass without effect.

She made the mistake of peeking up over the dash. The Ford was now so close that she could see the two men inside. With a little sound, she slid back down and returned to her task. Two more strikes with her feet and the glass shattered. But the pieces were held in place by the central sheet of plastic.

All at once the window cracked with the sound of thunder. Small sheets of the shattered pieces fell in on her. Someone had cracked the glass from the outside. Then one of the men from the black Ford reached in. She launched herself at him, but as soon as she grabbed hold of his arm the second man zapped her with a Taser.

Her body went limp. Together the men hauled her roughly out of the Pontiac. Through the awful buzzing in her head, she heard a gout of rapid-fire Arabic. An explosion of laughter. Their hands were all over her helpless body.

Then one of them put a gun to her head.

TWENTY-EIGHT

Martin Lindros, standing in the windowless cell deep underground in Dujja's Miran Shah complex, ran his hand over the walls. He had done this so many times since he'd been brought here he could feel the rebar like bones that crisscrossed beneath the rough concrete, reinforcing them.

Precisely fifteen paces to a side, each side equal, the only break a pallet hinged to one wall and, opposite, a stainless steel sink and toilet. Back and forth he paced, like a caged animal going quietly mad from its confinement. Three sets of purple-blue fluorescent lights were embedded into the ceiling. They were unguarded by wire mesh, being too high up for him to reach, even with his best to the hoop leap, therefore, they glared mercilessly down sixteen hours a day.

When they were turned off, when he lay down to sleep, they had the uncanny habit of snapping on just as he was sinking down into sleep, jerking him awake like a hooked fish. From these occurrences Lindros quickly determined that he was under continuous surveillance. After some detective work, he'd discovered a tiny hole in the ceiling between two of the sets of lights – another reason for the glare, no doubt – through which a fiber-optic eye observed him with all the dispassion of a god. All this possessed a level of sophistication befitting Dujja. It was confirmation, if he needed any, that he was at the heart of the terrorist network.

It was difficult not to believe that Fadi himself was keeping an eye on him, if not always in person, then by periodically reviewing the video tapes of him in his cell. How the terrorist must gloat every time he saw Lindros prowling back and forth. Was he looking forward to the moment when he imagined Lindros would make the break from human being to animal? Lindros was certain of it, and his fists turned white as they trembled at his side.

The door to his cell banged open, admitting Fadi, his face dark with fury. Without a word he strode to Lindros and struck him a massive blow to the side of the head. Lindros fell to the concrete floor, stunned and sickened. Fadi kicked him.

'Bourne is dead. Do you hear me, Lindros? Dead!' There was a terrifying edge to Fadi's voice, a slight tremor that spoke of being pushed to the edge of an emotional abyss. 'The unthinkable has happened. I have been cheated of the revenge I meticulously planned. All undone by the unforeseen.'

Lindros, recovering, hauled himself up on one elbow. 'The future is unforeseen,' he said. 'It's unknowable.'

Fadi squatted down, his face almost touching Lindros's. 'Infidel. Allah knows the future; He shows it to the righteous.'

'Fadi, I pity you. You can't see the truth even when it's staring you in the face.'

His face a twisted fist of rage, Fadi grabbed Lindros and threw him to the floor of the cell. His hands closed over the other man's throat, cutting off his breath.

'I may not be able to kill Jason Bourne with my bare hands, but here you are. I will kill you instead.' His eyes fairly bulging with fury, he squeezed Lindros's neck in a death grip. Lindros kicked and thrashed, but he had neither the strength nor the leverage to throw Fadi off him or to displace his hands.

He was losing consciousness, his good eye rolling up in its socket, when Abbud ibn Aziz appeared in the cell's open doorway.

'Fadi—'

'Get out of here!' Fadi cried. 'Leave me alone!'

Nevertheless, Abbud ibn Aziz took a step into the cell. 'Fadi, it's Veintrop.'

Fadi's eyes showed white all around. The Desert Wind – the killing rage – had taken possession of him.

'Fadi,' Abbud persisted. 'You must come now.'

Letting go of his hold, Fadi rose, turned on his second in command. 'Why? Why must I come now? Tell me this instant before I kill you as well.'

'Veintrop is finished.'

'All the safeguards are in place?'

'Yes,' Abbud said. 'The nuclear device is ready to be deployed.'

Tyrone was munching on a quarter-pound burger while watching with a self-taught engineer's eye the steady climb of a massive I-beam when the severely battered Pontiac came under attack. Two men in slick business suits ran out of a black Ford that had met the Pontiac head-on. They spoke to each other, but over the construction noise he couldn't make out the words.

He rose from a crate, his impromptu bench, and began to walk toward the men. One of them held a weapon: neither a gun nor a knife, Tyrone saw, but a Taser.

Then, as one of the men bashed in the driver's side window of the Pontiac, Tyrone recognized him as a guard he'd seen outside M&N Bodywork. These people were invading his turf.

Throwing aside his burger, he began to walk quickly toward the Pontiac, which looked as if some monster twenty-wheeler had tried its best to crush it. Having bashed in the safety glass, one of the men reached through it. Then the man with the Taser thrust his right arm through the opening, using the weapon on whoever was inside. A moment later, both men began to haul out the incapacitated driver.

Tyrone was close enough now to see that the victim was a woman. They manhandled her roughly to her feet, turned her so that he saw her face. He broke out into a cold sweat. Miss Spook! His mind racing, he began to run.

With the constant din of the construction site, the men did not become aware of him until he was almost upon them. One of them took the gun from Miss S's head, aimed it at Tyrone. Tyrone, his hands in the air, came to an abrupt halt a pace away from them. It was all he could do not to look at Miss S. Her head was hanging down on her chest; her legs looked rubbery. They had zapped her but good.

'Get the fuck out of here,' the man with the gun said. 'Turn around and keep walking.'

Tyrone put a frightened look on his face. 'Yessir,' he said meekly.

As he began to turn away, his hands sank to his sides. The switchblade slid into his right hand; he *snikked* it open and, as he whirled back, drove the blade to the hilt between the man's ribs, as he had been taught to handle the close-on street fights of turf wars.

The man dropped his gun. His eyes rolled up and his legs gave out. The other man groped for his Taser, but he had Miss S to consider. He threw her back against the crumpled side of the Pontiac just as Tyrone's fist shattered the cartilage in his nose. Blood flew out, blinding him. Tyrone drove a knee into his groin, then took his head between his hands, slamming it into the Pontiac's side mirror.

As the man crumpled to the ground, Tyrone delivered a vicious kick to his side, stoving in a handful of ribs. He bent, retrieved his switchblade. Then he hoisted Miss S over his shoulder, took her to the idling Ford, laid her carefully on the backseat. As soon as he slid behind the wheel, he once again checked out the construction site. Luckily, the Pontiac had blocked the workmen's view. They'd seen nothing of the incident.

He spat out of the side window in the direction of the fallen men. Putting the SUV into gear, he drove off, careful not to exceed the speed limit. The last thing he needed now was for a cop to pull him over for a traffic violation.

Snaking up the hillside, Bourne passed one wooden villa after another, built in the nineteenth century by Greek and Armenian bankers. Today they were owned by the billionaires of Istanbul, whose businesses, like those of their Ottoman ancestors, spanned the known world.

While he rode, keeping track of Muta ibn Aziz, he thought about Fadi's brother, Karim, the man who had taken Martin Lindros's face, his right eye, his identity. On the surface, he was just about the last person anyone would expect to be directly involved in Dujja's plan. He was, after all, the scion of the family, the man who had stepped in to run Integrated Vertical Technologies when his father had been incapacitated by Bourne's bullet. He was the legitimate brother, the businessman, just like the businessmen who had built these modern-day palaces.

And now, for the first time, Bourne understood the depth of the obsession the two brothers felt in avenging their sister's murder. Sarah had been the family's shining star, the repository of the Hamid ibn Ashef al-Wahhib honor that stretched back over the centuries, over the endless wastes of the Arabian desert, over time itself. Theirs was an honor embedded in the three-thousand-year history of the Arabian peninsula, of the Sinai, of Palestine. Their ancestors had come out of the desert, had come back from defeat after defeat, erasing ignominious retreat to take back the Arabian peninsula from their enemies. Their patriarch, Muhammad ibn Abd-al-Wahhab, was one of the great Islamic reformists. In the middle 1700s, he had joined forces with Muhammad ibn Saud to create a new political entity. A hundred fifty years later, the two families captured Riyadh, and modern Saudi Arabia was born.

Difficult as it was for a Westerner to understand, Sarah ibn Ashef embodied all of that. Of course her brothers would move heaven and earth to kill her murderer. This was why they had taken the time to weave Bourne's utter destruction – first of mind, then of body. Because it would not be enough for them merely to seek him out and put a bullet through the back of his head. No, the plan was to break him, then to have Fadi kill him with bare hands. Nothing less would do.

Bourne knew that the news of his death would send both brothers into a frenzy. In this unstable state they were more apt to make a mistake. All the better for him.

He needed to tell Soraya the identity of the man who was pretending to be Martin Lindros. Pulling out his cell phone, he punched in the country and city code, then her number. The act of dialing brought home to him that he hadn't heard from her. He glanced at his watch. Unless it had been badly delayed, her flight would have landed in Washington by now.

Once again, she wasn't answering, and now he began to worry. For security reasons he didn't leave another message. After all, he was supposed to be dead. He prayed that she hadn't fallen into enemy hands. But if the worst had happened, he had to protect himself from Karim, who would no doubt check her cell for incoming and outgoing calls. He made a mental note to try her again in an hour or so. That would be just after seven, less than an hour before Muta ibn Aziz was due to leave Büyükada to wherever Fadi was now.

'The endgame has begun,' the messenger had told Hatun. Bourne felt a chill run down his spine. So little time to find Fadi, to stop him from detonating the nuclear device.

According to the map he had purchased on the ferry, the

island consisted of two hills separated by a valley. He was now climbing the southern hill, Yule Tepe, on top of which sat the twelfth-century St. George's Monastery. As he rose in elevation, the road turned into a path. By this time, the palm trees had given way to thick, pine-forested swaths, shadowed, mysterious, deserted. The villas, too, had fallen away.

The monastery consisted of a series of chapels over three levels, along with several outbuildings. The blip that represented Muta ibn Aziz's position had remained stationary for some minutes. The way became too rocky and uneven for the bike. Plucking his satchel from the basket, Bourne set the bicycle aside, continuing on foot.

He saw no tourists, no caretakers; no one at all. But then the hour was growing late; darkness had descended. Skirting the ramshackle main building itself, he made his way farther up the hillside. According to the transponder, Muta ibn Aziz was inside the small building dead ahead. Lamplight glowed through the windowpanes.

As he approached, the blip started to move. Shrinking back under the protection of a towering pine, he watched as Fadi's messenger, holding an old-fashioned oil lantern, came out of the building and headed off between two colossal chunks of stone into the thicket of the pine forest.

Bourne made a quick recon of the area, assuring himself that no one was watching the building. Then he slipped in through the scarred wooden door into the cool interior. Oil lamps had been lit against the darkness. His map identified this building as having once been used as an asylum for the criminally insane. The interior was fairly bare; clearly it was unused now. However, evidence of its grisly past was evident. The stone floor was studded with iron rings, which presumably had been used to bind the inmates when they became violent. An open doorway to the left led into a small room, empty save for some tarps and various workers' implements.

He returned to the main room. Against a line of windows

facing north toward the woods was a long refectory table of dark wood. On the table, within a generous oval of lamplight, lay unfolded a large sheet of thick paper. Going over to it, Bourne saw that it was a map with a flight plan plotted on it. He studied it, fascinated. The air route led southeast across almost the entire length of Turkey, the southernmost tip of Armenia and Azerbaijan, out over the Caspian Sea, then, transversing a section of Iran, diagonally across the width of Afghanistan, with a landing in the mountainous region just across the border, in terrorist-infested western Pakistan.

So it wasn't a boat Muta ibn Aziz was going to use to leave Büyükada. It was a private jet with permission to enter Iranian airspace and enough fuel capacity to make the thirty-five-hundred-kilometer trip without refueling.

Bourne looked out the window at the dense pine forest into which Muta ibn Aziz had disappeared. He was wondering where in that mass a landing strip suitable for a jet could be hidden when he heard a noise. He was in the process of turning around when pain exploded in the back of his head. He had the sensation of falling. Then blackness.

TWENTY-NINE

Anne had never seen Jamil so angry. He was angry at the DCI. He was angry at her. He didn't hit her or scream at her. He did something far worse: He ignored her.

As she went about her work, Anne grieved inside with a desperation she had thought she had left behind. There was a certain mind-set to being a mistress, something you had to get used to, like the dull pain of a dying tooth. You had to learn to be without your lover on birthdays, Valentine's Day, Christmas, the anniversary of your meeting, the first time you slept together, the first time he stayed the night, the first breakfast, eaten with the naked delight of children. All these things were denied a mistress.

At first, Anne had found this peculiar aloneness intolerable. She tried to call him when he could not be with her on the days – and nights! – she craved him the most. Until he explained to her carefully but firmly that she could not. When he wasn't physically with her, she was to forget he existed. *How can I do that?* she had wailed inside her head while she smiled, nodding her assent. It was vital, she knew, that he believe she understood. Instinct warned her that if he didn't, he would turn away from her. If he did, she would surely die.

So she pretended for him, for her own survival. And gradually she learned how to cope. She didn't forget he existed, of course. That was impossible. But she came to see her time with him as if it were a movie she went to see now and again. In between, she could keep the movie in her head, as anyone does with the movies they adore, ones they long to see again and again. In this way, she was able to live her life in a more or less normal manner. Because deep down where she dared to look only infrequently, she knew that without him at her side her life was only half lived.

And now, because she had allowed Soraya to escape, he wasn't speaking to her at all. He passed by her desk on his way to and from meetings with the Old Man as if she didn't exist, ignored the swelling of her left cheek where Soraya's elbow had connected. The worst had happened, the one thing that had terrified her from the moment she had fallen deeply, madly, irretrievably in love with him: She had failed him.

She wondered whether he had gotten the goods on Defense Secretary Halliday. For a moment, she had been dead certain that he had, but then the Old Man had asked her to set up an appointment with Luther LaValle, the Pentagon intelligence czar, not Secretary Halliday. What was he up to?

She was in the dark, too, about Soraya's fate. Had she been captured? Killed? She didn't know because Jamil had cut her out of the loop. She didn't share his confidence. She could no longer tuck herself into his body, hot as the desert wind. In her heart, she suspected that Soraya was still alive. If Jamil's cell had caught Soraya, surely he would have forgiven her the sin of allowing her to get away. She felt chilled. Soraya's knowledge was like a guillotine hovering over her neck. Anne's whole life would be revealed as a lie. She'd be tried for treason.

Part of her mind went through the motions of her daily routine. She listened to the Old Man when he summoned her into his office; she input his memos and printed them out for him to sign. She made his calls, scheduled his long day with the precision of a military campaign. She protected his phone lines as fiercely as ever. But another part of her mind was frantically trying to figure out how she could reverse the fatal mistake she had made.

She needed to win Jamil back. And she had to have him, she knew that. Redemption came in many guises, but not for Jamil. He was Bedouin; his mind was locked in the ancient ways of the desert. Exile or death, those were the choices. She would have to find Soraya. Her bloodied hands were the only things that would bring him back to her. She would have to kill Soraya herself.

Bourne awoke. He tried to move, but found himself bound by ropes tied to two of the iron rings bolted to the asylum's floor. A man was crouched over him, a Caucasian with a lantern jaw and eyes pale as ice. He was wearing a leather flight jacket and a cap with a silver pin in the shape of a pair of wings stuck on it.

The pilot of the jet. From the look of him, Bourne knew he was one of those flyboys who fancied himself a cowboy of the sky.

He grinned down at Bourne. 'Whatcha doing here?' He spoke in very poor Arabic, reacting to Bourne's disguise. 'Checking out my flight plan. Spying on me.' He shook his head in a deliberately exaggerated fashion, like a nanny admonishing her charge. 'That's forbidden. Got that? For-bid-den.' He pursed his lips. 'You savvy?' he added in English.

Then he showed Bourne what he was holding: the NET transponder. 'What the fuck is this, you rat bastard? Huh? Who the fuck are you? Who sent you?' He pulled a knife, bringing the long blade close to Bourne's face. 'Answer me, goddammit, or I'll carve you up like a Christmas goose! You savvy Christmas? Huh?'

Bourne stared up at him with blank eyes. He opened his mouth, spoke a sentence very softly.

'What?' The pilot leaned closer to Bourne. 'What did you say?'

Using the power in his lower belly, Bourne brought his legs straight up in the air, scissoring them so that his ankles crossed behind the pilot's neck. His lower legs locked and he spun the pilot over and down. The side of the man's head struck the marble floor with such force, his cheekbone shattered. Immediately he passed out.

Twisting his neck, Bourne could see the knife on the floor behind his head. It was on the other side of the iron rings. Drawing his legs up, his body rolled into a ball, he rocked back and forth, gaining momentum. When he judged that he had enough force, he rocked backward with all his might. Though anchored by the rings to which his wrists were tied, he flew through the air in a backflip, passing over the rings, landing on his knees on the other side.

Extending one leg, he hooked the knife with the top of his shoe, kicked it so that the hilt clacked against the ring to which his right hand was bound. By moving the ring down until it was almost parallel with the floor, he was able to grab the knife. Laying the edge of the blade against the rope, he began to saw through it.

It was hard, cramped work. He couldn't apply the kind of pressure he'd have liked, so progress was frighteningly slow. From where he knelt, he couldn't see the transponder's screen; he had no idea where Muta ibn Aziz was. For all he knew, at any moment the messenger would walk in on him.

At length, he'd sawed through the rope. Quickly, he cut the rope binding his left hand, and he was free. Lunging for the transponder, he looked at the screen. Muta ibn Aziz's blip was still some way distant.

Bourne rolled the pilot over and methodically stripped off his clothes, which he donned piece by piece, though the shirt was too small, the pants too big. When he had arranged the pilot's outfit on his frame as best he could, he drew over his satchel and took out the various items he'd bought at the theatrical shop in Istanbul. Setting a small square mirror down on the floor where he could easily see the reflection of his face, he removed the prosthetics from his mouth. Then he began the process of transforming himself into the pilot.

Bourne trimmed and restyled his hair, changed the complexion of his face, added a pair of prosthetics to give his jaw a longer appearance. He had no colored lenses, but in the darkness of the night the disguise would have to do. Luckily, he could keep the pilot's cap low on his forehead.

He took another glance at the transponder, then went through the pilot's wallet and papers. His name was Walter B. Darwin. An American expat, with passports identifying him as a citizen of three different countries. Bourne could relate to that. He had a military tattoo on one shoulder, the words FUCK YOU, TOO on the other. What he was doing ferrying terrorists around the globe was anyone's guess. Not that it mattered now. Walter Darwin's flyboy career was over. Bourne dragged his naked body into a back room, covered it in a dusty tarp.

Back in the main room, he went to the table, gathered up the flight plan. It was twenty minutes to eight. Keeping an eye on the blip on the transponder screen, he stuffed the plan in his satchel, took up one of the lamps, and went in search of the airstrip.

Anne knew that Soraya was too smart to come anywhere near her apartment. Pretending to be Kim Lovett, Soraya's friend in the DCFD's Fire Investigation Unit, she called both Tim Hytner's mother and sister. Neither of them had seen or heard from Soraya since she had visited to break the news that Tim had been shot to death. If Soraya had gone there now, she would have warned them about a woman named Anne Held. But surely she'd want to talk to her best friend.

Anne was about to call Kim Lovett herself when she thought better of it. Instead, when she left the office that evening, she took a taxi straight to the FIU labs on Vermont Avenue and 11th Street.

Finding her way to Kim's lab, she went in.

'I'm Anne Held,' she said. 'Soraya works with me.'

Kim rose from her work: two metal trays filled with ash, charred bits of bone, and half-burned cloth. She stretched like a cat, stripped off her latex gloves, held out her hand for a firm shake.

'So,' Kim said, 'what brings you down to this grim place?'

'Well, actually, it's Soraya.'

Kim was instantly alarmed. 'Has something happened to her?'

'That's what I'm trying to find out. I was wondering whether you'd heard from her.'

Kim shook her head. 'But that's hardly unusual.' She considered a moment. 'It may be nothing, but a week or two ago there was a police detective who was interested in her. They met here at the lab. He wanted her to take him with her on some investigation or other, but Soraya said no. I had the feeling, though, that his interest in her was more than professional.'

'Do you remember the date, and the detective's name?'

Kim gave her the date. 'As for his name, I did write it down somewhere.' She rummaged through one of several stacks of files on the countertop. 'Ah, here it is,' she said, pulled out a torn-off strip of paper. 'Detective William Overton.'

How small the world is, Anne thought as she exited the FIU building. *How full of coincidence*. The cop who had been following her had been after Soraya as well. He was dead now, of course, but perhaps he could still tell her where to find Soraya.

Using her cell phone, Anne quickly found Detective William Overton's precinct, its address, and the name of his commanding officer. Arriving there, she produced her credentials, told the desk sergeant she needed to see Captain Morrell on a matter of some urgency. When he balked, as she knew he would, she invoked the Old Man's name. The desk sergeant picked up the phone. Five minutes later a young uniform was escorting her into Captain Morrell's corner office.

He dismissed the uniform, offered Anne a seat, then closed the door. 'What can I do for you, Ms. Held?' He was a small man with thinning hair, a bristling mustache, and eyes that had seen too much death and accommodation. 'My desk sergeant said it was a matter of some urgency.'

Anne got right to the point. 'CI is investigating Detective Overton's disappearance.'

'Bill Overton? *My* Bill Overton?' Captain Morrell looked bewildered. 'Why—?'

'It's a matter of national security,' Anne said, using the surefire catchall phrase that no one could refute these days. 'I need to see all his logs for the past month, also his personal effects.'

'Sure. Of course.' He stood. 'The investigation's ongoing, so we have everything here.'

'We'll keep you personally informed every step of the way, Captain,' she assured him.

'I appreciate that.' He opened the door, bawled 'Ritchie!' into the corridor. The same young uniform dutifully appeared. 'Ritchie, give Ms. Held access to Overton's effects.'

'Yessir.' Ritchie turned to Anne. 'If you'll follow me, ma'am.'

Ma'am. God, that made her feel old.

He led her farther along the corridor, down a set of metal

stairs to a basement room guarded by a floor-to-ceiling fence with a locked door in it. Using a key, he unlocked the door, then took her down an aisle lined on both sides with utilitarian metal shelves. They were packed with cartons in alphabetical order, identified with typewritten labels.

He pulled down two boxes and carried them to a table pushed up against the back wall. 'Official,' he said, pointing to the carton on the left. 'This other's his personal stuff.'

He looked at her, expectant as a puppy. 'Can I be of any help?'

'That's all right, Officer Ritchie,' Anne said with a smile. 'I can take it from here.'

'Right. Well, I'll leave you to it, then. I'll be in the next room, if you need me.'

When she was alone, Anne turned to the carton on the left, laying out everything in a grid. The files with Overton's logs she put to one side. As soon as she had assured herself that there was nothing of value to her in the grid, she turned her attention to the logs. She examined each item carefully and methodically, giving special attention to entries on and after the date Kim Lovett had given her, when Overton had met Soraya at FIU. There was nothing.

'Bollocks!' she muttered, turned her attention to the carton on her right, filled with Overton's personal effects. These turned out to be even more pathetic than she had expected: a cheap comb and brush sporting a thin mat of hairs; two packs of TUMS, one opened; a blue dress shirt, soiled down the placket with what looked like marinara sauce; a hideous blue-and-red-striped polyester tie; a photo of a goofily grinning young man in a football outfit, probably Overton's son; a box of Raisinets, and another of nonpareils, both unopened. That was it.

'*Merde!*'

With a convulsive gesture, she swept the gutter leavings of Overton's life off the table. She was about to turn away when she saw a bit of white sticking out of the breast pocket of the blue shirt. Bending down, she pulled it out with extended fingertips. It was a square of lined paper, folded in quarters. She opened it up, saw scribbled in blue ballpoint ink:

S. Moore – 8 & 12 NE (ck)

Anne's heart beat fast. This was what she was looking for. *S. Moore* was undoubtedly Soraya; *(ck)* could mean 'check.' Of course, 8th Street didn't cross 12th Street in Northeast – or in any quadrant of the district, for that matter. Still, it was clear that Overton had followed Soraya into Northeast. What the hell was she doing there? Whatever it was, she'd kept it secret from CI.

Anne stood staring at the memo Overton had made to himself, trying to work it out. Then it hit her, and she began to laugh. The twelfth letter of the alphabet was *L*. Eighth and L NE.

If Soraya was alive, it was more than likely she'd gone to ground there.

When Bourne passed between the two hulking chunks of stone, the lamplight revealed the path Muta ibn Aziz had taken. It went west for perhaps a kilometer before veering sharply to the northeast. He ascended a slight rise, after which the path headed almost directly north, down into a shallow swale that gradually rose onto the beginning of what appeared to be a plateau of considerable size.

All the while, he had been drawing closer to Muta ibn Aziz, who for the last minute or so hadn't moved. The pine forest was still dense, the thatch of brown needles underfoot deeply aromatic, deadening sound.

Within five minutes, however, the forest simply ended.

Clearly it had been cut down here to make room for a landing strip long enough to accommodate the jet he saw sitting at one end of the packed-dirt runway.

And there was Muta ibn Aziz, at the foot of the folding stairs. Bourne strode out from the path through the forest, heading directly for the plane, a Citation Sovereign. The pitch-black sky was strewn with stars, glittering coolly like diamonds on a jeweler's velvet pad. A breeze, dense with sea minerals, played across the cleared hilltop.

'Time to leave,' Muta ibn Aziz said. 'Everything in order?'

Bourne nodded. Muta ibn Aziz pressed a button on a small black object in his hand, and the runway lights flashed on. Bourne followed him up the stairway, retracting it as soon as he was inside. He went down the cabin to the cockpit. He was familiar with the Citation line. The Sovereign had a range of more than 4,500 kilometers and a top speed of 826 kph.

Seating himself in the pilot's chair, he flipped switches, turned dials as he went through the intricate pre-takeoff checklist. Everything was as it should be.

Releasing the brakes, he pushed the throttle forward. The Sovereign responded at once. They taxied down the runway, gathering speed. Then they lifted off into the inky, spangled sky, climbing steadily, leaving the Golden Horn, the gateway to Asia, behind.

THIRTY

'Why do they do it?' Martin Lindros said in very fine Russian.

Lying flat on his back in the infirmary in Miran Shah, he gazed up into the bruised face of Katya Stepanova Vdova, Dr. Veintrop's stunning young wife.

'Why do they do what?' she said dully as she rather ineptly administered to the abrasions on his throat. She had been training to be a physician's assistant after Veintrop had made her quit Perfect Ten modeling.

'The doctors here: your husband, Senarz, Andursky. Why have they hired out their services to Fadi?' Speaking of Andursky, the plastic surgeon who had remade Karim's face with his eye, Lindros wondered, *Why isn't he tending to me instead of this clumsy amateur?* Almost as soon as he had posed the question, he had the answer: He was no longer of any use either to Fadi or to his brother.

'They're human,' Katya said. 'Which means they're weak. Fadi finds their weakness and uses it against them. For Senarz, it was money. For Andursky, it was boys.'

'And Veintrop?'

She made a face. 'Ah, my husband. He thinks he's being noble, that he's being forced to work for Dujja because Fadi holds my own well-being over his head. He's fooling himself, of course. The truth is he's doing it to get his pride back. Fadi's brother sacked him from IVT on false allegations. He needs to work, my husband. That's his weakness.'

She sat back, her hands in her lap. 'You think I don't know how bad I am at this? But Costin insists, you see, so what choice do I have?'

'You have a choice, Katya. Everyone does. You have only to see it.' He glanced at the two guards just outside the infirmary door. They were talking to each other in low tones. 'Don't you want to get out of here?'

'What about Costin?'

'Veintrop's finished his work for Fadi. A smart woman like you should know that he's now a liability.'

'That's not true!' she said.

'Katya, we all have the capacity for fooling ourselves. That's where we get into trouble. Look no further than your husband.'

She sat very still, staring at him with an odd look in her eyes.

'We also all have the capacity to change, Katya. It only takes us deciding that we have to in order to keep going, in order to survive.'

She looked away for a moment, as people do when they're afraid, when they've made up their minds but need encouragement.

'Who did that to you, Katya?' he said softly.

Her eyes snapped back to him, and he saw the shadow of her fear lurking there. 'Fadi. Fadi and his man. To persuade Costin to complete the nuclear device.'

'That doesn't make sense,' Lindros said. 'If Veintrop knew Fadi had you, that should have been enough.'

Katya bit her lip, kept her eyes focused on her work. She finished up, then rose.

'Katya, why won't you answer me?'

She didn't look back as she walked out of the infirmary.

*

Anne Held, standing in a chill rain on the corner of 8th and L NE, felt the presence of the S&W J-frame compact handgun in the right-hand pocket of her trench coat as if it were some terrible disfigurement with which she had just been diagnosed.

She knew she would risk anything, do anything to rid herself of the feeling that she no longer belonged anywhere, that there was nothing left inside her. The only thing to do was to prove herself worthy again. If she shot Soraya dead, Jamil would surely welcome her back. She would belong again.

Pulling up her collar against the wind-driven rain, she began to walk. She should have been afraid in this neighborhood – the police certainly were – but strangely she was not. Then again, perhaps it wasn't strange at all. She had nothing left to lose.

She turned the corner onto 7th Street. What was she looking for? What kinds of clues would tell her whether she had deduced correctly that this was where Soraya had gone to ground? A car went by, then another. Faces – black, Hispanic, hostile, strange – glared at her as the vehicles cruised by. One driver grinned, waggled his tongue obscenely at her. She put her right hand in her pocket and closed it around the S&W.

As she walked, she kept her eye on the houses she passed – torn up, beaten down, singed by poverty, neglect, and flames. Rubble and rubbish filled their tiny front yards, as if the street were inhabited by junkmen displaying their woebegone wares for sale. The air was fouled by the stench of rotting garbage and urine, defeat and despair. Gaunt dogs ran here and there, baring their yellow teeth at her.

She was like a drowning woman, clutching at the only thing that could save her from going under. Her palm felt sweaty against the grip of the handgun. The day had finally arrived, she thought vaguely, when all her hours on the firing range would stand her in good stead. She could hear the deep, crisp voice of the CI firearms instructor correcting her stance or her grip while she reloaded the agency-issue S&W.

She thought again of her sister, Joyce, remembering the pain of their shared childhood. But surely there had been pleasure, too, hadn't there, on the nights they had slept in one bed, telling each other ghost stories, seeing which one of them would be the first to scream in fear? Anne felt like a ghost now, drifting through a world she could only haunt. She crossed the street, passing an open lot with weeds as high as her waist, tenacious even in winter. Tires, worn as an old man's face, empty plastic bottles, syringes, used condoms and cell phones, one red sock with the toe cap gone. And a severed arm.

Anne jumped, her heart pounding against the cage of her chest. A doll's arm only. But her heart rate didn't come down. She stared in grim fascination at that severed arm. It was like Joyce's aborted future, lying in a slagheap of dead weeds. What exactly was the difference between Joyce's future and her own present? she asked herself. She hadn't cried in the longest time. Now it seemed that she had forgotten how.

Day had descended into the grave of night, icy rain had turned to clammy fog. Moisture seemed to congeal on her hair, the backs of her hands. Now and again a siren rose in distress, only to fall again into uneasy silence.

From behind her came the grumble of an engine. She paused, her heart hammering, waiting for the car to pass. When it didn't, she began to walk again, more quickly. The car, emerging from the fog, kept pace just behind her.

All at once she reversed course and, with her hand gripping the S&W, walked back toward the car. As she did so, it stopped. The driver's-side window rolled down, revealing a long, withered face the color of old shoe leather, the bottom half of which was whiskery and gray.

'You look like you're lost,' the driver said in a voice gravelly with a lifetime of tar and nicotine. 'Gypsy cab.' He tipped his baseball cap. 'I thought you might need a ride. There's a crew down the end a the block lickin' their chops at the thought a you.'

'I can take care of myself.' Sudden fear caused her to sound defensive.

The cabbie eyed her with a downtrodden expression. 'Whatever.'

As he put the car in gear, Anne said, 'Wait!' She passed a hand across her damp brow. She felt as if a raging fever had broken. Who was she kidding? She didn't have it in her to shoot Soraya, let alone kill her.

Grabbing the rear door handle, she slid into the gypsy cab and gave the driver her address. She didn't want to go back to CI headquarters. She couldn't face either Jamil or the Old Man. She wondered whether she'd ever be able to face them again.

Then she noticed that the cabbie had turned around to scrutinize her face.

'What?' Anne said, a bit too defensively.

The cabbie grunted. 'You goddamn good lookin'.'

Opting for forbearance, she took out a clutch of bills, waving them in his face. 'Are you going to give me a ride or not?'

The cabbie licked his lips, put the car in gear.

As the car started off, she leaned forward. 'Just so you know,' she said, 'I've got a gun.'

'So do I, sister.' The grizzled cabbie leered at her. 'So do fuckin' I.'

The DCI met Luther LaValle at Thistle, a trendy restaurant on 19th and Q NW. He'd had Anne book a center table, because when he talked to LaValle he wanted them to be surrounded by raucous diners.

The Pentagon's intelligence czar was already seated when the Old Man arrived from out of the dense winter fog into the restaurant's roar. In a navy-blue suit, crisp white shirt, and red-and-blue-striped regimental tie pierced by an American flag enamel pin, LaValle looked out of place surrounded by young men and women of the next generation.

LaValle's boxer's torso ballooned the suit in the way of all overly muscled men. He looked like Bruce Banner in the process of transforming into the Hulk. Smiling thinly, he rose from his Scotch and soda to give the DCI's proffered hand a perfunctory squeeze.

The Old Man took the chair across from him. 'Good of you to meet me at such short notice, Luther.'

LaValle spread his brutal, blunt-fingered hands. 'What are you having?'

'Oban,' the Old Man said to the waiter who had appeared at his elbow. 'Make it a double, one ice cube, but only if it's large.'

The waiter gave a little nod, vanished into the crowd.

'Large ice cubes are best for liquor,' the DCI said to his companion. 'They take longer to melt.'

The intelligence czar said nothing, but looked at the Old Man expectantly. When the single-malt Scotch arrived, the two men raised their glasses and drank.

'The traffic tonight is insufferable,' the DCI said.

'It's the fog,' LaValle responded vaguely.

'When was the last time we got together like this?'

'You know, I can't recall.'

Both seemed to be talking to the young couple at the next table. Their neutral words sat between them like pawns, already sacrificed on the field of battle. The waiter returned with menus. They opened them, made their choices, and once again were left to their own devices.

The DCI pulled a dossier from his slim briefcase and set it on the table, unopened. His palms came down heavily on it. 'I assume you've heard about the utility truck that went out of control outside the Corcoran.'

'A traffic accident?' LaValle shrugged. 'Do you know how many of those occur in the district each hour?'

'This one is different,' the Old Man said. 'The truck was trying to run down one of my people.'

LaValle took a sip of his Scotch and soda. The Old Man thought he drank like a lady.

'Which one?'

'Anne Held, my assistant. Martin Lindros was with her. He saved her.'

LaValle leaned down, came back with his own dossier. It had the Pentagon's seal on its cover. He opened it and, without a word, reversed it, passing it across the table.

As the Old Man began to read, LaValle said, 'Someone inside your headquarters is sending and receiving periodic messages.'

The Old Man was shocked in more ways than one. 'Since when is the Pentagon monitoring CI communications? Dammit, that's a gross breach of interagency protocol.'

'I ordered it, with the president's okay. We thought it necessary. When Secretary Halliday became aware of a mole inside CI—'

'From Matthew Lerner, his creature,' the DCI said heatedly. 'Halliday has no business creeping into my shorts. And without me, the president is getting improperly briefed.'

'It was done for the agency's own good.'

Thunderclouds of indignation cracked open across the DCI's face. 'Are you implying that I no longer know what's good for CI?'

LaValle's finger stabbed out. 'You see, there. The electronic signal is piggybacking on CI carrier waves. It's encrypted. We haven't been able to break it. Also, we don't know who's doing the communicating. But from the dates it clearly can't be Hytner, the agent you IDed as the mole. He was already dead.'

The Old Man shifted aside the Pentagon dossier, opened his own. 'I'll take care of this leak, if that's what it is,' he said. Likely as not what these idiots had picked up was a clandestine Typhon communiqué with one of its deep-cover overseas operatives. Of course Martin's black-ops department wouldn't use normal CI channels. 'And you'll take care of the defense secretary.'

'I beg your pardon?' For the first time since they had sat down together, LaValle appeared nonplussed.

'That utility van I mentioned earlier, the one that tried to run over Anne Held.'

'To be candid, Secretary Halliday shared with me that he suspected Anne Held of being the mole inside—'

The appetizers arrived: colossal pink prawns dipped in blood-red cocktail sauce.

Before LaValle could pick up his tiny fork, the DCI held out a single sheet of paper he'd plucked from the dossier Martin had provided him. 'The van that almost killed her was driven by the late Jon Mueller.' He waited a beat. 'You know Mueller, Luther, don't bother pretending otherwise. He was with Homeland Security, but he was trained by NSA. He knew Matthew Lerner. The two were whoring and drinking buddies, in fact. Both Halliday's creatures.'

'Do you have any hard proof of this?' LaValle said blandly.

The Old Man was fully prepared for this question. 'You already know the answer to that. But I have enough to start an investigation. Unexplained deposits in Mueller's bank account, a Lamborghini that Lerner couldn't possibly afford, trips to Las Vegas where both dropped bundles of cash. Arrogance begets stupidity; it's an axiom old as time.' He took back the sheet of paper. 'I assure you that once the investigation gets to the Senate, the net that'll be thrown out will catch not only Halliday but those close to him.'

He folded his arms. 'Frankly, I don't fancy a scandal of this grave a scope. It would only help our enemies abroad.' He lifted a prawn. 'But this time, the secretary's gone too far. He believes he can do anything he wants, even sanctioning a murder using our government's men.'

He paused here to let these words sink in. As the intelligence czar's eyes rose to meet his, the Old Man said, 'Here is where I make my stand. I cannot condone such a recklessly unlawful act. Neither, I think, can you.'

Muta ibn Aziz sat brooding, watching the sky outside the jet's Perspex window glowing blue-black. Below him was the unruffled skin of the Caspian Sea, obscured now and again by streaks of clouds the color of a gull's wing.

He inhabited a dark corner of Dujja, performing the demeaning task of messenger boy, while his brother basked in the limelight of Fadi's favor. And all because of that one moment in Odessa, the lie they had told Fadi and Karim that Abbud had forbidden him to correct. Abbud had said he must keep quiet for Fadi's sake, but now, when Muta looked at the situation from a distance, he realized that this was yet another lie perpetrated by his brother. Abbud insisted on hiding the truth about Sarah ibn Ashef's death for his own sake, for the consolidation of his own power within Dujja.

Rousing himself, Muta saw the dark smudge of land coming into view. He glanced at his watch. Right on schedule. Rising, he stretched, hesitating. His thoughts went to the man piloting the jet. He knew this wasn't the real pilot; he'd failed to give the recognition sign when he'd emerged from the woods. Who was he then? A CI agent, certainly; Jason Bourne, most probably. But then he had received a cell phone text message three hours ago that Jason Bourne was dead, according to an eyewitness and the electronic tracker, which now resided at the bottom of the Black Sea.

But what if the eyewitness lied? What if Bourne, discovering the tracker, had thrown it into the ocean? Who else could this pilot be but Jason Bourne, the Chameleon?

He went up the central aisle, into the cockpit. The pilot kept his attention focused on the neat rows of dials in front of him.

'We're coming up on Iranian airspace,' Muta said. 'Here's the code you need to radio in.'

Bourne nodded.

Muta stood, his legs spread slightly apart, gazing at the back of the pilot's head. He drew out his Korovin TK.

'Call in the code,' he said.

Ignoring him, Bourne continued to fly the plane into Iranian airspace.

Muta ibn Aziz took a step forward, put the muzzle of the Korovin at the base of Bourne's skull. 'Radio in the code immediately.'

'Or what?' Bourne said. 'You'll shoot me? Do you know how to fly a Sovereign?'

Of course Muta didn't, which was why he'd gotten on board with the impostor. Just then the radio squawked.

An electronically thinned voice said in Farsi, '*Salām aleikom. Esmetān chīst?*'

Bourne picked up the mike. '*Salām aleikom,*' he responded.

'*Esmetān chīst?*' the voice said. What is your name?

Muta said, 'Are you insane? Give him the code at once.'

'*Esmetān chīst!*' came the voice from the radio. It was no longer a question. '*Esmetān chīst!*' It was a command.

'Damn you, radio the code!' Muta was shaking with rage and terror. 'Otherwise they'll shoot us out of the sky!'

THIRTY-ONE

Bourne put the Sovereign into such a sudden, steep bank to the left that Muta ibn Aziz was thrown across the cockpit, fetching up hard against the starboard bulkhead. As Muta ibn Aziz struggled to regain his footing, Bourne sent the jet into a dive, simultaneously banking it to the right. Muta ibn Aziz slipped backward, banging his head on the edge of the doorway.

Bourne glanced back. Fadi's messenger was unconscious.

The radar was showing two fighter planes coming up fast from beneath him. The hair-trigger Iranian government had wasted no time in scrambling its air defense. He brought the Sovereign around, caught a visual fix. What the Iranians had sent to intercept him were a pair of Chinese-built J-6s, reverse-engineered copies of the old MiG-19 used in the mid-1950s. These jets were so out of date, the Chengdu plant had stopped manufacturing them more than a decade ago. Even so, they were armed and the Sovereign wasn't. He needed to do something to negate that enormous advantage.

They'd expect him to turn tail and run. Instead he lowered the Sovereign's nose and put on a burst of speed as he headed directly toward them. Clearly startled, the Iranian pilots did nothing until the last moment, when they each peeled away from the Sovereign's path.

As soon as they'd done so, Bourne pulled back on the yoke and brought the Sovereign's nose to the vertical, performing a loop that set him behind both of them. They turned, describing paths like cloverleafs, homing in on him from either side.

They began to fire at him. He dipped below the crossfire, and it ceased immediately. Choosing the J-6 on the right because it was slightly closer, he banked sharply toward it. He allowed it to come under him, allowed the pilot to assume he'd made a tactical error. Taking evasive maneuvers as the chatter of the machine gun sprang up again, he waited until the J-6 had locked on to his tail, then he tipped the Sovereign's nose up again. The Iranian pilot had seen the maneuver before and was ready, climbing steeply just behind the Sovereign. He knew what Bourne would do next: put the Sovereign into a steep dive. This Bourne did, but he also banked sharply to the right. The J-6 followed, even as Bourne punched in every ounce of the Sovereign's speed. The plane began to chatter in the powerful shearing force. Bourne steepened both the bank and the dive.

Behind him, the old J-6 was shuddering and jerking. All at once a handful of rivets were sucked off the left wing. The wing crumpled as if punched by an invisible fist. The wing ripped from its socket in the fuselage. The two sections of the J-6 blew apart in a welter of stripped and shredded metal, plummeting end-over-end downward to the earth.

Bullets ripped through the Sovereign's skin as the second J-6 came after them. Now Bourne lit out for the border to Afghanistan, crossing it within seconds. The second Iranian J-6, undeterred, came on, its engines screaming, its guns chattering.

Just south of the position where he had crossed into Afghani airspace was a chain of mountains that began in northern Iran. The mountains didn't rise to significant height, however, until they reached Bourne's current position, just northwest of Koh-i-Markhura. With a compass heading of east by southeast, he dipped the Sovereign toward the highest peaks.

The J-6 was shuddering and shrieking as it flattened out the curve of its descent. Having seen what had happened to his companion, the Iranian pilot had no intention of getting that close to the Sovereign. But it shadowed Bourne's plane, dogging it from behind and just above, now and again firing short bursts at his engines.

Bourne could see that the pilot was trying to herd him into a narrow valley between two sharp-edged mountains that loomed ahead. In the confined space, the pilot sought to keep the Sovereign's superior maneuverability to a minimum, catch it in the chute, and shoot it down.

The mountains rose up, blocking out light on either side. The massive rock faces blurred by. Both planes were in the chute now. The Iranian pilot had the Sovereign just where he wanted it. He began to fire in earnest, knowing that his prey was limited in the evasive maneuvers it could take.

Bourne felt several more hits judder through the Sovereign. If the J-6 hit an engine, he was finished. The end would come before he had a chance to react. Turning the plane on its right wingtip, he waggled out of the line of fire. But the maneuver would help him only temporarily. Unless he could find a more permanent solution, the J-6 would shoot him out of the sky.

Off to his left he saw a jagged rift in the sheer mountain wall, and immediately headed for it. Almost at once he saw the danger: a spire of rock splitting the aperture in two.

The defile they were in was now so narrow that behind him, the J-6 had assumed the same sideways position. Bourne maneuvered the Sovereign ever so slightly, keeping the profile of his plane between the J-6 and the rock spire.

As far as the Iranian pilot knew, they were both going to fly through the aperture. He was so hell-bent on blowing the Sovereign away that when, at the last moment, his prey moved slightly to the right in order to pass through the rift, he had no chance to react. The spire came up on him, froze him with its frightful proximity, and then his plane smashed into the rock spire, sending up a fireball out of which a column of black smoke shot upward into the arid sky. The J-6 and its pilot, now no more than a hail of white-hot debris, vanished as if by a conjuror's hand.

Soraya awoke to the sound of a baby crying. She tried to move, groaned as her traumatized nerves rebelled in pain. As if her sound antagonized it, the baby started to scream. Soraya looked around. She was in a grimy room, filled with grimy light. The smells of cooking and closely packed human beings clogged the air. A cheap print of Christ on the cross hung at a slant on the grimy wall across from her. Where was she?

'Hey!' she called.

A moment later, Tyrone appeared. He was holding an infant in the crook of his left arm. The baby's face was so scrunched up in rage, all its features were sucked into its wrinkled center. It looked like a fist.

'Yo, how yo feelin' yo?'

'Like I just went fifteen rounds with Lennox Lewis.' Soraya made another, more concerted effort to sit up. As she struggled, she said, 'Man, do I owe you.'

'Take yo up on dat sumtime.' He grinned as he came into the room.

'What happened to the guys from the black Ford? They didn't follow you—?'

'They fuckin' dead, girl. Sure as shit, they won't bother yo no mo.'

The squalling baby turned her head, staring right into Soraya's eyes with that pure vulnerability only very young children had. Her screams subsided to gulping sobs.

'Here.' Soraya held out her arms. Tyrone transferred the baby to her. At once she laid her head against Soraya's breast, gave a tiny squawk. 'She's hungry, Tyrone.'

He left the room, returning several moments later with a bottle full of milk. He turned it over, tested the temperature on the inside of his wrist.

'S'okay,' he said, handing it to her.

Soraya looked at him for a moment.

'What?'

She put the bottle's nipple to the infant's lips. 'I never thought of you as being domesticated.'

'Yo evah thought a me havin' a kid?'

'This baby's yours?'

'Nah. Belongs t'my sis.' He half turned and called: 'Aisha!'

The doorway remained empty for a time, but Tyrone must have detected movement, because he said, 'C'mon, yo.'

Soraya saw a shadow of movement, then a thin little girl with big coffee-colored eyes stood framed in the doorway.

'Doan yo go bein' shy, girl.' Tyrone's voice had softened. 'This here's Miss Spook.'

Aisha crunched up her face. 'Miss Spook! Are you scary?'

Her father laughed good-naturedly. 'Nah. Looka how she holdin' Darlonna. Yo woan bite, will ya, Miss Spook?'

'Not if you call me Soraya, Aisha.' She smiled at the little girl, who was quite beautiful. 'Think you can do that?'

Aisha stared at her, winding a braid around her tiny forefinger. Tyrone was about to admonish her again, but Soraya headed him off by saying, 'You have such a pretty name. How old are you, Aisha?'

'Six,' the girl said very softly. 'What do your name mean? Mine means "alive and well."'

Soraya laughed. 'I know, that's Arabic. *Soraya* is a Farsi word. It means "princess."'

Aisha's eyes opened wider, and she took several steps into the room. 'Are you a real princess?'

Soraya, trying to keep the laughter down, said to her with exaggerated solemnity, 'Not a real princess, no.'

'She a *kind* a princess.' Tyrone contrived to ignore Soraya's curious glance. 'Only she not allowed to say so.'

'Why?' The child, fully engaged now, tripped over to them.

'Because bad people are after her,' Tyrone said.

The girl looked up at him. 'Like the ones you shot, Daddy?'

In the ensuing silence, Soraya could hear raucous sounds from the street: the sudden throaty roar of motorcycles, the teeth-rattling blare of hip-hop, the clangor of heated conversations.

'Go play wid yo aunt Libby,' he said, not unkindly.

Aisha gave one last glance toward Soraya, then whirled, skipped out of the room.

Tyrone turned to Soraya, but before he could say anything he took off one shoe, threw it hard and expertly into a corner. Soraya turned and saw the large rat lying on its side. The heel of Tyrone's shoe had nearly decapitated it. Wrapping the rat in some old newspaper, he wiped off his shoe, then took the rat out of the room.

When he returned, Tyrone said, 'About Aisha's mother, it's a old story hereabouts. She got hit in a drive-by. She was wid two a her cousins who pissed off some gangstas inna hood, skimmin' an shit off a drug run.' His face clouded. 'I couldn't let that go, yo.'

'No,' Soraya said. 'I don't imagine you could.'

The baby had drifted off, draining the bottle. She lay in Soraya's arms breathing deeply and evenly.

Tyrone fell silent, abruptly shy. Soraya cocked her head. 'What is it?'

'Yo, I got sumpin important to tell yo, leastways I think it's important.' He sat on the edge of the bed. 'Ain't a short story, but I'll try'tell it dat way.'

He told her about M&N Bodywork, how he and DJ Tank had been staking it out to use as the crew's new crib. He told her about seeing the armed men there one night and how he and DJ Tank had sneaked in after the men had left, what they'd found, 'the plastic explosive an shit.' He told her about coming upon the couple – the man and the woman – sawing up a man's body.

'My God.' Soraya stopped him there. 'Can you describe the man and woman?'

He began, painting frighteningly accurate word pictures of the false Lindros and Anne Held. *How little we know people*, Soraya thought bitterly. *How easily they fool us.*

'Okay,' she said at length, 'what happened then?'

'They set fire to the building. Burn it to the fuckin' ground.'

Soraya considered. 'So by that time the explosives had been moved.'

'True dat.' Tyrone nodded. 'There's sumpin else, too. Those two shitbirds I pulled offa you over Ninth and Florida? I recognized one a them. He were a guard that night outside that body shop.'

THIRTY-TWO

Muta ibn Aziz had begun to stir during the latter part of the aerial dogfight. Now Bourne became aware that he had regained his feet. He couldn't relinquish the controls in order to engage the terrorist, so he had to find another way to deal with Muta.

The Sovereign was nearing the end of the mountain chasm. As Muta ibn Aziz put the muzzle of the gun against his right ear, Bourne directed the Sovereign toward the mountain peak at the end of the chasm.

'What are you doing?' Muta said.

'Put the gun away,' Bourne said while focusing on the peak rising up in front of them.

Muta stared out the windshield, mesmerized. 'Get us out of here.'

Bourne kept the nose of the Sovereign headed directly for the peak.

'You're going to kill us both.' Muta licked his lips nervously. All at once he lifted the gun away from Bourne's head. 'All right, all right! Just—'

They were terrifyingly close to the mountain.

'Throw the gun across the cockpit,' Bourne ordered.

'You've left it too late,' Muta ibn Aziz cried. 'We'll never make it!'

Bourne kept his hands steady on the yoke. With a shout of disgust, Muta tossed his gun across the floor.

Bourne pulled back on the yoke. The Sovereign whooshed

461

upward. The mountain rushed at them with appalling speed. It was going to be close, very close. At the last instant Bourne saw the gap in the right side, as if the hand of God had reached down and cracked off half the mountaintop. He banked a precise amount; any farther and the passing crag would snap off the right wingtip. They passed just above the mountaintop, then, still climbing, pulled free of the chasm, blasting into blue sky.

Muta, on hands and knees, went scrabbling after the gun. Bourne was ready for this. He'd already engaged the autopilot. Unstrapping himself, he leapt onto the terrorist's back, delivered a savage kidney punch. With a muted scream, Muta collapsed onto the cockpit floor.

Quickly, Bourne took possession of the gun, then bound the terrorist in a coil of wire he found in the engineer's locker. Dragging him back across the cockpit, he returned to the pilot's chair, disengaged the autopilot, adjusted the heading a bit more south. They were halfway across Afghanistan now, heading for Miran Shah, just across the eastern border in Pakistan, the place circled on the pilot's map Bourne had studied.

Muta ibn Aziz expelled a long string of Bedouin curses.

'Bourne,' he added, 'I was right. You manufactured the story of your own death.'

Bourne grinned at him. 'Shall we call *everyone* by their real name? Let's start with Abu Ghazi Nadir al-Jamuh ibn Hamid ibn Ashef al-Wahhib. But *Fadi* is so much shorter and to the point.'

'How could you possibly know—?'

'I also know that his brother, Karim, has taken Martin Lindros's place.'

The shock showed in Muta's dark eyes.

'And then there's the sister, Sarah ibn Ashef.' With grim satisfaction, Bourne watched the messenger's expression. 'Yes, I know about that, too.'

Muta's face was ashen. 'She told you her name?'

At once Bourne understood. 'You were there that night in Odessa when we had the rendezvous set up with our contact. I shot Sarah ibn Ashef as she ran into the square. We barely managed to escape the trap with our lives.'

'You took her,' Muta ibn Aziz said. 'You took Sarah ibn Ashef with you.'

'She was still alive,' Bourne said.

'Did she say anything?'

Muta said this so quickly, Bourne knew that he was desperate for the answer. Why? There was more here than Bourne knew. What was he missing?

He was at the very end of what was known to him. But it was vital that he keep his opponent believing that he knew more than he did. He decided the best course was to say nothing.

The silence worked on Muta, who became extremely agitated. 'She said my name, didn't she?'

Bourne kept his voice neutral. 'Why would she do that?'

'She did, didn't she?' Muta was frantic now, twisting this way and that in a vain attempt to free himself. 'What else did she say?'

'I don't remember.'

'You *must* remember.'

He had Muta ibn Aziz. All that remained was to reel him in. 'I saw a doctor once who said that descriptions of things I'd forgotten – even fragments – could unlock those memories.'

They were nearing the border. He started the gradual descent that took them down to the hogback ridges of the mountain chain that did such an expert job at hiding many of the world's most dangerous terrorist cadres.

Muta stared at him incredulously. 'Let me get this straight. You want me to help you.' He gave a joyless laugh. 'I don't think so.'

'All right.' Bourne turned his full attention on the topography as it began to reveal its gross details. 'It was you who asked. I don't care one way or another, really.'

Muta's face contorted first one way, then another. He was under some form of terrible pressure, and Bourne wondered what it was. Outwardly he gave no sign that he cared, but he felt he needed to up the ante, so he said, 'Six minutes to landing, maybe a little less. You'd better brace yourself as best you can.' Glancing over at Muta ibn Aziz, he laughed. 'Oh, yeah, you're already strapped in.'

And then Muta said, 'It wasn't an accident.'

Unfortunately,' Karim said, 'LaValle was right.'

The DCI flinched. Clearly he didn't want to hear more bad news. 'Typhon routinely piggybacks on CI transmissions.'

'True enough, sir. But after some backbreaking electronic spadework, I discovered three piggybacked communiqués I can't account for.'

They sat side by side in the sixth pew on the right arm of the arc inside the Foundry Methodist Church on 16th Street NW. Behind them, affixed to the back, was a plaque that read: IN THIS PEW, SIDE BY SIDE, SAT PRESIDENT FRANKLIN D. ROOSEVELT AND PRIME MINISTER WINSTON CHURCHILL AT THE NATIONAL CHRISTMAS SERVICE IN 1941. Which meant that the service had taken place just three weeks after the Japanese attack on Pearl Harbor – dark days, indeed, for America. As for Britain, it had gained, through a painful disaster, an important ally. This spot, therefore, held great meaning for the Old Man. It was where he came to pray, to gain insight, the moral strength to do the dark and difficult deeds he was often required to do.

As he stared down at the dossier his second in command had handed him, he knew without a shadow of a doubt that another of those deeds lay dead ahead of him.

He let out a long breath, opened the dossier. And there it was in black and white: the fearsome truth. Still, he raised his head, said in an unsteady voice, 'Anne?'

'I'm afraid so, sir.' Karim was careful to keep his hands palms up in his lap. He needed to seem as devastated as the Old Man clearly was. The news had shaken the DCI to his roots. 'All three communiqués came from a PDA in her possession. One not CI-authorized, one we had no knowledge of until now. It seems she was also able to replace and doctor intel, falsely implicating Tim Hytner.'

For a long time, the DCI said nothing. They had kept their voices down because of the church's astoundingly fine acoustics, but when he spoke again his companion was obliged to lean forward in order to hear him.

'What was the nature of the three communiqués?'

'They were sent via an encrypted band,' Karim said. 'I have my best people working on a deciphering solution.'

The Old Man nodded absently. 'Good work, Martin. I don't know what I'd do without you.'

Today, at this moment, he looked every year of his age and then some. With his trusted Anne's terrible betrayal, a vital spark had gone out of him. He sat hunched over, his shoulders up around his ears, as if anticipating further psychic blows.

'Sir,' Karim said softly. 'We have to take immediate action.'

The DCI nodded, but his gaze was lost in the middle distance, focused on thoughts and memories his companion could not imagine.

'I think this should be handled privately,' Karim continued. 'Just you and me. What do you say?'

The Old Man's rheumy eyes swung around to take in his second's face. 'Yes, a private solution, by all means.' His voice was whispery. It cracked on the word *solution*.

Karim stood. 'Shall we go?'

The DCI looked up at him, a black terror swimming behind his eyes. 'Now?'

'That would be best, sir – for everyone.' He helped the Old Man to his feet. 'She's not at headquarters. I imagine she's home.'

Then he handed the DCI a gun.

Within several hours, Katya returned to the infirmary to check on the swelling of Lindros's throat. She knelt by the side of the low cot on which he lay. Her fingers stumbled over her previous handiwork so badly that tears came to her eyes.

'I'm no good at this,' she said softly, as if to herself. 'I'm no good at all.'

Lindros watched her, remembering the end of their last conversation. He wondered whether he should say something or whether opening his mouth would just push her farther away.

After a long, tense silence, Katya said, 'I've been thinking about what you said.'

Her eyes found his at last. They were an astonishing shade of blue-gray, like the sky just before the onset of a storm.

'And now I believe that Costin wanted Fadi to hurt me. Why? Why would he want someone to do that? Because he was afraid I would leave him? Because he wanted me to see how dangerous the world outside his world was? I don't know. But he didn't have to . . .' She put a hand up to her cheek, winced at the touch of her own delicate fingertips. 'He didn't have to let Fadi hurt me.'

'No, he didn't,' Lindros said. 'He shouldn't have. You know that.'

She nodded.

'Then help me,' Lindros went on. 'Otherwise, neither of us is getting out of here alive.'

'I . . . I don't know whether I can.'

'Then *I'll* help *you*.' Lindros sat up. 'If you let me, I'll help you change. But it has to be what you want. You have to want it badly enough to risk everything.'

'Everything.' She gave him a smile so filled with remorse, it nearly broke his heart. 'I was born with nothing. I grew up with nothing. And then, through a chance encounter, I was given everything. At least, that's what I was told, and for a time I believed it. But in a way that life was worse than having nothing. At least the nothing was real. And then Costin came. He promised to take me away from the unreality. So I married him. But his world was just as false as the one I'd made for myself, and I thought, *Where do I belong? Nowhere.*'

Lindros was moved to briefly touch the back of her hand. 'We're both outsiders.'

Katya turned her head slightly to glance at the guards. 'Do you know a way out of here?'

'Yes,' Lindros said, 'but it will take both of us.' He saw the fear in her eyes, but also the spark of hope.

At length, she said, 'What must I do?'

Anne was in the midst of packing when she heard a car's large engine thrumming on the street outside her house. As she picked her head up, it stopped. She almost went back to her packing, but some sixth sense or paranoia caused her to cross her second-floor bedroom and peer out the window.

Below her, she saw the DCI's long black armored car. The Old Man stepped out of it, followed by Jamil. Her heart skipped a beat. What was happening? Why had they come to her house? Had Soraya somehow got through to the Old Man, told him of her treachery? But no, Jamil was with him. Jamil would never let Soraya anywhere near CI headquarters, let alone allowing her access to the Old Man.

But what if . . . ?

Running purely on instinct now, she went to her dresser, opened the second drawer, scrabbled in it for the S&W she had returned to its customary hiding place when she'd returned home from the Northeast quadrant.

The bell rang downstairs, making her jump, even though she had been expecting it. Slipping the S&W into her waistband at the small of her back, she left her bedroom and descended the polished wood stairs to the front door. Through the diamonds of translucent yellow glass, she could see the silhouettes of the two men, both so important to her throughout her adult life.

With a slow exhalation of breath, she grabbed the brass handle, painted a smile on her face, opened the door.

'Hello, Anne.' The Old Man seemed to reflect her own lacquered smile back at her. 'I'm sorry to disturb you at home, but something rather pressing . . .' At this point he faltered.

'It's no bother at all,' Anne replied. 'I could use the company.'

She stepped back, and they entered the small marble-floored vestibule. A spray of hothouse lilies rose from a slender cloisonné vase on a small oval table with delicate cabriolet legs. She led them into the living room with its facing silk-covered sofas on either side of a red-veined whitestone fireplace, above which was a wooden mantelpiece. Anne offered them a seat, but everyone seemed inclined to remain standing. The men did not take off their coats.

She dared not look at Jamil's face for fear of what she might find there. On the other hand, the Old Man's face was no bargain. It was drained of blood, the skin hanging loosely on the bones. When had he grown so old? she wondered. Where had the time gone? It seemed like just yesterday that she had been a wild child at college in London, with nothing ahead of her but a bright, endless future.

'I expect you'd like some tea,' she said to his mummy's

face. 'And I have a tin of your favorite ginger biscuits in the larder.' But her attempt to retain a degree of normalcy fell flat.

'Nothing, thank you, Anne,' the DCI said. 'For either of us.' He looked truly pained now, as if he was fighting the effects of a kidney stone or a tumor. He took from his overcoat a rolled-up dossier. Spreading it out on one of the soft sofa backs, he said, 'I'm afraid we've been presented with something of an unpleasant realization.' His forefinger moved over the computer printout as if it were a Ouija board. 'We know, Anne.'

Anne felt as if she had been delivered a death blow. She could scarcely catch her breath. Nevertheless, she said in a perfectly normal voice, 'Know what?'

'We know all about you.' He could not yet bring himself to meet her eyes. 'We know that you've been communicating with the enemy.'

'What? I don't—'

At last, the DCI lifted his gaze, impaled her with his implacable eyes. She knew that terrifying look; she's seen it directed at others the Old Man had crossed off his list. She'd never seen or heard from any of them again.

'We know that you *are* the enemy.' His voice was full of rage and loathing. She knew there was nothing he despised more than a traitor.

Automatically, her eyes went to Jamil. What was he thinking? Why wasn't he coming to her defense? And then, looking into his blank face, she understood everything – she understood how he had seduced her with both his physical presence and his philosophical manifesto. She understood how he had used her. She was cannon fodder, as expendable as anyone in his cadre.

The thing that upset her most was that she should have known – from the very beginning, she should have seen through him. But she had been so sure of herself, so willing to rebel against the fussy old-line aristocracy from which she was descended. He had seen how eager she was to throw a bag of shit in her parents' faces. He'd taken advantage of her zeal, as well as of her body. She had committed treason for him; so many people would lose their lives because of her complicity. My God, my God!

She turned to Jamil now, said, 'Fucking me was the least of it, wasn't it?'

That was the last thing she ever said, and she never got to hear his reply, if he'd ever meant to give one, because the DCI had his gun out, and shot her three times in the head. He was still a crack shot, even after all these years.

Anne's blind eyes were on Jamil as her body collapsed from under her.

'Damn her.' The Old Man turned away. His voice was full of venom. 'Goddamn her.'

'I'll take care of the disposition of the body,' Karim said. 'Also, a news release with an appropriate cover story. And I'll call her parents myself.'

'No,' the DCI said dully. 'That's my job.'

Karim walked over to where his former lover lay curled in a pool of blood. He looked down at her. What was he thinking? That he needed to go upstairs, open the second drawer of her dresser. Then, as he turned the corpse over with the toe of his shoe, he saw that luck was still very much with him. He wouldn't have to go into her bedroom after all. He said a silent prayer of thanks to Allah.

Snapping on a pair of latex gloves, he pulled the S&W from its place at the small of her back. He noted the fact she'd had the presence of mind to arm herself. Staring down at her face for a moment, he tried to summon up even the tiniest bit of emotion for this infidel. Nothing came. His heart beat in the same rhythm it always did. He couldn't say that he'd miss her. She had served her purpose, even helping him dismember Overton. Which meant, simply, that he had chosen well.

She was an instrument he had trained to use against his enemies, nothing more.

He rose, stood straddling Anne's crumpled form. The DCI's back was still to him. 'Sir,' he said. 'There's something here you need to see.'

The Old Man took a deep breath. He wiped eyes that had been wet with tears. 'What is it, Martin?' he said, turning.

And Karim shot him quite neatly through the heart with Anne Held's S&W.

'It wasn't an accident.'

Bourne, concentrating more than he had to on his pre-landing routine, contrived to ignore this bombshell. They were overflying Zhawar Kili, a known al-Qaeda hotbed until the U.S. military bombed it in November 2001. At length, he said, 'What wasn't an accident?'

'Sarah ibn Ashef's death. It wasn't an accident.' Muta ibn Aziz was breathless, terrified, and liberated all at once. How he'd wanted to tell his abominable secret to someone! It had grown around his heart as the shell of an oyster excretes, layer by layer, over time becoming something humped and ugly.

'Of course it was,' Bourne insisted. He had to insist now; it was the only way to keep the spell going, keep Muta ibn Aziz talking. 'I should know. I shot her.'

'No, you didn't.' Muta ibn Aziz began to worry his lower lip with the ends of his upper teeth. 'You and your partner were too far away to make accurate shots. My brother, Abbud ibn Aziz, and I shot her.'

Bourne did turn to him now, but with a deeply skeptical look. 'You're making this up.'

Muta ibn Aziz appeared hurt. 'Why would I do that?'

'Let's go down the list, shall we? You're continuing to screw with my head. You did it to get Fadi and his brother to come after me.' He frowned. 'Have we met before? Do I know you?

Do you and your brother harbor a grudge against me?'

'No, no, and no.' He was annoyed, just as Bourne wanted him to be. 'The truth is . . . I can hardly say it . . .'

He turned away for a moment, and Bourne was listening closely for what was to come. The final approach to Miran Shah the pilot had laid out was coming up. It was in the center of a narrow valley – *defile* would be the more accurate term, now that Bourne saw it – between two mountains just inside the wild and woolly western border of Pakistan.

The sky was clear – a deep, piercing blue – and at this time of day the sun glare was minimal. The gray-brown mountains of altered volcanic rock from the Kurram River group – limestone, dark chert, green shale – looked stripped, barren, devoid of life. Automatically, he studied the vicinity. He scrutinized the furrowed mountainsides to the south and west for cave openings, east the length of the defile for bunkers, north through ruffled hillsides broken by a deeply shadowed, rock-strewn ravine. But there were no signs of Dujja's nuclear complex, nothing man-made, not even a hut or a campsite.

He was coming in a trifle hot. He slowed the Sovereign's speed, saw the runway in front of him. Unlike the one he'd taken off from, this was made of tarmac. Still no sign of habitation, let alone a modern laboratory complex. Had he come to the wrong place? Was this another in Fadi's endless bag of tricks? Was it, in fact, a trap?

Too late now to worry about that. Wheels and flaps were down. He'd reduced speed into the green zone.

'You're coming in too low,' Muta ibn Aziz said in sudden agitation. 'You'll hit the runway too soon. Pull up! For God's sake pull up!'

Bourne overflew the first eighth of the runway, guiding the Sovereign down until the wheels struck the tarmac. They were down, taxiing along the runway. Bourne cut the engines, much of the interior power. That was when he saw a rush of shadows coming from his right side.

He had only time to realize that Muta ibn Aziz must have phoned Bourne's identity to the people at Miran Shah before the starboard bulkhead blew inward with a horrific roar. The Sovereign shuddered and, like a wounded elephant, fell to its knees, its front wheels and struts blown out.

Flying debris made mincemeat of almost everything in the cockpit. Dials were shattered, levers sheared off. Wires dangled from ripped-apart bays in the ceiling. The trussed Muta ibn Aziz, who'd been on the side of the plane that was now crumpled in on itself, was lying underneath a major piece of the fuselage. Bourne, strapped in on the far side of the cockpit, had escaped with a multitude of minor cuts, bruises, and what felt to his dazed brain like a mild concussion.

Instinct forced him to push the blackness from the periphery of his vision, reach up, and release his harness. He staggered over to Muta ibn Aziz, a frozen tundra of shattered glass crunching underfoot. He choked on air full of broken needles of metal, fiberglass, and superheated plastic.

Seeing that Muta was breathing, he hauled the twisted wreckage, charred and scored and still burning hot, off to the side. But when he knelt down, he saw that a shard of metal, roughly the size and shape of a sword blade, had lodged itself in Muta's gut.

He peered down at the man, then slapped his face hard. Muta's eyes fluttered open, focusing with difficulty.

'I wasn't making it up,' he said in a thin, reedy voice. Blood was leaking out of his mouth, down his chin. It pooled in the hollow of his throat, dark, throwing off the scent of copper.

'You're dying,' Bourne said. 'Tell me what happened with Sarah ibn Ashef.'

A slow smile spread across Muta's face. 'So you *do* want to know.' His breath sawing in and out of his punctured lungs sounded like the scream of a prehistoric beast. 'The truth is important to you, after all.'

'Tell me!' Bourne shouted at him.

He grabbed Muta ibn Aziz, hauled him up by the front of his shirt in an attempt to rattle the answer out of him. But at that moment a cadre of Dujja terrorists swarmed through the rent in the fuselage. They hauled him off Fadi's messenger, who lay coughing up the last of his life.

Chaos ensued – a rushing of bodies, a jumble of spoken Arabic, clipped orders and even more clipped responses – as they dragged him half conscious across the bloody floor, out into the arid wastes of Miran Shah.

BOOK FOUR

THIRTY-THREE

Soraya Moore, on the corner of 7th Street NE, a well-armed Tyrone standing lookout beside her, called CI headquarters – from a pay phone, not from her cell.

When Peter Marks heard it was her, his voice lowered to a whisper.

'Jesus Christ,' he said, 'what the hell have you done?'

'I haven't done anything, Peter,' she replied hotly.

'Then why is there an all-department directive posted to report any appearance, any phone call, any contact whatsoever with you immediately and directly to Director Lindros?'

'Because Lindros isn't Lindros.'

'He's an impostor, right?'

Soraya's heart lifted. 'Then you know.'

'What I know is that Deputy Director Lindros called a meeting, told us you'd gone over the edge, completely lost it. It was Bourne's death, right? Anyway, he said you were making insane accusations about him.'

Oh, my God, Soraya thought. *He's turned everyone at CI against me.*

She heard the naked suspicion in Marks's voice, but plowed gamely on anyway. 'He's lied to you, Peter. The truth is too complicated to get into now, but you've got to listen to me. Terrorists have put into motion a plan to blow up headquarters.' She knew she sounded breathless, even a little bit mad. 'Please, I'm begging you. Go to the Old Man, tell him it's going to happen in the next twenty-four hours.'

'The Old Man and Anne are at the White House, meeting with the president. They'll be there for some time, Deputy Director Lindros said.'

'Then contact one of the directorate chiefs – better yet, *all* of them. Anyone but Lindros.'

'Listen, come in. Give yourself up. We can help you.'

'I'm not crazy,' Soraya said, though increasingly she felt as if she was.

'Then this conversation is over.'

As Katya turned toward the two guards outside the infirmary, her delicate fingers undid the top two buttons of her blouse. She had never worn a bra. She had beautiful breasts, and she knew it.

The guards were playing the same game they always did, the rules of which she could never fathom. Of course, no money changed hands; that would make it gambling, which was forbidden by Islamic law. The object seemed to be to sharpen their reaction time.

To turn her mind away from her present situation, she conjured up the rush of her old life, the one Costin had insisted she give up. As the guards became aware of her, she stood in profile, as she would on a Perfect Ten shoot, her back slightly arched, her breasts thrust out.

Then slowly, disarmingly, she turned toward them. Their eyes were nailed to her body.

She felt the ache in her breastbone, where she had instructed Lindros to hit her. She opened her blouse wide enough so that they could see the bruise, so new that the skin was bright red, just starting to puff up.

'Look,' she said, quite unnecessarily. 'Look what that bastard has done to me.'

With these words, the guards roused themselves suffi-

480

ciently to rush past her into the infirmary. They saw Lindros flat on his back, his eyes closed. There was blood on his face. He seemed to be scarcely breathing.

The taller of the two guards turned to Katya, who was standing directly behind him. 'What have *you* done to *him*?'

At that precise moment, Lindros drew back his right leg, opened his eyes, and slammed the heel of his right foot as hard as he could into the shorter guard's crotch. The guard gave a little grunt of surprise as he collapsed in on himself.

The taller guard, slow in turning back, received the tightly curled edge of Lindros's knuckles in his throat. He coughed, his eyes going wide, his fingers scrabbling for his sidearm. Katya, as Lindros had instructed her, kicked the back of his left knee. As he pitched over, the side of his head made violent contact with Lindros's fist.

The two of them spent the next five minutes stripping the guards, then tying and gagging them. Lindros dragged first one, then the other to the utility closet, stowing them away like so much rubbish. He and Katya climbed into their clothes, she in the smaller guard's outfit, Lindros in the taller one's.

As they dressed, he smiled at her. She reached out and wiped the blood from his pricked finger off his cheek.

'How was that?' he said.

'We're a long way from being free.'

'How right you are.' Lindros gathered up the guards' weapons – sidearms and semiautomatic machine guns. 'Do you know how to use these?'

'I know how to pull a trigger,' she said.

'That'll have to do.'

He took her hand, and together they fled the infirmary.

Bourne was not treated as roughly by the terrorists as he had expected. In fact, once they'd dragged him out of the wrecked

Sovereign, he wasn't treated harshly at all. They were all Saudis, this cadre. He could tell not only by the way they looked, but by the Arabic dialect they spoke as well.

As soon as his shoe soles hit the scorched earth of the runway, they stood him up straight and frog-marched him onto the shale, where two armored military all-terrain vehicles, veiled in heavy camouflaging, stood waiting. No wonder he'd missed seeing them from the air.

They took him around to the larger of the two vehicles, which on close inspection looked like a mobile command center. The rear doors banged open, two burly arms extended, and he was hauled bodily up and in. Immediately the metal doors slammed shut.

From out of the inky darkness, a familiar voice in a beautiful clipped British accent said, 'Hello, Jason.'

Red lights flickered on, making Bourne blink as his eyes adjusted. By the odd illumination he could see banks of electronic equipment, silently emitting mysterious readouts, like communications from another planet. To one side, a young bearded Saudi sat hunched over an islet of equipment. He had on a pair of professional earphones. Occasionally, he jotted a sentence or two from whatever he was listening to.

To his left, close to where Bourne stood, was the huge, overmuscled man who must have hoisted Bourne into the mobile command center. He stared at Bourne without any emotion whatsoever. With his shaved head, his rocklike arms crossed over his equally muscular chest, he might have been a eunuch guarding a sultan's harem.

However, this one was guarding the third person in the truck, who sat at the command console. He must have swiveled the chair around as soon as Bourne had been hoisted aboard. He grinned from ear to ear, which belied his regal bearing.

'We must stop meeting like this, Jason.' His ruby-red lips pursed. 'Or no, perhaps it is kismet that we do so at the most propitious times.'

'Goddammit,' Bourne said, recognizing the slim, dark-eyed man with the beak of a nose. 'Feyd al-Saoud!'

The chief of the Saudi secret police fairly jumped out of his chair and rushed to embrace Bourne, kissing him happily and moistly on both cheeks.

'My friend, my friend. Thank Allah you're still alive! We had no idea you were inside. How could we? It's Fadi's plane!' Waggling an admonishing forefinger, he said with mock anger, 'And in any event, you never tell me what you're up to.'

Bourne and Feyd al-Saoud had known each other for some time. They had worked together once, in Iceland.

'I'd heard a rumor that the Saudis had a line on Fadi, though they vehemently denied it.'

'Fadi is Saudi,' Feyd al-Saoud said, sobering quickly. 'He is a Saudi problem.'

'You mean he's a Saudi embarrassment,' Bourne said. 'I'm afraid he's made himself everyone's problem.'

He went on to brief his friend on Fadi's identity, as well as on what he and his brother, Karim al-Jamil, had planned, including the infiltration of CI. 'You may think you've homed in on Dujja's main camp,' Bourne said in conclusion, 'but I can assure you this isn't it. What is here, somewhere, is the nuclear facility that's enriching the uranium and manufacturing the nuclear device they plan to detonate somewhere in the United States.'

Feyd al-Saoud nodded. 'Now things are starting to make sense.' He swung around, brought up a tactical pilotage chart of the area in order to orient Bourne. Next, he switched to a series of close-up IKONOS satellite images.

'These were taken last week, at two-minute intervals,' he said. 'You'll notice that in the first image we see Miran Shah as we do now – barren, desolate. But here, in image two, we see two jeeplike vehicles. They're heading more or less north-west. Now what do we see in image three? Miran Shah is once again barren, desolate. No people, no vehicles. In two minutes, where did they go? They could not possibly have driven out of the IKONOS range.' He sat back. 'Given your intel, what must be our conclusion?'

'Dujja's nuclear facility is underground,' Bourne said.

'One must believe so. We have been monitoring terrorist communications. From whence, we had no idea – until now. It's coming from beneath the rocks and sand. Interestingly, it's from *within* the facility. There have been no communications from the outside world for the three hours we've been here.'

'Just how many men did you bring with you?' Bourne asked.

'Including myself, twelve. As you've discovered, we had to pose as members of Dujja ourselves. This is North Waziristan, the most deeply conservative of Pakistan's western provinces. The local Pashtun tribespeople have profound religious and ethnic ties to the Taliban, which is why they welcome al-Qaeda and Dujja alike. I couldn't afford to bring more of my people in without awkward questions being raised.'

At that moment the man with the headphones tore off the top sheet of paper on which he'd been frantically scribbling. He handed it to his chief.

'Something in the rock or perhaps the facility's lead shielding is interfering with the monitoring.' Feyd al-Saoud scanned the sheet quickly, then handed it to Bourne. 'I think you'd better have a look at this.'

Bourne read the Arabic transcription:

'[?] both missing. We found the guards in [?] closet.'
'How long?'
'[?] twenty minutes. [?] couldn't say for sure.'
'Mobilize [?] you can spare. Send [?] to the entrance. Find them.'

484

'And then?'
'Kill them.'

Lindros and Katya sprinted through the modern catacomb under Miran Shah. The alarm was blaring from loudspeakers spaced along the walls of the facility. The entrance had been in sight when the alarm had gone off, and immediately Lindros had reversed course. Now they were heading deeper into the facility.

From snatches of overheard conversations as well as his own observations, Lindros had deduced that the Dujja facility was on two levels. The upper contained living quarters, kitchens, communications, and the like. The infirmary was on this floor. But the surgical facilities where Dr. Andursky had taken Lindros's right eye, where he had remade Karim's face, were below, along with the laboratories: the cavernous centrifuge room where the enriched uranium was concentrated even further, the double-walled fusion lab, and so on.

'They know we're missing,' Katya said. 'What now?'

'Plan B,' Lindros replied. 'We have to get to the communications room.'

'But that's farther away from the entrance,' Katya said. 'We'll never get out.'

They raced around a corner, were confronted by a long corridor that ran down the spine of the facility. Everything in the place – the rooms, corridors, stairwells, elevators – was oversize. No matter where you stood, you felt insignificant. There was something inherently terrifying about such a facility, as if it were designed not for people, but for a machine army. Humanity had been excluded from the premises.

'We have to think first about survival, then escape,' Lindros said. 'That means letting my people know where we are.'

Though he was nervous, he slowed them down to a fast

walk. He didn't like this long, wide corridor stretching out in front of them. If they got trapped here, there was nowhere to hide or to run.

As if reading his worst fear, two men appeared at the far end of the corridor. Seeing their quarry, they drew their weapons. One of them advanced down the corridor while the other held his position. His semiautomatic swung up to aim at them.

'I've got to find a way to warn everyone inside CI headquarters,' Soraya said.

'But yo heard fo yoself they be illin' on yo,' Tyrone replied. 'Ain't gonna get no props from them no matter what yo do.'

'I can't stop trying, can I?'

Tyrone nodded. 'True dat.'

Which was why they were hid out, as Tyrone would say, in a tobacco shop where an old, grizzled Salvadoran was hand-rolling Cuban-seed shit he grew himself into Partagas, Montecristos, and Coronas, selling them to eager customers at a premium price over the Internet. As it happened, Tyrone owned the place, so to him went the lion's share of the profits. It was just a ratty hole-in-the-wall on 9th Street NE, but at least it was legit.

In any event, today its grease-streaked window afforded them a more or less clear view of the black Ford that Tyrone had stolen from the two Arabs he'd offed at the construction site. Tyrone had parked it directly across from the tobacco shop, where it now sat, waiting along with them.

They had come up with the idea together. Since Soraya could no longer simply walk through the doors of CI headquarters, couldn't even call anyone there without the threat of it being traced back to her, she needed another way in.

'I know my vehicles, girl,' Tyrone had said, 'an that some

tricked-out beast. Them shitbirds know by now they two ain't comin' home. Think they just let that go? Shit, no. They be comin' afta it *an* you. Ain't gon let either a yo be. Sure as shit they be comin' here to Northeast 'cause that's the last place they knowd you be.' He'd grinned, wide and handsome. 'When they get here, we on 'em like flies on shit.'

It was a dangerous plan, but a good one for all that, Soraya had to admit. Besides, she couldn't think of any alternative that wouldn't get her either thrown in a CI cage or, more likely, killed.

'Fadi has taken prisoners,' Feyd al-Saoud said.

'I might know one of them,' Bourne said. 'My friend Martin Lindros.'

'Ah, yes.' The security chief nodded. 'The man whom Fadi's brother is impersonating. He may still be alive, then. And the other?'

'I've no idea,' Bourne said.

'In any case, we must hurry if we're to have any chance of saving them.' He frowned. 'But we still have no idea how to gain entrance.'

'Those vehicles on the IKONOS imagery,' Bourne said. 'They had to go somewhere. Somewhere within a radius of a thousand meters of where we are now.' He pointed at the screen. 'Can you make a printout of that?'

'Of course.' Feyd al-Saoud tapped a computer keyboard. There came a soft whirring sound; then a sheet of paper was spewed out of the printer slot. The security chief handed it over.

Bourne exited the mobile command post, followed by Feyd al-Saoud and his immense bodyguard, whose name, the security chief had told Bourne, was Abdullah.

He stood on the southeast side of the runway, staring at the topography and comparing it with the IKONOS map.

'The trouble is, there's nothing here.' Feyd al-Saoud's fists were on his hips. 'As soon as we arrived, I sent out a recon of three men. After an hour, they returned without success.'

'And yet,' Bourne said, 'those vehicles must have gone *somewhere*.'

He walked straight ahead, onto the runway. To his right was the wreck of the Sovereign, which would never fly again. To his left was the beginning of the strip. In his mind's eye, he could see the Sovereign coming in too hot.

All at once Muta ibn Aziz came into his mind. *'You're coming in too low,'* he'd said. *'You'll hit the runway too soon.'* Why had he become so agitated? The worst that would have happened was that the Sovereign's wheels would have struck the tarmac at its near end. Why would that concern Muta ibn Aziz? Why would he even care?

Bourne began to walk to his left, along the tarmac toward its beginning. He kept his eyes on the landing strip. He was now at the near end, the place Muta ibn Aziz was adamant he avoid. What would he be afraid of? Three things occurred when a jet touched down: high-level applications of friction, heat, and weight. Which one had worried him?

Bourne crouched down, put his fingertips on the runway. It looked like tarmac, felt like tarmac. Except for one crucial thing.

'Feel this,' Bourne said. 'The tarmac should be burning hot from the strong sunlight.'

'It's not.' Feyd al-Saoud moved his hand around. 'It's not hot at all.'

'Which means,' Bourne said, 'it's not tarmac.'

'What could Dujja be using?'

Bourne rose. 'Don't forget that they have access to IVT's technology.'

He walked farther down the runway. When he reached the place where marks showed he'd set the Sovereign down, he knelt again, put his hand to the tarmac. And snatched it away quickly.

'Hot?' Feyd al-Saoud said.

'This is tarmac.'

'Then what's back there?'

'I don't know, but the man I was with – Fadi's messenger – didn't want me to land there.'

Returning to the end of the runway, Bourne traced a route across the full width of it. In the back of his mind he was furiously working on a plan. They needed to gain access to the underground facility, get to Fadi before his men found the prisoners. If there was any chance that one of them was Lindros . . .

Once again, he scanned the IKONOS topographic readout, compared it with the visual survey he'd taken on his way in. A facility enriching uranium required water – a lot of it. Which was where that deeply shadowed, rock-strewn ravine came in. He'd noted it from the air, and it had stayed in his mind like a beacon.

What he was considering might work, but he knew Feyd al-Saoud wasn't going to like it. And if he couldn't sell his friend on the plan, it wasn't going to work. It might not work even *with* the security chief's cooperation, but he didn't see any viable alternative.

Reaching the near side of the runway, he once again knelt down, scrutinizing the edge. Then he said to Abdullah, 'Can you help me with this?'

Together Bourne and Abdullah heaved up, curling their fingertips around the end. With a titanic effort, they began to peel the surface back.

'What we have here,' Bourne said, 'is a strip of landing material.'

Feyd al-Saoud came forward, bending his body from the waist. He was looking at the material, which was perhaps six centimeters thick and the precise color and texture of tarmac.

Clearly, it wasn't tarmac. What it was, exactly, there was no way of telling. Not that it mattered in the least. What was of intense interest to them, what they were all studying with a fierce concentration of joy and triumph, was what lay beneath the peeled-back layer.

A metal hatch, large as the door of a two-car garage, set flush with the ground.

THIRTY-FOUR

What are you doing here?' the lead terrorist shouted. He was clearly agitated, which meant he was on hair-trigger alert.

'We've been sent to the—'

'Turn into the light! You're not one of us! Put your weapons down now!'

At once Lindros raised his hands. Having a semiautomatic rifle leveled at you was a threat that needed to be taken very seriously.

'Don't shoot!' he said in Arabic. 'Don't shoot!' To Katya, he muttered, 'Walk in front of me. Do exactly as I say. And for God's sake, whatever happens, keep your hands in the air.'

They began to walk toward the front man, who was in a semi-crouch. While keeping him in the periphery of his vision, Lindros watched the cover man farther down the corridor. At this moment, he was the real problem.

'Halt!' the terrorist said when they were several paces from him. 'Turn around!'

Katya obeyed. As she was turning, Lindros drew out a bottle of alcohol he'd taken from the infirmary, opened the top, and threw the contents in the terrorist's face.

'Down!' he shouted.

Lindros leapt over Katya as she dropped to the floor. Lunging for the recoiled terrorist, he grabbed his semiautomatic and pressed the trigger, spraying the corridor with bullets. Several struck the cover man in the arm and leg, spinning him back against a wall. He returned fire, but his aim was wild.

With a short, precise burst, Lindros brought him down.

'Come on!'

He slammed the butt of the semiautomatic into the base of the skull of the terrorist, still clawing at his face, then went roughly through his clothes for other weapons. He found a handgun and a thick-bladed knife. With Katya behind him he sprinted down the corridor, snatched up the cover man's semiautomatic, handed it to Katya.

They made their way to the communications room, which according to Katya was around to the left at the far end of the corridor.

Two men were inside, busy at their equipment. Lindros stepped up behind the one on the right, put his hand under his chin, and, as shocked tension came into the frame, quickly brought his head up and back, slashing his throat. As the second man turned, coming up out of his seat, Lindros threw the knife into his chest. With a small gurgle, he arched backward, his lungs already filling up with blood. Even as he slid, lifeless, onto the floor, Lindros took his seat, began to work the communications system.

'Don't just stand there whimpering,' he ordered. 'Guard the door. Shoot at anything that moves, and keep shooting till it stops!'

Feyd al-Saoud's earpiece crackled. He put a hand up to it to press it more firmly into his ear canal. In a moment, he nodded. 'I understand.' To Bourne, he said, 'We must return to the command center. At once.'

The three men covered the several hundred meters to the vehicle in very little time. Inside, they found the communications officer gesticulating wildly. When he saw them, he ripped off his headphone and pressed a cup to his left ear, so he could hear them and what was coming out of the earphones simultaneously.

THIRTY-FIVE

Bourne ran straight at the oncoming vehicle, leapt off his feet, and landed on its hood. Using a combination of the vehicle's momentum and his own strength, he lowered his shoulder as his entire body was driven into the windshield.

The glass shattered from the force, and Bourne used his leading elbow and forearm to sweep aside the remaining shards. Scrambling through the rent, he found himself in the seat next to a man who, given his close facial similarity to Muta ibn Aziz, could only be his brother, Abbud.

Abbud ibn Aziz had a gun at the ready, but Bourne lunged at the wheel, turning it hard to the right. Centrifugal force slammed his body into the terrorist's. The gun fired, deafening them both, but the bullet went awry, embedding itself in the doorpost. Abbud ibn Aziz squeezed off two more shots before the vehicle slammed into the concrete wall.

Bourne, who had prepared for the impact by willing his body to go completely slack, was slammed forward, then back against the seat. Beside him, Abbud ibn Aziz smashed into the top of the steering wheel, causing a great bloody gash in his forehead as well as a fracture in the bone over his right eye.

Wresting the gun from his slack fingers, Bourne slapped him hard across the cheek. He knew he had little time, but he was determined to get to the bottom of the mystery of Sarah ibn Ashef's death.

'What happened that night in Odessa, Abbud?'

He deliberately left off the last half of the terrorist's name, a clear sign of contempt.

Abbud ibn Aziz's head lolled against the back of the seat. Blood, coming from several places, leaked from him. 'What d'you mean?'

'You shot Sarah ibn Ashef to death.'

'You're insane.'

'Muta told me. He *told* me, Abbud. You shot Fadi's sister, not me. This whole vendetta could have been avoided if only you'd told the truth.'

'The truth?' Abbud spat blood. 'In the desert, there is no such thing as the truth. The sands shift constantly, like the truth.'

'Why did you lie?'

He began to cough, blood vomiting out of his mouth.

'Tell me why you lied about Sarah ibn Ashef's death.'

Abbud ibn Aziz spat again, almost choked on his own blood. When he'd recovered sufficiently, he muttered, 'Why should I tell you anything?'

'It's over for you, Abbud. You're dying. But you already knew that, didn't you? Your death from a car accident won't get you to heaven. But if I kill you, you will have a martyr's death, filled with glory.'

Abbud looked away, as if in that way he could escape the fate awaiting him. 'I lied to Fadi because I had to. The truth would have destroyed him.'

'Time's running out.' Bourne held a knife to his throat. 'I'm the only one who can help you now. In a moment, it will be too late. You will have lost your chance at *shahada*.'

'What do you, an infidel, know of *shahada*?'

'I know that without jihad there can be no martyrdom. I know that jihad is the inclusive struggle for truth. Without your confession of the truth, there can be no jihad, there can be no *shahada* for you.

'Without my help, you won't be able to stand witness to

the truth that is Allah. Therefore, your holy struggle in the cause of Allah – your entire existence – will be meaningless.'

Wholly unbidden, Abbud ibn Aziz felt tears stinging his eyes. His enemy was right. He needed him now. Allah had placed this final terrible choice in front of him: testify to the truth, or be condemned to the eternal fires of damnation. In this way, at this moment, he understood that Muta ibn Aziz had been right. It was the shifting sands of the truth that had buried him. If only he had spoken the truth at once. For now, in order to die righteously, in order to be clean in the eyes of Allah and all that he held holy, he would have to betray Fadi.

He closed his eyes for a moment, all the defiance drained out of him. Then he stared up into his enemy's face.

'I shot Sarah ibn Ashef, not Muta ibn Aziz. I *had* to shoot her. Six days before the evening of her death, I discovered that she was carrying on a love affair. I took her aside and confronted her. She didn't bother denying it. I told her that the law of the desert dictated that she commit suicide. She laughed at me. I told her that committing suicide would relieve her brothers of the stress of killing her themselves. She told me to get out of her sight.'

Abbud paused for a moment. Clearly, reliving the shock of the confrontation had robbed him of his remaining strength. Presently, however, he gathered himself. 'That night, she was late, hurrying across town to meet her lover. She had ignored me. Instead she was continuing to betray her own family. I was shocked, but not surprised. I had lost count of the times she had told me that we inverted Islam, that we twisted Allah's holy words to further our cause, to justify our . . . what did she call it? . . . Ah, yes, our death dealing. She had turned her back on the desert, on her Bedouin heritage. Now the only thing she could bring her family was shame and humiliation. I shot her. I'm proud of it. It was a virtue killing.'

Bourne, sick at heart, had heard enough. Without another word, he slashed the blade of the knife across Abbud ibn Aziz's throat, slipping out of the vehicle as the gout of blood flooded the front seat.

The moment Abbud ibn Aziz had taken off against his orders, Fadi drew out a gun, aimed it at his back. Truly, if it hadn't been for the hail of gunfire, he'd have shot his second dead. So far as he was concerned, there was no excuse for insubordination. Orders were to be obeyed without either thought or question. This was not the UN; others did not get their moment to wade in with options.

As he ran toward the comm room, this last thought rolled around his head, raising echoes he didn't want to hear. In his opinion, the Aziz brothers had been acting strangely for some time. Their verbal battles had long since become legendary – so much so that they were now expected, never remarked upon by the others. Lately, however, their fights had occurred behind closed doors. Afterward, neither wanted to talk about the subject, but Fadi had noted that the growing friction between them was beginning to interfere with their work. Which was why, at this crucial juncture, he had sent Muta ibn Aziz off to Istanbul. He needed to break the brothers up, give them both space to work out their enmity. Now Muta ibn Aziz was dead, and Abbud ibn Aziz had disobeyed orders. For one reason or another, he could no longer rely on either of them.

He saw the carnage the moment he turned the corner to the comm room. Soberly, angrily, he high-stepped between the corpses like a jittery Arabian horse. He checked each body, as well as the room itself. Eight men down in total, all dead. Lindros must have taken more weapons.

Cursing under his breath, he was about to return to the ramped entrance when his earpiece sizzled.

'We've sighted the fugitives,' one of his men said in his ear.

Fadi's body tensed. 'Where?'

'Lower level,' his man said. 'They're heading for the uranium labs.'

The nuke, Fadi thought.

'Shall we close in?'

'Keep them in sight but under no circumstances are you to engage them, is that clear?'

'Yes sir.'

This conversation had driven all considerations of revenge clear out of his head. If Lindros should find the nuke and the heli, he would have it all. After all this time, all the sacrifice, all the endless work and bloodshed, he would be left with nothing.

He ran down the corridor, turned left, then left again. The open door to a freight elevator yawned in front of him. He stepped smartly in, punching the bottom button on the panel. The doors slid shut, and he began to descend.

At some point, as they advanced along the warren of lower-level labs, Lindros became aware that they were under surveillance. This disturbed him, of course, but it also frightened him. Why weren't these watchers closing in, as the first group had?

As they ran, he could see that Katya was crying. The violence and the death she'd been exposed to would have shaken anyone up, especially a civilian inexperienced with incarceration and violence. But to her credit, she kept pace with him.

All at once she pulled away and lunged out for an open doorway then, leaning over, vomited up whatever was in her stomach. Lindros put one arm around her to try to hold her steady, the butt of the semiautomatic on his opposite hip. That was when he glanced into the lab they had come to. It

503

was the surgery where Dr. Andursky had carved out his eye, where he had transformed Karim into a terrifying doppelgänger. When he was finished with his infernal business, Andursky had trotted Lindros out to see his handiwork, so the new Martin Lindros could ask the original Martin Lindros to populate his mind with Lindros's memories – enough, anyway, to fool the CI interrogators and Jason Bourne. That's when Lindros had devised a code he hoped would reach Jason.

At first the surgery looked deserted, but then he saw cowering behind one of the two surgical tables the thin, weasely face of Dr. Andursky.

Soraya, her arms wrapped tightly around Tyrone's rock-hard waist, sat behind him on his Passion Red Kawasaki Ninja ZX-12R. The motorcycle was on 5th Street NE, following both the reappropriated black Ford and the white Chevy. They were turning northwest onto Florida Avenue.

Tyrone was a superb driver who, Soraya could see, knew his way around D.C., not just his neighborhood. He wove in and out of traffic, never staying in the same position. One moment he was three car lengths behind their quarry, the next five. But Soraya never felt that they were in danger of losing their targets.

On Florida Avenue, they crossed over into the Northwest quadrant, turned right onto Sherman Ave NW, heading due north. At the junction of Park Road NW, they made a slight jog to the right onto the beginning of New Hampshire, then almost an immediate left onto Spring Road, which, in turn, led to 16th Street NW, onto which they made a right.

They were traveling due north once again, more or less paralleling the eastern edge of Rock Creek Park. Skirting the park's northeastern boundary, the two cars pulled into the loading bay of a large mortuary. Tyrone turned off the Ninja's engine, and they dismounted. As they watched, the inner wall of the right side of the loading bay began to slide down.

Once they crossed the street, they saw the closed-circuit TV guarding the loading bay. The camera was on a wall mount that moved it slowly back and forth to cover the entire area.

Both vehicles drove through the aperture and slowly down the concrete ramp. Soraya, one eye on the CCTV, calculated that if they followed the vehicles the camera would immediately pick them up. It was rotating away, but slowly, so slowly. The concrete wall was rising up from its slot in the floor.

They edged closer, closer. Then, with the wall halfway up, she clapped Tyrone on the back. Sprinting for the disappearing aperture, they leapt through the opening at the last instant. After landing on the concrete ramp, they picked themselves up.

Behind them, the wall slid home, encasing them in fumy darkness.

Feyd al-Saoud stood at the southwestern end of the rock-filled ravine. At last his men were in place, the charges set. Incredible as it seemed, Dujja had the technology to tap into the underground river. His men had discovered three huge pipes, clearly with wheelcocks inside the facility, to regulate the water flow. It was these wheelcocks they had to destroy.

He moved back several hundred meters and saw that his splendidly disciplined men ringed the ravine. Lifting his arm, he caught the attention of his two explosives experts.

In the heat and utter stillness of the moment, his mind flashed back to the moment when Jason Bourne had described the plan to him. His initial response had been incredulity. He had told Bourne that the plan was an insane one. He'd said, 'We'll go in the old-fashioned way. With a frontal assault.'

'You'll be committing your men to certain death,' Bourne

had told him. 'I'm reasonably sure that Fadi monitored my conversation with Lindros, which would argue for him having monitored your communication with your recon party earlier.'

'But what about you?' Feyd al-Saoud had said. 'If you go in by yourself, his men will mow you down as soon as you show your face.'

'That's where you're wrong,' Bourne had replied. 'Fadi needs to kill me himself. Anything else is unacceptable to him. Besides, his weakness is that he thinks he's gotten inside my mind. He's expecting a diversion. Lindros will give him one, to lure him into a false sense of complacency. He'll convince himself he's gotten my tactic right, that the situation is under control.'

'Which is where we come in.' Feyd al-Saoud nodded. 'You're right. The plan is unorthodox enough that it just might work.'

He glanced at his watch. Now that he was committed, he itched to get started. But Bourne had insisted they stick to the plan. 'You have to give me fifteen minutes to do what must be done,' he said.

Ninety seconds left.

Feyd al-Saoud stared at the jumbled bottom of the ravine, which, as it turned out, was not a ravine at all. Bourne had been right: It was a dry riverbed whose bottom was slowly collapsing into the underground waterway that had once, along ago, been on the surface. The underground river was where the Dujja facility was getting its needed supply of running water for the nuclear manufacturing. His men had set their charges at the facility end of the riverbed. The attack would serve two purposes: It would either drown or flush out every member of Dujja, and it would render the canisters of enriched uranium safe until a full complement of CI and Saudi experts could take over the facility permanently.

Fifteen seconds to go. Feyd al-Saoud took one long look

around at each of his men. They'd been briefed; they knew what the stakes were. They knew what to do.

His arm swept down. The detonators were activated. The twin blasts exploded several seconds apart, but to Feyd al-Saoud and his men they sounded like one long percussion, a ripping wind, a hailstorm of rocky debris, and then the sound they were all waiting for: the deep, earthbound roar of water rushing along the course it had carved out of the bedrock.

Down in the Dujja facility, the mighty blasts felt like earthquake temblors. Everything on the shelves of the surgery smashed to the floor. Cupboard doors flew open, their contents exploding out into the room, coating the floor with a lake of liquids, shards of glass, twisted ribbons of plastic, a pickup-sticks welter of metal surgical instruments.

Katya, clinging both to Lindros and the door frame, wiped her mouth and said, 'Come on! We've got to get out of here!'

Lindros knew she was right. They had very little time now to get to a place of safety where they could stay until the worst was over.

And yet he couldn't budge. His eyes were riveted on the face of Dr. Andursky. How many times during his recovery from the surgical rape Andursky had subjected him to had he dreamed of killing this man. Not simply killing. My God! The *methods* he had devised for Andursky's end! Some days, those increasingly elaborate fantasies were the only things that kept him from going insane. Even so, time and again he'd awaken from a dream of ravens plucking at the man, his flesh peeled back, exposing the bones of his skeleton for the windborne sand to scour clean of whatever mocking semblance of life he still clung to. This dream was so detailed, to keenly felt, so *real* that sometimes Lindos couldn't help feeling he'd crossed the line into insanity.

507

Even now, though he felt the imperative to get to safety, he knew there would be no solace for him as long as Andursky lived. And so he said to Katya, 'You go. Get as close to the nuclear lab as possible, then climb up into the nearest HVAC vent and stay there.'

'But you're coming with me.' Katya tugged at his arm. 'We're going together.'

'No, Katya, there's something I have to do here.'

'But you promised. You said you'd help me.'

He swung around, fixed her with his one good eye. 'I have helped you, Katya. But you must understand, if I don't stay here and do this, I will be like the walking dead.'

She shivered. 'Then I'll stay with you.'

The entire facility gave a great shudder, moaning as if in terrible pain. Somewhere not so far ahead, he could hear the shriek of a wall splitting apart.

'No,' he said sharply, returning his attention to her. 'That's not an option.'

She hefted the semiautomatic. 'And I say it is.'

Lindros nodded. What else could he do? They'd run out of time. He could hear a distant roaring, becoming louder, harsher, closer with each beat of his heart. *Water!* he thought. *Good Lord, Jason's flooding the facility!*

Without another word he strode into the surgery, Katya following several paces behind, her rifle at the ready. In the last few minutes since they'd left the comm room, she'd studied Lindros, thought she had a semblance of knowledge of how to use this instrument of death.

Lindros advanced on Dr. Andursky who, through all of this, had remained in the same position, cowering behind the table on which he had taken out Lindros's eye. His gaze was locked on Martin much as a rabbit will crouch, mesmerized, as the owl swoops silently down out of the twilight to snatch it up in its powerful talons.

As he went through the surgery, Lindros had to struggle

to keep his gorge down, to keep the sickly sweet scent of the anesthetic from clogging his nostrils. He had to fight all over again the terror of helplessness and rage that had all but paralyzed him upon awakening to discover what had been stolen from him.

And yet here was Dr. Andursky in front of him, here he was gripped by Lindros's taloned fingers, scoring the flesh of his chest.

'Hello, Doctor,' Lindros said.

'No, please don't. I didn't want to. They made me.'

'Please enlighten me, Doctor. After all the little boys they supplied you – they made you pluck out my eye? They insisted you do it – or what? They would refuse to service you?'

'Martin,' Katya called, wide-eyed with fear. 'Our time has run out. Come on now! Please, for the love of God!'

'Yes, yes, listen to her. Have mercy.' Andursky was actually weeping now, his body quaking in much the same way as the walls around them had begun to quake. 'You don't understand. I'm weak.'

'And I,' Lindros said, 'gather strength with every breath I take.' He drew Andursky to him, until they stood intimate as lovers. Now it was different. The end would not be the same.

Drawing on an enormous wellspring of strength, Lindros pressed his thumbs into Andursky's eyes.

Andursky shrieked and thrashed about, desperately trying to get away. But Lindros had him in an unbreakable death grip. Every fiber of his being was directed toward one end. In a kind of ecstatic semi-trance, he felt the soft, springy tissue of the eyeballs beneath the pads of his thumbs. He drew in a breath, expelled it as he drove his thumbs slowly, inexorably into Andursky's eye sockets.

The surgeon shrieked again, a sharp inhuman noise abruptly cut off as Lindros shoved his thumbs all the way in. Andursky danced for a little, his autonomous nervous system flickering with whatever galvanic energy remained inside his body. Then that, too, was gone and, released from Lindros's grip, he slithered to the floor as if all his bones had dissolved.

THIRTY-SIX

Fadi heard the screams of pain from the facility he had designed and helped build, saw the cracks shoot through the reinforced concrete as if lightning was streaking through it. Then a throaty roar echoed through the corridors and he knew the water was coming, gallons of water, tons of it flooding the labs, and all he could think of was the nuclear device.

He tore along the corridors past the elevator. He pushed past milling guards, who looked to him for guidance. He ordered them to the front entrance to find Bourne, then he forgot about them. They were all cannon fodder anyway. What did it matter if they died? There were more where they came from, an endless supply of young men clamoring to follow him, eager to die for him, to martyr themselves for the cause, the dream that one day they would live in a world of righteousness, a world without the infidel.

That this frankly brutal outlook had been forced on him by his enemies was a given, a watchword by which he'd lived his entire adult life. He told himself as much several times a day, although it never occurred to him that he needed to justify to himself any of his decisions or actions. His mind, his heart, and his hand were guided by Allah; this he believed absolutely. The possibility that their plan might not succeed had until now never entered his mind. Now that thought superseded all others, even his obsessive need to revenge himself for the crippling of his father or the death of his sister.

Racing down the stairs, he found the lower level already calf-deep in water. He pulled his Glock 36, checked the .45 to make sure it was fully loaded. The water lapped at his legs, rising with every step he took. He felt as if he were walking against the tide, the sensation bringing him back to the encounter with Bourne under the pier in Odessa. How he wished he'd finished him off there. Except for the damn dog, he felt certain he would have.

But this was no time for recriminations, and he was not a man who dwelled on what-ifs. He was a pragmatist, which dictated that he get to the heli with its all-important payload. What was unfortunate was that the secret exit to the camouflaged helipad was at the rear of the lower level. This location had been deliberate, for the exit was nearest the nuclear facilities where, Fadi had surmised, he would need to be if the facility was ever discovered and raided.

What he hadn't counted on was the raiding party discovering the underground river. The section of the facility he sought was also where the water was gushing in at the fastest rate. Once he got to his destination, however, he'd be all right, since the helipad had wide drainage apertures all around its perimeters. This thought occupied him as he ran past the open door to the surgery and saw Katya. Ludicrously, she held one of his own semiautomatics in both hands. But it wasn't Veintrop's wife that so arrested him. Rather, it was the sight of Martin Lindros standing, bloody-handed, over the corpse of the man who had maimed him, Dr. Andursky.

The singsong lilt of Arabic threaded through the darkness beneath the mortuary. Karim's men were praying, their bodies bowed toward Mecca. From the bottom of the ramp illumination spread upward like the fingers of a hand. Tyrone was wearing sneakers, but Soraya had taken off her shoes to silence her footfalls.

Moving cautiously toward the lower end of the ramp, Soraya and Tyrone peered into the basement. The first thing Soraya saw were the two vehicles they had been following: the white Chevy and the black Ford. Behind them was what looked to be a gleaming black limo. On the left side of the Ford, four men were lined up, kneeling on small prayer rugs, their foreheads to the low nap. To the right was a glass-paned door. Soraya craned her neck but could not get a good angle at which to see through the door's glass.

They waited. At length, the prayers ended. The men rose, rolled their rugs, and stowed them away. Then the group broke up. Two of the men disappeared up a stainless-steel spiral staircase to the mortuary proper. The remaining pair snapped on latex gloves, opened the Ford's doors, and proceeded to go over it as thoroughly and meticulously as a professional forensics team.

Soraya, curious about what lay behind the glass-paned door, signed to Tyrone to stay put and cover her, if necessary. He nodded, produced a Saturday-night special, the grips wrapped in black elecrician's tape, and stepped back into deep shadow. Not for the first time in the last several hours, Soraya felt comforted to have him with her. He was street-savvy, knew the district in far more detail than she did.

Watching the two men examine the Ford, she waited until both their backs were turned to the mouth of the ramp, then ran silently to the door. Twisting the knob, she opened it and slipped through.

At once she was suffused with a deep chill that emanated from the cold rooms where the corpses were kept. She was confronted with a short, wide corridor off which six open doorways presented themselves. Peeking around the corner of the first one, she came upon the bodies of the two men who had attacked her at the construction site. In accordance with austere Saudi Islamic tradition, they had been placed on bare wooden slabs and were draped in the simplest cloth robes. There would be no embalming of these men.

Her heart leapt. The corpses were the first hard evidence she had that Karim was working with a cadre of Dujja terrorists inside the district. How had they all missed this Dujja sleeper cell right under their noses? State-of-the-art surveillance equipment was all well and good, but even the best electronic net couldn't catch every human being who slipped inside America's borders.

The second and third rooms she came to were empty, but in the fourth a dark-complected man with his back to her was bent over an embalming table. He wore latex gloves and was using a machine to pump the body laid out on the table with the ghastly pink embalming fluid. He would stop every so often, put aside the probe, then use his hands to knead the fish-white flesh in order to effect the even circulation of fluids through the corpse's veins and arteries.

As he moved from the corpse's right side to its left, Soraya was able to see the head, then the face of the deceased. As soon as her brain passed though its shock phase and was able to process the image, she was compelled to bite her lip in order to stop herself from screaming.

No, she thought. Fear and panic fought for dominance inside her. *It can't be*.

And yet it was.

Here in the mortuary owned and operated by Dujja was the corpse of the DCI. The Old Man was dead, a bullet hole drilled through his heart.

The moment he had memorized the schematic of the facility affixed to the wall, Bourne ran out of the parking area. At once he saw a group of armed Dujja running his way. Ducking back away from their fire, he climbed into the smallest vehicle. Fortunately it, like all the others, had the key already in it; there was no need to waste time hot-wiring the ignition.

He roared into the corridor, then pressed the accelerator to the floor, shooting the vehicle ahead like a bolt released from a crossbow. It plowed into the clutch of terrorists, flinging them under it or to either side. He sped down the spine of the facility until he came to the freight elevator.

As the doors opened, he drove in, crushing four more armed men. Climbing out, he pushed the button for the lower level. He grabbed one of the semiautomatics as the oversize cab began to descend.

Reaching its destination, the elevator came to a halt, but its doors refused to open. Water was leaking in from the corridor outside. Opening the panel in the side wall, he pressed the manual release. This, too, was inoperative.

Bourne climbed onto the vehicle's roof. Bracing himself, he slammed the butt of the semiautomatic repeatedly against the small square door in the cab's roof. Finally it gave. He shoved it out of the way and, slinging the weapon across his back, hoisted himself up. On top of the cab, he knelt down by the side of an oblong control box and opened it. Inside he found the circuit that operated the doors. He took its wires and diverted them to the lift mechanism's power source. The doors slid open, a heavy slosh of water roiling into the elevator.

Back behind the wheel, he put the vehicle in gear, then screeched out into the waterlogged lower level. He headed toward the nuclear labs, gunning the engine as the water level rose. In a moment it would be high enough to flood the engine. Unless he kept going it would conk out altogether, and his advantage would disappear.

But a moment later, the vehicle's use ran its course anyway. Dead ahead of him he saw Fadi standing in the center of the corridor, blocking his way. Held in front of him in the crook of Fadi's powerful left arm was Martin Lindros. In Fadi's right hand was a Glock 36, the muzzle pressed to Martin's temple.

'My pursuit of you ends here, Bourne!' Fadi shouted over the roar of the incoming water and the noise of the vehicle's engine. 'Turn off the ignition! Out of the car! Now!'

Bourne did as Fadi ordered. Now, closer, he saw something in Fadi's right ear. A wireless earpiece. He *had* been monitoring the communications.

'Get rid of that rifle! All your weapons! Now, keeping your hands where I can see them, walk very slowly toward me.'

Bourne sloshed through the water, his eyes on Martin's ruined face. His one eye glared at Bourne with a fierce pride. He intuited that Lindros was going to make a move, and wanted to warn him against it; Bourne had his own plan for dealing with Fadi. But Lindros had always wanted to be a hero.

Sure enough, a scalpel appeared in Martin's left hand. As he drove it into the meat of Fadi's thigh, Fadi fired the Glock. He'd been aiming for Lindros's brain, but the stab caused an involuntary spasm of shock and pain so that, instead, the bullet ran along Lindros's jaw. Still, it was a .45. Martin's body was launched through the doorway, into the surgery beyond.

Bourne leapt. His leading shoulder struck Fadi in the solar plexus as the terrorist was wrestling the scalpel out of his muscle. Both of them fell backward into the water, now as high as their knees. Bourne got his hand on the Glock and wrestled it upward, so that it fired harmlessly into the air. At the same time Fadi wrenched the scalpel out of his thigh and, seeking to finishing what he had started, stabbed it toward Bourne's left side.

Bourne was ready. He lifted the Glock, and Fadi's right hand with it, so that the blade skimmed off the gun's thick barrel. Fadi realized the gun was useless in the water, released it, and, grabbing Bourne by the shirtfront, flipped him over onto his back. Using his right elbow, he kept Bourne's head under the water while he stabbed downward again and again with the point of the scalpel.

Twisting and writhing his torso, Bourne sought to keep the keen-edged blade away from him. At the same time he reached up so that his hands and forearms were out of the water. Marshaling all the power of his shoulders, he slammed the heels of his hands against Fadi's ears. The terrorist arched back, his hands clutching his right ear. Bourne's blow had driven the wireless transceiver through his eardrum, rupturing it and the canal behind it.

Fadi lost the scalpel, then his balance. Bourne, sensing this, scissor-kicked, twisting himself onto one hip as he did so. The maneuver threw Fadi off far enough for him to rise up above the waterline.

He reached for Fadi. As he did so, he heard a ferocious roar from farther down the corridor. Fadi appeared to be trying to shake off the effects of his ruptured eardrum, blood leaking out of his right ear. Bourne reached for him, felt the bite of Fadi's serpent-bladed knife as it drew blood along the back of his hand.

Tearing off his belt, Bourne wrapped it around and around his knuckles, using the layers of leather to fend off Fadi's knife thrusts. Inevitably, however, the struck leather began to come apart. A moment more and he would be defenseless.

The roaring increased to a howl. What was coming? Fadi, seeing his advantage, stepped up his attack with precise swipes, lent unnatural power by his desperation. Bourne was forced back toward the surgery.

Then out of the corner of his eye he saw a blurred movement. Someone had darted from the doorway to the surgery. A woman: Katya. Tears were streaming down her face. Her hands were red with blood – Martin's blood. It was she who had attempted to escape with Martin. But then Fadi had found them. Why hadn't Martin led her to shelter as Bourne had warned him to do? Too late now.

'Look what they've done to him!' Katya wailed.

Bourne saw something metallic gleaming in her hand.

Wading out into the corridor, Katya came toward him. At that moment the roar reached a fever pitch. Katya turned her head to stare down along the corridor. Bourne, following her gaze, saw a wall of water filling the corridor from floor to ceiling, heading toward them.

Fadi's knife blade swept across his makeshift shield one last time. All the layers fell away, baring his bloody knuckles.

'Get back!' he shouted to Katya. 'Take shelter!'

Instead she continued to wade toward him. But now the water was waist-deep, the rush of it so powerful that she could no longer make headway. Fadi tried for a killing stab, but Bourne kicked out through the rushing water, throwing him off balance. The blade turned; Bourne's bruised defensive forearm struck the flat of it, sending it up and away.

Katya, realizing she was stymied, tossed the metallic object toward Bourne.

He reached out, caught the metallic implement at its midsection – a Collins twenty-two-centimeter amputating knife. In one smooth motion he reversed it, plunged the wicked blade into the soft spot at the base of Fadi's throat, then drove it downward through his collarbone, into his chest.

Fadi stared at him, openmouthed. At the moment of his death, he was paralyzed, helpless, without thought. Frozen in time. His eyes, in the process of glazing over, revealed that he was trying to understand something. In this, too, he failed.

The roiling wall of water was almost upon them. There was nothing else Bourne could do except clamber up Fadi's split upper torso. He locked his curled fingers through the holes in the HVAC vent in the ceiling, levered himself up. Then he reached back for Katya. Afterward, he never knew whether she could have made it to him. She stood there, staring at nothing while he shouted to her.

He was about to go after her when the water struck him with the fury of a giant's fist, knocking all the breath out of him. Howling like the demon that lived atop Ras Dejen, it ripped Fadi's corpse from under him and swept Katya into its furious heart. It roared and foamed through the Dujja facility like Noah's flood, drowning all in its wake, scouring everything clean.

THIRTY-SEVEN

There was in Feyd al-Saoud's brave heart a rising conviction that one day – not soon, perhaps not even in his lifetime – the war against the tribespeople intent on setting the world on fire in order to destroy his country would be won. It would take great sacrifice, stern conviction, an iron will, as well as unconventional alliances with infidels like Jason Bourne, who had caught a glimpse of the Arab mind and understood what they had witnessed. Most of all, it would take patience and perseverance during the inevitable setbacks. But the reward would be days such as this one.

Having used a second set of C-4 charges to divert the underground river, his men entered the Dujja facility via the blast hole. He stood on the edge of the camouflaged helipad, which looked like the bed of a flat-bottomed well. Above him the opening in the rock widened as it neared the top, which had over it the specially designed camouflage material that made it indistinguishable from the rock around it.

The waters had receded, swallowed at last by the huge drains built into the facility's lower level.

Directly in front of Feyd al-Saoud, in a raised platform undamaged by the flood, squatted the helicopter meant, he was certain, to take Fadi to his rendezvous with the nuclear device. Another of his men held the pilot under guard.

Though he very much wanted to know how Bourne had made out, he was understandably reluctant to leave the device to anyone else's care. Besides, the fact that he was standing here, rather than watching the copter lifting off as Fadi made his escape, spoke eloquently of Bourne's victory. Still, he'd sent his men in to find his friend. He very much wanted to share this moment with him.

However, the individual they brought back was an older man with a high, wide forehead, prominent nose, and steel-rimmed glasses, one lens of which was cracked.

'I ask you for Jason Bourne and you bring me this.' Feyd al-Saoud's annoyance masked his alarm. Where was Jason? Was he lying injured somewhere in the washed-out bowels of this hellhole? Was he still alive?

'The man says his name is Costin Veintrop,' the team leader said.

Hearing his name amid the blur of fast-paced Arabic, the newcomer said, '*Doctor* Veintrop.' He followed this up with something in such poor Arabic as to be incomprehensible.

'Speak English, please,' Feyd al-Saoud said in his impeccably accented British.

Looking visibly relieved, Veintrop said: 'Thank God you're here. My wife and I have been held prisoner.'

Feyd al-Saoud stared at him, mute as the Sphinx.

Veintrop cleared his throat. 'Please let me go. I need to find my wife.'

'You tell me you're Dr. Costin Veintrop. You tell me that you and your wife were being held prisoner here.' Feyd al-Saoud's growing anxiety as to his friend's fate was making him ever more testy. 'I know who was being held prisoner here, and it wasn't you.'

Veintrop, properly cowed, turned to the man who'd brought him here. 'My wife, Katya, is in the facility. Can you tell me if you've found her?'

The group leader, taking his cue from his chief, stared at Veintrop in stony silence.

'Ah, God,' Veintrop moaned, lapsing in shock and worry into his native Romanian. 'My God in heaven.'

Completely unmoved, Feyd al-Saoud gave him a look of disdain before turning at the sound of movement behind him.

'Jason!'

At the sight of his friend, he rushed to the entrance of the helipad. With Bourne was another of Feyd al-Saoud's detachment. They were supporting between them a tall, well-built man whose face and head looked as if they had been put through a meat grinder.

'Allah!' Feyd al-Saoud cried. 'Is Fadi dead or alive?'

'Dead,' Bourne said.

'Who is this, Jason?'

'My friend Martin Lindros,' Bourne said.

'Ah, no!' At once, the security chief called for his group surgeon. 'Jason, the nuclear device is in the heli. Incredibly, it's contained within a slim black briefcase. How did Fadi manage that?'

Bourne stared at Veintrop balefully for a moment. 'Hello, Dr. Sunderland – or I should say Costin Veintrop.'

Veintrop winced.

Feyd al-Saoud raised his eyebrows. 'You know this man?'

'We've met once before,' Bourne said. 'The doctor is an extremely talented scientist with a number of specialities. Including miniaturization.'

'So he was the one who built the circuits that allowed the nuke to fit into the briefcase.' Feyd al-Saoud's expression was dark, indeed. 'He claimed that he and his wife were prisoners.'

'I *was* a prisoner,' Veintrop insisted. 'You don't understand, I—'

'Now you know about him.' Bourne talked over his response. 'As for his wife—'

'Where is she?' Veintrop gasped. 'Do you know? I want my Katya!'

'Katya is dead.' Bourne said this bluntly, almost brutally. He had no sympathy to spend on the man who had connived with Fadi and Karim to destroy him from the inside out. 'She saved me. I tried to save her, but the wall of water took her.'

'That's a lie!' Veintrop, white-faced, fairly shouted. 'You have her! You have her!'

Bourne grabbed him and took him into the chamber from which he'd first come. In the aftermath of the deluge, the Saudi team was lining up the corpses they'd found. Next to Fadi's was Katya's. Her head lay at an unnatural angle.

Veintrop gave out a low moan that seemed almost inhuman. Bourne, watching him sink to his knees, felt a pang for the beautiful young woman who had sacrificed herself so that he could kill Fadi. She had wanted Fadi's death, it seemed, as much as he did.

His gaze slid over to Fadi. The eyes, still open, seemed to stare at Bourne with a hateful fury. Bourne took out his cell. Crouched down, he took several shots of Fadi's face. When he was finished, he rose and dragged Veintrop back to the helipad.

Bourne addressed Feyd al-Saoud. 'Is the pilot inside the heli?'

The security chief nodded. 'He's under guard.' He pointed. 'And here is the case.'

'Are you certain that is the device?' Veintrop said.

Feyd al-Saoud looked to his expert, who nodded. 'I've opened the case. It's a nuclear bomb, all right.'

'Well, then,' Veintrop said with an oddly vibrant note to his voice, 'I'd open it again if I were you. Perhaps you haven't seen everything inside.'

Feyd al-Saoud glanced at Bourne, who nodded. 'Open it,' the security chief said to his man.

The man laid the case carefully down on the concrete floor and snapped the lid open.

'Look on the left side,' Veintrop said. 'No, nearer the rear.'

The Saudi craned his neck, then recoiled involuntarily. 'A timer's been activated.'

'That happened when you opened the case without using the code.'

Bourne recognized the note in his voice: It was triumph.

'How much time?' Feyd al-Saoud said.

'Four minutes, thirty-seven seconds.'

'I created the circuit,' Veintrop said. 'I can stop it.' He looked from one man to the other. 'In return, I want my freedom. No prosecution. No negotiation. A new life, paid in full.'

'Is that all?' Bourne hit him so hard that Veintrop bounced off the wall. He caught him on the rebound. 'Knife,' he said.

Feyd al-Saoud knew what was required now. He handed one to Bourne.

The moment Bourne took possession of the knife he buried the blade just above Veintrop's kneecap.

Veintrop screamed. 'What have you done?' Then he began to weep uncontrollably.

'No, Doctor, it's what *you've* done.' Bourne crouched down beside him, holding the bloody blade in his line of vision. 'You've got just under four minutes to disable the timer.'

Veintrop, holding his ruined knee, rocked back and forth on his backside. 'What . . . what about my terms?'

'Here are *my* terms.' Bourne flicked the blade and Veintrop screamed again.

'All right, all right!'

Bourne looked up. 'Put the open case in front of him.'

When that had been done, Bourne said, 'It's all yours, Doctor. But rest assured I'm going to be watching every move you make.'

Bourne stood, saw Feyd al-Saoud staring at him, his heavy lips pushed out in a silent whistle of relief.

Bourne watched while Veintrop worked on the timer. It took him just over two minutes, by Bourne's wristwatch. At the end of that time, he sat back, arms folded protectively around his ruined knee.

Feyd al-Saoud signed for his man to take a look.

'The wires are cut,' the man said. 'The timer's dead. There's no chance of detonation.'

Veintrop had returned to his mindless rocking. 'I need a painkiller,' he said dully.

Feyd al-Saoud called for his surgeon, then went to take possession of the nuclear device. Bourne got to it before him.

'I'm going to need this to get to Karim.'

The security chief frowned deeply. 'I don't understand.'

'I'm taking the route Fadi would have taken to Washington,' Bourne said in a tone that brooked no interference.

Even so, Feyd al-Saoud said, 'Do you think that's wise, Jason?'

'I'm afraid at this juncture wise doesn't enter into it,' Bourne replied. 'Karim has put himself into a position of such power inside CI he's all but untouchable. I've got to go another route.'

'I expect you have a plan, then.'

'I always have a plan.'

'All right. My surgeon will take charge of your friend.'

'No,' Bourne said. 'Martin comes with me.'

Again, Feyd al-Saoud recognized Bourne's steely tone of voice. 'Then my surgeon will accompany you.'

'Thank you,' Bourne said.

Feyd al-Saoud helped his friend load Martin Lindros into the helicopter. While Bourne laid down the law to Fadi's pilot, the security chief sent his man off the copter, then knelt to help his surgeon make Lindros as comfortable as possible.

'How long does he have?' Feyd al-Saoud said softly, for it was clear Lindros was dying.

The surgeon shrugged. 'An hour, give or take.'

Bourne was finished talking to the pilot, who now slipped into his chair. 'I need you to do something for me.'

Feyd al-Saoud rose up. 'Anything, my friend.'

'First, I need a phone. Mine is fried.'

The security chief was handed a cell by one of his men. Bourne transferred the chip that held all his phone numbers into the new model.

'Thanks. Now I want you to phone your contacts in the U.S. government, tell them that the plane I'll be taking is a Saudi diplomatic mission. As soon as I speak with the pilot, I'll send you the flight plan. I don't want any problems with Customs and Immigration.'

'Consider it done.'

'Then I want you to call CI, tell them the same thing. Only give them an ETA forty minutes later than the actual one I'll give you when the pilot has checked the weather.'

'My call to CI will alert the impostor—'

'Yes,' Bourne said. 'It will.'

Feyd al-Saoud's face was wreathed in concern. 'You play a terribly deadly game, Jason.'

Having delivered this warning, he embraced his friend warmly.

'Allah has given you wings. May He protect you on your mission.'

He kissed Bourne on both cheeks then, bending over, stepped out of the heli. The pilot threw a switch that retracted the camouflaged top of the helipad. When he was certain that all ground personnel were well clear of the rotor, he started the engine.

Bourne knelt beside Lindros and took his hand. Martin's good eye fluttered open. He stared up at Bourne, smiled with what was left of his mouth, and gripped Bourne's hand all the tighter.

Bourne felt tears come to his eyes. With an effort, he held them back. 'Fadi's dead, Martin,' he said over the mounting noise. 'You've got your wish. You're a hero.'

THIRTY-EIGHT

Karim was deliberately late to the directorate admin meeting. He wanted all seven of the directorate chiefs around the table when he walked in. The conference room was by design located adjacent to the DCI's office suite. In fact, there was a connecting door from the Old Man's suite into the conference room. Also by design, it was through this door that Karim made his entrance. He wanted to reiterate to the Seven, without having to utter a word, where he stood vis-à-vis them in the CI hierarchy.

'The DCI sends his regrets,' he said briskly, taking the Old Man's seat around the table. 'Anne, who's with him, tells me that he's still closeted with the president and the Joint Chiefs.'

Karim opened a thick dossier, only the first five pages of which were real – if you could call real disinformation he had carried in his head for months.

'Now that the imminent threat posed by Dujja has been eliminated, now that Dujja itself is a shell of itself, it's time we moved on to other matters.'

'One moment, Martin,' cut in the steely voice of Rob Batt, chief of operations. 'If I may, before we close the door on this one there's still the matter of Fadi himself to consider.'

Karim sat back, twisting a pen through his fingers. The worst thing he could do, he knew, was cut off this line of inquiry. As the meeting several days ago had indicated, he was on Batt's shit list. He wasn't about to do anything to raise Batt's level of distrust.

'By all means,' Karim said, 'let's discuss going after Fadi.'

'I agree with Rob,' Dick Symes, chief of the Intelligence Directorate, said. 'I'm in favor of committing a significant percentage of personnel to his capture.'

There were nods from several of the other chiefs arrayed around the table.

In the face of this rising wave, Karim said, 'In the absence of the Old Man, we'll naturally implement what the majority thinks best. However, I'd like to point out several things. First, having wiped out Dujja's most important base of operations, we have no idea whether Fadi is alive or dead. If he was in or near the facility in South Yemen, there's no doubt that he was incinerated along with everyone else. Second, if he was elsewhere at the time of the raid, we have no idea where he might be. For sure, he will have gone to ground. I say we allow time to pass, see what we pick up on the Dujja network. Let the terrorist world believe we've turned our attention elsewhere. If Fadi is alive, he'll begin to stir, and then we'll get a line on him.'

Karim looked from face to face. There were no frowns, no dissenting shakes of the head, no covert glances among the Seven.

'Third, and perhaps most important, we have to get our own house in order,' he continued. 'I can confirm the rumors that the Old Man has been under attack by Defense Secretary Halliday and his Pentagon lackey, Luther LaValle. Halliday knew about our mole, and he knew about the computer virus attack. It turns out that the late Matthew Lerner was also Halliday's man.'

This caused quite a stir around the table. Karim held up his hands, palms outward. 'I know, I know, we've all felt the turmoil caused by Lerner's attempt to realign CI. And now we know why the changes felt so alien to us – they were mandated by Halliday and his henchmen at NSA.

'Well, Lerner's dead. Whatever clandestine influence the defense secretary had here is gone. And now that the mole has been dispatched, we're free to do what should have been done years ago. We need to remake CI into an agency better equipped than any other to wage war on global terrorism.

'That's why my first proposal is to hire the uniquely qualified Arabs and Muslims drummed out of the various agencies in the wake of September 11. If we have any chance of winning this new war, we have to understand the terrorists who make up our patchwork enemy. We have to stop confusing Arab with Muslim, Saudi with Syrian, Azerbaijani with Afghani, Sunni with Shia.'

'Hard to argue with any of that,' Symes said.

'We can still take a vote on Rob's suggestion,' Karim said smoothly.

As all eyes turned to the chief of operations. 'That won't be necessary,' Batt said. 'I hearby withdraw my suggestion in favor of Martin's.'

Bourne sat on the floor of the helicopter facing the Saudi surgeon and his large black bag. Between them lay the bloody body of Martin Lindros. The doctor was continuing to give Martin something intravenously for the pain.

'The best I can do,' the surgeon had said as they had sped away from Miran Shah, 'is to make him as comfortable as I can.'

Bourne stared down into Lindros's ruined face, conjuring up an image of his friend as he had been. He wasn't entirely successful. The .45 bullet from Fadi's gun had exploded along the right side of his head, destroying the eye socket and half the brow ridge. The surgeon had been able to stop the bleeding, but because the gun had been fired from close range, the damage had been massive enough to cause the shutdown of Martin's vital organs. According to the surgeon, the cascade effect had progressed far enough as to make any attempt at saving Martin's life fruitless.

Martin was in a period of uneasy sleep now. Watching him, Bourne felt a combination of rage and despair. Why had this happened to Martin? Why wasn't he able to keep him alive? He knew his distress came from helplessness. It was the same feeling he'd had on seeing Marie for the last time. Helplessness was the one emotion Bourne could not abide. It got under his skin, buried itself in his psyche like an itch he couldn't scratch, a mocking voice he couldn't silence.

With a guttural growl, he turned away. They had reached a high enough altitude to be clear of the mountains, so he opened his cell phone, tried Soraya again. It rang, which was a good sign. Once again, she didn't answer, which wasn't. This time, he left a brief voice-mail message that evoked Odessa. It would be cryptic to anyone but Soraya herself.

Then he called Deron's cell. He was still down in Florida.

'I've got a problem only you can handle,' Bourne said without preamble.

'Shoot.'

This kind of abbreviated conversation was typical with them.

'I need a full kit.'

'No problem. Where are you?'

'About ten hours out of Washington.'

'Kay. Tyrone's got my keys. He'll get it all together. Dulles or Reagan International?'

'Neither. We're scheduled to set down eighteen kilometers south of Annandale,' Bourne said, giving Deron the coordinates in Virginia he'd gotten from the pilot. 'It's on the extreme eastern edge of property owned by Sistain Labs.' Sistain was a subsidiary of IVT. 'Thanks, Deron.'

'No biggie, my man. I just wish I was there myself.'

As Bourne disconnected, Martin stirred.

'Jason.'

Martin's reedy whisper caused him to put his head beside his friend's. The odor of lacerated flesh, of impending death, was nauseating.

'I'm here, Martin.'

'The man who took my place—'

'Karim. Fadi's brother, I know. I worked it all out, Martin. It started with the Odessa mission Conklin gave me. I was with Soraya at the meet with her contact. A young woman came running toward us. It was Sarah ibn Ashef, Karim and Fadi's sister. I shot at her, but I didn't hit her as I assumed I had. It was one of Fadi's men. He shot her dead because she was having an affair.'

Martin's one remaining eye, red-rimmed, burning still with life, fixed on Bourne. 'It's Karim . . . you have . . . to get, Jason.' He was wheezing, his breath coming in herky-jerky gasps, clotted with pink phlegm and blood. 'He's the wily one, the . . . chess player . . . the spider sitting at the . . . center of the . . . Jesus, of the . . . web.'

His eye was open wide, moving to the spasms of pain racking him. 'Fadi . . . Fadi was just the . . . front, the rallying . . . point. Karim is the . . . truly . . . dangerous one.'

'Martin, I heard every word you said, and it's time to rest now,' Bourne said.

'No, no . . .' Lindros seemed to have been seized by a peculiar frenzy. The energy of a small star radiated from him, bathing Bourne in its glow. 'Plenty of time to . . . rest when . . . I'm . . . dead.'

He had started to bleed again. The surgeon leaned over, wiped the blood away with a gauze pad that soon enough was soaked through.

'For Karim it isn't . . . simply America, Jason. It's CI itself. He hates us – all of us with . . . every fiber of his . . . being.

That ... that's why he ... was willing to ... gamble ... everything, his entire ... life and soul to ... get ... inside.'

'What does he mean to do? Martin, what does he mean to do?'

'Destroy CI.' Martin looked up at Bourne. 'I wish I knew more. Christ, Jason, how I fucked up.'

'It wasn't your fault, Martin.' Bourne's expression was stern. 'If you blame yourself for any of this, I'll be extremely angry with you.'

Lindros tried to laugh, but with all the blood he brought up he didn't quite make it. 'We can't have that, now, can we?'

Bourne wiped his mouth.

Like a momentary loss of electricity through a power grid, something flickered across Lindros's face – a window to a dark, cold place. He began to shiver.

'Jason, listen, when this ... is all ... over, I want you to send a dozen red roses to Moira. You'll find her address in ... my cell phone at home. Cremate my body. Take my ashes to the Cloisters in New York City.'

Bourne felt a burning behind his eyes. 'Of course, I'll do whatever you want.'

'I'm glad you're ... here.'

'You're my best friend, Martin. My *only* friend.'

'It's sad, then, for ... both of us.' Lindros tried to smile again, gave up, exhausted. 'You know ... the thing ... between us, Jason ... what bound us? You ... can't remember your past and ... I can't ... bear to remember ... mine.'

The moment came, then, and Bourne could feel it. An instant ago Martin's good eye was regarding him with grave intelligence; now it was fixed in the middle distance, staring at something Bourne had sensed many times, but never seen.

*

Soraya, horrified not only by what she saw but also by its implications, stood transfixed, staring at the half-embalmed corpse of the Old Man. It was like seeing your father dead, she thought. You knew it had to happen someday, but when that day came you couldn't wrap your mind around it. To her, as to everyone else at CI, he had seemed indestructible as well as invincible. He had been their moral compass, the font of their worldwide power for so long that now with him gone she felt naked and horribly vulnerable.

In the wake of the first shock, she felt a cold panic grip her. With the Old Man dead, who was running CI? Of course, there were the directorate chiefs, but everyone from the upper echelons on down knew that Martin Lindros was the DCI's anointed successor.

Which meant that the false Lindros was heading up CI. *God in heaven*, she thought. *He's going to take CI down – this was part of the plan all along*. What a coup for Fadi and Dujja to be able to destroy America's most effective espionage agency just before they detonated a nuclear bomb on American soil.

In the blink of an eye, she saw it all. The barrels of C-4 Tyrone had seen were meant for CI headquarters. But how on earth was Dujja going to get the explosives past security? She knew Fadi had devised a method to do so. Perhaps it would be easy now that the false Lindros had effected a coup.

All at once Soraya snapped back into the here and now. Given the Old Man's murder, it was imperative she gain access to CI headquarters. She had to inform the seven directorate chiefs of the truth, her own safety be damned. But how? The false Lindros would have her picked up the moment she showed her ID to CI security. And there was absolutely no way to sneak into HQ undetected.

*

As the helicopter descended through the clouds toward the private airstrip in Mazar-i-Sharif, Bourne sat beside Martin Lindros, his head bowed. His mind was filled with connections, some to memories, others that went nowhere because the memories were lost to him. In that very important respect, connections were of paramount importance to him. Now a key one was gone. It was only now, in the aftermath, that Bourne understood how important Martin had been to him. Amnesia could engender many things in the mind, including insanity – or at least the semblance of it, which more or less amounted to the same thing.

Being able to connect with Martin after Conklin was murdered had been a lifeline. Now Martin was dead. He no longer had Marie to come home to. When the stress level became too great, what would prevent him from slipping into the madness that came from the forest of broken connections within his brain?

He held on to the briefcase as the pilot set the helicopter down on the tarmac.

'You're coming with us,' Bourne said to the pilot. 'I need your help for a bit longer.'

The pilot rose and, together with Bourne, picked up Lindros's body. With some difficulty, they maneuvered it off the helicopter. A larger high-speed jet was sitting on the tarmac, fueled and ready. The two men made the transfer, and Bourne spoke with the jet's pilot. Then Bourne ordered the copter pilot to ferry the surgeon back to Miran Shah. Bourne warned him that Feyd al-Saoud's team would be monitoring both his flight progress and his communications.

Ten minutes later, with the two men and the corpse on board, the jet rolled down the runway. Gathering speed, it lifted off into the slate-gray clouds of an oncoming storm.

*

Ever since he'd taken the call from Soraya, Peter Marks had found it impossible to concentrate on his work. The encrypted communications from Dujja seemed like so much Martian to him. Feigning a migraine, he finally had to hand them off to a colleague.

For some time, he sat at his desk, brooding. He couldn't help but examine every aspect of that call, as well as his response to it. At first, he'd had to get over his anger. How dare Soraya try to get him involved in whatever mess she had made for herself? That was the moment he'd almost picked up the phone and punched Lindros's extension, to report her call.

But with his hand halfway to the receiver, something had stopped him. What was it? On the face of it, Soraya's story was so outlandish that it didn't even rate considering. First, they all knew that the Dujja nuclear threat had been averted. Second, Lindros himself had warned everyone that Soraya had been unhinged by Jason Bourne's death. And she certainly had sounded nuts on the phone.

But then there was her warning about the danger to the CI headquarters building. With all his years of training, it would be remiss of him to ignore that part of her story. For the second time, he almost punched Lindros's extension. What stopped him was the hole in his reasoning. Namely, why would one part of her story be true and the other made up? He couldn't believe anyone – let alone Soraya – would be that unhinged.

Which meant that he was back to square one. What to do about her call? His fingers drummed a tattoo on the desktop. Of course, he could do nothing, simply forgetting the conversation had ever taken place. But then if something did happen to headquarters, he'd never be able to forgive himself. Assuming, of course, he was still alive to feel the insupportable guilt.

Before he could second-guess himself into inaction, he

grabbed the receiver and dialed his contact at the White House.

'Hey, Ken. Peter here,' he said when the other answered. 'I've got an urgent message for the DCI. Could you scare him up for me? He's in with the POTUS.'

'No, he's not, Peter. The POTUS is meeting with the Joint Chiefs.'

Peter's heart skipped a very small beat. 'When did the DCI leave?'

'Hold on, I'll access the log.' A moment later, Ken said, 'You sure about your intel? The DCI hasn't been here today, and he isn't on the POTUS's or anyone else's schedule.'

'Thanks, Ken,' Peter said in a strangled voice. 'My mistake.'

Oh, dear God, he thought. *Soraya is as sane as I am.* He looked through the open door to his cubicle. He could just see a corner of Lindros's office. *If it isn't Lindros, who the hell is running Typhon?*

He lunged for his cell phone. As soon as he could get his fingers to work properly, he punched in Soraya's number.

THIRTY-NINE

Tyrone was waiting patiently for Soraya when she poked her head out of the glass-paned door. As she did so, she felt her cell phone vibrate. Tyrone signaled to her and she ran silently into the shadows at the ramp's mouth.

'The two shitbirds finished,' he said in a low voice. 'They upstairs now wit they peeps.'

'We'd better go,' she said.

But before she could move back up the ramp, he took hold of her arm. 'We ain't finished here, girl.' He pointed. 'See that past the Ford?'

'What is it?' She craned her neck. 'A limo?'

'Not jus' any limo. This one got government plates on her.'

'Government plates?'

'Not ony that, they's CI plates.'

Catching her sharp glance, he said, 'Deron taught me t'look out for 'em.' He motioned with his head. 'Yo, check it out, yo.'

Soraya stole around the flank of the Ford. Immediately she saw the gleaming expanse of the limo and its license plates. She almost gasped out loud. Not only were they CI plates, they were the plates on the Old Man's limo. All at once she understood why they had taken the trouble to embalm the DCI. They needed the body, which meant two things: It had to be malleable, and it must not stink.

Her cell buzzed again. She pulled it out, looked at the

screen. It was Peter Marks. What the hell did he want? Crab-walking her way back to Tyrone, she said, 'They've killed the director of CI. That's his limo.'

'Yeah, but what they doing wit it?'

'Maybe that's where they killed him.'

'Mebbe.' Tyrone scratched his chin. 'But I seen 'em foolin' wit the inside.'

For the third time her cell buzzed. This time, it was Bourne. She needed desperately to tell him what was going on, but she couldn't risk a prolonged conversation now. 'We've got to get out of here now, Tyrone.'

'Mebbe you,' he said, his eye on the limo. 'But I'm gonna stay here awhile longer.'

'It's too dangerous,' Soraya said. 'We're both leaving now.'

Tyrone raised his gun. 'Doan give me no orders. I done tol yo what I was doin'. You make yo own choice.'

Soraya shook her head. 'I'm not leaving you here. I don't want you any more involved than you already are.'

'Yo, I killed two men fo yo, girl. How much more involved could I get?'

She had to admit he had a point. 'What I don't get is why you got involved in the first place.'

He gave her a grin because he knew she was done fighting him. 'Yo mean what in it fo me? Hood where Deron an I brought up, homeboys only do things f'two reasons: t'make money or t'fuck sumbody over. Hopefully both. Now I watch Deron for a while. He pull hisself outta the shit; he make sumpin of his bad self. I admire that, but I always thought: That him, not me. Now wit this shit, I see I got a shot at a future.'

'You've also got a shot at getting killed.'

Tyrone shrugged. 'Yo, ain't no more than every day inna hood, yo.'

At that moment, he pulled out a PDA.

'I didn't know you had anything but a burner,' she said, referring to the throwaway cell phones she'd seen him carry.

'Only one person knows bout this PET. One who give it t'me.'

'PET?'

'Yeah. Personal Electronic Thingy.'

He checked the PET, obviously reading an e-mail. 'Shit.' Then he glanced up. 'What a we waitin' fo? Let's get the fuck outta Dodge.'

They walked back up the ramp to the panel they'd found for the lights and the automatic door opener. 'What changed your mind?'

Tyrone put a disgusted expression on his face. 'Deron say I gotta split right this fuckin' minute. I got yo man Bourne's back.'

Peter Marks, lurking in the corridor near the elevator, caught Rob Batt's eye as the Seven emerged from the conference room. Marks had worked for Batt before being chosen by Martin Lindros for Typhon. In fact, metaphorically speaking, he'd cut his eyeteeth on Batt's methodology; he still considered the chief of operations his rabbi within CI.

So it was not surprising that Marks, having caught the older man's eye, got his attention immediately. Batt peeled off from the others and turned a corner into the corridor where Marks stood.

'What are you doing here, Peter?'

'Waiting for you, actually.' Marks glanced nervously around. 'We need to talk.'

'Can it wait?'

'No, sir, it can't.'

Batt frowned. 'Okay. My office.'

'Outside would be best, sir.'

The chief of operations gave him a curious glance, then shrugged.

They took the elevator down together and walked across the lobby, then out the front door. There was a rose garden on the east side of the property, which is where Marks led them. When they were a reasonably safe distance from the building, he told Batt word for word what Soraya Moore had told him.

'I didn't believe it, either, sir,' he said, seeing the look on Batt's face. 'But then I called a buddy of mine at the White House. The Old Man isn't there, never was there today.'

Batt rubbed his blued jowls with one hand. 'Then where the fuck is he?'

'That's just the thing, sir.' Marks, already ill at ease, was getting more nervous with every moment that passed. 'I've spent the last forty minutes on the phone. I don't know where he is, and neither does anyone else.'

'Anne?'

'Also AWOL.'

'Christ Jesus.'

Marks rechecked their immediate environment. 'Sir, incredible as it might seem on the face of it, I think we have to take Soraya's story seriously.'

'Incredible is right, Peter. Not to mention insane. Don't tell me you believe this—' Batt shook his head as words failed him. 'Where the hell is she?'

'That I don't know,' Marks conceded. 'I've put in a couple of calls to her cell, but she hasn't gotten back to me. She's terrified of Lindros finding her.'

'I should hope to fuck she is. We need to get her in here, pronto, process this crap out of her before she causes a panic inside the agency.'

'If she's wrong, then where's the Old Man and Anne?'

Batt headed back out of the rose garden. 'That's what I'm going to find out,' he said over his shoulder.

'What about Soraya—?'

'When she calls you, make her believe you're on her side. Get her in here, pronto.'

As the chief of operations disappeared inside headquarters, Marks's phone sang. He checked the incoming call. Punching a button, he said, 'Hi, Soraya. Look, I was thinking about what you said, and I checked at the White House. Both the Old Man and Anne are missing.'

'Of course they are,' he heard her say in his ear. 'I've just seen the Old Man. He's laid out on a mortuary slab with a bullet hole in his heart.'

Along with the Seven, Karim sat in the conference room adjacent to the Old Man's suite. They were all listening to the message from the Saudi secret service informing them of the takeover of the Dujja nuclear facility in Miran Shah. Unlike the others, however, he received the communiqué with equal parts confusion and trepidation. Was this a ploy by his brother because of the heightened terror alert, or had something gone horribly wrong?

He knew there was only one way to find out. He left the conference room, but on the way to the elevator he glimpsed Peter Marks out of the corner of his eye. This was the second time he'd noticed Marks up here where he didn't belong. A warning bell went off in his head and, instead of entering the elevator with some of the other chiefs, he turned to his left. The corner behind which he stood gave him a view of the conference room door. As Rob Batt emerged, Marks approached him. They spoke for a moment. Batt, initially cool, nodded, and together they walked back into the conference room, shutting the door behind them.

Karim walked very quickly into the DCI's suite, past the desk where a young man from Signals was filling in for Anne. The man nodded to him as he went into the Old Man's office.

Once behind the desk, he toggled on a switch. Two voices from the conference room became audible.

'. . . *from Soraya,*' Marks was saying. '*She claims to have seen the DCI's body in a morgue with a bullet hole through his heart.*'

'*What is this woman on? I spoke to Martin. He's heard from the Old Man.*'

'*Where is he?*'

'*On personal business, with Anne,*' Batt said, with what sounded like a yawn.

'*Soraya's also heard from Bourne.*'

'*Bourne's dead.*'

'*He isn't. He found the real nuclear facility. It's in Miran Shah, on the border of—*'

'*I know where Miran Shah is, Peter,*' Batt snapped. '*What is this crap?*'

'*She said you can verify everything with Feyd al-Saoud.*'

'*That's just what I need, go crawling to the chief of Saudi security for our own intel.*'

'*She also said Bourne killed Fadi. He's on his way here in Fadi's jet.*'

There was more to the conversation, but Karim had heard enough. His skin felt as if ants were crawling all over it. He wanted to scream, to tear himself limb from limb.

Bolting from the office, he took the elevator down. But instead of picking up a CI vehicle in the basement parking area, for which he'd have to sign, he hurried out the front door and walked off the grounds.

The night was well advanced in the district. The low sky, full of glowering clouds, seemed to absorb the spangle of lights from the city. Shadows rose to monument height.

He stopped at the corner of 21st and Constitution and called a taxi service. Seven agonizing minutes later, the cab pulled up and he got in.

Thirteen minutes after that, he alit in front of an Avis

rental and began to walk away from it. When the taxi had disappeared, he reversed course, went into the Avis office, and rented a car, using false ID. He paid cash, took possession of the GM car, asked for directions to Dulles airport, then drove off.

In fact, he had no intention of going to Dulles. His destination was the Sistain Labs airstrip south of Annandale.

The jet, banking low over Occoquan Bay, turned north heading toward the airstrip on the fist-shaped peninsula that jutted out into the water. The pilot, following the glide path of the lights, brought the jet down in a whisper of a landing. As they taxied along the runway, losing speed with every meter, Bourne saw Tyrone astride his Ninja, a hard-sided black leather case strapped across his back. He glanced at his watch. They were right on time, which meant he had approximately thirty-five minutes to prepare himself for Karim.

En route, he'd spoken to Soraya several times. They had brought each other up to date with news that was both shocking and gratifying. Fadi was dead, Dujja's nuclear threat thwarted, but Karim had killed the Old Man, consolidating his power inside CI. Now he was planning to destroy CI headquarters and everyone in it, coordinating the devastating attack with the detonation of the nuke. Soraya had one ally inside CI – the Typhon agent named Peter Marks, but Marks wasn't a rebel by nature. She didn't know how far he would bend the regs for her.

As for the Old Man's death, Bourne had mixed feelings. He had been made to feel like the prodigal grandson, a wayward who, on returning home, was subject to his grandfather's spiteful wrath. More than once, the DCI had tried to have him killed. But then he'd never understood Bourne, and so had been deeply frightened of him. Bourne could blame the Old Man for many things, but not for that.

Bourne had never fit into the CI scheme – he'd been shoehorned into an agency that despised individualists. He'd never asked for the association, but there it was. Or rather, there it had been.

Now he turned his attention to Karim.

The plane had come to a stop on the tarmac; the engines whined down. Bourne, taking the pilot with him, went down the cabin aisle, opened the door, and lowered the stairs for Tyrone, who had driven up beside the jet.

Tyrone came up the stairway, dropping the black leather case at Bourne's feet.

'Hey, Tyrone. Thanks.'

'Yo, need some light in here, yo. Can't see a thing.'

'That's the point.'

Tyrone was peering at him. 'Yo look like a fuckin' Arab.'

Bourne laughed. He pulled the bag up, went over to a set of facing seats, opened it up. Tyrone became aware of the Arab pilot, a dark-skinned, bearded man who glowered at him, half defiant, half fearful.

'Who the fuck is this?'

'Terrorist,' Bourne said simply. He paused in unloading the bag long enough to drink in the situation. 'You want to get a taste?'

Tyrone laughed. 'Killed two of 'em was about to do for Miss Spook.'

'Now, who would that be?'

Tyrone's dark eyes flashed. 'I know yo an Deron are close, but doan fuck wid me.'

'I'm not fucking with you, Tyrone. Excuse me for this, but I'm on a deadline.' Bourne turned on one of the overhead seat lights, opened his cell, and brought up the photos he'd taken of Fadi's face. Then he set about opening small pots, jars, tubes, and various oddly shaped prosthetics. 'Would you please tell me what you're talking about?'

Tyrone hesitated for a minute, studying Bourne to see if

he was still fucking with him. Apparently, he decided he'd been wrong. 'Talkin' 'bout Miss Spook. Soraya.'

Bourne, glancing at the photos of Fadi, placed several prosthetics in his mouth and worked his jaws around experimentally. 'Then I owe you a thank-you.'

'Yo, what the fuck happened to yo voice, man?'

Bourne said: 'As you can see, I'm becoming a new man.' He continued with his transformation, finding a thick beard from the pile inside the case, shaping it with a scissors so that it was the exact replica of Fadi's. He applied the beard, took a look at himself in the magnifying mirror he pulled from the case.

He handed his cell to Tyrone. 'Do me a favor, would you? How much do I look like the man in these photos?'

Tyrone blinked, as if he couldn't believe what Bourne had asked of him. Then he looked at the photos one by one. Before moving on to the next one, he studied Bourne's face.

'Fuck me,' he said finally. 'Yo, how yo do that shit, man?'

'It's a gift,' Bourne said, meaning it. 'Now, look. I need you to do me another favor.' He glanced at his watch. 'In just over eleven minutes, this bastard Soraya's been after is going to be coming here. I want you out of the way. I need you to take care of something for me. Something important. In the next cabin is my friend, Martin Lindros. He's dead. I want you to contact a mortuary. His remains need to be cremated. Okay? Will you do that for me?'

'Got my cycle, so I gots t'sling him across my lap, that okay?'

Bourne nodded. 'Treat him with respect, Tyrone, okay? Now take off. And don't use the front entrance.'

'Never do.'

Bourne laughed. 'I'll see you on the other side.'

Tyrone looked at him. 'The otha side a what?'

FORTY

Driving into Virginia, Karim called Abd al-Malik at the mortuary.

'I need three men at the Sistain Labs location at once.'

'That will leave us with no one to spare.'

'Do it,' Karim said shortly.

'One moment, sir.' After a slight pause. 'They're on their way.'

'Is the DCI's body prepared?'

'Forty minutes, possibly a bit more, sir. This isn't your normal embalming job.'

'How does he look? That's what's most important.'

'Indeed, sir. His cheeks are rosy.' Abd al-Malik made a pleased sound in the back of his throat. 'Believe me, security will be convinced he's still alive.'

'Good. As soon as you're finished, get him into the limo. The timetable has been accelerated. Fadi wants the CI building taken out as soon as humanly possible. Call me when you're in position.'

'It will be done,' Abd al-Malik said.

Karim knew it would. Abd al-Malik, the most accomplished member of his sleeper cell in the district, and its leader, had never failed him.

Traffic was light. It took him thirty-eight minutes to arrive at the main entrance, on the western side of the Sistain Labs property. The place was deserted. He'd had to restrain

547

himself twice on the drive down here – once when a kid in what the Americans called a muscle car cut him off; again when a trucker had come up behind him, sounding his air horn. Both times, he'd pulled out his Glock, was ready to pull the trigger, when he'd caught himself.

It was Bourne, not these poor fools, he wanted to kill. His rage – the Desert Wind he'd inherited from his grandfather – was running high, giving him hair-trigger responses to stimuli. But this wasn't the desert; he wasn't among Bedouins who would know better than to antagonize him.

It was Bourne; it was always Bourne. Bourne had murdered innocent Sarah, the pride of the family. Karim had forgiven her her impious views, her unexplained absences, her wanting her independence, putting those things down to the same English blood that pulsed through his veins. He'd overcome his Western blood, which was why he had embarked on a program to reeducate her in the ways of the desert, the Saudi ethos that was her true heritage.

Now Bourne had killed Fadi, the public figurehead. Fadi, who had relied so heavily on the planning and the funds of his older brother, just as Karim had counted on his younger brother to protect him. He'd forgiven Fadi his hot blood, his excesses, because these traits were vital to a public leader, who drew the faithful to him with both his fiery rhetoric and his incendiary exploits.

They were both gone now – the innocent and the commander, one the tower of moral strength, the other of physical. He, of all of Abu Sarif Hamid ibn Ashef al-Wahhib's children, remained. Alive, but alone. All that was left were the memories he held close to him of Fadi and Sarah ibn Ashef. The same memories held by his father – maimed, paralyzed, helplessly bound to his bed, needing a special harness to get into the wheelchair he despised.

This was the end for Bourne, he vowed. This was the end for all the infidels.

He made his way through the long, curving drives that skirted the low, sleek green-glass and black-brick lab buildings. A final swing around to the left brought the airfield into sight. Just beyond the parked jet was the fat gray-blue crescent of water adjacent to Occoquan Bay.

Nearing the landing strip, he slowed, took a long, careful survey of the area. The jet sat alone on the tarmac, near the far end of the runway. No vehicles were in sight. No boat plied the wintry waters of Belmont Bay. No helicopters hovered anywhere in the vicinity. Yet Fadi was dead, and Bourne sat inside the jet in his place.

Of course there wouldn't be anyone here. Unlike him, Bourne had no support to back him up. He pulled the car over out of sight of the jet, lit a cigarette, waited. Quite soon the black Ford carrying his men arrived, pulling up alongside him.

He got out and gave them their instructions, telling them what to expect and what they should do. Then he leaned against the front fender of the car, smoking still as the Ford drove onto the tarmac.

When it reached the plane, the door swung inward and the stairway was lowered. Two of the three men got out, trotted up the stairs.

Karim spat the butt from his mouth, ground it beneath the heel of his shoe. Then he climbed into the rental car and headed back along the drive to the lab building hunkered eerily alone, on the northern fringe of the property, hard against the waste dump.

I can help you, Soraya,' Peter Marks said, his cell to his ear, 'but I think we should meet.'

'Why? You have to be my eyes and ears at HQ. I need you to keep track of the impostor.'

'I don't know where Lindros is,' Peter said. 'He isn't in his office. In fact, he's nowhere in the building. He didn't check out with his assistant. Is this an epidemic?'

He heard the sharpness of Soraya's indrawn breath. 'What is it?'

'Okay,' Soraya said. 'I'll meet you, but I pick the place.'

'Whatever you want.'

She gave him the address of the mortuary on the northeast edge of Rock Creek Park. 'Get there,' she said, 'fast as you can.'

Marks checked out a CI vehicle, making the trip in record time. He pulled up across the street and down the block from the rear of the mortuary, then sat in his car as Soraya had directed. Before leaving headquarters, he'd toyed with the idea of contacting Rob Batt, of getting permission to take several agents with him, but the urgency of the meet made it imperative that he not take the time to persuade Batt to divert personnel.

Soraya tapping on the glass of the passenger window caused him to jump. He'd been so wrapped up in his thoughts that he hadn't seen her approach. This made him doubly nervous, because he was out in the field where she had the distinct advantage over him. He'd been nothing but a desk jockey his entire career – which, he supposed, was the real reason he hadn't wanted to take anyone with him. He had something to prove to his rabbi.

He unlocked the doors and she slipped into the passen-
's seat. She certainly didn't look as if she'd cracked.

nted you to come here,' she said a bit breathlessly,
his is the mortuary where the Old Man is.'

d to these words as if they were part of a dream

550

he was having. He had wrapped his hand around his gun when she was opening the door and he was out of sight to her. Now, as if he himself were in a dream, he brought the gun to her head and said, 'Sorry, Soraya, but you're coming back to headquarters with me.'

The two terrorists who boarded the jet blinked in the semi-darkness. They looked stunned when they recognized him.

'Fadi,' the taller of the men said. 'Where is Jason Bourne?'

'Bourne is dead,' Bourne said. 'I killed him in Miran Shah.'

'But Karim al-Jamil said he would be on board.'

Bourne held up the briefcase with the nuclear device. 'As you can see, he was mistaken. There's been a change in plan. I need to see my brother.'

'At once, Fadi.'

They didn't search the plane, didn't see the pilot Bourne had tied and gagged.

As they led Bourne to the black Ford, the tall man said, 'Your brother is nearby.'

They all got into the Ford, Bourne in the backseat with one of the men. Bourne kept his face averted from the runway lights, the only light source. As long as he kept his face in semi-shadow, he'd be fine. These men were reacting to a familiar voice, familiar body language. These were a mimic's most powerful weapons. You needed to convince the mind, not the eye.

The driver left the airfield, looped around to the north, stopped at the side of a black-brick building that stood some distance away from the others. Bourne could see the slag pit as they opened a huge corrugated-iron door and led him inside.

The interior was huge and empty. There were no interior

walls. Oil stains on the concrete floor indicated that it was, in fact, an airplane hangar. Light came in through the door, as well as through square windows set high up in the walls, but it soon dissipated in the vastness, swallowed up by great swaths of shadow.

'Karim al-Jamil,' the tall man called, 'it was your brother who was on the plane, not Jason Bourne. He's with us, and he has the device.'

A figure appeared out of the shadows.

'My brother is dead,' Karim said.

Behind Bourne, the men tensed.

'I'm not going anywhere with you,' Soraya said.

Marks was about to reply when the wall at the back of the mortuary loading bay slid down.

'What the hell—?' he said.

Soraya took advantage of his surprise and bolted out of the car. Marks was about to go after her when he saw the DCI's limo emerge, then head down the street away from him. He forgot all about Soraya. He put his car in gear, peeling out after the limo. The Old Man was supposed to be away on personal business. What was he doing here?

As he raced after the limo, he dimly heard Soraya shouting for him to turn back. He ignored her. Of course she'd say that; she was sure the Old Man was dead.

Up ahead, the limo stopped at a red light. He pulled up alongside it, scrolled down his window.

'Hey!' he called. 'Peter Marks, CI! Open up!'

The driver's window remained in place. Marks put the car in PARK, got out, pounded on the window.

He pulled out his ID. 'Open up, dammit! Open up!'

The window slid down. He caught an instant's glimpse of the Old Man sitting bolt upright in the back. Then the driver aimed a Luger P-08 at his face and pulled the trigger.

The detonation burst his eardrums. He flew backward, arms outstretched, dead before he hit the pavement.

The limo's window slid back up and, as the light turned green, it rolled swiftly down the street.

Karim stood staring intently at Bourne. 'It can't be. Brother, I was told you were dead.'

Bourne raised the briefcase. 'And yet,' he said in Fadi's voice, 'I come in the guise of destruction.'

'Let the infidel beware!'

'Truly.' Even though Bourne knew he was looking at Karim, it was unnerving to face this man who was a dead ringer for his best friend. 'We're together again, brother!'

Martin had warned him that Karim was the dangerous one. *'He's the chess player,'* Martin had said, *'the spider sitting at the center of the web.'* Bourne held no illusions. The moment Karim asked him an intimate question, one only his brother would know, the masquerade would be over.

It didn't take that long.

Karim beckoned. 'Come into the light, brother, that I may once more look upon you after so many months.'

Bourne took a step forward; light flooded his face.

Karim stood stock-still. His head rocked a little, as if he had developed a palsy. 'You're as much a chameleon as Fadi was.'

'Brother, I've brought the device. How could you mistake me?'

'I overheard a CI agent say—'

'Not Peter Marks.' Bourne took a shot because it was all he had left. Marks was the only one in CI Soraya had contacted.

Confused again, Karim frowned. 'What about him?'

'Marks is Soraya Moore's conduit. He's repeating the disinformation we fed her.'

Karim gave a wolfish grin; the doubt cleared from his eyes. 'Wrong answer. CI believes my brother was killed in the raid on the false Dujja facility in South Yemen. But you wouldn't have known that, Bourne, would you?'

He gave a sign and the three men behind Bourne grabbed him, then held his arms at his sides. Without taking his eyes from Bourne's, Karim stepped forward, wrenched the briefcase out of his hand.

Soraya was running to where Peter Marks lay dead, spread-eagled on the curb, when she heard the deep-throated roar of a motorcycle approaching from behind. Pulling her gun, she swung around and saw Tyrone on his Ninja. He had just dropped Lindros's corpse at the mortuary.

Slowing, he allowed her to climb aboard, then took off.

'You saw what happened. They killed Peter.'

'We gotta stop them.' Tyrone jumped a red light. 'You put alla pieces t'gether – C-Four explosive, a replica of yo boss's limo, yo boss hisself lyin' flat-out on a embalming table, whattaya got?'

'That's how they're going to get in!' Soraya said. 'Security will take one look at the Old Man in the backseat and wave the limo through into the underground parking lot.'

'Where the foundation of the building is.'

Tyrone, bending low over the Ninja's handlebars, put on a burst of speed.

'We can't shoot at the limo,' Soraya said, 'without running the risk of setting off the C-Four and killing who knows how many bystanders.'

'An we can't allow it t'get to CI headquarters,' Tyrone said. 'So what d'we do?'

The answer was provided for them as one of the limo's rear windows slid down and someone began firing at them.

*

Bourne stood without trying to move. He tried to clear his mind of the image of Martin Lindros's ruined face, but in fact he found he didn't want to. Martin was with him, speaking to him, demanding retribution for what had been done to him. Bourne felt him; Bourne heard him.

Patience, he whispered silently.

Centering himself, he felt where each of the three men was in relation to himself. Then he said: 'My one regret is that I never finished what I started in Odessa. Your father is still alive.'

'Only you would call that kind of existence living,' Karim snapped. 'Every time I'm in his presence, I vow anew that I'll make you pay for what you did to him.'

'Too bad he can't see you as you are today,' Bourne said. 'He'd take a gun and shoot you himself. If only he was able.'

'I understand you, Bourne, better than you think.' Karim stood barely a pace away from Bourne. 'Look at you. To everyone but ourselves you're Fadi and I'm Lindros. We're in our own separate world, locked in our circle of revenge. Isn't that what you're thinking? Isn't that how you planned it? Isn't that why you've made yourself up to look like my brother?'

He shifted the briefcase from one hand to the other. 'It's also why you're trying to bait me. An angry man is easier to defeat, isn't that how the Tao of Bourne goes?' He laughed. 'But in fact, with this last chameleon act of yours you've done me an incalculable service. You think I'm going to shoot you dead, here and now. How wrong you are! Because after I detonate the nuclear device, after I destroy CI headquarters, I'm going to take you back to whatever is left of CI. I'll shoot you there. And so, having killed Fadi, the world's most notorious terrorist, Martin Lindros will become a national hero. And now that I've killed the DCI, who do you think a grateful president will elevate to the post?'

He laughed again. 'I'll be running the agency, Bourne. I'll be able to remake it in my own image. How's that for irony?'

At the mention of the fate of CI headquarters, Bourne felt Martin's voice stirring inside him. *Not yet*, he thought. *Not yet*.

'What I find ironic,' he said, 'is what happened to Sarah ibn Ashef.'

Fire leapt into Karim's eyes. He backhanded Bourne across the face. 'You who murdered her are not fit to speak my sister's name!'

'I didn't murder her,' Bourne said slowly and distinctly.

Karim spat in Bourne's face.

'I couldn't have shot her. Both Soraya and I were too far away. We both were using Glock 21s. Sarah ibn Ashef was all the way across the plaza when she was shot dead. As you well know, the Glock is accurate up to twenty-five meters. Your sister was at least fifty meters away when she was killed. I didn't realize it at the time; everything happened too quickly.'

His face a taut mask, Karim struck Bourne again.

Bourne, having expected the blow, shook it off. 'Muta ibn Aziz refreshed my memory, however. He and his brother were in the right position that night. They were at the right distance.'

Karim grabbed Bourne by the throat. 'You dare to make a mockery of my sister's death?' He was fairly shaking with rage. 'The brothers were like family. To even insinuate—'

'It's precisely because they *were* like family that Abbud ibn Aziz shot your sister to death.'

'I'll kill you for that!' Karim screamed as he began to strangle Bourne. 'I'll make you wish you'd never been born!'

*

Tyrone zigzagged the Ninja through the streets, following the limo. He could hear the bullets whizzing past them. He knew what it was like to be shot at; he knew the agony of having a loved one shot dead in a drive-by. His only defense was study. He knew bullets the way his crew knew gangsta rappers or porn stars. He knew the characteristics of every caliber, every Parabellum, every hollow-point. His own Walther PPK was loaded with hollow-cavity bullets – like hollow-points on steroids. When they impacted with a soft target – human flesh, for instance – they expanded to the point of disintegration. The target felt like he had been hit by an M-80. Needless to say, the internal damage was extreme.

The man was shooting .45s at them, but his range was limited, his accuracy low. Still, Tyrone knew he needed to find a way to stop the shooting altogether.

'Look up ahead,' Soraya urgently said into his ear. 'See that black-glass building six blocks away? That's CI head-quarters.'

Putting on another burst of speed, Tyrone brought the Ninja up very fast on the limo's left flank. This brought them within range of the Luger, but the distance was also of bene-fit to him.

Drawing her ASP pistol, Soraya aimed and fired in one motion. The hollow-core struck the terrorist full in the face. There was an explosion of blood and bone out the open win-dow.

'They killed Sarah ibn Ashef and covered up their complicity,' Bourne managed to get out. 'They did it to protect you and Fadi. Because sweet, innocent Sarah ibn Ashef was carrying on a torrid love affair.'

'Liar!'

Bourne was having trouble breathing, but he had to keep

talking. He'd known going into this that psychology was his best weapon against a man like Karim, the only one that might bring him victory. 'She hated what you and Fadi had become. She made her decision. She turned her back on her Bedouin heritage.'

He saw something explode onto Karim's face.

'Shut up!' Karim cried. 'These are the foulest of lies! Of course they are!'

But Bourne could sense that he was unsuccessfully trying to convince himself. He had finally put all the pieces of Sarah's death together, and it was killing him.

'My sister was the moral core of my family! The core you destroyed! Her murder set my brother and me on this course. You brought this death and destruction on yourself!'

Bourne was already on the move. He stepped backward and planted his heel hard onto the instep of the man directly behind him. As he did so, he twisted his torso, breaking the hold of the man on his right. Burying a cocked elbow into the solar plexus of the man on his left, he struck outward with the edge of his other hand, slashing it into the side of the third man's neck.

He heard the crack as the vertebrae fractured. The man went down. By this time the man directly behind him had thrown his arms around Bourne, gripping him tight. Bourne bent double, sending the man head over heels into Karim.

The man on his left was still bent over, trying to catch his breath. Scooping up a Luger that had fallen to the floor, Bourne slammed the butt into the crown of his head. The man he'd sent tumbling into Karim had drawn his gun. Bourne shot him and he collapsed in a heap.

That left Karim. He was on his knees, the attaché case directly in front of him. His eyes were red with a kind of madness that sent a shiver down Bourne's spine. Once or twice before, Bourne had seen a man teetering on the edge of madness, and he knew that Karim was capable of anything.

As he was thinking of this, Karim produced a small stainless-steel square. Bourne recognized it instantly as a remote detonator.

Karim held the device aloft, his thumb pressed against a black button. 'I know you, Bourne. And knowing you, I own you. You won't shoot me, not while I can detonate twenty kilos of C-Four in the parking ramp under CI headquarters.'

There was no time for thought, no time for second guesses. Bourne heard Martin's ghostly whisper in his mind. He pointed the Luger and shot Karim in the throat. The bullet passed through the soft tissue, then severed the spinal column. In near-paralyzing pain, Karim sat down hard. He stared at Bourne, disbelieving. He tried to work his fingers, but they wouldn't respond.

His eyes, the light in them fading, found the knuckles of one of his downed men. Bourne, understanding what was about to happen, lunged toward him, but with one last effort, Karim toppled over.

The detonator slammed against the bared knuckles.

At last, Bourne was able to let Karim go. At last, Martin's voice in his head was silent. Bourne stared down at Karim's right eye – Martin's eye – and thought about his dead friend. Soon enough he'd send a dozen red roses to Moira, soon enough he'd take Martin's ashes to the Cloisters in New York.

One thing lingered in his mind, like an angler's unbaited hook. When he had the chance, why hadn't Karim tried to detonate the nuke? Why the limo, which would have a far more limited effect?

He turned, saw the attaché case lying on the concrete floor. The snaps were open. Had Karim done that in the vain hope of engaging the timer? He crouched down, about to close the snaps, when a chill passed through him, the force of it making his teeth chatter.

He opened the case. Peering inside, he searched for the timer, seeing that it was indeed inactive. The LED was dark, the wires disconnected. Then what . . . ?

Probing beneath the nest of wires, he looked closer and saw something that injected the chill into his bones. A secondary timer had been activated when Karim had popped the snaps. A secondary timer that Veintrop had installed, but deliberately never told them about.

Bourne sat back on his haunches, beads of sweat rolling down his spine. It looked as if Dujja – and the doctor – were going to get their revenge after all.

FORTY-ONE

Four minutes and one second. That was the amount of time Bourne had left, according to the readout of the secondary timer.

He closed his eyes, conjured up an image of Veintrop's hands working on the timer. He could see every move the doctor had made, every twist of the wrist, every curl of a finger. He'd needed no tools. There were six wires: red, white, black, yellow, blue, green.

Bourne remembered where they had been attached to the primary timer and in what order Veintrop had disconnected them. Twice, Veintrop had reattached the black wire – first to the terminal on which the end of the white one had been wound, then on the terminal for the red.

Remembering what Veintrop had done wasn't Bourne's problem. Though he saw that the secondary timer, like the primary, was powered by another set of six color-coded wires, the two were physically different. As a consequence, none of the terminals to which the wires were attached was in the same place.

Pulling out his cell, Bourne called Feyd al-Saoud's number in the hope that he could get Veintrop to tell him the truth about deactivating the secondary timer. There was no answer. Bourne wasn't surprised. Miran Shah, mountainous as it was, was a disaster for cell service. Still, it had been worth a try.

3:01.

Veintrop had started with the blue wire, then the green.

Bourne's fingertips gripped the blue wire, about to unwind it from its terminal. Still, he hesitated. Why, he asked himself, would the secondary timer deactivate in the same way? Veintrop had designed this ingenious trap. The secondary timer would come into play only if the primary had been disabled. Therefore, it would make no sense to design it to be disabled in the same way.

Bourne lifted his hands free of the secondary timer.

2:01.

The question here was not how to deactivate the timer; it was how Veintrop's fiendish mind worked. If the primary had been disabled, it would mean that someone had known the right order in which to detach the wires. In the secondary, the order in which the wires needed to be detached could be reversed, or even scrambled in so many possible combinations it would be virtually impossible to stumble upon the right one before inadvertently detonating the nuclear device.

1:19.

The time for speculation had passed. He had to make a decision, and it had to be the right one. He decided to reverse the order; he grasped the red wire, about to unwind it when his keen eye spotted something. He leaned in closer, studying the secondary timer in a different way. Pushing aside the nest of colored wires, he discovered that the timer was attached to the main part of the device in a wholly different way than was the primary.

:49.

Bourne tipped the primary out of its niche, the better to see what was underneath. Then he pulled it free of the detonator, to which it was attached by a single wire. Now he saw the secondary timer unimpeded. It was resting directly against the detonator. The trouble was, he couldn't see where the two were attached.

:27.

He moved the wires away, careful not to detach any of

them. Using a fingernail, he lifted the right edge of the secondary timer up and away from the detonator. Nothing.

:18.

He slipped his nail beneath the left edge. It wouldn't budge. He applied more pressure and slowly, up it came. There, beneath, he saw the wire, coiled like a tiny snake. His finger touched it, moved it slightly, and like a snake, it uncoiled. He couldn't believe his eyes.

The wire wasn't attached to the detonator!

:10.

He heard the voice of Dr. Veintrop. *'I was a prisoner,'* he'd said. *'You don't understand, I . . .'* Bourne hadn't allowed him to finish his thought. Again, the problem was to solve the riddle of Veintrop's mind. He was a man who enjoyed playing mind games – his research proved as much. If Fadi had held him against his will, if Fadi had used Katya against him, Veintrop would have tried to gain a measure of vengeance against him.

Bourne took up the primary, checked the wire dangling from it. The insulation was intact, but the bare copper core at the end felt loose. It came away in his fingers, no more than a couple of centimeters in length. The wire was a fake. He removed his hands from the device, sat back, watched the timer face count down its final seconds. His heart beat painfully against the cage of his chest. If he was wrong . . .

:00.

But he wasn't wrong. Nothing happened. There was no detonation, no nuclear holocaust. There was only silence. Veintrop had gained his revenge against his captors. Under Fadi's nose, he'd secretly disarmed the device.

Bourne began to laugh. Veintrop had been made to accurately rig the primary trigger, but with the backup he'd somehow cleverly fooled Fadi and Dujja's other scientists. He closed the attaché case, took it as he rose. He laughed all the way out of the building.

FORTY-TWO

In the aftermath of the C-4 explosion, Soraya invoked the power of her CI credentials. The surrounding buildings, thick, hulking government edifices, had sustained superficial damage, but nothing structural. The street, however, was a disaster. An enormous hole had been blown out of it, into which the incinerated remains of the limo had dropped like a flaming meteor. The one saving grace was that at this time of the evening, there were no pedestrians in the general vicinity.

Dozens of police cars, fire engines, ambulances, and various emergency and utility agency personnel were swarming over the area, which had been cordoned off. Power was out in a two-and-a-half-square-kilometer radius, and the immediate area was without water, as the mains were ruptured.

Soraya and Tyrone had given statements to the police, but already she saw Rob Batt and Bill Hunter, chief of the Security Directorate, on the scene, taking over. Batt saw her and gave her a *sit tight* nod as he spoke to the police captain nominally in charge of the scene.

'All this official shit make me nervous as a priest wid the clap,' Tyrone said.

Soraya laughed. 'Don't worry. I'm here to protect you.'

Tyrone gave a snort of derision, but she saw that he stayed close to her. With the din of workers moving equipment, shouting to one another, vehicles pulling up, they seemed to be engulfed in a web of sound.

Above them, a news helicopter hovered. Soon it was joined by another. With a roar, air force jets, scrambled and weapons loaded, did a flyby. Their wingtips waggled, then they were gone into the clear blue sky.

New York was fogbound the morning Bourne arrived at the gates of the Cloisters. He passed through, holding the bronze urn containing Martin Lindros's remains close against his chest. He'd sent the dozen roses to Moira, then discovered when she'd called him that they were a silent good-bye from Martin to her.

He'd never met Moira. Martin had only mentioned her once, when he and Bourne had gotten very, very drunk.

Bourne saw her now, a slim, shapely figure in the mist, dark hair swirled about her face. She was standing where she said she would be, in front of the tree that had been trained to spread against the stone blocks of a building wall. She had been overseas on business; had arrived home, she said, only hours before Bourne's call. She had, it seemed, done her weeping in private.

Dry-eyed, she nodded to him, and together they walked to the south parapet. Below them were trees. Off to the right, he could see the flat surface of the Hudson River. It looked dull and sluggish, as if it were the skin of a serpent about to be shed.

'We each knew him in different ways.' Moira said this carefully, as if fearful of giving away too much of what she and Martin had had together.

Bourne said, 'If you can know anyone at all.'

The flesh around her eyes was puffy. No doubt she had spent the last several days crying. Her face was strong, sharp-featured, her deep brown eyes wide apart and intelligent. There was an uncommon serenity about her, as if she was a woman content with herself. She would have been good for Martin, Bourne thought.

He opened the top of the urn. Inside was a plastic bag filled with carbon dust, the stuff of life. Moira used her long, slender fingers to open the bag. Together they lifted the urn over the top of the parapet, tipped it, watched as the gray matter floated out, became one with the mist.

Moira stared into the indistinct shapes below them. 'What matters is we both loved him.'

Bourne supposed that was the perfect eulogy, one that brought a kind of peace to all three of them.